THE
TEMPLAR
SUCCESSION

MARIO READING

CORVUS

Published in paperback in Great Britain in 2016 by Corvus,
an imprint of Atlantic Books Ltd.

10 9 8 7 6 5 4 3

A CIP catalogue record for this book is available from the British Library.

Paperback ISBN: 978 1 78239 535 5
OME ISBN: 978 1 78239 924 7
E-book ISBN: 978 1 78239 536 2

Printed and bound by CPI Group (UK) Ltd, Croydon, CR0 4YY

Corvus
An imprint of Atlantic Books Ltd
Ormond House
26–27 Boswell Street
London
WC1N 3JZ

www.corvus-books.co.uk

THE
TEMPLAR
SUCCESSION

Mario Reading is a multi-talented writer of both fiction and non-fiction. His varied life has included selling rare books, teaching riding in Africa, studying dressage in Vienna, running a polo stable in Gloucestershire and maintaining a coffee plantation in Mexico. An acknowledged expert on the prophecies of Nostradamus, Reading is the author of eight non-fiction titles and seven novels published in the UK and around the world.

For my nephew, Ole Rummel

'...and what I do shall be done by all men in the years unborn. Yes, they shall talk together across the wide spaces of the earth, and the lover shall hear her lover's voice although great seas roll between them. Nor perchance will it stop at this; perchance in future time men shall hold converse with the denizens of the stars, and even with the dead who have passed into silence and the darkness.'

She and Allan, Henry Rider Haggard

ONE

Katohija, Kosovo

The first Lumnije Dardan heard of the event that would shape the rest of her life was the sound of her mother's raised voice.

But Jeta Dardan never raised her voice. She was a placid woman, content with her lot, happily married to Burim Dardan, associate professor of politics at Pristina University, and just now taking a well-earned rest at their country cottage in the village of Katohija, a few kilometres north of Pejē, with her husband and her two children, Azem, just turned eighteen, and Lumnije, sixteen and a half.

The next thing Lumnije heard was the crackle of heavy tyres.

'It is the Serb police,' she said to herself. 'They are returning.'

The Serb police had visited them three times already that summer. They had behaved themselves, for the most part,

1

limiting their aggression to shouting and ordering people to register – Serbs on one side, Albanian Muslims on the other – together with a little minor theft. Chickens, mainly, and the occasional lamb. Always from the Albanians and never from their fellow Serbs. But rumours were rife of more extreme outrages in other parts of the country. And the minority Albanians were understandably cautious. There was a long history of ethnic hatred between the Albanians and their Serbian neighbours.

Lumnije and her family were Albanian Muslims. The last time the police had come they had ordered any Serbians to paint a large S onto the door of their houses, to differentiate themselves from their non-Christian neighbours. There had been an active discussion amongst the villagers as to whether everybody ought to paint the S onto their doors as a form of protest at this infringement of their liberties by the authorities. It was finally decided, however, that no harm could come from obeying the new law, so the situation had been allowed to lapse into abeyance. The S on every other house was hardly noticed any more.

Lumnije could hear her mother shouting louder now, her voice interspersed with those of other women, and the raucous, baritone cries of angry and frightened men. She began to run. This was the first time the Serb police had come when the men, too, were resident in the village – her brother Azem on leave from his university studies, and her father, given the political situation, on an enforced sabbatical from his professorial duties. Maybe the Serbs were threatening him? Or angry about something one of the villagers had done? Or Azem was mouthing off to the police in the way young men with pent-up political opinions occasionally do?

Lumnije burst into the village square, her hair flowing behind her, her dress flattening against the front of her thighs. It was to be the last time in her life that she was ever able to view anything as remotely normal.

The big trucks she had heard earlier were just pulling up, but paramilitaries on foot, and heavily armed, had infiltrated the village first. Paramilitaries, not policemen.

The soldiers were splitting the men from the women and herding them into two groups. Lumnije was just in time to see her brother and her father being dragged away from her mother, who was shrieking and screaming, her face afire, her cheeks awash with tears.

Lumnije stopped in her tracks. No one had ever dared treat her family with disrespect.

Now Lumnije added her voice to the screaming and wailing of the women. She ran to her mother's side. A soldier hurried her on her way with a glancing blow from his boot. Lumnije sprawled on the ground, her dress hoicked up, her underwear showing. The soldiers jeered. Lumnije began to retch.

The officer in charge of the soldiers ordered all ethnic Serbs to return to their houses. This they did, hurrying away without backward glances, abandoning their neighbours with every appearance of relief.

Lumnije looked for her father and her brother amongst the men, but she could not see them.

The Captain of the soldiers took a piece of paper out of his pocket. He consulted it for a moment, then called out her father's name in a loud voice. The Captain towered by more than a head over his nearby men. His face was square. He had a massive jaw below an unexpectedly feminine nose. He was dressed entirely in camouflage fatigues. A red beret surmounted by a cap badge decorated with a Greek cross was tipped casually over one eye. The man's face was criss-crossed with charcoal stripes and white chalk, giving him an otherworldly, almost animalistic appearance. Even his webbing was camouflaged. To Lumnije, the man seemed like an alien, transposed by error onto the familiar ground of her childhood.

Lumnije's father stepped forward. As the most notable individual amongst the Albanian population of the village, it was natural that he should be called first. He began to protest on behalf of the non-Serb villagers. Lumnije knew the tone he was using well. It was her father's public voice. His professional voice, the voice he used beyond the confines of the home.

The Captain unbuckled his holster and raised his pistol. At just this moment, their family dog, Peta, ran in from the periphery of the group, where he had been circling and barking, and leapt into her father's arms. It was his party trick. The thing he knew would always gain him attention and, if he was absurdly lucky, a treat.

The Captain's shot took Peta behind the head. He and her father both fell to the ground. Peta was dead, her father still alive. One of the Serb soldiers ran over and slit her father's throat with his knife. Then four more soldiers took his body up, dragged it to a nearby Albanian house, threw it inside and followed its passage in with two grenades.

'Three times,' said the Captain to the howling women. 'We have killed this filth three times.'

It was then that the machine guns opened up. Lumnije sat, cradled in her mother's arms, and watched as the men fell to the ground like scythed corn. Her brother tried to run towards them, shouting for his mother, but he was killed before he took two paces. Any woman who tried to move towards the men was struck down with a rifle butt or, if she was young and pretty, slapped to the ground by a soldier's hand.

Later, as the women watched, still wailing and weeping, a bulldozer was brought into the village and the bodies of the men were raised up on the hoist and dumped into an empty truck bed.

It was at this point, watching the bulldozer manhandling the bodies of her husband and son, that Lumnije's mother broke. She ran at the Captain, screaming her husband's name. The Captain shot her. It was done so swiftly, and with such contemptuous dispatch, that, for a moment, Lumnije did not realize her mother, too, was dead.

One of the soldiers dragged Lumnije to her feet and pushed her towards a small group of young women that was being gathered together at the edge of the village. Lumnije knew them all. Each girl was weeping and shrieking, just like her. Some had covered their heads with kerchieves and scarves in a bid to make themselves less noticeable to the soldiers. Others were too deeply lost in shock even for that. Some of the girls were unable to stay on their feet. When they were raised up they fell down again, like rag dolls. Finally, their friends held them, fearing that the soldiers would lose patience and kill them.

When the clearing of the men was complete, the girls were loaded onto a covered truck. There were only young women left. The older women and the children had been herded towards the edge of the village and told to leave for Albania. If any turned back, they were warned once and then shot. The bodies of those who disobeyed were loaded onto the same truck that was carrying the dead men.

Two kilometres out of the village, at an abandoned quarry, there was a snarl-up. The truck containing the young women stopped. Lumnije, her hands shaking, lifted the tarpaulin to see where they were being taken. She saw the truck containing the dead men tipping its contents into a shallow trench. She thought she saw her father and her brother tumbling with the others. She could not see her mother, although she knew she was with them. As she watched, the Serbs threw cornhusks onto the piled-up bodies and lit them. Soon, great plumes of smoke rose into the air. The heat from the fire became so intense that the rubberized tarpaulin of the truck she was sitting in began to smoke.

The truck lurched forwards. Lumnije hugged the girl beside her. The girl hugged her back. The two young women remained that way, clasped in each other's arms, for the remainder of the two-hour journey.

TWO

It was the Captain himself who came for her in the isolated room in which she was being held. For some time now, Lumnije had been hearing the screams of her friends and other young women she did not know as the soldiers raped them next door. As a result, she had retreated far inside herself to a place nobody could touch. A dark place, of shadows and mist and the shortages of winter. A place which bore no resemblance to the substance of her normal dreams.

'You. Come with me.'

Lumnije followed the Captain. It was the first time she had been outside the room in thirty-six hours. She had been having her period, and this had saved her from the initial free-for-all that had occurred a few minutes after their arrival in what the soldier who brought her food insisted on calling the 'rape house'. Now it was her turn.

As she walked through the main rooms of the house she saw naked girls walking around in a daze – many with dried blood down their legs, over their breasts, on the inside of their thighs. Some were being made to clean with mops and brooms and besoms. Others were lying on the floor as if dead. There were Serb soldiers sprawled everywhere, drinking rakia and beer and smoking Domacica. As she walked behind the Captain the soldiers called out to her, and made foul movements with their hands. Lumnije thought the Captain would hand her over to them, but he continued walking and she followed him. What else could she do?

He took her to a private room in the back of the house and told her to undress and lie on the bed.

'I am a virgin,' she said.

'You are all virgins,' he said. 'That is the point of this.'

'I do not understand,' she said.

'You do not need to understand. You are not a human being. You are an Albanian. You were born a whore. I am merely here to remind you of this. Has your period ended?'

Lumnije nodded.

'Then you stay here sixteen days. I've decided to make you exclusively mine. I don't like sharing. Half these morons that I command are diseased, and they will pass this on to the girls. For my part, I draw the line at catching the clap. I am their Captain. So what I say goes. You must remain in this room at all times. You will not mingle with the other girls. And you will keep yourself clean. Do you understand me? From now on, when I come in, you are at my complete disposal. If you fight, I give you to my soldiers. If you cry, I give you to my soldiers. If you try to talk to me when I do not wish to be spoken to, I give you to my soldiers. Do you understand me?'

Lumnije nodded again, although she had not understood half of what he had said.

When the first rape was over, she sat on the bed in the corner of the room and wept in mourning for her virginity. No husband could possibly want her now. An Albanian bride needed to enter her marriage intact. No man in his right mind would wish to father children by a woman who had been soiled by a Serb. From here on in she would be considered 'touched'. Impure. What had been done to her could never be undone. Her few remaining relatives would turn away from her in shame. Lumnije rocked to and fro, clutching her groin in an effort to minimize the pain of the Captain's intrusion.

Later, when the pain began to ebb away, she thought about her father and her brother and her mother, but her memories of them were now overlaid by the horror of their recent deaths. This became her pattern of thought over the next few days – first regret, then realization, finally despair. Outside, she could hear the screams of the other girls as they were taken by whoever felt the urge. But she, for whatever reason – perhaps the Captain's morbid fear of infection by what he had mysteriously termed 'the clap' – was secured from the soldiers inside this room. She was the Captain's property. As clearly his as if she had been marked by a brand.

'You are lucky,' said the Captain one day.

'I am lucky?' said Lumnije.

'Yes,' said the Captain. 'You could be with those other ones. Instead you are safely in here with me.'

Lumnije curled up on the bed and hid her head inside her hands. She could feel the Captain watching her. Could feel his eyes travelling over her body.

Lumnije hated her body. Hated her femaleness. Hated the way her hair fell across her face. The way her breasts stood up. She wished she might obliterate all that made her desirable to men, but she knew that was an impossible dream.

So the Captain came back. Sometimes he would be drunk. At these times he used soft words when he was raping her. But the soft words did not help. They only made it worse. She wanted her father's words. Her brother's kisses. Not this man's. She wanted her mother's arms round her – to smell the starch in her apron – the dough on her hands from the bread she was baking. Not this man's hands, which were rough, and intrusive, and cold as grave ice.

'Why sixteen days?' she asked him once.

'So you get pregnant,' he said. 'Have a Serb baby.'

'Why?' she said.

'Why?' he said. 'I do not know why. Why is there always a why? Think yourself lucky. Have I mistreated you?'

Lumnije stayed silent.

'You fucking Albanians have no idea,' the Captain said. He sat down on the edge of the bed. 'You know how many I have killed these last six months?'

Lumnije shook her head.

He held out his hand. He pointed to the palm with his other hand. 'Imagine that is full of rice. That is how many I have killed. And still there are more of you. Like locusts. Like ants.' He raised his hand as if to hit her.

Lumnije turned towards the wall. She waited a long time. Eventually she heard him get up and walk to the door. He stood there watching her.

She did not turn round.

Finally, without a word, he left.

THREE

On the fourteenth day of her incarceration Lumnije tried to commit suicide. She tore up the bedsheets and knotted them into ropes. Then she tied the ropes together and attached them to the light bracket. She made a rough noose and placed it round her neck. Then she stood on the bed and jumped off.

Her weight brought the light bracket down. She lay on the floor and looked up at the hole left in the ceiling.

One of the soldiers came in, attracted by the noise. He looked at her lying there, and then at the trailing light. He dragged her to her feet by the rope, and for one moment Lumnije thought that he would take her out into the main room and give her to his brothers. But he contented himself with beating her about the arms and shoulders with his belt. She was the Captain's woman. More would have been inappropriate.

He unknotted the rope from round her neck and left her lying on the bed. Five minutes later, the Captain came in and beat her some more.

'Will you try this again? If so, you are of no more value to me, and I give you to my men now. Take your clothes off.'

Lumnije shook her head. 'I will not try it again.'

'You swear to this on Allah's head?'

Lumnije nodded.

The Captain threw something on the bed. 'Look. I brought you a shawl.'

'I do not want a shawl.'

The Captain looked at her for a long time. Then he left.

Lumnije picked up the shawl and threw it into a corner of the room.

That night, with no sheets left, she was forced to retrieve the shawl and use it to keep warm. The Captain came in around midnight, drunk, and raped her again. As usual, he spoke soft words to her. As usual she closed her ears and her heart to anything he said. She had given up trying to fend him off. The Captain was so massive and so overwhelmingly strong that he could hold her at bay with one hand while he did whatever he wanted to do with the other. Now she merely lay still, like a rag doll, and let him handle her as he saw fit.

'Are you pregnant yet?'

'How can I know?' Lumnije said. 'Don't you understand females, how we work? How can I possibly know?'

She would never have spoken to him like this when he was sober.

He looked at her and made a sign of disgust with his hand. 'You are not a female. What am I thinking? You are an Albanian. I kill Albanians.'

'Then kill me. Kill me like you killed my mother and my father and my brother. Do you have a family?'

The Captain looked at her in drunken incomprehension. 'I have a son,' he said. 'And a wife.' For a moment he sounded almost human. As if he felt flattered that she had asked the question.

'Then I hope somebody kills them.'

They looked at each other across the bed. Lumnije was beyond hatred. Beyond fear. Now she simply existed. Two more days, she told herself. In two more days he will let me go and I will have to stand no more of this.

'I like you,' he said, on the eve of the sixteenth day. The day he had promised to release her. 'You suit me. That's why I have given you these special privileges. I take no pleasure in breaking in new girls. I take no pleasure in rape. So I have decided to keep you.'

FOUR

Dushkaje Province, Kosovo

19 SEPTEMBER 1998

John Hart watched the teenager moving in front of him through the woods. Was the boy taking him on a wild goose chase? Had he offered him too much money? Was he being led into a trap?

He shifted the weight of his cameras and adjusted his backpack. The pair had been walking for eight hours now and Hart was tired. At twenty-five years old he was fitter than he had any right to be given his binge-drinking and his thirty-a-day smoking habit, but his fitness was as nothing compared to that of the boy. The boy seemed hardly to be sweating. In fact the boy seemed barely to notice that they were moving at all.

Hart called for a stop. 'How much further is it now?'

'Not long,' said the boy.

'What is not long?'

'The time to smoke thee cigarettes. Maybe four.'

'Maybe five? Maybe six?'

'No. Four. Four certain.'

'And you know this place exists?'

'Yes. Many Serb soldiers. Young girls in house. There is screaming.'

Hart could feel the saliva poaching in his throat. What insanity had started him on this trip? Was it the desire to make his name after the catastrophic series of damp-squib failures that constituted his career over the past few years? To get the photo scoop to end all photo scoops? The one cool shot that would play and play forever. Like Nick Ut's napalm snap of the burned and naked girl in Trang Bang in 1972. Or Robert Capa's loyalist militiaman at the point of death in Cerro Muriano in 1936.

Now, thanks to his foolishness, he would more than likely get killed for his trouble. The Serbs didn't play nursery games. He had seen that during the bombing of Sarajevo in 1994, which he had covered as a wet-behind-the-ears twenty-one-year-old, having lied about his age to the newspaper that employed him. As a result of his experiences during the bombing, Hart still jumped whenever he heard a loud noise, and woke up unexpectedly on selective nights not knowing where he was or what he was doing. Out here in the woods, with no company but the boy, he felt vulnerable and fragile again, as if he was crawling out onto the edge of an eerily familiar precipice with no way back but down.

'Why don't your people do anything about this?'

17

'Because we are weak and they are strong.' The boy's face hardened. 'And because the girls aren't worth saving.'

'What do you mean?'

'They have been touched.'

'Touched? I thought this was a rape house.'

The boy twisted his head to one side and spat. 'When a girl has been touched she is never clean again. Her family is besmirched. Her people are shamed. It is better for her to die.'

Hart watched the boy. He was slowly beginning to understand the depths of hatred between the two groups that made up the Kosovan population. Neither thought the other was entirely human. The worst thing you could do was to take one of the other side's young women and rape them. For an Albanian Muslim, this was tantamount to psychological murder. The girl would be shamed and exiled or, if she was lucky, forced into a silence that could last a lifetime. She could never tell her husband. Her father. Her mother. And if she was made pregnant she faced ostracism and the forcible adoption of her baby. In Bosnia, Hart knew that there had been cases of girls killing their own children at birth. Killing themselves while still pregnant. Rape was a war aim. Everybody knew the cost. That's why they did it.

'If your sister was raped, would you turn your back on her?' he said.

'If my sister was raped I would kill her. Then I would kill the man who raped her.'

Hart shook his head. 'Then why are you taking me to this place?'

'The money,' said the boy. 'I need the money.'

'To buy clothes?' said Hart. 'To buy a fucking motor car?'

'No. To buy weapons.'

They left it at that. Neither liked the other. It was a visceral hatred, made up of illogic and youth. Hart didn't trust the boy and the boy disdained him as an interloper and as a voyeur of other people's pain. There was no bridging the gap.

'And you will wait for me while I take my pictures?' said Hart.

'That is the deal.'

'But will you keep to it?'

'Your question is stupid.'

Hart knew his question was stupid, but still he had to ask it. He couldn't break through this boy's carapace. Couldn't read him. He was left with honesty.

They continued on their way.

Four cigarettes. How long a time does it take to smoke four cigarettes? thought Hart. An hour? Fifteen minutes per cigarette?

An hour later the boy signalled him down. They began to crawl. In the distance Hart could hear male voices and the revving of machines.

'What are they doing?'

'Maybe they are going?' said the boy. 'Maybe they are packing up? Maybe you will miss your pictures?'

Hart felt the shame burning his cheeks. He knew what the boy meant. Here he was, an observer, with a safe hotel to return to. A comfortable bed. And here the boy was, a participant, with no home left, let alone a secure place to sleep. How the kid must despise him.

Hart crawled behind the boy to the edge of the clearing. The house stood back a little, in honour of its importance. It had been the home of a lawyer, maybe, or a government official. There were decorative flourishes on the roof and windows – money flourishes, designed to impress. In front of the house men were climbing into trucks. Hart fumbled with his telephoto lens. No. No women. Maybe this was just a barracks after all, and the Serb soldiers were going out on exercise?

'They're leaving. This isn't a rape house. I knew these places didn't exist. You've brought me all the way out here to watch a bunch of Serb paramilitaries heading out on fucking exercise.'

'No. Look.'

Two Serb soldiers were sealing the house from the outside. Iron bars at the windows, wooden beams propped against the doors. They were doing it casually, as if it had been done many times before.

'What does that prove? Only that they're securing the house for their return.'

'You a fool,' said the boy. 'You don't lock from outside in when you secure. They locking people in, not out.'

Hart watched the trucks disappear up the track, leaving a dust cloud in their wake. 'Will there be guards?' he said.

'Why?' said the boy. 'There are only girls inside. No one will come to save them. No one care.'

His face was haunted by unseen ghosts.

FIVE

Two hours later, the boy melted away. One moment he was there; the next he was gone.

Hart cursed under his breath, but there was nothing he could do. He was marooned near a Serb outpost with a clutch of cameras, two bottles of water and a Sujuk sandwich. He felt like every sort of a fool.

He gave it ten minutes and then stood up. In the two and a half hours he had been watching the house he had heard and seen nothing. He held up his press pass and stepped out into the clearing. Part of him expected to be shot. Another part, still flush with the confidence of youth, reckoned he could talk himself out of nearly anything, given half a chance. Hand out a few cigarettes. Explain that he had been looking for the monastery the boy had been muttering about. Visoki something or other. That he had wanted to photograph the tomb of St Stefan. That would be sure to appeal to the Serbs.

He stood in the clearing and looked around. Nothing stirred. It was past mid-September but it was still hot. Hot enough to fry an egg on the bonnet of your car. Maybe thirty degrees. The cicadas were chirruping as if it were high summer.

Hart took a sip of his water and looked at the house. It sat there like a physical manifestation and stared back at him, revealing nothing.

Hart walked closer. He could feel the back hairs on his neck rising. Had it turned cold all of a sudden? Maybe there had been a zephyr of wind on this otherwise windless day? A fluttering of leaves?

Then he heard it again. The moan. It was long drawn out. The distillation of despair.

Hart looked around himself in consternation. Yes. It had been a human moan. And it had come from inside the house. He caught himself taking a step backwards preparatory to running.

He was a photographer. A photojournalist. Not a participant in this crazy civil war. If someone was locked inside the house he should leave them, shouldn't he? And what if there were Serb soldiers? They would kill him. Or at the very least confiscate his cameras and beat him up.

He took a few more steps towards the house. He had come out here, into the depths of the countryside, to get a scoop. No one had succeeded in photographing one of the so-called 'rape houses' before. No one was even sure they existed. The

Serbs maintained that they were Albanian propaganda. The Albanians maintained that the Serbs were using rape as a weapon of war. The Serbs countered with the fact that the Albanians were doing the same thing. But, like Samuel Goldwyn had once famously proclaimed, the consensus was that 'nobody knows anything'.

John Hart had made it his business to force the issue. He had gone around asking questions until someone, somewhere, responded. Then he had bribed them to take him to see one of the houses for himself. The man who had given him the information had sent the boy instead of coming personally. Hart had hesitated. But in the end he had gone for it. What did he have to lose? He had no reputation to speak of yet. No contract to imperil. He was a freelancer. Had been since Sarajevo. He was lucky to sell five photographs a month. Sometimes less. But all it would take would be one classic. The one shot that everyone needed. Then he would be a made man. Write his own ticket. Hart was in a hurry. He was young. He was still in love with his profession.

He walked to the front door of the innocuous house in the clearing and prodded the beam. It was hammered tight. Hart stood back and kicked it. The beam stirred a little, but remained in place. He kicked it again. It stirred a little more.

He looked around to see if anyone had noticed the noise he was making. The cicadas had shut up, but the clearing itself seemed alive. It seemed to be waiting for him to do something. As he watched, mesmerized by the sudden silence, the cicadas began to saw again. He swallowed, but the saliva would not come. All his instincts told him to run back towards the shelter of the woods. Retrace his steps. Lose himself inside the greenery.

He kicked at the beam a third time. This time it moved. Hart heard the moan again. Then there were more moans. Female voices. High-pitched. Close to hysterical. Probably scared that the Serbs were coming back.

Oh Christ, what am I doing, thought Hart.

He kicked the beam fully out of the way and yanked at the door. It opened. His nostrils were immediately assailed by a noxious mixture of sweat, faeces, semen, urine, blood and ammonia. Hart clamped a handkerchief to his mouth and ventured inside.

At first, still blinded by the daylight, he could make nothing out. Then he saw them. Eight or nine naked girls cowering against the wall. Most of them were covered in filth and caked blood. Some were protecting their breasts and pudenda from his gaze – others simply stood in place, their heads bowed.

Hart threw the door wide open to let more air in. He was close to gagging. He beckoned to the girls, but none of them approached him. The cameras on his chest weighed on him like a sackful of stones. The stones of conscience.

He backed outside and smiled. Then he urged them anew. No one moved. When he made to enter the room again one of the girls screamed. Hart edged as far away from the girl as

25

he could and towards another door, situated further inside the property. He threw that door open too. The room was empty. A collection of sex toys was grouped together on a nearby table, as if being readied for some perverted game of chess.

He backed out of the room and sidestepped round the girls until he came to a further door. He talked all the time to them. In English. Tried to calm them. But not a single one of them seemed to speak his language. His body was dripping sweat. His shirt and trousers were wringing. He feared that at any moment a detachment of Serb soldiers would burst in and shoot him.

He reached the second door and tried the handle. This one was locked. He signalled for a key, but the girls shook their heads. Hart kicked at the lock. It began to splinter. He kicked again. The sound was obnoxiously loud in the confined space, but Hart sensed, from the way the girls were behaving, that something or someone of significance lay concealed behind the locked door.

At his third kick, the door swung open. A young woman was tied, more or less fully clothed, on a bed. Her body was half covered by a bloodstained shawl. Long withheld nausea overwhelmed Hart's defences. He tried to hold back but he couldn't. He vomited on the floor, retching and choking, one hand on the door frame, the other trying to hold his cameras back against his chest so that they would not be soiled.

When he was finished being sick he wiped his mouth on his

shirtsleeve, then stared at what he had done with disbelief. Eventually he looked at the girl. She had bruises on her cheeks and about her eyes. There was blood caked beside her mouth and in her hair. He took out his pocket knife and untied her.

'Do you speak English?' he said. 'English? My name is John Hart.'

The girl hesitated. Her gaze drifted to the open doorway behind him.

'Please,' he said.

The girl stirred as if awakening from a dream. Her eyes flared. Her face took on the rictus of normality, as of one who rarely speaks.

'My name is Lumnije Dardan. I speak English. You must go from here and lock the doors again. Just as you found them. Or when they come back the soldiers will kill us all.'

SIX

Lumnije watched the tall young man with the golden hair standing beside the door. She could smell his fear. This one was not a soldier. He carried no pistol. The soldiers she knew did not vomit when they saw young girls. They picked one and took her. The girls were too scared or too broken to argue.

The week before, a girl had succeeded in killing herself with one of the soldier's knives. Lumnije had been made to watch her body being dragged out of the house. The Captain, after a loaded glance at Lumnije, had ordered the girl to be jointed and fed to the pigs. The rest submitted. There was nothing else to do. The cost could be counted later.

'You must come with me,' the man said to her.

Lumnije almost laughed.

'Please. We must hurry. There are no soldiers here now. But they will return.'

'No soldiers?' she said.

'None. I broke in here. No one stopped me. The soldiers have gone away for the time being. You must tell the others to come with me.'

'Why?'

'Why?' he said.

'Yes. Why should we come with you? Can you protect us?'

The tall young man with the golden hair looked down at his cameras. 'No. I can't protect you.'

She watched him from across the floor. Then something stirred inside her. Some echo of possible salvation. She got up from the bed and crossed the floor towards him. She saw him flinch when he caught the stench from her body. She walked past him. He followed her.

'You. All of you,' she said to the cowering girls. 'This man is taking us away. We must go with him.'

No one moved. Some were from her village. Some were not. Lumnije clapped her hands together to capture their attention.

One of the girls stepped forward. A girl she did not know.

'You are the Captain's whore. Why should we listen to you?'

Lumnije walked to the front door and looked out. It was true. There were no soldiers. 'We are all whores now. You can go or you can stay. I don't care. I go with this man.'

'What is he?' said one of the others. 'Why does he have cameras and not guns?'

'What are you?' said Lumnije to the tall young man with the golden hair.

'What am I?'

'My friend wants to know what you are doing here. Why you carry the cameras? Why you don't have a gun?'

The golden-haired young man looked as if he was about to cry.

Lumnije took pity on him. 'Find any clothes you can,' she told the girls.

'Why do you have clothes and we have not?' said the first girl. The one who had called her the Captain's whore.

'Because I am the Captain's whore. See?' She lifted up her stained blouse to show the bruises on her stomach. Then she turned to show the stripes on her back from his belt. 'I am so beautiful he gave me special attention. This is why I have clothes and you have none. Take sheets, coverlets, anything to cover yourselves with. The sun is hot and we are no longer used to it.' Lumnije squinted at the sunlight outside. 'Shoes, too, if you can find them. They will be sure to follow us.'

Some of the girls began to moan again.

'Those who wish to stay, stay. But believe this. They will kill you.'

She looked at the man.

'Now we go,' she said in English. 'Do not fear. They will follow. In their own time. Sure. But they will follow.'

SEVEN

Hart led the girls back along the path the boy had taken him. He thought he would remember the first mile. Then maybe he would remember some more, maybe not.

Three of the girls had decided to join the one who spoke English. The rest elected to stay behind. Hart found this fact almost impossible to grasp. He had tried to persuade the girl they called the Captain's whore to force her friends to accompany him, but she had looked at him with pity and shaken her head.

'What is your name?' he asked her.

'Lumnije,' she said. 'I told you this back at the house.'

'What?'

'Lumnije. Lumnije Dardan.'

'And the others?'

'I do not know their names.'

Hart was tempted to continue with his questioning, but he

suspected he would get nowhere. He was still in shock. His hands, when they clutched his cameras for comfort, shook. He took no photographs.

'The soldiers,' he said.

'The soldiers will come for us. They will kill the other girls and they will come for us.'

'Why will they kill the others?'

'Because they wish to use the house again. It is convenient for them.'

'Why did the soldiers leave?'

'I do not know. But sometimes this happens. There is a call. They all go. Maybe it is to kill a village? To take more girls? That is why they have this house.'

Hart slowed his pace. Some of the young women were struggling. Two of the three had found no shoes.

'Where are we going?' said the girl called Lumnije.

'Going?' said Hart. 'You are asking me where are we going?'

'Yes. Where are you taking us?'

Hart felt an unholy calm descend on him. A preternatural tranquillity. As of a murderer who has finally come to terms with the fact of his execution. 'We are going to a monastery. Called Visoki, I think.'

Lumnije threw her head back and stared at Hart as if he had taken leave of his senses. 'You mean Visoki Dečani? But that is a Serb monastery. I know of this place – it is Orthodox Christian. But we are Albanians, Sunni Muslim.'

'The monks are protecting Albanians. I have heard this.'

32

'And you think the Serb soldiers who have been holding us will value this?'

'I don't know what they will value.' Hart shook his head. 'I don't even know the way to the monastery.'

Lumnije looked at him. She saw a young man, not so much older than herself, suddenly responsible for four touched girls. Girls whom the Serbs had destroyed. 'I know the way to the monastery,' she said. 'It is ten kilometres from my village. Up a long valley. I have never been there but I know where it is.'

'You do?'

She nodded. 'We must stick to the high ground, away from the roads. So that the Captain can't use his vehicles.'

'Are you so sure he will follow us?'

'He will follow, yes. It will be a game for him. A change from his usual routine.'

'And the monastery? You agree with me?'

Lumnije shrugged. 'Why should the monks care what happens to us?'

'Then why are we going?'

She looked him directly in the eyes. 'Because there is nowhere else.'

EIGHT

The Captain stood looking at the open door. Then he walked in. The five remaining girls were huddled together near the unused fireplace.

'Where is the one from my room?' he asked them.

'She went. With him,' one said.

'Him? Who is him?'

'The golden-haired one.'

'A soldier?'

'No. He had cameras.'

'Cameras?'

'Yes. Many.'

'There were others?'

'No. Only him.'

'And the other ones are with him too?'

'Yes.'

'Why did you not go with them?'

'We are naked.'

The Captain was tempted to laugh. Months ago, one of his men had suggested that they keep the girls naked so that they would not escape. The Captain had thought it was a good joke. He had never expected the plan to work.

'So they are in bare feet?'

'Yes. Except your one and one other. These have shoes.'

The Captain looked at his corporal. The corporal looked back at him.

'Please let us live,' said the girl who had been speaking to him. 'We stayed when we could have gone. Some of us may be pregnant.'

The Captain looked round the room. At the accumulated filth on the surfaces. The blood on the floor and on the walls. He took a coin out of his pocket and flipped it. He looked at it in the palm of his hand. 'You are lucky. You live. Now clean up here. My men will bring you water and bleach and whitewash. When I get back I want this place sparkling. You understand me?'

'Yes. Yes. We understand.'

The Captain walked outside with his corporal. He nodded back towards the house. 'When they have finished cleaning, kill them. Kill them all.'

The corporal nodded.

'We close this place. I want no record here of what this was.'

'In case the other ones get through? Them and the man with his cameras?'

'They will not get through,' said the Captain.

NINE

Two hours into their trek Hart shared his water and his remaining sandwich with the girls. None of them would come near him, so Lumnije took the bottles round and split up the sandwich into four parts. She also took Hart's penknife and made rough shoes out of the sheets the girls had draped themselves with.

'Why won't they come near me?'

'Why do you think?'

'But I have not done them any harm.'

'You are a man.'

Hart sat with his hands in his lap and stared back at the path down which they had travelled. 'Then why do you? Why do you come near me?'

'Because I am different.'

'How?'

'I cannot tell you. Do not ask me.'

Hart nodded. He wanted to appear wise, but he was out of his depth. 'Thank you for talking to the others and persuading them.'

'It would have been better if they had not come.'

'What?'

'You heard me. They will slow us down. It would have been better if they had stayed behind.'

'But I had to bring them.'

'Yes. You had to. You did the right thing. But we will suffer for it.'

Hart stared at her. 'Do you always tell the truth like this?'

'No. Before, I did not do this. But I have had much time to think in these past few weeks.'

Hart swallowed. He looked at the prison pallor on Lumnije's face. At her bruises and her cuts. He remembered the terrible flash of her wounds as she revealed her stomach and her back for the other women. 'Are you in pain?'

'Pain?' said Lumnije. 'The Captain killed my mother and my father and my brother. This is pain. I have no pain. Just…' She searched for words. 'Numb.'

An hour later they reached a thin river, trickling through a wide, empty bed. In winter it would be a torrent. But now it scarcely qualified as anything waterborne. More like a rivulet.

Hart absented himself while the women washed themselves and drank. Later, he filled the empty water bottles.

Lumnije came back with berries and they all ate.

'How long have we got?' he asked her.

'Until the soldiers come back from whatever they are doing. If we are lucky we have until nightfall. We must keep walking through the night.'

'But these women need sleep,' said Hart.

'They have done nothing but sleep for two weeks. That and the rest. Now they can walk.'

'Why are you so hard on them?'

'Because I want to survive.'

'What? To bear witness to what the soldiers have done to you?'

'No. That I will never say.'

'Then why?'

Lumnije shook her head. 'If you do not know I cannot tell you.'

TEN

'They are going high, Captain. Up in the hills where our vehicles cannot follow them.'

'Then we will follow them on foot.'

The corporal pointed at the ground. 'Look. They stopped here for a while to rest. There are pieces of torn sheet.'

The Captain inspected the remnants of cloth. 'They have been making themselves shoes. How many are we looking for again?'

'Three. Plus the one from your quarters. Plus the man.'

'We will soon have them. We can walk twice as fast as them.'

'Yes, Captain. We will soon have them.'

The Captain glanced up the track ahead. 'You know this country. Where are they going?'

The corporal shrugged. 'There is nowhere for them to go. Everything is Serb-held here. Maybe there is a village. But most have been cleared. I think maybe they cross over into Albania. Or maybe Montenegro. We would be rid of them then.'

The Captain thought back to the girl. The daughter of Burim Dardan. She was no peasant like the others. That was why he had chosen her to be his own. That, and the fact that she was beautiful. And unsullied. 'We will never be rid of them. These females have tongues. And the man is a journalist.'

'How can you know this?'

'What of his cameras? You heard the description. Who walks around with cameras in these hills?'

'Ah, yes.'

'Ah, yes,' said the Captain. 'He will have photographs. Of the house. Of the girls. Perhaps of us.' He paused for thought. 'Radio back. Tell Marković not to kill the whores after all. The men can keep them. Later, maybe, when it is safe, we will set them free. That way their deaths cannot come back to haunt us.'

'Do we stay on at the house?'

'No. That is dead. This bastard may have a phone.'

'But there is no reception in these hills.'

'A satellite phone then.'

'Is that likely?'

The Captain shrugged. 'Only one way to find out. We cut the man's heart out and see if he is connected.'

The corporal burst out laughing. The Captain laughed too. Both men enjoyed the chase. Enjoyed the focus accorded by having an enemy in common. The Captain was a professional soldier, in the army since just after puberty. In civilian life the corporal had been a car mechanic. Both relished the power they had been given to do anything they wanted to the enemy. Each understood the other. It was the closest of all bonds. The bond of shared guilt.

'Shall I call for more men?'

'No. We do this ourselves. We are armed; they are not. What is the one with the cameras going to do? Ambush us? Pelt us with females?' The Captain stood up. 'When did the girls last eat?'

'Last night.'

'They will be weak then. Short of water.'

'There is a stream.'

'Where?'

'One hour north of here. We will cross it on this track.'

'We make for the stream then. Maybe we catch them there.'

ELEVEN

The first of the girls dropped out just before dark. Like the boy who had been guiding Hart, she just disappeared.

'We have to find her.'

Lumnije shook her head. 'No. She knows where she is going. Her village may be near here. She will go back.'

'Why don't we all go there?'

'Because there will be nothing. The Captain has cleared all the Albanians out of the villages in this area. Only Serbs left. They will give us in.'

'Won't they give her in?'

'No. She will go quietly. Secretly. Take a few things. Whatever the looters have left behind them. Photographs, maybe. Of the people who have been killed. Then she will cross the border.'

Hart shook his head. What insanity was this? 'Shouldn't we cross the border too?'

Lumnije looked at the two remaining girls. Then at herself. She thought of the Serb police. The stories she had heard. About them picking out the prettiest of the refugees at the border crossings and taking them away to be raped. Then handing them back, ruined, to their families. 'No. We go to the monastery.'

'But I thought you said…'

'I know what I said. We go to the monastery.'

Hart watched Lumnije as she strode ahead of him up the track. Compared to the two other girls who followed on behind, she was relatively fit and healthy. And yet he had seen her cowering in that room. Seen what the man they called 'the Captain' had done to her. The rest was easy to imagine.

Each man on earth held within him the capacity for doing what the Serbs were doing. Why was he any different? Why should Lumnije see him as different from them? And yet he knew in the deepest part of his soul that under no circumstances could he ever give himself up to the sort of bestiality that these girls had encountered. Where had this decency sprung from? Or was it just common humanity? And what was happening in Kosovo was a freak show, like the Bosnian ethnic cleansing that preceded it, in which even the churches and the mosques bore the brunt of the people's rancour?

'Why are you here, Anglez?'

Hart looked up. Lumnije had fallen back towards him and was walking by his side.

'Why have you come here?' she said again.

'To take photos.'

'Why?'

'To record things. Things that would otherwise not be recorded.'

'And yet you have not taken photos of us.'

'No.'

'Why is that?'

'I don't know.'

'You do not know much, do you?'

Hart tried to shrug but failed. The movement he succeeded in making looked more like a nervous tic. 'I'm learning.'

'You better learn fast. When the Captain catches up to us he will kill you first. Then us. And that will be the end of your life. No more learning.'

'How can you be so sure?'

'Some things one is sure of in this world.'

Hart raised the tempo of his walking. But soon he had to lower it again, as the two non-English-speaking girls were finding it hard to keep up, despite the strips of sheet they had wrapped around their feet.

'We must hide,' said Hart. 'The soldiers will catch up and ambush us otherwise. Maybe if we cut off this track and lie up somewhere? Find ourselves a cave?'

'The Captain will trail us and kill us.'

'He's not a bloody superman.'

Lumnije looked back at the two young women following them. She lowered her voice, even though she knew the girls would not be able to understand her. 'Compared to us? As we are now? Yes, he is. I don't think you understand. For weeks these girls have been constantly raped. By anybody who felt like raping them. Ten, twenty times a day. Then hardly fed. Porridge, maybe. A little stale bread. I hear it all the time, what goes on. Through the walls. I am the lucky one. Only the Captain touch me. He make me his own. He say he do not like to share. Do not like to get disease.'

Hart shook his head as if he wished to rid it of a tinnitus.

'Listen to me, Anglez. You need to know this. Before the rapes these girls see their family killed. Or sent away to starve. So already they are…' She searched for the right phrase in English. 'They are touched. Destroyed. The world…' She stopped, as if lost for words. Then she continued, each sentence breaking free from the other, as if it were a train, unhitching. 'The world has changed for them. No time for thinking. No time for mourning. Only live for the next minute. The next hour. So the Captain. Yes. He is Superman. He is force. He is…' She hesitated again. 'Inevitable.' Her face had taken on a haunted look in the dusk's half-light.

'You talk as if we might as well lie down in the middle of the road and give ourselves up.'

'Not lie down. No. But we will never make it to the monastery. The soldiers will be very close to us now.'

'Why are you so sure they will follow us?'

Lumnije pointed at Hart's cameras. 'Because you wear these.'

Hart looked down. He started to take the cameras from around his neck.

'No. It is too late for that now. Later, if we are still alive, maybe you take pictures then. For your newspapers. Maybe I talk to you. Tell you things for you to write. Maybe I don't. For me, there is no close family left to shame. The Captain. He killed them all. Just like I described.' Lumnije's face, always so contained, so tightly held under control, seemed to break into a thousand pieces. To become malleable all of a sudden, like melting rubber.

Hart took a step towards her, but she raised both arms against him in the shape of a transversal cross. She began to sob.

One of the young women hurried towards her. Took her by the shoulders. Led her away.

Hart was left standing in the clearing, the early moonlight settling on his face, bereft.

TWELVE

'They are close,' said the corporal. He shone his torch onto the ground. The moonlight was so strong, though, that he scarcely needed it. 'Look.'

The Captain leant forwards. 'Menstrual blood.'

'Yes.'

'Then one, at least, is not pregnant.'

'Yes.'

'Incredible. How did she manage that, do you think?'

The corporal shrugged. 'Maybe her body closed down? Killed the baby? This can happen. I have heard of it. If you hate enough, your body listens to you.'

The Captain squinted at his subordinate. 'Where do you learn this claptrap?'

The corporal swallowed. 'I don't know. I listen to the women sometimes.'

'In between raping them?'

'Yes, sir. In between raping them.'

'Then you are a stupid ass. Who listens to women?'

'I don't know.' The corporal consciously closed down. He knew what his commander was capable of. Had seen it a hundred times. They were alone out here. He did not want to die.

'Of course you don't know. You are an idiot.' The Captain thought for a while. 'How far ahead?'

The corporal looked at the blood. He touched it with his finger. It had scarcely had time to clot. 'Ten. Fifteen minutes at the most.'

'Good. We catch them up within the hour.'

'Yes, Captain.'

They began walking again, this time at a faster pace. The Captain unslung his gun. The corporal, seeing him, unslung his too. He wondered for a moment if he should use it to kill the Captain. Then run back. Say they had been ambushed by the KLA. The Captain scared him. The man was visibly out of control. In recent weeks he had taken to playing God. Sometimes, when they were purging villages, the Captain spared people on a whim. All those with glasses, maybe. Or bald ones. Totally at random. Other times, he killed old people or a child – someone you would usually let escape, encourage towards the border. Why would a man kill old people and children? There were more than enough men of fighting age left to kill in the normal run of things.

He twitched the barrel of his gun away from the Captain's

back to forestall temptation. It would be so easy. Later, he could shoot himself in the fleshy part of the arm just before his return and act wounded. Pretend he was a hero. Who was to know the KLA hadn't dragged off the soldiers he would claim to have shot? A man made his own way in this world. The Captain's days were numbered. He sensed it. You couldn't go on killing as the Captain did and not have it affect you.

'Move on ahead. What are you lingering behind me for? Who is meant to be the guide here? You or me?'

'Me, Captain.'

'Then guide. Don't fuck around waving your gun at my arse.'

'Yes, Captain.'

They came upon the two girls forty minutes later, running back down the track towards them. At first the corporal thought he was seeing ghosts. Then he realized that the girls were wrapped in white sheets, like ponchos. Even so, he had come perilously close to shooting them.

'Stop.' The Captain walked past him. 'Where do you think you are going?'

One of the girls fell to the ground. The other stood on the track. Frozen. The corporal saw that she was pissing herself.

'You heard me,' said the Captain. 'Where are you going?'

'We are coming back.'

'Bullshit. Where were you going? I will ask it once more.'

Both girls were weeping.

The corporal looked at the Captain. The Captain was lighting a cigarette. It was what he always did before executions.

'Shall I take them back to the house?' said the corporal quickly. 'You could go on alone.'

The Captain appeared to consider. He looked at the two girls. Then at his cigarette. 'Yes. You better get them out of here. The bastard has probably already photographed them.'

'He will have their faces, yes,' said the corporal. He didn't know why he was trying to defend the girls. He had raped them both numerous times. Had used them like toilet roll. But somehow, out here, away from their hysterical companions, they seemed more human to him.

'How far are the other three ahead?'

The girl on the track looked up at him uncomprehendingly. It was the standing one who answered him.

'Not three of them. Two. Short distance. Not far. Five. Ten minutes.'

'Who is this man? What is his name?'

She shook her head. 'Anglez.'

'An Englishman? What is he doing here? Is he a journalist?'

The girl shook her head again.

'Why did you run?'

Both girls shook their heads.

'Did the other one run?'

A nod.

'Was it the one from my room?'

Another shake of the head.

'Are your villages near here? Was that why you ran?'

Silence.

The Captain took out his pistol.

'Look,' said the corporal, 'I take them with me, heh? I get them back. Then I go and get the other one. Soon we have them all.'

The Captain paused. He took aim at the supine girl's head and made a *paf* sound with his mouth. Then he did the same to the standing girl. She fell down.

'*Paf!*' The Captain said again. '*Paf! Paf! Paf!* They all fall down.' He laughed. 'Go on. Take them back with you.' He started up the track. Then he stopped. 'Corporal?'

'Yes, sir?'

'Your heart. It's mush. It's mashed potato. It's old stew. You need to harden it. If not, we never win. Do you hear me?'

'Yes, sir.'

'Then understand this. When you get back, tell Marković I am rescinding the final part of my orders. Let the first part stand.'

The corporal swallowed. He looked at the two girls. They might as well be dead now. He knew that if it wasn't for the sound a gun makes, and which might risk spooking their quarry, the Captain would have killed them on the spot. 'Yes, sir.'

'Tomorrow I return. Make sure the house is cleaned before I get back. Sparkling. No mess left.'

Before the corporal could reply the Captain turned on his heel and disappeared up the track.

THIRTEEN

When Lumnije came back, she was alone. The other two girls were gone.

'Did you tell them to go?' Hart said. 'Did you encourage them to leave?'

'No. Why would I do that?'

'I don't know. Maybe they have villages near here too?'

'No. They are both from my village.'

Hart looked at her. There was no sign at all that Lumnije had been weeping. Her face was blank. Shut off from him. In another place entirely. 'Then why?'

'They think you will rape them.'

'You can't be serious.'

'I am very serious.'

Hart took a step towards her. 'Couldn't they see that I was trying to help them?'

Lumnije echoed his movement, but backwards, as if they

54

were engaged in a formal dance neither knew the rules to. 'They are beyond help. Can't you see that?'

'Are you beyond help too? Is that what you are telling me?'

'Yes.'

'So why do you stay with me?' Hart was really angry now. He could feel the seeds of outraged virtue building inside him. He had tried to help these girls and they had spurned him. What were they thinking of? He was a decent man. Not like the filth who were perpetrating this. 'Why did you come back? Why didn't you run off too?'

Lumnije turned away from him. 'I don't know. I cannot tell you this.' She put her hand on her chest as if she might somehow be able to control the frequency of her breathing. 'I no longer know myself. I am not myself. I no longer exist.'

'What are you saying? Of course you exist. You have your whole life in front of you.'

'No. I no longer exist.'

'Bullshit. What age are you? Twenty? Twenty-two?'

'I am sixteen.'

Hart felt the anger leach out of him. He was like a bladder someone has just popped. He wanted to reach out and hug her, but he knew she would probably scream, and then he would lose her for good. And for some obscure reason he knew he had to keep her. Keep this last one. That it meant something. Held some deep significance for his future life. For him now, even.

'We need to move on,' he said.

'Yes,' she said.

'They can't be far behind us,' he said.

'No,' she said.

They were writing their relationship in words, not movements. He realized that. She was staying with him for the comfort of words. Not even in her own language. Just words. It wasn't about him. He was just a conduit. He could be anyone. It was the first time in his life that he truly felt the tenor of his own insignificance.

They hurried through the woods, still keeping to the track. Hart knew that it was a dangerous thing to do, but veering off would only slow them down. They would get lost, stumble off into the void. For some reason the track represented security, even though it was the one thing that made them the most vulnerable.

'How far is the monastery?'

'By walking? Maybe two days.'

'What?'

'Two. Maybe three. Now there is just the two of us I think two.'

'Are you still okay?'

Lumnije looked at him. How could she tell him about the cramps she was getting in her stomach? The pain in her back and hips? The burning in her vagina and anus where the Captain had entered her, sometimes three or four times in a row. How could she tell this man such things? How could she tell any man? Anybody?

'I am okay.'

'Maybe the Captain is not after us. Maybe we're just imagining it?'

'He is after us. We are not imagining.'

Hart felt excluded. Out of the loop. He was in a country he did not understand, doing something he did not know how to do. 'Can I photograph you?'

'No.'

'It might serve to protect you. If I can get the photos out, that is. I could photograph the bruises on your front and back – what you showed the other girls. It might help.'

'No.'

'Okay. I was just asking.'

'Don't ask.'

'No. I won't. I won't ask again.'

He did not know why he kept the cameras now. They were only slowing him down. He was cluttered up with paraphernalia. But maybe he could take some distant shots of the Serb soldiers, if he somehow managed to avoid them killing him. Get some faces on film. Hand the results over to the International Criminal Tribunal.

Because there would sure as hell come a time when all this bestiality would have to be paid for. You don't destroy a country, rape its women, kill its men and boys, without some comeback some time. If not now, then later, a few years down the line. Any photographs he took would be evidence. He wanted to kick himself for not taking any photos of the house when he had had the chance. Bloody fool. He had come all this way to photograph a rape house, and when he found one all he did was escape from it with a bunch of girls who then left him because they thought he would do the same thing to them the soldiers had done. It wasn't a pretty story. He felt his twenty-five years of life like a lesson only partially learned. A botched project, half finished.

'We need to go higher.'

'Are you sure you know where we are?' Hart said.

Lumnije moved her head around as if she was sniffing the air. The first fingers of dawn were lighting the trees. 'No. I do not know for certain. Only the direction.' She touched the moss on the back of a tree. 'This is south.' She touched the bald side of the tree. 'This is north. We need to go east.'

'That's it? That's all you know?'

'It is enough.'

FOURTEEN

The Captain sensed that the two of them, the man and the girl, were picking up speed. It had been a clever thing of them to get rid of the two whores clothed in sheets. He would have done the same thing in their position. Driven them off. Maybe not killed them, but driven them off. Hell, maybe he would have killed them just for slowing him up.

This set the Captain to thinking back to the first man he had ever killed. It was during the Bosnian War. At Srebrenica/Potočari, following the break-up of the Socialist Federal Republic of Yugoslavia into warring factions made up largely of Serb Christians and Bosniak Muslims. He had been a junior lieutenant in the Scorpions, 12–13 July 1995. He and the other Serbs had held back until then, not sure how the Dutch UNPROFOR troops who were nominally maintaining peace would react. But when the Dutchbat forces refused to intervene in what the Serbian forces were doing at the place they called the White House, something broke in him. Something was liberated.

First he joined in the gang rape of a young Bosniak girl by three other Serb soldiers. Then he asked to be able to shoot a Bosniak prisoner. Some kid they had captured. He shot the kid, and one of the soldiers with him cut the kid's nose, ears and lips off. Why, he couldn't tell.

But it freed him. There was a craziness in the air. He suddenly realized he could do anything he wanted with these people and no one would care. No one would protect them. No one would fight back. It was total power. Something he had never experienced before.

All through that night and into the next day, he raped and killed with impunity. The Dutch soldiers just stood by and watched. Maybe they were getting a kick out of it too?

By the second night he and his people were killing the Bosniaks on an industrial scale. Lighting up the killing fields with arc lights. Carting the bodies away in trucks and bulldozers. Burying them in mass graves. Raping women when they wanted a break from the killing. Sometimes in front of their fathers and mothers. In front of their children. Some of the victims they just buried alive. Nothing much counted any more. Dutch soldiers were watching all this happening. Some had Walkmans on. They were listening to music while the raping and killing and mutilation went on. How do you account for that?

He himself was crazy by then. His unit was out of control.

They had gone too far to ever stop. Stories were coming back that people were committing suicide in the refugee camp rather than waiting for the Scorpions to come get them.

That was power, thought the Captain. That was total war. Action, pure and simple. No thought, no holding back. You acted just as you saw fit. When and how you saw fit. You were God. There was no God. How could there be? How could God let this happen if He existed? Or didn't He care about people? A Serbian Orthodox priest had even blessed his unit before they started killing. How could anyone take God seriously after that? When even priests reckoned God was on your side while you murdered people?

It was well after dawn when the Captain heard the noise ahead of him. He upped his pace. He was carrying his automatic rifle unslung all the time. Part of him wondered whether Marković had killed all the girls back at the camp yet. Because now, by virtue of the orders he had given, he was killing even when he wasn't killing. That was a neat trick. But everything needed tidying up back there. The corporal would deal with the two white-sheeted girls somewhere along the road home. Dump them in a ditch. Probably rape their dead bodies. That was something he had never tried. Some people swore by it. They killed the women just as they were ejaculating inside them. Crazy. Crazy what this war had thrown up in the way of pleasure.

He came into the clearing at the half-run. There were ten people there, all Albanians. He could tell. Refugees, heading for the border, half men and half women. Some of the men were fighting age. The Captain raised his rifle and shot them before they could get away. Then he shot the old men. The women were shrieking and howling like they always did on these occasions, so he shot them too.

Ten. He'd just killed ten people. No one had escaped. Their bodies lay scattered along the track like debris from a runaway train. He kicked them one by one down into the gulley and watched them tumble away, their limbs flailing.

Shit. Now he'd warned the two he was following. He should have kept one of these ones alive and asked them questions. Whether the two had passed them by, stuff like that. But he'd needed to be quick. They'd been scattering in all directions by the time he'd decided to shoot.

He stood at the top of the gulley and looked down. He was the master. The master of everything. What he said, mattered. What he did, counted.

He was the Captain.

FIFTEEN

Hart and Lumnije looked at each other when they heard the gunshots.

'The soldiers have killed them,' said Hart. 'Those people we saw.'

'It was the Captain,' said Lumnije.

'Him and all the others.'

'No,' said Lumnije. 'That was only one gun.'

'How can you tell?'

Lumnije stared at him as if he was mad. 'I hear before. Soldiers practising. At the house. They shoot the walls. The trees. When they not raping us, or drinking, or smoking, they practising.'

'Are you saying we're being followed by just one man?'

'The Captain. Yes.'

'How can you possibly know that?'

'I know.' She hesitated. 'He want me.'

'You mean he wants to kill you?'

'No. He want me back.'

Hart stared at her. 'Is that what this is all about then? Him wanting you?'

'No.' Lumnije shook her head. 'I rather die than let him touch me again.'

They were jogging by this time. Away from the direction the shots had come from.

The sun was fully risen now, its face above the trees. Hart was sweating. The perspiration was dripping down his back and leaching into his trousers. It was beyond his understanding how Lumnije could keep going after all that had happened to her. Just like the damned boy who had abandoned him at the clearing, she seemed tireless.

The two of them had been on the run for close on eighteen hours now, with no sleep. Hart could feel himself beginning to hallucinate, humming under his breath to the rhythm of the cameras striking his chest, struggling to keep his eyes open. All he wanted was to curl up somewhere safe. Meanwhile the girl just hustled on, her arms pumping, her head jacked to one side as if she was listening out for something.

'We've got to stop. We've got to hide up.'

'No. He will find us.'

'He's not a superman,' said Hart. 'I told you that.'

'He's worse.'

Hart continued jogging, although it was more a flailing movement by now. The last three days had taken it out of him – the preparation, the walk to the rape house and what happened afterwards. He could feel the familiar tightening in his chest, which the cigarettes usually took care of. But he had no more cigarettes. Hell of a time to go cold turkey.

He started fantasizing about setting traps for the Captain. Bending back trees, maybe, like they did in Vietnam. He could hardly cut punji sticks, though, with only a three-inch penknife. He cursed himself for venturing out so stupidly unprepared. Talk about an amateur. Hunger was a yawning void in his stomach and they had drunk the remainder of the water hours ago. The empty plastic bottles clattered uselessly against his back. He imagined pouring himself a Coke from a pinch-waisted glass bottle into a tall glass with ice and lemon. It did no good.

The bullet took him in the small of the back and drove him forward. His body slithered up the track as though propelled by an explosive charge. He lay face down in the dirt but he was conscious. He could hear everything.

He heard the Captain's footsteps behind him and felt rather than saw the Captain stoop to look down at him. He felt the Captain's fingers as they disentangled the cameras from about his neck, ripping out the film to expose it.

It was then that he heard the cry. She had come back for him. Lumnije had come back for him.

The Captain dropped the cameras and began to run. Hart could hear the clomp of the Captain's boots disappearing up the track ahead of him. He was going after Lumnije.

Hart sat up. Why wasn't he dead? The Captain had shot him. He felt behind himself. Touched his rucksack. Opened it. Fished out his telephoto lens. The big one. The one he had mortgaged his soul to pay for.

It was bent and skewed out of shape. The lens was shattered. It had taken the full force of the Captain's bullet and deflected it somehow away from him.

Hart stood up. He felt as though someone had struck him between the shoulders with a polo mallet. At full swing. From horseback. He dropped to his knees and teetered, ready to fall. But the Captain was running after Lumnije. He must do something before it was too late.

He looked to his right. The Captain's rifle lay on the track like a dead snake. The Captain must have heard Lumnije come back and run straight after her. The man probably had a pistol strapped to his waist. He didn't need the rifle. And Hart was dead. As far as the Captain was concerned, Hart was dead. You don't shoot a man in the back only for him to rise up again like the Firebird. Like the bringer of doom. Lumnije had saved his life by coming back. Her return had prevented the Captain from checking inside his rucksack and finding the telephoto lens, putting two and two together.

Hart grabbed the rifle and shucked off the rucksack. Lightning doesn't strike twice in the same place. The next time, whatever happened, the Captain would kill him. Probably slit his throat.

Hart started up the track. First at a hobble. Then at a jog.

SIXTEEN

The Captain ran. He could hear the patter of the girl's feet ahead of him. He was catching up. He was still a young man. Fighting fit. Well fed. The girl was wrecked. She would be his shortly. Nothing was beyond him now. He could feel the testosterone surging through his limbs.

How easy it had been to kill the man. He had seen him flailing through the trees and taken a snap shot. The bastard had rocketed forwards like someone launched out of a cannon. A human cannonball. Later, when he had the girl, he would go back and check for more film in the man's backpack and expose that too. Bust the data cards. Then he would be safe. Maybe he would even take the man's ears as a souvenir to prove to the other men back at the camp that he had got him.

He saw the girl fifty metres ahead of him. The crazy bitch had come back when she heard the shot. Why had she done that? She could have been three or four hundred metres further ahead now. Half a kilometre maybe. Given herself a chance to escape.

He caught himself laughing. Well, he would have got her anyway. It was inevitable. He could probably sniff her out by this stage. There'd been no water to speak of at the house, just an outside rain bucket. They brought all their drinking water in. Some of the girls were pretty ripe after two weeks of not washing. But his soldiers didn't seem to care. Fucked them anyway.

Thirty metres now. He slapped the pistol on his hip. Stupid to have left his rifle behind, but he hadn't wanted it cluttering him up while he was running. The pistol would do. He didn't want to actually kill the girl. She'd gotten to him for some reason, probably because she didn't fear him. Even after nearly three weeks she didn't fear him. She lay there and let him do what he wanted, but he was unable to break her, unable to get through to her, not to where it counted. Any other girl he would have killed but this one was special. She was Burim Dardan's daughter – Albanian royalty. And she didn't frighten. But he bet she was frightened now. Oh yes. Sure enough she was frightened now.

He caught up with her in a small clearing next to a gorge. He could hear water pissing away below them. In another world, at another time, you might have gone fishing down there for trout, or held a picnic. It was that scenic. But people didn't do those sorts of things any more. Not in Kosovo. Not with the war on.

The girl stood looking at him from the centre of the clearing. She was breathing like the bulls you see in those Spanish films with the lances in their backs, thought the Captain. Great, heavy breaths that shake the entire body. As if the body is a lung.

He drew his pistol, but let the weight of it carry his hand down to his side. 'Come here, girl.'

'No. You will have to kill me.'

'I won't have to kill you. I'll just wound you. In the arm, maybe. Or the upper leg. Just above the knee.'

'Then you'll have to carry me.'

'That won't be a problem.'

'Why won't you kill me? You've killed all the rest.'

'It would be too easy,' said the Captain. 'And I am tired of killing.'

'No you're not. You say that for effect. You killed those people we passed, didn't you? There must have been ten of them. You killed them all.'

'Them? Oh, they don't count. Those aren't people. They're just numbers. Another ten to add to the tally. I thought you meant real killing. Like your father. Like the Anglez. Killing that counts.'

The Captain was walking towards her all the time. But Lumnije could not move, not any longer. She thought of her father and her mother, of her brother and the Anglez, of what had happened to her these last few weeks. About the sweetness of escape and the bitterness of being captured again. The Captain must indeed be a superman. Had to be. Everything he did he won at. Everyone who opposed him he beat.

She summoned up a residue of strength from somewhere deep inside her body and began to edge towards the top of the gorge.

The Captain quickened his step. 'Stay where you are.'

Now Lumnije was running towards the gorge and the Captain was sprinting to cut her off.

'No. Stop.'

He was levelling his pistol at her.

She tripped and fell. Right on the edge of the gorge she tripped and fell. She could feel the tears of frustration clouding her eyes. Her body ached and her legs would no longer obey her. She turned onto her front and began to crawl.

The Captain slowed up. He had her now. She was his.

Hart appeared at the furthest edge of the clearing. He raised the rifle. His hands were shaking.

'Stop. Don't move. Drop your pistol.'

The Captain must surely have been astonished at Hart's sudden re-emergence from the dead but, if he was, he showed no sign of it. Maybe he didn't quite believe it? Maybe he didn't hear Hart call out to him? Maybe he was so concentrated on the girl he had no time for anything else?

Hart fired a single shot. It wasn't meant as a warning shot, but it missed the Captain cleanly. It severed the upper branch of a tree ten feet to the man's right.

The Captain fired three closely spaced shots at Hart with his pistol, but Hart was way out of range and the shots petered out long before they could do any damage. The Captain continued towards Lumnije. It was clear that he intended to take her alive and use her as a bargaining tool.

Hart raised the rifle and shot at him again, making due allowance for the rightward drift of the first bullet, just as he'd been taught during Corps practice at Bisley while he was still at school.

He saw the Captain spin, then disappear over the edge of the hillside towards the river.

Hart let the rifle drop and sat down. Then he turned onto his side and curled up into a foetal ball.

SEVENTEEN

It was nearly midday. Four hours after Hart had shot the Captain.

'He's still following us,' said Lumnije. 'He's still on our trail.'

Hart turned towards her, his eyes wide with shock. 'Impossible. I shot him. You saw me do it. You're imagining things. You're seeing ghosts.'

'Look.' Lumnije pointed far down the valley behind them.

A solitary figure was making its way along the trail. Even at a distance of nearly a kilometre, it was clear to both of them that the figure was that of the Captain. It was wearing military camouflage and a combat cap. At one point the sun glinted off the pair of dark glasses the Captain had been wearing when they last saw him, brandishing his pistol at the edge of the clearing.

'Jesus Christ. What is the bastard made of? Granite? Do bullets bounce off him?'

'What? Like they bounce off you?'

'My telephoto lens, not me.' Hart shaded his eyes. 'Does he have the rifle? Lumnije, does he have the rifle? I know I should have chucked it over the gorge.' He squinted against the sunlight. 'My long sight isn't good. Can you see?'

'No. No. He doesn't have it. But he is limping. You must have hit him after all.'

'I should have checked he was dead. Gone down after him. I thought he fell into the gorge and we were rid of him.'

'How could you check? The man is invulnerable. Nothing can kill him.'

Hart made a face. 'He must have hooked up onto a tree or something.'

The two of them stared at the approaching figure as if hypnotized.

'He is going to catch us,' said Lumnije. 'Nothing can stop him.'

'No, he's not.' Hart tried to take Lumnije's hand but she snatched it away. They both began to run. 'He is limping,' said Hart, between breaths. 'So I must have hit him. Or else he damaged his leg falling. Trying to get away from the rifle. Maybe both. So he's sure to be losing blood. So we'll be getting stronger. And he'll be getting weaker. Don't you see?'

'You really think so?'

'I know so.'

73

They forged ahead in silence for a while. The fright seemed to have galvanized them. They had both forgotten, for the time being at least, just how hungry and thirsty they were.

'Thank you for coming back for me,' said Hart. 'I've been meaning to say.'

'I thought you were dead.'

'Then why did you come back?'

Lumnije flapped one hand at him as if she was batting off a fly. They continued for a while at the half-jog. Both were functioning at the outer edges of their capacities. Close to total exhaustion.

'Why did you come back then?' Hart repeated. 'Tell me.'

Lumnije shook her head. 'Because I was scared.'

'Scared people don't return to the lion's den voluntarily. You knew what he would do to you, and yet still you came back.'

Lumnije stopped and stared at Hart. Her face was a mask of pain. She said nothing. Only looked at him.

'Your parents?' he said. 'And your brother? You didn't want to lose me too?'

She nodded.

'Come on.' He took her hand again and was gratified this time that she didn't snatch it back. If anyone had asked him, he would not have been able to explain why he felt so pleased. But he suspected that it had something to do with his vision of himself as a fundamentally kind man. A man whom women could trust. Nothing like the monster who was pursuing them.

'We need to break trail. We need to go higher. Where he will have difficulty following us now that he's limping.'

'We need water. And food. Not detours,' said Lumnije.

'Water, yes. We can manage without food for a while longer.'

'We could head down for the gorge. There is water down there for sure.'

'No. That would only suit him,' said Hart. 'We have to risk going higher. He is injured. It will make it harder for him to follow us. Believe me in this.'

'But there will be no snow melt. Not this time of the year. The streams will be dry.'

'Still.'

At the first available opportunity they cut upwards onto a deer track. Hart backed down the trail again and did his best to cover their footsteps as he did so. Then he continued further up the main track, making sure to leave a few random boot impressions as he walked. He'd read about doing this somewhere. In a John Buchan novel probably. A hundred yards further on he cut back up through the woods, walking gingerly from stone to stone, trying to leave no trail.

'That will not fool him,' said Lumnije, when he rejoined her.

'But I had to try.'

'Yes.' She nodded. 'You had to try.'

'Are you really only sixteen?' he said later.

She didn't answer.

Hart looked down at her feet. The shoes she was wearing were coming apart. He looked down at his own. He felt a stab of guilt when he realized how effective his own were in comparison to hers. How intact. But what could he do? His were size elevens. Hers were maybe a size five. You could fit two of her feet into his one. It let him well and truly off the hook.

'Maybe he continued along the trail?' he said at last. 'Maybe we tricked him?'

She shook her head. 'No. You must know him by now. He will have seen where we went. He will out-think us.'

'We can't always assume that. It will weaken us to assume that.'

Lumnije sat down by the side of the deer trail. The movement was so abrupt that Hart nearly ran into her. He sat down beside her.

'I need water,' she said.

Hart looked around. He closed his eyes and listened. Then he cupped his ears. 'Maybe up high? Maybe we can find a lake?'

'Maybe,' she said.

They heard a scrabbling sound far below them. Both stood up.

'Do you think it's him?' said Lumnije. 'That close?'

'It might be a deer. Or a sheep. They probably have wild goats here too. Could be anything.'

'But on the trail behind us? How likely is that?'

'Not very likely.' The expression on Hart's face reflected his inner feelings. He was beyond masking anything any more. Beyond prevarication.

They started up again. It was late afternoon by now, but the day was still warm. 'He didn't want to kill you. Why?' said Hart at last. He was snatching breaths whenever he could, like a man with asthma.

'I told you. He wants me.'

'But the rest – the other girls. What makes you so different from them?'

Lumnije shrugged. 'Luck,' she said. 'I was having my time of the month when they caught us. The soldiers put me aside for later. Knowing they hadn't touched me, the Captain took me for his own. He told me later that he was scared of getting a disease.' After she said it she seemed shocked at her own immodesty. Shocked that she was telling him this. That the obscene could seem so pedestrian. Something, though, held her back from adding that the soldiers' overriding intention was to see to it that all the Albanian girls got pregnant. That it was a war aim. Designed to damage the enemy psychologically.

'You call that luck?' Hart said.

Lumnije laughed. It was the first time she had laughed since Hart met her. She threw back her head and laughed. But there was bitterness in her laugh. Something metallic. As if it was witness to its own reflection. Not intrinsically true.

77

By nightfall, the Captain still hadn't caught them.

'His leg wound. It must be worse than we thought,' said Lumnije.

'How much further do you think it is to the monastery?'

Lumnije looked bereft. 'I do not know where it is. I no longer know where it is.'

Hart looked at her. Her eyes were hollow from lack of sleep. Her face was pale and drawn. It was clear that she was only holding herself together through sheer willpower. 'I'm going to suggest something that you need to do,' he said. 'I want you to listen to me, please, and not just reject it out of hand.'

'What is it?' Lumnije's face held not even the faintest trace of hope.

'I'm going to cut back down the hill. Then I'm going to ambush him. He has to be in pain. Probably losing blood. He won't be on his guard. It's him or us. I want it to be him.'

'And I wait here for you, is that it?'

'No. You continue on your way. You keep on walking until you can't walk any more.'

'He will kill you.'

'He tried that before. He failed.'

'Through stupid luck. A one in a thousand chance. It will not happen again.'

'But I will have the advantage of surprise. I will hide myself at the side of the track. Up high maybe. With a rock. He will have no chance. He is crippled, remember. Not walking normally. He has to use the track.'

Lumnije stared at Hart. 'Why? Why do you have this urge to sacrifice yourself for me?'

'Sacrifice has nothing to do with it. It's to save myself. Nothing more complicated than that. It's what I would do if I were alone and he was following me.'

'Don't you think he knows that?'

Hart shook his head. 'I don't care. A few more hours of this and I won't be able to ambush him. I'd just topple onto the track in front of him with my legs in the air like a cockchafer.'

Lumnije laughed again. But this time it was a purer laugh, with nothing held back. It made her look like a young girl. The girl she had been before the Captain came to her village three weeks before.

'So you're okay with that? I go?'

She gave him a half nod.

If he hadn't been looking out for it he wouldn't have seen it.

EIGHTEEN

The Captain stopped for a moment to inspect the wound in his side. It was only a flesh wound. Had to be, or he would be dead by now. But it hurt like a thousand biting ants.

He carried morphine on him but he didn't dare take it. Morphine made you drowsy. And other stuff too. But it was the drowsiness part he needed to avoid.

Once, eighteen months before, he'd been caught by a ricochet from one of his own soldiers' bullets. The ricochet had taken him in the shoulder. Torn through bone and muscle. He'd taken morphine for that. Slept for three days. Become claustrophobic. Couldn't pee. Couldn't shit. He daren't risk the same thing happening again. The Anglez would come back and kill him. Hell. He was probably on his way back even now.

The Captain checked around himself, just as he had done every five minutes into his climb. If anyone was approaching him, he'd hear. Morphine also wrecked your hearing. Gave you tinnitus. It felt like someone was testing a bust loudspeaker inside your head. You couldn't make out anything inside that din.

The Captain changed his dressing. Cleaned away the Celox blood coagulant. Threw on some sulphonamide powder. Hoped he wasn't allergic to the stuff. He didn't want to get urticaria. Or Stevens-Johnson syndrome. He'd seen both of those in the field and knew how much he needed to avoid them. But the danger of an infection was greater. The bullet had passed through his clothing. Carried chunks of it through his wound. That's how Reinhard Heydrich had died in Poland in 1942. Not by bullet or by grenade. But by the bits of leather car seat and stuffing the grenade had blown into his wounds. Sulphonamide, the new wonder drug, would have saved him. Theodor Morell, Hitler's personal physician, had advocated its use. But Gebhardt, the asshole Himmler sent out to look after his pet, overruled him, thinking Heydrich was getting better.

The Captain wouldn't make Gebhardt's mistake. When he died he wanted it to be of old age. Extreme old age. There were too many things he wanted to do in this world before then.

He forced himself to his feet and started back up the trail. He still couldn't work out how the Anglez had survived his shot. He'd hit him in the back. Seen it clear as day. Surely the bastard wasn't still wearing his Kevlar vest beneath the rest of his kit? Those things could weigh twenty kilograms. It would have been the first thing he'd have discarded if he knew he was being chased. But maybe this Anglez was a coward? Maybe he feared being shot in the back? But he'd come after the girl, hadn't he, just as the girl had come after him? Crazy. But then he too had been crazy to leave his rifle back in the clearing, beside the body.

The Captain caught himself nodding off. He flared his eyes, mimicking wakefulness. He rested his head against a tree but refused to lie down again. The man *had* been dead. You didn't suddenly get up after you'd been hit in the spine by a 7.62 mm bullet from an assault rifle. You stayed down. You stayed put.

But why had he left the rifle behind him after he'd shot the Anglez? Because he'd wanted the girl, of course. Thought he might have to run. Didn't want to weigh himself down with useless junk. He had intended to go back for the rifle later. You had to make compromises in this life. All the time. You had to make compromises. Nobody was perfect. He'd made the right call.

The Captain drifted into unconsciousness. Still standing. Still half leaning against the tree.

He woke up some time later, the sweat dry on his face. *You've been dozing again*, he told himself. *Maybe your wound is worse than you think? Maybe you've been having a fever?*

He rechecked his watch. No. It was okay. He'd only been out for ten, twenty minutes tops. Not surprising really. One didn't get shot every day. And by one's own gun. Bloody stupid. Bloody stupid thing to do. Even though he'd got away with little more than a puncture wound. No vital organs involved. He'd been incredibly lucky. The pair of them could have seen him off, no problem. Silly fuckers not to come and check on him when he fell over the gorge. Scared shitless probably. He'd only landed six feet down. All they'd needed to do was walk to the edge and he'd have been theirs.

He felt down for his pistol. His skin flashed cold as if the wind had kissed it. Or as if he'd just swum through an icy current out at sea. The pistol was gone. He felt again. Then he straightened up and looked around. Maybe it had jumped out of his holster while he was walking? But it was attached by a lanyard. It would have bobbed along the track behind him until he noticed it.

He checked the end of the lanyard. It had been cut. Neatly cut. The Anglez then. He must have come along while he was asleep and taken the pistol. The Captain straightened up. He peered round the glade, more in curiosity than apprehension. Did the Anglez have him covered from somewhere? And if not, why not? Why hadn't the man killed him? The Captain shook his head.

Insane. These foreigners were insane. The Anglez could have shot him in his sleep. Been done with it all. But here they both were with nothing changed. Nothing fundamentally changed. Except that now he knew the Anglez's weak spot. The man was a bleeding heart. If it had been the girl who found him first, she would have slit his throat. No ifs or buts about that. And taken his ears as trophies.

No wonder they said the West was dying. It was emoting itself to death. Like the turgid death scene in some opera, where the heroine lies on a bed and coughs up tiny gouts of blood from behind a handkerchief while the hero sits and weeps into his hands. Inconsolable.

The Captain shook his head to clear it. Slapped himself on both cheeks. Grinned. Then set off after his quarry again.

NINETEEN

'I got his pistol. He is disarmed.'

Lumnije looked at Hart. 'So he is dead then?'

'Dead? No?'

'What do you mean, not dead?' Lumnije was staring now. 'How can you disarm such a man without killing him?'

'He was asleep. Dozing. I crept up behind him and cut his lanyard. Took his pistol.'

'And you did not kill him?'

'There seemed no point. What did you want me to do? Kill an unarmed and wounded man?'

'Yes. Yes, you fool.'

Hart fingered the pistol in his hand. 'I will kill him if he comes after us. Obviously. But I could not kill him while he was asleep.'

'So why didn't you wake him up?'

Hart hesitated. 'Then I would have had to kill him. Don't you see?'

Lumnije made a disgusted motion with her hand. The sort of motion a woman will make when she has decided that a man she had formerly believed in is no longer for her.

Hart felt the motion bitterly. He had seen the Captain was dozing from the far side of the glade. At first he had thought the Captain was waiting for him, like in a cowboy film. Lulling him into a false sense of security, like Clint Eastwood under his poncho in *For A Few Dollars More*. But the longer he looked, the more he realized that the Captain had genuinely fallen asleep standing up. Which wasn't surprising. The man clearly wasn't the superman Lumnije thought him to be. He was wounded. And he was succumbing to his wound. Like any normal man.

Hart had taken the opportunity to check the wound out while he was stealing the Captain's gun. It didn't look good. In fact it was a miracle that the Captain had travelled so far with it. As Hart stared at it, he had felt almost detached from himself. It was he, Hart, who had caused that wound. He'd shot a man. With no malice. With no forethought. Simply shot him because it had seemed the only sane thing to do at the time. And the result was this.

Hart looked down at the pistol in his hand. Knock the man out? Should he do that? But the pistol felt heavy and alien. Quite enough to kill someone with if you overdid the blow. Tie the man up? With what? What should he do?

Hart held the pistol up to the Captain's head. It would be so simple. No one would hear the shot. No one would witness what would amount to an assassination. A murder.

Before he knew it Hart found himself walking up the track again, away from his sleeping enemy. There was no way the Captain could catch them any more in the condition he was in. No way in hell. And there was no way Hart could murder a wounded man.

On his way back to Lumnije, Hart had been tempted to chuck the pistol over the side of the defile next to the track. But then they would have no means of defence. The Captain wasn't the only soldier in this world and there might be others ahead of them. The possession of the pistol might save their lives.

Hart checked the pistol out as he walked. Its weight was oddly comforting. There were five bullets left in the magazine. More than enough.

Now here was Lumnije telling him, in so many words, that he was a coward for not killing a helpless man. A man who had raped and brutalized her. Killed her family. Destroyed her life.

What the hell was the world coming to? How did a man know which way to turn?

He and Lumnije continued along the trail, twenty yards between them, like two strangers. Hart wished he had his cameras back. He felt unclothed without them, like someone sent to cover a wedding in only a pair of shorts.

When next he looked up Lumnije was squaring up to him across the track.

He stopped.

'Give me the gun,' she said. 'I will go back and kill him.'

'No you won't.'

She took a step towards him. 'Give me the gun.'

There was something so absurd about the situation that Hart was tempted to burst into peals of hysterical laughter. Here was this sixteen-year-old girl. Dishevelled. Beaten down. Brutalized. Deprived of everything that had meant anything to her in this world. And here he was, John Hart, budding photojournalist in the prime of life, freak survivor of a dedicated murder attempt, fortunate denizen of the West and proud inheritor of its fifty-year peace dividend. And here they both were arguing over the possession of a pistol, like children squabbling in a public playground.

'You're not going back,' Hart said. 'I forbid it.'

'You said yourself that he was weak. Badly wounded. That he could not catch us if he tried.'

'Yes. I said that.'

'Then why try to stop me? What do you care what happens to me? Who am I to you? I'm just a weight round your neck.'

'No you're not. You're more to me than that.'

'Then give me the gun.'

'No.'

Lumnije made a lunge at him. It was so unexpected that Hart countered automatically by raising both his arms. The pistol was tucked into his belt. Lumnije tried to grab it. Hart threw her off.

He hoped that would be enough to dissuade her, but he saw by the set of her face that she was about to come at him again. This was no longer play. Or anything remotely like it. He tried to grab her by the arms and turn her away from him so that she could neither bite, nor gouge, nor kick. He was probably a foot taller than her and outweighed her by five stone. In principle, at least, there should have been no contest between them.

Lumnije threw herself back against him and the pair of them pitched to the side of the track. Then she carried on over his body, borne by her own physical momentum, and disappeared down the defile.

Hart watched in horror as she rolled and tumbled down the rocks. He lunged after her but he was too late.

She came to rest at the bottom of the slope, some thirty yards below him.

Hart scrabbled down the face of the slope until he fetched up beside her. He tried to disentangle her limbs, fearful of what he might find. The sheer anarchy of her fall had rocked him to the core. Lumnije had flailed and pitched down the incline like a rag doll. Angrily, almost. As if her body relished the punishment it was taking.

A noise alerted him to the presence of someone nearby. Hart turned round. The Captain was approaching them along the track. He was half running, half dragging his injured leg. By a serial mischance, Lumnije's fall had brought them down to a parallel trail, maybe a half-kilometre behind their previous position in terms of pure walking distance, and straight into the Captain's path.

Hart felt for his pistol. It was no longer in his belt. He looked back up the slope behind him. The pistol had fallen out ten yards above him. He could see it nestling amongst the scraggle and the scree.

He launched himself up the slope, half aware that the Captain was paralleling his movements twenty yards across from him.

But Hart wasn't wounded. He had full use of all his limbs. And the slope was steep.

He reached the pistol first and turned it on the Captain.

The Captain watched him, unblinking. 'You will not shoot.' The Captain's accent was faux-American, as if his English had been learnt from a bunch of straight-to-video Steven Seagal movies.

'Are you so very sure?'

Hart saw the Captain's confidence falter. He was in pain. The blood from his wound had drenched through his combat overalls, making a darker stain against the original camouflage design.

'Get back down to the track,' said Hart. 'I'm covering you all the way, remember? I'm the unwounded one. You can't get away. If you try to run I shall shoot you. Believe me. This time I will do it in cold blood.'

The Captain, to Hart's astonishment, obeyed. Was it something in his face? Had something changed him in these past few hours? From a nominal non-combatant into someone who has finally chosen which side they wish to fight on?

'Now get out your first-aid pack.'

'What first-aid pack?'

'Don't fuck with me, Captain. All frontline soldiers carry them.'

The Captain smiled. He was always smiling. 'I've used it all up. How do you think I got here behind you so quick?'

Hart wavered. But then he saw the Captain's eyes. Hart had watched many people being interviewed in the course of his five-year career. Photographed them even. He knew what their eyes did when they were lying. The micro-expressions that slipped through the net to reveal the liar's true intentions. The movement to the right that a right-handed person's eyes will make when they are fabulating. The Captain was maintaining far too much eye contact with him. It was unnatural. There were thoughts and motivations going on behind the impermeable mask. Hidden agendas.

'Throw the pack towards Lumnije. Otherwise I'll come on over and beat it out of you. After shooting you again first, of course. Where it really hurts. I'd enjoy that.'

The Captain felt in his left thigh pocket. He tossed a flat black packet onto the path.

'Now lie down. On your front. Arms behind.'

'You're joking, surely? The girl is dead. Can't you see that? She's probably broken her neck, the silly bitch. Whatever set us against each other is gone. I've got no quarrel with you. Take the pistol. Take the morphine pack. And piss off. My men will already be following us along the track. They will be coming soon to find me. If you leave me now, I will not follow you. I am badly wounded. Worse than I thought. I've got no taste for this any more. Now that the Albanian cunt has finally managed to kill herself you are free.'

Lumnije groaned. She turned partially over onto one side. For a moment Hart could see the Captain's eyes widen and become uncertain. If Lumnije woke, there was only one possible outcome to this piece of Grand Guignol theatre they were taking part in, and the Captain knew it.

'Lie down, I said.'

The Captain made a big thing about being forced onto his stomach. Like a professional footballer who is trying for a foul, everything the man did was thought out and pre-calculated. Hart realized that now. The Captain was a calculating machine. He functioned outside any normal person's orbit.

Once the Captain was flat on the ground he craned his head back over his shoulder to look at Hart. 'Go on. Tell me. How did you survive my shot? It took you in the back. I saw it clear as day. From that distance I don't miss. You pitched up the track like you'd been kicked by a horse. People don't survive that. It was Kevlar, wasn't it? You were wearing Kevlar?'

'No.'

'Then how?'

Hart hesitated. But what harm could it do? It might even work in his favour. Puncture the man's morale just that little bit more. 'Your bullet hit my telephoto lens. The one in my backpack. It shifted the slug away from my body. I felt as if I'd been hit across the back with an iron bar. You lucked out, Captain. Not everyone you kill stays down.'

The Captain's eyes turned inwards. 'Maybe my luck is running out?' He refocused on Hart again. 'Your telephoto lens, you say? Makes a change from the Bible, anyway.' His face broke into its customary grin. But the effect was macabre. Like a piranha fish leering at its prey from below the waterline, its features exaggerated by the water.

Hart positioned himself over the Captain and pinioned the man's arms with his legs. He was scared. The man below him was a killer. And a rapist. And a torturer. A man for whom morality played no part. A man who would kill you as soon as look at you. A man for whom the words 'regret' and 'empathy' did not exist.

Hart felt under the Captain's belly and undid his belt. While he did this he held the Captain's own pistol tight against his ear. Maybe he should let it off by mistake? Who could blame him for firing under these circumstances? Who would ever know? Who would even care? The man's brains would spatter over the undergrowth and it would all be ended.

'Tempting, isn't it?' said the Captain.

'I'm not like you,' said Hart. 'I don't kill on a whim.'

'More fool you,' said the Captain.

Hart retrieved the Captain's belt and used it to tie his hands behind his back. Then he rifled through the Captain's pockets. No knives. No spare pistols. Nothing useful. Just a carnelian rosary, some American cigarettes and a windproof lighter. Hart pocketed the cigarettes and the lighter. After a brief hesitation he pocketed the rosary too. He didn't know why.

When he turned the Captain over, he was forced to look at the man's face close to. The Captain was smiling. Grinning from ear to ear. Hart lurched sideways so that the Captain would not be able to knee him between the legs. He could imagine the Captain biting a chunk out of his windpipe like an attack dog. Worrying at him despite his ligatured hands.

In the top pocket of the Captain's combat outfit he found a pair of flexicuffs.

The Captain grinned some more when Hart took them out. 'You know what I use those for?'

'I don't want to know.'

'I used them on her, amongst other things. When I wanted to do things to her that caused her to squirm too much. I tied her hands together and locked them round the bed head. Then I could do whatever I wanted to her. Didn't matter how much she squirmed. I've never known a girl to squirm and scream so much. I reckon she secretly enjoyed it, don't you? Some women do, you know. I tell you, once…'

Hart stood up. He wanted to start beating the Captain around the head with his own pistol. To batter his head to a pulp. But a single glance at Lumnije's recumbent body was enough to show him how much he would be needing this man in the coming hours. And, following that, how much he would relish handing him in to the authorities.

Lumnije was groaning. Hart locked the Captain in his own handcuffs and replaced the man's belt around his waist. Then he went over to attend to his patient.

The Captain had heard Lumnije's groans too, and recognized their significance to him. 'I'd give her some morphine. Quick. She's bound to be in pain when she wakes up.'

'What do you care? You're only looking to cover your back. If she wakes, she'll kill you. And do you know what? I'll let her. If she needs morphine, I'll give it to her in my own time. Life or death? It's a throw of the dice as far as you're concerned.'

'Isn't everything?' said the Captain, grinning.

TWENTY

Lumnije had a heavy concussion. Hart realized that much. The pupils of her eyes, when he twitched open her lids, were uneven – one considerably larger than the other. She was bleeding out of one ear. She was breathing maybe forty times a minute. Hart thought that the normal baseline might be half that. Maybe less.

He let his hands travel over her body. He felt almost guilty as he did so. As though he were betraying her trust in some way. Putting himself on a par with her aggressors.

'Like that, did you?'

It was the Captain. Hart ignored him.

On the surface he could see and feel no real damage beyond countless small abrasions and tears. He treated these with swabs, antiseptic and sulphonamide. He tried to remember if he had heard somewhere that one shouldn't use morphine for head injuries, but he couldn't remember. His main fear was that he might have missed something in his cursory body check. Something serious. So he gave her the morphine anyway.

'Hey. How about me with the morphine?' said the Captain. 'I've been shot.'

'I need you,' Hart said. 'I need you walking. You are going to carry her.'

'The fuck I am.'

'It's either that or a shot to the guts. I've got no more time to argue with you. You can die alone, by the side of this track, in agony, if that's what you want. No water. No morphine. Nothing. It's a more decent fate than you've ever offered your victims. Either that or you carry her.'

'Well,' said the Captain. 'When you put it like that.'

'I do.'

The Captain sighed. 'Why have I begun to believe you all of a sudden?'

'Maybe because what I am saying is true?'

The Captain tried to crane his head backwards to stare at his wound, but his prone position made that impossible. 'You know what your best bet would be?'

'What?'

'To leave us both here and fuck off back home where you belong. You're intact. Unwounded. A walking miracle. Why throw away your life? My men will find me eventually. And I'll always think kindly of you.' The last part was said with heavy irony.

Hart pulled the Captain to his feet. He looked down at Lumnije. This was impossible. Impossible.

Hart took off the Captain's belt again and used it to tie Lumnije's hands together. Then he hung her across the Captain's shoulders, with the belt hooked through the man's battledress pockets, so that her legs trailed behind like the tails of a skirt.

He slid the pistol into his waistband and took Lumnije's legs in either hand.

'Now walk. No more talking. Just walk.'

TWENTY-ONE

Hart imagined the three of them leaving a slug trail behind them. Seen from above they must present a strange picture. What would a circling buzzard make of them, for instance? Some previously unknown creature, perhaps, slithering and stumbling up the slope? The beast with two backs? But there was no way on earth that Hart could carry Lumnije alone. He needed the Captain. Needed a human packhorse.

It took them the better part of two hours to make their way back to the spot where he and Lumnije had had their falling out. Hart looked back down the defile. How had Lumnije survived the fall? Someone must have been smiling on them both. Or making a mockery of them. Playing the long game.

As soon as he allowed the 'smiling' analogy to enter his head he was tempted to laugh out loud. Smiling on him, maybe. Hardly on Lumnije. He tried to get his head round what she might feel when she woke up and saw their changed situation – the killer of her parents and her brother – her tormentor and rapist – carrying her. But he soon gave up. He would deal with that as and when he came to it.

At the beginning of their trek the Captain had tried to work on him psychologically. Predictably. To tell him stupid stories. Disgust him. Draw him into his own world view. But soon the Captain was fighting for breath so hard that he no longer had the energy left to talk.

Hart was grateful for that. The Captain's stories did work on him. And the worst thing was that he suspected they were all true.

The Captain, for his part, delighted in disgusting Hart. Testing his parameters. And he paid no mind, at least at first, when Hart told him to shut up. He knew that Hart needed him now, and this knowledge was precious to him. The Captain only had to wait. Hart would have to sleep some time and then the Captain's moment would come. And he would relish every second of it.

His wound was bad. Sure. No doubt about that. But not so bad that he could not walk. He felt weak, too. Very weak. But not quite as weak as he made out. The heavy breathing was largely for effect.

How old was this Anglez, the Captain wondered. Twenty-five? Twenty-six? Probably scared shitless at what had happened to his calm, well-ordered life. The Captain had seen it countless times before. Had used it to his advantage. Ruthlessness has its very own logic. And it was kinder in the long run. Why make people suffer unnecessarily? Just kill them and get it over with. That way you can gather in more victims. Like a soul harvest.

The Japanese had been masters of it. The Germans too. And the Russians. Races with iron in their guts. Not like the English, with their fuzzy principles and pissant pieties. When did they last have a war on their own territory? The Captain didn't know. But it was one hell of a long time ago for sure. Yet still they persisted in meddling in other people's wars. They should keep their snouts out. War hurt. The strong always dominated the weak. War was like a river in spate, washing everything away before it. Best get yourself a raft right at the beginning. Then cling to it like merry fuck and let no one else aboard.

The Captain hated the Anglez. He realized that now. Hated him with a bitter and resentful hatred. At first he had brushed aside the humiliation of his present condition. Ignored it. But now he knew that if his men came across him like this, with him trussed up, a prisoner, and the Anglez behind him, forcing him to carry the whore like a beast of burden, he would never be able to hold his head up again. Could never hope to control them in the way he had been doing.

He would have to do something. Anything. And soon. Before he got too weak. Before the blood loss finally got to him.

TWENTY-TWO

'Give me your arm.' Hart held out his hand.

'What the fuck for?'

'I'm going to inject you with morphine.'

'No you're fucking not.'

Hart sighed. 'If you don't collaborate I'll shove the needle in your neck.'

The Captain looked up at Hart. Maybe the Anglez did have some balls after all? Did have some sense in his head? The morphine would put him to sleep, as it was laced with a strong tranquillizer. The Anglez needed sleep, that much was a certainty. And the only way he could sleep was to be damned certain the Captain was sleeping too. People had been known to work their way out of fibre cuffs before – even chew their way through them if they were desperate enough and were given enough time.

The Captain proffered his arm. Well. He needed sleep

too. And the pain was intense. About as bad as it could get and you not pass out. The Captain had been complaining for the past hour that he could no longer carry the whore. The Anglez had seemed not to be listening. But now he had thought up this little ploy for himself.

Full on, thought the Captain. The pain was full on. He suddenly knew he would welcome the morphine. There was time. A whole lot of time. He knew where they were going now. And the whore showed no signs of waking up. She'd probably scrambled her brains falling down the hill. What a dumb cunt. To fall down a hill like that. What had she been thinking of? Had she been trying to off herself again? Maybe twenty per cent of the girls in the rape house tried to kill themselves over the course of time. Some succeeded. Some didn't. But it was fun beating them up and then raping them again afterwards. The Captain had taken quite a liking to it. Him and some of his men. He liked seeing their frightened faces. Making an example of them in front of the other girls. It had become compulsive. Like the killing.

The more he thought about it, the more he didn't know what he'd do when the war was over and Serbia was victorious. Maybe hire himself out as a mercenary? That's what most of the guys did. Once you were bitten by the need for action it was almost impossible to shake it. You had to follow it like you would the leader in some dance. Snaking and reeling behind him. A dance of death.

The Captain began drifting off. It was good. Maybe the

Anglez had slipped him an overdose? Get rid of him that way? The fool clearly couldn't face murder head on. Didn't have the balls for it. Few people had.

It took a special sort of person to kill dispassionately. A person like him.

The Captain.

TWENTY-THREE

Hart had found the rock spring while reconnoitring up the track ahead of them during a rest period. The water seemed clean and fresh. It was this that had given him the idea of doping the Captain.

Truth to tell, he hadn't known what to do with the man. As a child he had always fantasized about how easy it would be to kill someone in warfare. He had read trashy mags like any other boy his age, and played soldier games and watched war movies. But when it came down to it, the real thing was a little different. Killing a man in cold blood – even a man who boasted to you of the most bestial of crimes – was another thing entirely. Different from taking a snap shot at them when the odds were against you. A snap shot that just happened to hit its mark.

But the rock spring changed the dynamic. Changed it totally.

When he was sure the Captain was out cold – that the tranquillizers had cut in and that the morphine was biting – he dragged the man's prone body past the rock spring and farther along the track. Way beyond the point where the Captain could possibly hear the water pinkling into the natural basin that housed it behind him. Then he walked back down the track, clearing any sign of their progress with a cut branch. The Captain would wake up and continue on his way. Dehydrated from the morphine. Woozy from the tranqs. Like an automaton. While he and Lumnije would have drunk their fill. Hart knew this. Was counting on it.

He scooped up the water in his palm and tipped it into Lumnije's mouth. Then he massaged her throat so that she would swallow. Whenever she gagged, he waited. Then he began again. Only when she had drunk her fill did he drink himself.

Then he stood up. Next step.

He would carry Lumnije himself now. He fastened her hands around his neck with the cuffs, and attached her to his waist by the belt. He slipped her legs through his arms, with his thumbs tucked through his own belt for stability. He didn't trust the Captain. Didn't believe he could dominate the man all the way to the monastery. And where would he find any UN forces to hand him in to when he got there? No. The man was more trouble than he was worth. That's why Hart had dosed him with enough morphine to fell a horse. One thing he had to say for the Serb paramilitaries.

They came prepared. Their first-aid packs were second to none. They clearly expected to be shot at some point in their careers and wished to survive when it happened. And largely out of pain with it.

The rehydrating effects of the water soon wore off. Hart went from feeling semi-euphoric to depressed in under thirty minutes. Lumnije groaned louder now. It sounded to him as though she was hallucinating. Yes. That seemed to be it. Her body jerked and thrashed on his back. Maybe she was reliving all that had happened to her? That was the most likely scenario.

Hart had to stop and rest every five hundred metres. He counted the steps out loud to himself. The last hundred were always the worst. By the end of each section he was mewling with exhaustion. Muttering to himself. Asking himself where he was. What he was doing. Why he was there. Cursing. Cursing his destiny. Then it began all over again.

The countryside around them was gradually changing. Becoming less mountainous. They'd been on the lower, wooded slopes of a vast granite range for most of their journey. Now, in the far distance, maybe twenty miles away as the crow flies, Hart could make out villages and habitations. Farms. Barns. Churches. Blurred, but definitely there. It was inconceivable that he wouldn't come across somewhere similar very soon along their trail. And if it was Serb-held, and they refused to offer him food and water, he would hold them up with his pistol. Give them a taste of their own medicine. Christ, but he was angry enough for that now. It was the anger that was carrying him onwards. The anger and the outrage.

There was something about carrying another human being on your back that profoundly changed your manner of thinking. Because that person was reliant on you for everything. Lumnije seemed real to him, all of a sudden, like nobody else. She was part of him. Her fragile body locked to his by sweat and blood. Symbiotic. Almost related.

Once he felt her pissing down the backs of his legs. He laughed. This was a good thing, he decided. The spring water must have passed through her kidneys. Flushed her out. He felt like a father with his child.

Another time he stopped and checked her pupils. The difference in size was lessening. But still he gave her more morphine. He couldn't afford to have her awake and out of her head on his back. He needed her docile. His to do with as he saw fit.

Like the Captain, he caught himself thinking. Just like the Captain.

TWENTY-FOUR

He sensed the monastery before he saw it. There was something neat about the trail he was following. As if many people had walked it. It was no longer simply a bare mountain trail. It was heading downwards. It was going somewhere. Leading to some precise destination.

First came the vines, as if bearing witness to incipient civilization. On a south-facing hillside. Heavy with grapes. Cared for and nourished. Nearly ripe for harvest. The fundamental signs of domestication.

Hart picked his way along the trail, Lumnije tight against his back. He thought of calling out to see if anyone would answer, but decided against it. There might be Serbian soldiers. Guards, protecting the vines. Protecting the crops. For there were apple trees. Cherry trees. Almonds. Walnuts. Quinces. Hanging in clusters all around him. Like the bloody Garden of Eden.

Then he saw the monastery itself in the valley below him. An island of neatness in a mass of late summer vegetation. The land all around was cleared and planted. The buildings were bright with whitewash. The roof tiles shone in the late afternoon sun. There was a wall surrounding the monastery. Great trees sprang up inside it. Cedars. Poplars. Yews. And a river. It was a crazy place. Like a film set almost. As he watched, the bells in the campanile began to ring. Compline, maybe. It was too early for vespers.

Hart realized that he did not know which day of the week it was any more.

There were dark figures in the fields below him. As he watched them, they turned from their chores and headed down towards the abbey.

He shifted Lumnije to a better position and started down too.

It took him an hour to reach the monastery gates. He could hear the monks chanting. The first shadows of evening were beginning to fall.

He dropped Lumnije onto the grass halfway to the abbey entrance. He stumbled onwards. Threw open the abbey doors. Far down the aisle he could see the monks standing in a semicircle. A large congregation attended them. The monks had their backs to the congregation. Serb, he thought. These are Serbs. And I have brought them an Albanian Muslim. Am I insane?

He shouted once and then turned back. A figure was

entering the monastery precincts behind him. A figure in camos. Dragging one leg. The Captain.

Hart ran towards Lumnije. He had his pistol out now. Held in both hands like they'd taught him in Weapon Familiarization during the Hostile Environment Training course that all war-zone journalists took. He was going to kill the Captain. Have done with it once and for all.

He felt rather than saw the monks run past him, their black clothing flapping in the wind. One of them stopped him and took the pistol from his hand. Very gently. As you would prise something dangerous away from a child. Others placed themselves between Lumnije and the Captain, their arms held high.

Civilians. People who had not been inside the abbey but only in the purlieus. They were coming down the steps from the surrounding buildings. Hart watched them. Men, women and children, so many of them, some of the women with headscarves. The monks seemed like black crows in the larger field of colour they made.

One man, the abbot probably, was standing in front of the Captain. The Captain was talking to him and gesticulating. Pointing to Lumnije, then at Hart.

The abbot was shaking his head. Hart knew it was the abbot. The man had a long grey beard, forked in the middle, a high black hat whose material fell down his back, a staff with a silver top, a gold pendant on his chest with eight points inlaid with rubies. The abbot raised his staff and pointed it at the Captain.

Some of the women who had run down from the buildings were already gathering Lumnije up.

Hart felt infinitely tired. He sank to his knees. The monks were leading the Captain away. The Captain was unwilling. But many of the younger monks seemed vital and strong. Not men to take no for an answer. Their hair hung long behind their heads or was gathered up like a woman's, in a bun. But these were no women. The Captain had no choice but to go where they led him. Perhaps they would tend to his wounds? Make him strong again so that he could take Lumnije back with him? They were Serbs, after all. On the same side. What had he done?

Hart saw the abbot coming towards him. He tried to get to his feet but he was unable.

The abbot fluttered his hand, as if he were drawing attention to something on the path in front of him.

'He's a bad man,' said Hart. 'An evil man. You must protect the woman. He wishes her ill.'

'Evil,' the abbot said. 'It is all around us. You are safe now, my son. The woman too. St Stefan will protect you.'

'But she is a Muslim. You are Christian.'

The abbot shrugged.

Hart found himself thinking about the end of a film. A Billy Wilder film. When Jack Lemmon takes off his wig and reveals to Joe E. Brown that he is really a man underneath.

But the abbot didn't say 'Nobody's perfect'. All he did was to make the sign of the cross and motion to two of his monks to take Hart by the arms and help him to his feet.

Then he turned and indicated all the people who had come running down the steps from the surrounding buildings to help Lumnije, and who were now standing and watching their intercourse. He waved his hand.

'All these,' he said. 'All these are our guests. These are Muslim too.'

TWENTY-FIVE

Hart saw Lumnije three more times before he left the monastery. On the first two occasions he sat beside her bed and held her hand, while one of the monks acted as chaperone. Which was a neat turnaround, thought Hart. A Christian Serbian monk acting as chaperone to an Albanian Muslim woman who had been repeatedly raped by a Christian Serbian war criminal. It almost gave one hope for the future.

On these first two occasions, Lumnije had been far too groggy to formally acknowledge his presence. On the second occasion she had, however, managed what passed for a smile, and once, significantly, she had squeezed his hand when he had told her that she was safe from the Captain because – no doubt thanks to the excellence of the monks' medical ministrations – the man had abandoned his sickbed, stolen the abbot's car and absconded back to his unit during the night.

'The abbot has promised me, though, that Serbian war units are not allowed within the precincts of the monastery. This rule is strictly upheld by the Serbian high command. At the abbot's instigation, the army has posted sentries round the entire periphery of the monastery precincts. The abbot had been arguing for such a thing for months, so he is very pleased that they have finally relented. If the Captain or his men were to breach the guard line he would be subject to an immediate court martial. There is no danger of the Captain coming back, therefore. The abbot agrees with me that the man is addicted to danger and to killing. The prospect of losing his commission and his consequent right to bear arms would be too much for the bastard to bear. Still. It might be wise to leave here as soon as you are able. Would you like me to accompany you to Pristina? I may be able to swing things with the British Consulate there to get you a temporary visa to Britain. Asylum seeker seeking refugee status. That sort of thing.'

Lumnije had shaken her head. Another short squeeze of the hand had followed.

On the third occasion, Lumnije had been able to talk. Hart had come in to say his final goodbyes, and to try one last time to persuade Lumnije to let him help her. His taxi was waiting outside.

'Yes. And the Captain will be waiting too. Further down the road.'

'What? For me?' said Hart.

'No. For me.'

Hart shook his head. 'But they are sending an escort with me.'

'Then you will get through. If I were to travel with you, the escort would melt away. You are an Anglez and I am an Albanian. The two things are very different. If you were to be assassinated on the way to the airport they would fear bad publicity. With me, no one would care. Just another Muslim who got in the way of a bullet.'

Hart had shaken his head, unconvinced. 'You still think the Captain is this superman figure you've created for yourself, don't you? Yet we beat him, Lumnije. We beat him at his own game.'

'But he will win in the end,' she said. 'Such men always do.'

'What? Against me?'

'No, John. Against me.'

Hart had not fully understood then what she had meant. He had put it down to post-traumatic stress. The understandable reaction of a woman who had been brutalized beyond her ability to bear it. Only later, much later, did he come to understand her true meaning.

Before he left she had asked him one last favour.

'Anything. I'll agree to anything,' he said. 'You know that.'

'But this is a hard thing I intend to ask of you.'

'Still. Ask away. It's yours. I owe you that much.'

Lumnije had looked away from him. Out through the window. Her gaze taking in the distant hills as if somewhere far beyond them lay the answer to her question. 'What I want to ask you is this.' She hesitated, measuring her words. 'Never to write about what happened to me. Never to tell about what you know and what you have seen.'

'But my newspaper.' Hart had shaken his head mournfully. 'I've promised them I will talk to one of their reporters about the rape houses. Blow the lid off what the Serbians are doing to you Muslim women. That way, even without any photographs to show, I'll be able to do some good.'

Lumnije placed one hand on her heart. 'I told you what I would ask you would be difficult.'

Hart spread his hands out in a final gesture of appeal. 'But can't I tell them anything?'

'Yes. Tell them about the Captain. About what he told you he had done. But spare my family name. Never mention me. Or the other girls who escaped with us and whom you knew. Don't even change their names and think you will protect them that way. It would murder them. And their families. Because it would be known. Inferred. They could never hold their heads up again. No one must know what they did to us.'

Hart saw his story disappearing before his eyes. If you couldn't give examples – mention real people in a newspaper feature – mine direct quotes – you might as well piss into the wind and have done with it. 'Okay. I promise.' The words stuck in his craw.

'I am sorry, John. Sorry to ask this of you.'

117

'It's okay,' he lied. 'I blew the whole fucking thing right from the beginning when I didn't take any pictures. I was dead in the water then.'

She met his gaze. And she knew he was lying. And he knew she knew.

But he kept to his word.

It was one of the few times in his life when a human relationship impinged on his ability to tell the objective truth.

If he ever met Lumnije again, though, he would be able to look her directly in the eye. At least there was that.

But he never did. And he couldn't.

TWENTY-SIX

Tal Afar, Iraq

16 JUNE 2014

Back in Iraq. Back in the shit.

John Hart squinted down his viewfinder. IS troops dressed in black, with black balaclavas and face shrouds, were moving through the fields a hundred metres ahead. Some of them were wearing white sports trainers on their feet, which gave them an almost comical air, like prancing ponies at a school gymkhana. They were ushering a group of camo-clad prisoners ahead of them.

'I don't like the look of this. I don't fucking like the look of this.'

Hart carried on filming without paying any attention to his companion. Rider always complained. It was a nervous tic. His words simply washed over them all and dispersed in the surrounding ether.

Amira Eisenberger, Hart's ex-girlfriend, crawled towards him along the drainage canal.

119

'John?'

'Yes?'

'I got through. With the last of my battery I got through.'

'I suppose they're going to send in the SAS for us? Or a helicopter gunship? Maybe a battalion of tanks?'

'Nope.'

'You surprise me.'

Amira eased herself up beside him and looked out at the prisoners being shepherded ahead of them. 'They're going to kill them, aren't they?'

'I suspect so. They've done it with all the others.' He glanced across at her. 'What do they say?'

'They say we must get ourselves into Kurdistan. As far as Dohuk. They'll have someone waiting there to get us out.'

'I like Dohuk. Good food. Great nightlife. Shame it's forty kilometres away. Through IS-held territory.'

'We only have ourselves to blame.'

'Well, there is that.' Hart collected all his cameras together and eased himself into a more comfortable position, so that his legs and back were supported against the banked-up sides of the canal, and his head was no longer visible to a sniper. He looked at the four other journalists surrounding him. Two France-Presse boys, Amira and bloody Rider. What a gang to be caught out in no-man's-land with. Amira was the only one he really knew. She'd made a stab at dressing herself up as a man, but she wouldn't pass muster for two minutes if anyone took a close look at her.

'We'll need a car,' he said.

'Perhaps you can go into Tal Afar and hire one for us? Don't forget to put me on as named driver.'

'Ha ha. Very funny.'

The firing began again from a little way in front of them.

'Oh God,' said Amira. 'They are killing them.'

All the journalists fell silent, listening. Rider was the oldest, at forty-five. One of the France-Presse boys was about thirty, the other a year or so older. They'd all of them seen and heard this sort of thing before. Between them, Amira and Hart had spent upwards of forty years in the field. He was forty-one and she was a couple of years younger than him. Or maybe the same age. Or maybe older. He'd never really been able to work it out. Either way, the chances of their reaching their next birthday seemed a little remote.

Hart cocked his head at the others. 'We'll wait until nightfall. I'll go and film the carnage those bastards have left. Then we'll dump the helmets and body armour and try and walk out of here. Steal a car if we can. Do you think the Kurds will have secured the border?'

'Yes. It'll have been the first thing they did. If they've got any sense, the Peshmerga will use this chaos to grab as much land as they can before IS get their hands on it. They've got a standing army. They're weaponed-up. This is their big chance.'

Hart hadn't smoked for ten years. But watching Amira light up and take a long drag on her cigarette was almost too much to bear. 'We'll never get through the border in the normal way. IS will be patrolling the roads. They'll have checkpoints everywhere.'

'What do you suggest then? That we stand up and come clean? Admit that we're here? That we've allowed ourselves to be cornered in a war zone and would now like to get out, with our pictures and our stories intact, please?'

'It wasn't a war zone when we entered it.'

'They never are.'

Amira ground out her cigarette before it was finished. It was her way of limiting her smoking. 'IS are targeting old mosques and temples. Blowing them up.'

Hart eased his legs into a more comfortable position. 'It's a grand old tradition. I visited an early Assyrian site once. Not far from here. Wall carvings, fifty feet high. Four thousand years old. Saddam Hussein's troops shot them to pieces with their AK47s. Now IS are calling Saddam a martyr. What did Adolf Hitler say? *What today is known as history, we will abolish altogether.* IS are just rearranging history. They'll get to the Yazidi shrines and the Christian churches next and finish demolishing the pre-Islamic world. The Kurds have the right idea. Seal yourselves off. Fortress Kurdistan. If I were them I'd attack Mosul. Take that before it's too late. Then declare themselves an independent country. The West will fall over itself recognizing them.'

Amira was lighting another cigarette. 'One good field doesn't make a harvest.'

'But it's a start. When it comes down to it, a country is only as good as the quality of life it affords its people.'

Amira crinkled up her nose and smiled at him. 'You're a philosopher at heart. I always suspected it.' She glanced across at the two Frenchmen. Then at Rider. 'Do you think they'll want to work together as a team? Or go their own way?'

Hart followed the line of her glance. 'We'll stick together. Those guys aren't under any illusions. There's safety in numbers. If we get taken, we'll have a better chance the more of us there are.'

'I don't think IS will kill us.' Amira's face had taken on a faraway look.

'You don't?'

'No. We'll be worth far too much to them as collateral.'

Hart shook his head. 'One look at my film and they'll know what we've seen. These guys like to manipulate their own propaganda. They don't want freelance stuff getting out. Or stuff they can't control.'

'Then destroy your film.'

'No.'

'How did I know you'd say that?'

'Because you're the same as me, Amira. You'd swallow a story and shit it out later if you had to, just to keep a hold on it.'

'Not a pretty image, but I can't fault you for accuracy.' Amira ground out that cigarette too. It was her sixth in ten minutes.

'Is something bothering you by any chance?' Hart said. 'I mean something other than the prospect of being beheaded.'

Amira sighed.

'Come on then. Spit it out. There'll never be a better place to do it. The clock is ticking.'

Amira looked at him. Her eyes seemed preternaturally large. Like those of some night-time prey animal on the lookout for predators. 'I want us to begin again.'

'Oh Christ.'

'No. Listen to me, John.'

'I am listening. I've got nowhere else to go. I'm a captive audience. My only out is to run screaming towards the enemy, imploring them to take me in.'

'You just aren't funny. You're not funny.'

'Sorry. It's my nerves. I always crack stupid jokes when the odds are stacked against me.'

'Why won't you?'

'Why won't I what?'

'Try again?'

'Do you want the full director's cut? Or the expurgated version?'

Amira threw some dirt at him and slithered off to talk to Rider.

Hart didn't feel proud of himself. But, truth be told, he was scared of Amira. She didn't take prisoners. They'd been on and off with each other for years. Until, three years before, she'd aborted their child without telling him. This

124

had tipped him over the edge. He'd left her. And he'd had a number of affairs since then. Even fancied himself in love. He assumed Amira had too. Their emotional cat's cradle was now too complicated ever to untangle. At least as far as he was concerned. He knew he didn't have the energy even to attempt it. Not to mention the will. If Amira had been the sort of woman you could have had a casual affair with, no strings attached, he would have taken up her offer with alacrity. But she wasn't. And that was that.

'Okay,' he said, as loudly as he dared. 'We'd better roll. It's getting dark. Jean-Claude? Grégoire? Rider? Are you with us?'

The three men nodded. No one wanted to be left alone behind IS lines. There was security in numbers.

'Amira?'

'I'm coming.'

'If we get stopped, lose yourself behind us. Walk away if you can. We'll make a lot of racket up front to occupy their minds. Wave our press passes. Gesticulate. Feign outrage.'

'Fuck off. I'm not going anywhere without you. Who do you think I am? Barbara fucking Cartland?'

The Frenchmen laughed. Rider sniggered. Hart stifled a nervous yawn.

'Does anyone know how to hotwire a car?' she said.

Rider held up his hand. 'I do.'

'Well, you're good for something at least,' said Amira. 'Miserable bloody bastard that you are.'

125

TWENTY-SEVEN

Hart looked down at the pit. IS were so confident of their position here at Tal Afar that they hadn't even bothered to fill it in. The freshly killed bodies were piled up on top of each other, leaching flies.

'For Christ's sake, don't use a flash.'

Hart ignored Rider's comment. He set up his portable tripod, screwed on his camera and got on with it. Even the tiniest bit of camera shake would wreck the shots in this light.

'Come on, man. Let's get out of here.'

The two Frenchmen were nodding too. The place reeked of blood and death and excrement. Only Amira was striding round taking everything in. Filtering it through that journalist's brain of hers. Stamping it onto her memory. Later, she'd look at Hart's shots. He knew that. But even without them her piece would be just as good. She had a mind like a combine harvester.

At first they stuck to single file and walked along the edge of fields. One blessing was that there were unlikely to be mines yet. No one had ever thought, three days ago, that IS were going to attack. Nor that the Iraqi military would up sticks and run, abandoning their matériel for the enemy to use as they saw fit.

People in the villages tended to go to bed early too. So if they skirted settlements, and kept their eyes skinned for patrols, they had a fair chance of slipping through. Each of them carried a navigation aid, so at least they knew where they were. And where they were was too far behind enemy lines. They would have to lie up for another day at least if they didn't find a car soon, vastly increasing their chances of being found.

'What's that?' Grégoire, who had the best eyes of all of them, was pointing into the distance.

Hart focused his telephoto lens on the object. 'Looks like a 4x4. Non-military.'

'Why not let's take that?'

'Do you think IS will have all the roads sewn up?'

'Only one way to find out. Anyway, we can avoid the roads and run with our lights switched off. It's bright enough. With a car we'd have a fair chance of breaking through to Dohuk tonight.'

'If the Kurds don't shoot us up.'

'I'll call ahead. Rider tells me he has some battery left on his phone. He's got one of those sunshine charger gizmos.

Our people can warn the border guards that we are coming through.'

'When we know which actual crossing we shall be using.'

'Yes. There is always that. But I'm going to do it anyway. The Kurds are well organized. Not like the Iraqi army.'

They made their way to the 4x4. It was parked near a house. The house was made of concrete. It was grander, by far, than the houses around it. It even had its very own court-yard, sealed off from the outside world. And a sheet-metal roof that glistened in the moonlight like liquid mercury.

'We're going to have to push the car. We can't afford to start it here. We'd wake everybody up.'

'Rider. Get in and do your bit.'

Rider looked worried. 'You'd better pray there isn't an electronic handbrake. Or a faulty alarm.'

'Rider, just do it.'

Rider tested the doors. They opened. Rider slid into the front seat. After a moment he waved his hand. The two Frenchmen, Amira and Hart began pushing. Rider steered the car. When it was three hundred metres away from the house, they stopped.

'That's bloody clever how you managed to bypass the steering lock,' said Hart.

Rider held up a car key. Then he grinned. Hart made a pretend fist. But he was privately relieved. Maybe their luck was changing? Three days ago they'd come to Tal Afar because it was safe, and the perfect place to report on the situation in Mosul, seventy kilometres down the road. That had been the plan anyway. But things had moved too fast for the journalists. They'd found themselves boxed in before they knew it. And here was the result. Pushing a stolen vehicle down a road at two in the morning, in fear for their lives.

'Is there any petrol in the thing?' said Hart.

'Full,' said Rider. 'The only stuff these people have left is petrol.'

'Then I suggest we get in, start it up and drive full-throttle for the border.'

'You can't be serious?'

'Do you have an alternative? If we drive like snails we'll be picked up. If we drive like the devil is behind us, maybe they'll think we're IS soldiers on a mission. Who would expect five idiot journalists to be in the car? Sometimes one has to think laterally.'

'Who's going to drive?' said Amira.

Hart looked round. 'It was my idea. I'm happy to do it.'

'So says the man who infiltrated himself inside Iran last year, and came out with his hide intact. If you can't do it, nobody can. They don't call you the Templar for nothing.'

Hart tried to make out if Amira was joshing him, but it was impossible to pin down the expression on her face in the half-light of the moon. It was Amira herself who had coined the 'Templar' epithet for him following a bloody fiasco in Germany two years before in which he had infiltrated an extreme right-wing party which was using the Holy Lance as its symbol. The whole thing had ended badly, but the 'Templar' nickname had stuck. All the more so because Hart's direct ancestor, ex-Templar Johannes von Hartelius, had been made the Guardian of the Holy Lance way back in the twelfth century by one of Frederick Barbarossa's sons. It had been the perfect 'silly season' fodder. And Hart had been saddled with the name ever since. Even his editors insisted he use it when signing off material. Amira, tongue firmly in cheek, called it the price of fame – Hart's fifteen minutes in the headlights. Hart called it a bloody irritation.

'Okay. Get in.' Hart started up the car and pulled away. 'I hope to heck whoever owns this vehicle doesn't decide to come outside for a romantic moonlit drive.'

'Keys must have been in it for a reason.' This was Rider. 'Maybe he was dropping off his girlfriend? Maybe he'll be out in a minute when she finishes blowing him?'

'Shut up, Rider.' The three of them said it in tandem this time. It would have been four, but one of the Frenchmen didn't speak English.

TWENTY-EIGHT

Hart took the Zammar road. He'd checked out the Askï Mawşil dam three days before, for background shots, and was pretty sure he'd noticed a service road running round it. What he did know for certain was that the far side of the dam belonged to the Kurds. Why would IS have any reason to guard a dam? It was a natural barrier. And how did you guard a dam anyway?

He kept the 4x4 at a steady 100 kilometres an hour. There was little or no traffic on the roads at night. Everyone scared to venture out, probably. But he knew from experience that one was apt to over-endow new conquerors of a province with too much organizational capacity. In reality, after a putsch of any sort, there was usually an interim period of utter chaos, in which old rivalries were sorted out, revenges taken and infrastructures secured. It was during this short window that one still had the chance to move more or less freely about. If one had the balls for it. Or was foolish enough to try.

Hart saw the checkpoint half a kilometre ahead.

'Shit.'

He pulled up at the side of the road using the engine brakes only and left the engine running. The vehicle lights were off. As long as nothing came up behind them and lit them up like a baseball diamond, they were safe.

'Do we try and bullshit our way through?' said Rider.

'Christ, no,' said Hart. 'These people have no sense of humour. They'd shoot you as soon as look at you. And ask questions afterwards.'

Hart checked out the fields on either side of the road. On one side the dirt was plastered flat, as if it had been recently harrowed. The other side was impassable. Corrugated and uneven. Full of ha-has and revetments.

'I'm going right. Do I take it fast or slow?' He looked round the interior of the cab for guidance.

'I say fast,' said Amira. 'We've only got one shot at this. And they're going to be suspicious of any vehicle travelling in the middle of the night anyway. With luck the checkpoint will only be manned by a couple of men.'

'Yeah. With AK47s,' said Rider.

'There is that.'

Hart slipped the vehicle into four-wheel drive. 'Any of you want to get down on the floor? Or want out?'

The Frenchmen shook their heads. 'We'll take our risks

with you,' said the one who spoke English.

Hart looked at Rider. Rider nodded. Hart didn't even have to check with Amira. He knew what her answer would be.

He put his foot down and cut right.

'If we're lucky they may not hear us,' said one of the Frenchmen.

'What? You mean they may be sleeping on duty?' Amira let out a guffaw. 'IS would probably martyr them.'

It was at that exact moment that the shooting started. Hart could hear the distant crackle of semi-automatic weapons. Only he had the strange impression that it was not they who were being targeted, but someone else.

'You don't think the Yanks have drones up?' said Rider. 'That they'll think we're IS charging the border and simply vaporize us?'

'Rider, shut the fuck up.'

A loose round smashed through the back window. Almost immediately one of the Frenchmen choked and fell forward. Amira threw herself across the intervening seats and forced him upright. 'It's his shoulder, I think. Ricochet maybe. Lot of blood.'

'Fuck.' Hart was trying to keep the 4x4 on a roughly straight course across the field. He was busy devastating somebody's seasonal corn crop but he didn't care. He passed a house. The lights came on. There was more shooting behind them, but none of it accurate. He reckoned privately that they were now out of range. If the checkpoint guards had instant access to vehicles, of course, they would be piling into them right about now. That would be another matter entirely.

'I can see moonlight reflecting off the reservoir,' he said.

'Which way do we go?' said Amira.

'Lottery. I don't remember the map.'

'Think, man, think. Make a call.'

'Right. I think Dohuk is right.' Hart could see vehicle headlights flaring and swooping behind them. 'I need to switch my lights on. I can't see shit. They'll catch us otherwise.'

'No. Keep them off. It's our only chance.' Amira touched him on the shoulder. 'Their lights will destroy their night vision. We still have ours. It might make a difference.'

Hart took the ramp leading up to the service road at about sixty miles an hour. The 4x4 was protesting. Bits were falling off it. It had no acceleration to speak of. Hart recognized it as a jeep. But a bottom-of-the-range one. An old-style Patriot, or something like that. He remembered that air conditioning cut power output so he switched it off. Was he imagining it, or did the vehicle surge forwards?

He hit the rock two miles further along the shoreline, with the lights in the rear-view mirror steadily edging up behind them. The front right tyre blew. The Patriot swerved violently back and forth across the service road in the shape of an elongated S.

'The boat,' said Rider. 'Make for the boat.'

'I don't see any boat,' said Hart.

134

'There. There. Can't you see it?' Rider was pointing out of the side window.

'We'll be sitting bloody ducks.'

'We're already sitting bloody ducks,' yelled Rider. 'The fucking tyre's gone.'

Hart slewed the Patriot off the service road and down towards a small dock. Three boats were tied up there. Metal-bottomed. Tourist crap. The motors were shipped.

'See if you can start one, Rider,' said Hart.

'They'll shoot us to pieces.'

'Rider! Fuck it! This was your idea. Try the fucking engines.'

'Switch on the headlights then. Give a sucker an even break.'

Hart shone the headlights towards the boats.

There was a *crump* out on the lake. Maybe a hundred metres from where they were standing.

'Bloody heck,' said Hart. 'That was a rifle grenade. Someone's shooting from the back of the cab approaching us.'

Rider had found one antediluvian engine that started with a pull on the toggle. He blipped the throttle. A thick pall of smoke rose from the exhaust.

'Get in, all of you,' said Hart.

'We need to sink these other boats,' said Amira.

'Too late. Let's take them with us and then abandon them. We don't want them following us.'

135

'Good idea.' Amira was pressing a pad down on the wounded Frenchman's neck. Her arms were covered in blood up to the elbows.

Despite their situation, Hart was impressed with the way everyone was working together. These were all professionals. Used to emergencies. There were no wasted words. No pointless arguments. No grandstanding. Everybody simply got on with whatever they were doing.

Two minutes into the exercise they were out on the reservoir, heading east. Behind them there was another *crump*.

'Bastard's shot up our Patriot,' said Rider. 'Full tank too. Whoever we stole it from is going to be major pissed off.'

'Do you reckon he'll take that up with IS, do you, Rider? Ask for compensation?' Hart was squinting into the darkness in front of him.

Rider grinned one of his grins. He knew he irritated people. It was his stock-in-trade. Do enough of it, and you were apt to learn things. All journalists have their wrinkles. This one was Rider's. 'I would,' he said. 'I'd sharia the bastards so they'd know they'd been shariahed. Fuckers wouldn't know what hit them.'

This time they found themselves bracketed by rifle grenades. Then the small arms started. Bullets zipped off the water, pinged off the metal surrounds of the two attached boats.

'Cut them loose, for pity's sake,' shouted Hart. 'Give them some targets other than us to aim at.'

The vehicle on the shore had a searchlight. It was bracketing the reservoir.

Grégoire, the uninjured Frenchman, cut the two empty boats free. His friend groaned. Amira was still trying to staunch the blood loss from his shoulder. She was having to be rough about it.

One of the boats drifted immediately into the searchlight beam. A heavy machine gun opened up and cut it to pieces.

'Did you see that?' Rider yelled. 'Those were cannon shells, not bullets.'

Then the beam cut across to the second boat.

'Get down,' shouted Hart.

The metal-bottomed boat reared out of the water as if it had been speared.

Hart lay almost flat on the deck of the third boat. He had the throttle twisted to full. If the searchlight found them they'd be dead. Heavy machine guns had awesome ranges. Not like the popguns that were firing at them before.

He watched the luminous white wake behind them over the gunwale. He waited for the shells to hit. Waited to be blown to bits.

But there was silence. Except for the ludicrous popping of their tiny engine.

'The stupid bastards have deafened themselves,' said Rider. 'Serves them fucking well right. They can't hear us over the din in their ears. They think they've blasted us out of the water.'

Hart looked down the length of the tourist boat. 'For once in your life, Rider, you may finally have got something right.'

TWENTY-NINE

'Kurdish, do you think?' Hart was monitoring the checkpoint through his telephoto lens.

'The flag gives it away, don't you think?' said Amira.

'What flag?' said Hart.

'The Kurdish flag over there that you can't see because your lens is too narrow.' Amira was grinning.

Hart shook his head. Amira loved catching him out. It was a sort of sport with her. 'How the hell do we warn them that we're coming through? They can't have failed to hear the gunfire on the reservoir.'

'Maybe they thought it was IS conducting a military exercise?' said Rider.

'Why don't you go over and check that out,' said Hart. 'I'm sure it hasn't made them itchy-fingered. In fact they're probably stretched out on a carpet somewhere having breakfast.'

Rider looked at him, but didn't answer. There wasn't anything to say.

'Look,' said Hart. 'We haven't got much time. When IS discover the empty third boat they'll know someone got away.'

'What do you think they're going to do then?' said Rider. 'Invade Kurdistan?'

'Possibly. Yes. I wouldn't put anything past them.'

'So what do you suggest we do, oh mighty Templar person?' It was Rider at his most cynical. 'Wave a flag of truce? Offer to parley? The phones are fucked thanks to the drenching we got when we waded ashore. Your film is probably fucked too.'

'No it's not,' said Hart.

'How come?'

'Because I seal each memory card inside a waterproof package when I'm finished with it,' said Hart. 'I learned to do that on Lake Atitlan in Guatemala, when the place flooded.'

'Shame you didn't think to do that with the phones before we went for our brief dip in the lake,' said Rider, content that he'd achieved the last word.

Hart grunted. He stood up and began walking towards the Peshmerga lines. He heard someone say 'Oh fuck' behind him. Rider, probably. The man swore for England.

Hart held up his press pass in one hand and his drenched cameras in the other. They'd be watching him through infrared, the soldiers, even though it was well beyond dawn now. It gave that tiny extra edge.

There was a burst of machine-gun fire.

Over my head, Hart said to himself. They are not firing at me. They are firing over my head.

He stopped and waited. If an IS sniper got him at this point he'd never know anything about it. He'd just pitch onto the track in front of him and bleed out. No luckily positioned telephoto lens like in Kosovo, sixteen years before. You don't get that sort of a break twice in a lifetime.

He watched the soldiers approaching him. He never moved his arms. Cameras, press pass. It was all he could think of to do. At least he didn't look like an IS soldier in disguise. He was blonde-haired, clean-shaven – give or take a couple of days – and only lightly tanned. Not dark-haired, bearded, and wrapped up like a mummy in the Cairo museum.

'Down. Flat.' It was one of the approaching soldiers.

Hart knelt down and slithered onto his stomach. 'There are four more journalists behind me. Two French. Two English. One of the Frenchman is injured. We are all unarmed.'

'Where?' said the Kurdish soldier.

'Fifty metres. Straight back. Can I call them?' said Hart.

'Yes. Call.'

'Okay.' Hart raised his voice. 'Come on out. Arms high. Press passes on show. These are Peshmerga.'

'What was the shooting?' said one of the soldiers. An officer, surely.

'IS were chasing us,' said Hart. 'On the reservoir. We

escaped in boats. They used rifle grenades. And what sounded like cannon fire.'

The soldiers exchanged glances.

'Are we in no-man's-land?' said Hart.

'No-man's-land? No. There is no no-man's-land,' said the officer. 'What do we need with no-man's-land? You are in newly liberated Kurdistan.'

THIRTY

'What made you do it?' Amira was looking at Hart over her cup of Kurdish tea. 'Risking your life like that? I've seen you do stuff like that before. Something comes over you, you stand up, and act like a suicidal maniac.'

'Someone had to do it,' said Hart.

'Yes, but why always you?'

Hart sipped his tea. He shrugged. He looked across at the two Frenchmen. Then at Rider. Everyone was sipping their tea and eating unleavened bread and honey. Most had inane grins on their faces. Even the Frenchman that Amira had patched up. Each one knew that getting unscathed out of IS-controlled territory constituted a near miracle. The sort of thing you'd tell your grandchildren about, when they deigned to listen.

'You want the truth?' Hart said.

'No, John. I want a lie. I want you to concoct the juiciest, most idiot-demeaning lie you possibly can, and then tell it to me.'

Hart sighed. Amira was on the warpath. He'd ducked out from under her suggestion that they get back together again, and she wasn't about to forgive him in a hurry. No woman likes her overtures spurned. Hell. He could understand that. If he'd made a similar overture, and Amira had chucked it back in his face, he'd have been livid.

'I don't know why I did it,' said Hart. 'But I had a sudden flashback. To Kosovo.'

'Kosovo?' Amira made a face. 'Kosovo?'

'Yeah. I was there in ninety-eight,' said Hart.

'You never told me that.'

'You never asked me.' Hart shrugged, instinctively making light of something that held a particular significance for him.

Amira pulled the blanket the Peshmerga had provided her with further over her shoulders. 'So what happened?'

'It's complicated,' he said.

'I suppose it involves a woman?' she said.

'Collaterally only.' Hart gave a brief nod. 'Yes. I suppose it did.'

'What do you mean collaterally only?'

'I mean that the woman involved was not involved with me.' Hart waved an impatient hand. 'Look. This isn't important. It happened a long time ago. I don't know why I'm suddenly thinking of it. Maybe because I thought an IS sniper was going to take me out while I stood there like a prune waving my press pass at the Peshmerga.'

'Someone shot you in Kosovo?'

'Yes. A Serb war criminal they called "the Captain". He shot me in the back. Only the telephoto lens in my backpack deflected the bullet.'

'You're kidding me?'

'No.' Hart raised his eyes to meet hers. 'The force of the bullet knocked me about ten feet up the path I was walking on. If the bullet had hit me in the normal run of things it would have punched a six-inch hole clear through my spine. I still get twinges on thundery nights. A distinct sort of muscle memory.'

'What happened to the collateral woman?' said Amira.

'I don't know. She'd been badly treated.' Hart hesitated. He could feel the past beckoning to be let back in. 'Well, systematically raped, if you must know. Before that the Captain had killed both her parents and her brother in front of her eyes. I abandoned her in a Serb monastery. She was injured, you see. The abbot promised me he would look after her. The monastery was famous for protecting Albanian Muslims as well as Serb Christians. It seemed the right thing to do at the time.'

'But you wrote about it at least?'

'About her? No. She made me promise not to. About the rest? Yes. Someone else wrote the piece on my behalf. But the whole thing fell flat as a pancake without any personal testimony or photographs. I might as well have been making it all up.'

'And – don't tell me – you never kept in contact?' Amira was staring at Hart as if he had just emerged from a lengthy sojourn in an insane asylum.

'She fell off the ends of the earth,' said Hart.

'How do you mean?'

'A week after I left, when I finally got through to the abbot to ask about her, he told me she had disappeared. When I asked him where to, he couldn't say. I traced her back to her village. No luck. After the war was over she never returned. Look, Amira. Some of those women who were raped were so ashamed of what had happened to them that they couldn't face their families again. I'm not telling you anything you don't know already. You've been around, same as me.'

'And that was that?' she said.

'Pretty much,' he said.

'What are you *not* telling me?' she said.

Hart waved her question away. 'Nothing. It was bad. That's all. Probably the worst thing that's ever happened to me on assignment.'

'How old were you then? It was 1998, you said?' Amira tried to work it out in her head.

'Twenty-five.'

'And I suppose you thought you could change the world?'

'No. I didn't,' said Hart. 'Not after Sarajevo. But I admit I was naïve. I did think I could make a small difference. But I couldn't. Not really. When it came down to it, nothing had changed. Lumnije – that's what she was called – Lumnije –

146

she still had to deal with all that had happened to her. And the Captain was free to carry on his campaign of gang rapes and ethnic cleansing and murder until NATO finally got its act together and intervened.' Hart sighed. 'I might as well have spat into the Pacific Ocean and expected it to raise a tsunami for all the good I could do.'

'Nice image,' said Amira.

'I thought so,' said Hart.

Amira eased herself across the raised carpet on which she and Hart were sitting. She opened up her blanket. 'Cuddle? No strings?'

Hart nodded.

She snuggled up against him.

'You're cold,' he said.

'Somewhat,' she said. 'Do you actually remember what just happened to us? Or are you still loitering somewhere in Kosovo sixteen years ago with a collateral female?'

Hart didn't answer.

'How old was she, by the way?' said Amira.

'Sixteen.'

Amira sat back and stared at him. 'Sixteen?'

'Yes. When I got her out of the rape house, though, she looked ten years older. And she'd had it easy. Or so she said. The Captain had reserved her for himself because he didn't want to catch the clap.' Hart shook his head. 'Don't glare at me like that, Amira. That's exactly what she told me. I'm not making it up.' He only allowed himself to relax when he saw that Amira was prepared to accept that he hadn't been being flippant. 'What happened to the others doesn't bear thinking about. Anyone who wanted to could take them. Do anything they liked. Humiliate them in whatever way they chose.'

'And all this is still haunting you?' said Amira.

'It never goes away,' said Hart. 'Every war zone I'm in, every photo I take, I remember those girls. First they lost their families. Then they were dragged through hell and back. Then they were shamed. Sometimes I look at myself in the mirror, when I'm feeling at my most self-pitying, and I remember. And it's all happening again. IS – or what the Arabs call the Daesh – are doing the same thing with the Yazidis and with the Kurds and with the Shia. You saw them massacring a bunch of unarmed Shia pretty much in front of our eyes. Nothing changes. The strong still dominate the weak. That's the way of things. Sometimes we think the situation is improving. But we're only kidding ourselves. The first chance people get to lord it over other people, they take it. We're the world's worst animals. Because we do it for fun.'

'And this is why you get up and offer yourself to the fates?' said Amira. 'Put yourself in the way of danger? Play the martyr?'

Hart looked down at Amira as she lay in the crook of his arm. 'Maybe.' He hesitated. 'Yes. Maybe.'

THIRTY-ONE

There are days you don't care to remember. Other days that pass you by. And then there comes a day that gets a grip on you and never lets you go. Such a day happened to Hart three days after his return to England from Iraq.

He was winding down from his assignment. Six, seven days. It usually took that long. At first everything and everyone seems strange when you come back from a war zone. Trivial. Uncaring. You walk amongst the civilians and you say to yourself, what the hell are these people doing? People are dying out there. And here you all are, boozing and flirting and pissing your lives away.

Then, slowly, you begin to swing with the tide again. You remember that life is for the living. Not the dead. That if you are offered precious freedoms, it is an insult not to clasp them to your breast and hug them to death.

Hart was beginning to notice the pretty girls in their

summer dresses in the London parks. The taste of a cold beer on a sunny day. The smell of coffee outside a grindery in Camden Town. He walked round the British Museum and the V&A. Admired the Ardabil carpet. Had lunch at Fernandez & Wells in South Kensington, sitting outside eating chorizo, fried eggs and sourdough bread, while he watched the world go by.

And then he got the phone call.

Later, when he thought about it, it had a sort of inevitability. Like when you remember an old friend you haven't thought of for years, and he contacts you out of the blue, a few hours later, explaining that he'd found himself thinking of you at the exact same time you were thinking of him and decided to get in touch. Didn't have your number but, what the hell, he'd looked you up on the internet and found a number for you in amongst all the dross and tack that people wrote.

That's what happened with Lumnije.

Hart had changed his telephone number maybe six times in the intervening sixteen years since they had last seen each other. But she knew exactly where to find him. All she'd needed to do was to trawl through a newspaper article or two to confirm his name, and then subscribe to the BT phonebook for his home number. He'd never thought to go ex-directory. No one phoned him on his landline anyway, unless they were trying to cold call him about notional car accidents or phantom problems with his computer.

When he heard the heavily accented voice he'd almost put the phone down with his customary 'I'm sorry. I never take unsolicited phone calls.' I mean, why offend people? They had tacky enough jobs as it was. People being impolite to them just added to their misery.

But something about the voice had struck a chord somewhere. Deep in his unconscious mind. He hung, midway between slamming the telephone down and asking for more information.

'John?' she'd said. 'John Hart? Is that you?'

So he'd sat down with the portable house phone, looking out of his opened window towards the park, and he'd sunk back into the past.

'Lumnije?' he said.

'Yes.'

'This is crazy. I was thinking about you. Just a few days ago. In Iraq. We got into trouble. Bad trouble. I was remembering.'

There was a long silence on the other end of the line.

'Are you still there?' he said.

'Yes, I'm still here.'

Her English was better than before. He noticed that straight away. More fluent. As if she'd spent time on a course, maybe. Or been forced to use it for work.

'Where are you now?' he said. He could feel the guilt mounting to his cheeks as he mouthed the question. 'I tried to trace you all those years ago. Called the monastery. They had no news.'

'And then you gave up,' she said.

He watched a woman getting into her car in the street below. Her husband putting their young child into its car seat and getting in himself. Tidy. The perfect nuclear family. The answer to someone's dream. 'And then I gave up. Yes. I reckoned you didn't want me to contact you.'

'I didn't,' she said.

'Oh.'

The pause was a long one. Hart held the phone to his ears. For some reason his heart was beating uncontrollably fast. As though the Captain was still pursuing them through the Kosovo woods. As though he could hear the man's boots closing in on the trail behind him.

'I live in Macedonia now,' she said. 'On the shores of Lake Ohrid. Near Struga. A village called Radožda.'

Another long pause.

'Do you know Macedonia?' she said at last.

'No,' he said. 'It's one of those places that has escaped me. I'm not even entirely sure where it is. The only thing I know is that it's not in Greece.'

She laughed. He remembered her laughing way back then. It had been a rare-enough occurrence to warrant mention. He tried to imagine what she looked like now. She'd be, what, thirty-two years old? Prime of life still. Probably married with five children. But he didn't ask her. Men don't ask such questions.

'I want you to visit me,' she said.

'What?'

'You heard me, John. I am asking a favour of you. I have something for you. Something important. I want you to visit me and collect it.'

'But I can't just get on a plane to Macedonia...' His voice fell away.

'Why not?' she said. 'Are you working?'

Hart sighed. 'No. I'm on leave. Recovering from the thing that happened in Iraq.'

'Do you have a girlfriend then, perhaps? Will she be unhappy if you come to visit me?'

Hart smiled. He remembered Lumnije's way with the truth. She thought of a question and she asked it. No beating about the bush. 'No. No. I don't have a girlfriend.'

'Then book a ticket to Skopje,' she said. 'Please. For tomorrow. Come tomorrow. I need to see you. Very much. And this thing I have for you. You will be pleased. It is important. For your work. It will make you very famous.'

'I don't want to be famous,' he said.

Lumnije laughed again. 'But you are. I have been reading all about you. You are already famous. They call you the "Templar". After what you did in Germany.'

'That's all nonsense,' he said.

'I knew you would say that. You have to say that.' There was a catch in her voice. An odd little hesitation. 'Come to Skopje tomorrow. I will pick you up at the airport. Take the Vienna flight. Will you do that for me? Will you, John? Please?'

Hart closed his eyes. He could see Lumnije's face clearly now. Remember her deadweight on his back as he had carried her, seemingly forever, with the Captain hard behind them. All thanks to his stupidity in not killing the man when he had the chance. Flashes of this, flashes of that kept coming back to him. Sixteen years wasn't so long.

He remembered again the pang he had felt on leaving her at the monastery. As though he were betraying her in some way. Abandoning her to the fates. Abandoning her to the Captain.

'All right,' he heard himself saying. 'I'll come.'

Quietly, gently, she put down the phone.

THIRTY-TWO

Lumnije loved the springs at Crn Drim. To her eyes, they were the most beautiful place on earth. They were situated on the opposite side of Lake Ohrid to her house. The shortest way to get to them would have been through Albania, but that was impossible. For her it was impossible.

So she drove the long way round the lake in her little Simca, through Struga, through Ohrid, past Peštani. All safely inside Macedonia. She'd made the journey a hundred times before but still she loved it.

When she arrived at the springs she parked her car and walked down to the restaurant for lunch. As she ate she watched the tourists being ferried by rowing boat the length of the springs. She could hear their cries of delight when they saw how crystal clear the water was. When they saw the springs bubbling through the silt underneath them like tiny volcanic eruptions. When they spotted a snake circling away through the riffle, perhaps, or a water rail flitting ahead of them through the dappled light given by the trees.

All year round the water temperature remained at a constant ten degrees centigrade. Look deep into it, and you could see every detail of the bottom. Every curl of leaf. Each rib of weed. Forty-five separate springs, half from Lake Prespa, 148 metres higher and eighteen kilometres away, and half from somewhere deep inside the Galičica Mountains. Constantly feeding the springs and keeping them pure. It was a miracle.

Later, after lunch, the musicians came and played the Czardas, Jovano Jovanke, and then Black Eyes, when no one could think of any more Macedonian folk songs. Two violins, an accordion, a guitar and a bass. People slipped banknotes in between the strings of the lead violinist as a tip.

One of the tourist parties made a circle, with more and more people joining in as the music rose in intensity. Lumnije joined it too, and danced the Hora with them, her head held high, three steps forward and one back, her dress bouncing to the rhythm. The simplest of all the Macedonian dance steps. But satisfying for all that.

Later that afternoon she slept a little in her car. Then, when she saw the tourist buses leaving and the souvenir shops being shut, she moved her car out of the main car park and a few hundred metres towards the St Naum Monastery. She knew there were cleaners there who came in at night. Her car would not be noticed in amongst theirs.

When dusk fell she crossed the open expanse of grass towards where they moored the rowing boats at Crn Drim. They were chained. She had expected this.

She sorted through the keys she had brought with her until she found one that fitted the padlock of the prettiest of the boats. She unshipped the single oar and stood on the oarsman's platform. Then she pushed away from the shore.

The rowing boat glided through the water. Lumnije enjoyed the sound her oar made as it kissed the surface. The moon was rising. Soon everything would be clear as day.

She waited a little at the picnic place near the tiny chapel at the far end of the springs. Waited for the moon. She ate the sandwich she had brought with her, and drank a little rakia for strength. She could feel the spirit burning her throat. She felt alive. So alive. As if every sinew, every nerve in her body was attuned to this miraculous place.

When the moon was at its highest, and full to bursting with light, she eased the rowing boat away from the shore. Soon, almost too soon, she reached her private place and anchored the boat. She dipped her hand in the water and felt the cool springs caressing her fingers beneath the surface. She smiled. She felt like a young girl again. Like the girl she had once been before the Captain and his men came to her village and killed her mother, and her father, and her brother, Azem. Before the Captain stole her off to his rape house and used her like a discarded piece of rag.

She looked up at the moon. It was beautiful. Very

157

beautiful. Lumnije stepped over the side of the boat and let herself sink into the water. She could feel her dress ballooning beside her. The springs below her tickled her feet. It was easy to stand. The water was nowhere more than four feet deep, so even she, at a little over five feet tall, felt secure. Even so, she attached herself to the side of the boat with a loop of rope.

She reached across the gunwale for her bag. She felt inside. Yes. There was her father's razor. She had rescued it from their house after she left Visoki Dečani Monastery, and before she came to Macedonia, all those years ago, alongside some photographs and a few trinkets that hadn't been looted yet. She had had to be silent and furtive. There had been only Serbs left in her village. Katohija had been ethnically cleansed of all Albanians. Not a single one had been left behind. The village had been struck by a human whirlwind whose winds were driven by hate.

She looked at her wrists. They seemed so thin. So vulnerable in this white light.

She cut downwards as she had been told, and saw the blood well up out of the artery, as if it, too, was fed by secret springs deep in the mountains. When she touched bone, she withdrew her father's cut-throat razor and moved to the other arm. Just looking at the blood made her feel weak.

She botched the other side at first. She had not counted on the strength in her cut arm melting away so fast. But finally she had it.

She dropped the razor and watched it float away beneath her. Then she lay back in the water and let it take her.

Ah, it felt so good. Her head felt light, as if she were about to faint. She looked to her left and to her right. It was so beautiful here. The most beautiful place on earth. She had chosen well.

The blood pulsed away from her in the water. She felt part of the water.

Slowly, without meaning to, she tipped onto her front.

Soon she could scarcely breathe. But that didn't matter. The springs were taking her. She was becoming part of them. They would never forget her.

Later, just before the end, she heard the cry of an owl. Heard something rustle behind her, as if an animal were coming down to drink.

She closed her eyes. How soft the water was. How delicate its lapping sound. How sweet its grip.

THIRTY-THREE

John Hart cursed himself all the way to Skopje. He cursed himself in London when he boarded the plane. He cursed himself in Vienna, where he had his stopover, and he cursed himself on the final leg when the plane cut down through the clouds and drifted to a halt.

What would he and Lumnije find to say to each other after sixteen years? Even when they were together, they had spoken little, as if they were two beings swept up on a deserted island but speaking different languages. Why had she chosen to call him to her now, with so much water under the bridge? What did she have to give him?

Hart thought back to London and to the satisfaction he had just started taking in life again. Well. One good thing had already come out of Lumnije's call. He had been due to visit his dementia-suffering mother and her semi-deranged lover, Clive. That had had to be cancelled. He loved his mother.

But Clive? Clive came as part of the package, unfortunately. The prospect was a nightmare. Seeing Lumnije again was infinitely preferable. Anything was preferable to Clive.

As his flight progressed, though, and their meeting loomed, Hart was grudgingly forced to admit that he had wondered about Lumnije many times over the past decade and a half. How had she dealt with the past? What had happened to her? Where had she gone? What had she done with her life? There was a certain satisfaction to be had in readdressing the past. In unlocking its mysteries.

Hart looked round the Arrivals section of Skopje Airport. He sensed that he would recognize Lumnije immediately. You don't change that much between sixteen and thirty-two. Do you?

He waited an hour. He had no number for her, of course, because she had put down the phone so quickly after he had agreed to come, almost as if she had feared him changing his mind. And he would have, given half the chance. When he had eventually thought to dial BT Call Back the automated voice had told him, in so many words, to go to hell. They didn't give out international mobile numbers.

He waited another hour. Part of him was tempted to arrange for his open return to be used again that day. An instant turnaround. Maybe he would stop off in Vienna for a day or two and do the museums. Take in an opera. Drink some coffee and eat some cake. Chalk the whole thing down to experience.

Damn it all to hell. He couldn't do that. He owed Lumnije. Owed her big. And her out-of-the-blue call had piqued his curiosity. He couldn't deny it. The girl had been a force of nature. He was more than a little tantalized to know what the woman had become.

He walked across to the nearest car-hire desk. What had she said? I live on Lake Ohrid. Near Struga. A village called Rad something or other. Shouldn't be so hard to find. What had her surname been? Burdin? Burdem? No. Wait. Dardan. Lumnije Dardan. It was all coming back to him now.

He cast one more look round the airport and went out to where they allocated the cars. Macedonia. He was standing in Macedonia on a sunny day in June and he didn't know anyone. Had no connection here whatsoever. It was like the sort of practical joke they foist on you on some godforsaken TV programme at number 643 on the list of satellite channels. Sad man standing in sad country looking sad. Then everyone bursts out of the undergrowth and tells him he has been taken for a god almighty sucker. And expects him to join in the joke.

In the end he stopped at Ohrid, a few miles short of his destination, and booked himself into a hotel overlooking the lake. Time enough to go looking for Lumnije tomorrow. Maybe she had stepped under a bus? Had a stroke? Fallen off her bicycle and lost her memory?

Hart went to bed at nine o'clock and slept the sleep of the disenchanted. When he awoke again two hours later

162

he couldn't even be bothered to go down to the hotel lobby and order himself a drink. He lay in bed and thought his way back to Kosovo and the rape house, and the girls he had seen there. Thought back to the Captain and the monastery and to the callousness of youth that had seen him intervene and then run away from his intervention at the first available chance. That was it, wasn't it? That was the crux of the matter. He had been a moral coward. The action stuff was all very well. But when it came to cementing some sort of real human relationship, he was a blast.

He drifted off to sleep again around three in the morning, his brain tired through with thinking, and his conscience stricken.

THIRTY-FOUR

He tried Radolišta first. The name of the village began with Rad. And it was about five kilometres inland from Struga.

He walked around town and asked whoever looked remotely amenable to questioning if they knew of a Lumnije Dardan. No one did. He went to the football pitch. Watched the game for a few minutes. Made the circuit of the spectators, asking the same question. No. No one had heard of her. Some pricked up their ears at the name Dardan, as if at the mention of a one-time historically important figure who has now been forgotten. Sir Cloudesley Shovell. Someone like that. Where the name is more memorable than the activities the person themselves engaged in. But no one knew of a Lumnije.

Hart began to wonder if Lumnije had taken on a new identity following her move to Macedonia. Maybe she was walking past him on the street at that very moment and he would never find her. Never recognize her.

'You should try Radožda,' an old woman told him. 'That starts with Rad. It's ten kilometres away. Right on the lake. Tight up near the Albanian border. You can't get any closer.'

What had Lumnije said? *I live in Macedonia now. On the shores of Lake Ohrid.*

Not in the bloody hinterland.

Hart thanked the woman who had given him the information.

As he attempted to step away from her, she caught his arm. 'Wait. Maybe I am wrong about this. Lumnije Dardan is an Albanian Muslim name. Here, in this village, we are all Albanians. All Muslim. In Radožda they are all Christians. Macedonian Christians. No. She won't be there. On second thoughts do not bother to go. I misled you. I did not think.'

Hart drove to Radožda anyway. Straight away he could see that the old woman was right about the village demographics. The place was oozing churches. Hart counted at least seven, for a population of, what, seven or eight hundred? Why would Lumnije move here, amongst people who were both ethnically and religiously different from her? It didn't make sense.

Then he saw the Muslim graveyard tucked away inside a curve in the hills, instantly recognizable thanks to its low grave markers and to the lack of crosses and other Christian accoutrements. A funeral was taking place. Four men were carrying the body of the deceased, which was wrapped in a *kafan* cloth to protect its modesty. Three other men were processing behind them. A single young woman stood off to one side, well beyond the borders of the graveyard, and watched as the body was laid in the grave, while verses from the Quran were read out over it. Then the grave was covered and more prayers were intoned. Some of the men stamped the earth down onto the grave as this was happening.

Hart didn't at first understand what kept him watching. True, one of the mourners, by definition Muslim, might know of Lumnije's whereabouts. But the truth was far simpler than that. It was because he couldn't rightly think of what else to do. What sort of person, he tried to tell himself, walks up to mourners straight after a funeral and starts asking them questions about their community? They'd probably stone him.

For some reason, though, he still hung around. Made himself as inconspicuous as possible. Blended into the landscape.

Finally, only the young girl remained. The seven men walked off in the direction of the village without seeming to acknowledge her presence at all. Maybe they were paid mourners? The Macedonian equivalent of a rent-a-crowd funeral cortege? Hart heard two cars start up. Then the men drove past him and back towards Struga. Hart checked out the number plates. *OH*. Not local then. These men came from way across the lake in Ohrid.

The girl stood for some time staring down at the grave. Then she walked towards him.

Hart looked around himself in consternation. He wasn't on any normal track. Neither was he particularly near the road. When he'd noticed the cemetery he'd made a point of picking his way across an abandoned piece of scrubland to position himself beneath a convenient and relatively inconspicuous sycamore tree. Inconspicuous, my arse.

He watched the girl approach with a sinking heart. Yes. She was making straight for him. No ifs or buts about it. He wondered whether to turn round and head swiftly back for his car. Jog even. Or should he attempt to brazen it out? The worst that could happen would be for her to upbraid him for his voyeurism. He'd respond by saying that he'd never seen a Muslim funeral before. Which was why he'd been standing three hundred yards away from the cemetery. Under a tree. He hadn't meant any disrespect. Thank God the men hadn't seen him. Seven against one didn't bear thinking about. He could surely handle the girl via a mixture of grovelling apology and playing the dumb foreigner.

The girl stopped directly in front of Hart and looked up into his face. 'So you've come then?'

'I've come?' Hart said. He had never been more surprised by an opening line in his life.

'Majka said she'd called you.'

'Majka?'

'It means mother in Macedonian.'

'Ah. And who is your mother?' But Hart already knew. The girl looked enough like Lumnije had looked at her age to cement the recognition. He'd have staked his life on it.

'Lumnije Dardan.' The girl seemed irritated more than anything. There were few signs of mourning on her face. In fact she looked as if she had just come from a job interview that had not quite gone according to plan. Whoever she had been burying – grandmother? Grandfather? Distant uncle? – had clearly not meant much to her.

Hart nodded. Might as well act normal, he decided. Pretend that he had known who the girl was all the time. 'And where is she, your majka? She was meant to pick me up yesterday at the airport. I waited three hours, you know.' He hadn't meant to sound petulant. Especially in the prevailing circumstances. But guilt can do that to a man.

The girl watched him for a moment. She appeared to be weighing him up. Measuring him in some way. Then she hitched her chin over one shoulder.

'She's in there. In that grave. Now you know why she didn't pick you up at the airport yesterday.' She turned away and started towards the road. 'Still. I'm sorry indeed for your wait.'

THIRTY-FIVE

Hart followed along behind her. He felt a little sick. What had he got himself into? Should he climb back into his car and head straight for Skopje? He had nothing whatsoever to do with this angry young girl. No possible connection. His business had been with Lumnije. Now that was over. The fact that Lumnije had a daughter was irrelevant to him.

'Will you drive me?' the girl said. 'Our house is just outside the village.'

Well. He couldn't very well say no, could he? There was nothing for it then. Hart opened the car door for her and she got in.

'My name is Biljana. It means herb.'

'My name is John Hart.' He was tempted to add 'which doesn't mean a thing', but he didn't.

'I know that. My mother told me all about you.'

'Oh.' Hart was tempted to ask what Lumnije had said. How

far she had gone. Instead he said. 'How did your mother die? I can hardly believe it. I only talked to her two days ago. She could only have been in her early thirties. What happened? A car accident?'

'She cut her wrists and drowned,' said the girl. 'Just across the lake from here. In Islam suicide is a sin, you know. This is why no one came to her funeral.'

'She committed suicide?' Hart gripped the steering wheel a little harder. He looked sideways at the girl, more shocked than he cared to acknowledge. Each person whose life you save becomes a part of you. Lumnije had been a part of him. It was as simple as that. What was it she had said to him that last time he had seen her at the monastery? *But the Captain will win in the end. Such men always do.* 'What? Against me?' he *had answered, naively. 'No, John,'* she had said. *'Against me.'*

And now he had. The Captain had won.

'So you did hire those men at the graveyard,' said Hart. 'I suspected as much.'

'Yes.'

'But you still couldn't walk with them? Behind your own mother?'

'No. Only men can do this. Women make too much noise. We wail and we weep. So we are kept apart. The Quran orders it so.'

'But you are not wailing and weeping?'

'No.'

They didn't talk for the rest of the journey. Hart, because

he was trying to work out why Lumnije would invite him over to Macedonia and then kill herself a few hours later, before she had a chance of seeing him. The girl for her own reasons. Maybe she was mourning? In shock? But it certainly didn't look like it.

'How old are you?' Hart said at last, more to break the ice than for any ulterior motive. Privately he put her age at fourteen. Still a minor then. But if so, why was her father not present at the funeral? Or maybe fourteen was considered an adult in Macedonia? It was an odd sort of a country, after all. Yes. Maybe it was that.

'I am fifteen.'

'Fifteen?' said Hart. 'You're fifteen?' After the initial shock had worn off, he began a feverish series of calculations in his head. 'Are you sure?'

Biljana stared at him. 'Of course I am sure. My birthday was two days ago. The day my mother killed herself. The day I came of age as a legal adult. Why shouldn't I know my own age?'

It's true, thought Hart. This girl must be the Captain's daughter. Has to be. The dates match completely. Because by any stretch of the imagination he couldn't imagine the Lumnije he knew leaving Visoki Dečani Monastery and letting another man anywhere near her. For months. If not years. If not for ever.

So it had to be the Captain. Unless she had been raped again at some border crossing. Which was something he doubted very much. Lumnije had learned her lessons the hard way. She was not the sort of woman who needed telling twice.

'And your father?' said Hart lamely. 'Is he waiting for you at home, perhaps? Shall I get to meet him?'

'You are my father,' said the girl, with a disdainful sideways glance. 'That is why my mother called for you. Is it not?'

THIRTY-SIX

How was he to play it? Hart had made a solemn vow to Lumnije, before he had left her that final time at the monastery, that he would never speak to anyone about what had happened to her. Never reveal a word of her shame.

'An Albanian woman's life is over once her people know that she has been "touched",' she had told him. 'If a woman is made pregnant, she will kill her own baby, or give it away, rather than bring up the rape child of a Serb. Her own community will abandon her. Her husband will disdain her. She will be forced to lie for the rest of her life. That is the future I face if I find I am pregnant. That is the future all we women face. Can I trust you?'

Hart had sworn that she could. On his life and that of his future children. Lumnije had been implacable. The oath had meant that much to her.

Since that time Hart had followed the aftermath of the

Kosovo War as closely as he was able. He had read books. Studied articles. Read witness reports. He had learned that what Lumnije had told him was true. He knew of numerous examples of Albanian women giving birth to rape children, kissing their babies one final time, and then breaking their necks or suffocating them beneath their blankets. Others gave them up to monstrous orphanages, where the children received no affection and no stimulation and were disdained by those who ought to have been caring for them. They were rapists' children after all. Serbian children. The neglect they suffered was worse than being killed. Far worse.

Still other women – the lucky ones, Hart supposed one might call them – somehow managed to lie to their families and to their husbands, who were persuaded to think that the babies were their own. It was an unendurable position to find oneself in. Few, very few, ever asked for help from the outside world. Wartime rape for an Albanian Muslim woman was a private grief, to be dealt with privately. It was an unsalvageable calamity.

So maybe Lumnije had made the right moral decision? The decision to keep her child after all? To give her innocent little girl a chance of life? Maybe this was why she had moved to a Christian village in Macedonia where questions wouldn't be asked? Because if the girl thought that Hart was her father, she sure as heck didn't have the remotest idea of the real circumstances behind her birth.

'No. I am not your father.'

'You have to say that. You want to check me out first. Make sure I am who I say I am. Well. That's all right. I can understand.'

'No. It's not that.'

'If you are not my father, then why did my mother keep all your cuttings? Follow your career all these years since my birth? Did you or did you not know her…' she began counting on her fingers, 'fifteen years and nine months ago?'

Hart closed his eyes. A sense of the inevitability of life washed over him. 'Yes, I did.'

'See. I knew it. You even look like me.'

'No I don't.' Hart couldn't prevent himself stealing a glance at the girl. This was ridiculous. Here he was, checking out a total stranger as if by some parthenogenetic miracle she could be his daughter, when he had never so much as kissed her mother, far less made love to her. Instead he had carried her on his back for twenty hours and then abandoned her, an Albanian Muslim, at a Serbian Orthodox monastery in the middle of a civil war. It had been all he could manage at the time. But it didn't look good on paper. No. It certainly did not.

'I can wait for you to check me out. I'm in no hurry.'

Hart sighed. How was he going to extricate himself from this one without causing havoc? Was he to overturn the girl's life by telling her that she was the child of the Serbian war criminal they called 'the Captain', who had locked her mother in a rape house and abused her unmercifully for close

175

on a month? After first killing her parents and her brother in front of her eyes? No. He could not do it. Far less so, given that Lumnije was now dead and he had vowed to her, while she was still living, that he would treat what had happened to her with terminal discretion.

Or had Lumnije meant her suicide as a message to him? How else to explain the timing? But surely, in that case, she would have mentioned something over the phone? Or maybe not. Either way, it was enough to drive a man mad.

'Your mother said she had something for me.'

'I don't know about that.'

'It's why she wanted to see me.'

'Maybe she meant me?' Biljana's eyes never left his face.

Hart swallowed. He could imagine his ex-girlfriend Amira's voice now, berating him from back in London when he called her with the news. 'You're like a piece of human flypaper, John. Stories stick to you like glue. Now you've really bought the lottery ticket.'

'Have you brothers or sisters at least?' Hart said.

'No. My mother never had another man after you.'

Hart rolled his eyes. What was he going to do? Take her for a DNA test? Hard to do in Macedonia. And he certainly wasn't going to ferry her back to England with him. No way was he going to risk opening that particular can of worms.

'Listen to me, Biljana. I am not your father. Your mother phoned me out of the blue two days ago. I hadn't heard from her before that for nearly sixteen years. She asked me to come over here to visit her. That she had something for me. Something that was important for my work. Something that would make me famous.'

'Is that what you want to be? Famous?'

Hart felt like whacking the steering wheel with his fore-head. 'No. No, I don't. I am just telling you her words.'

'They could as well be referring to me.'

'What? You being my daughter would make me famous?'

Both sides fell silent. Biljana indicated with a wave of her hand that Hart should turn off the main road and go down a track towards the lake.

Hart decided that he had no choice but to go with the flow. He owed Lumnije that much. And any fifteen-year-old girl, who had just lost her mother to suicide, was bound to be feeling fragile. However effectively this particular one was attempting to disabuse him of the notion.

He couldn't just abandon her, could he? Couldn't just leave her to her fate as he had done with her mother?

THIRTY-SEVEN

It rapidly became clear to Hart that Biljana had not been exaggerating her situation. She had no one. She and her mother had lived alone in this house, in a Christian village, far from any possibility of contact with anyone from their own community of Albanian Muslims.

Biljana did not attend high school, but was instead being home taught. Such a thing was more or less legal in Macedonia, she assured him, to the extent that nobody really cared what anyone else did. Plus the Christians did not tangle with the Muslims, and vice versa. History was too close at hand. Tempers too raw. Macedonia had so far avoided being caught up in any of the Balkan conflicts, and the majority of its citizens, whatever their religious affiliation, wished only to maintain the status quo.

Biljana had, however, been attending an external TEFL course in Struga, given by an Englishwoman of Balkan origin. Every three months her teacher would pop over some convenient border and then come back in again possessed of a brand-new three-month visa. This was the way things were done here. And this was why Biljana spoke such good English.

'Are you close to your English teacher? Could she help you out in any way?'

'No.'

'And you have no idea what your mother left for me? Why she called me over here just a few hours before she committed suicide?'

'I've told you. She left you me. That must be clear to you by now.'

Hart had given up declaring to Biljana that he was not her father. It simply washed over her. She had made up her mind on the subject and that was that. He decided to ride the tiger for the time being until a reasonable opportunity presented itself for him to get out from under. Meanwhile he needed to get to the bottom of just what Lumnije had intended when she had called him across from England. He owed her memory that much.

'Do you mind if I go through your mother's things?'

'If you must.'

Hart had no experience dealing with teenagers. And certainly not angry ones, with attitude, who were busy blocking any grief they might be feeling on the false premise that, despite having just lost a distant mother, they might conceivably have inherited an even more distant father on the back of it. Albeit one who was resolutely refusing to recognize them as such.

Christ, Hart told himself, he didn't even like the girl. She was clearly so angry with him that her movements, when he was in her vicinity, took on a nightmarish quality, as if she were a doll that someone else was manipulating. Someone with a powerful grudge against him. If he were to approach her for a hug, for instance, due to some misguided attempt at sympathy, he suspected that she would probably stab him. A chip off the old block then.

He sat at Lumnije's desk and looked around himself. Where to start? And might this not all be some grand misunderstanding, and Lumnije had never had anything for him in the first place? Maybe she had just wanted a temporary stopgap to look after her daughter in the wake of her suicide and felt that he owed her? And who better? Suicides were self-obsessed by default. And he was one of only two men on earth who knew her full story. Who would understand the ramifications of her actions and not feel the need to tell tales out of school. How was she to know her daughter would jump to all the wrong conclusions and imagine that her wayward daddy had finally decided to come home?

Hart trawled back through his recent telephone conversation with Lumnije. To the exact tone she had used. But Lumnije's voice had always been next to impossible for him to read.

Something deep inside her appeared to have closed down at the rape house. For ever, he now realized. What had happened to her there had been the equivalent of a ticking bomb. She had chosen to wait for her fifteen-year-old daughter to reach some sort of spurious emotional majority before finally stepping off the merry-go-round. And how could he possibly criticize her for her actions? He had never suffered anything as remotely traumatic in his life as what had happened to her. He had no conceivable idea how he would have responded in her place. Maybe even in the same way? Although he suspected not. His emotional core was tender. Lumnije's was hard as ice. And there was the rub.

'Here,' said Biljana. 'Here is what my mother left for you.'

Hart took the papers from Biljana's hand. 'Where did you suddenly find these?'

'In the rice bin. Where she keeps her money.'

'Oh.' He glanced at the papers. They were handwritten. In block capitals. Fastidiously. In English. 'Have you looked at them?'

'Yes.'

Hart glanced up at her. 'Look. I haven't asked you this yet. But I need to. Was there a suicide note? Did your mother try to explain anything to you in writing? About why she did what she did?'

Something passed across the girl's face. Some fleeting emotion that Hart could not interpret. 'No.'

'And there was nothing else? Only this?'

That same look again. 'Only this.'

This time Hart caught the look. The girl was lying. There had been something else. But this was all he was going to get for the time being. That much was clear.

He was in Biljana's house. On her terms. In her territory. She was the injured party, not him. She would play this thing as she saw fit.

And not, he was forced to admit, without some justification.

'Right,' he said. 'I'll get on and read this, shall I?'

THIRTY-EIGHT

It proved to be nonsense, of course. Some guff about the Knights Templar and their lost great treasure. All derived from dubious books about the final days of the confraternity, following the arrest of their last Grand Master, Jacques de Molay, on 13 October 1307, and his public burning, seven years later, on 18 March 1314. The winding up of the old Order. Stuff that could be found anywhere, and from a variety of sources.

Hart was inured by now to Templar fantasies. As the direct descendant of ex-Templar Johannes von Hartelius, twelfth-century Guardian of the Holy Lance, he had suffered more than his fair share of false trails and wish fulfilment fantasies, culminating in his recent illegal incursion into Iran on God's own wild goose chase that had nearly seen him blown up on a mountain track twenty feet behind his *kulbar* guide during an ill-advised attempt to recover King Solomon's Copper Scrolls.

Despite all this, the 'Templar' nickname that his journalist ex-girlfriend Amira had publicly foisted on him following his infiltration into an extreme German right-wing organization two years before seemed to have stuck for good. And Lumnije had fallen for it, hook, line and sinker. She had clearly felt she needed some additional pretext to lure him over, and she had done her homework well. She'd had that sort of brain.

The more he read, the more he realized that she had gone considerably beyond merely secondary sources to devise a theory of her own about the location of the Templar's lost treasure. And she had pinpointed this to the original site of the last great Paris temple in the Marais. To the exact place where Jacques de Molay and his unfortunate acolytes had first been imprisoned.

The snag, as Hart knew only too well, was that the entire temple precincts and the former keep had been flattened under Napoleon, and was now represented by a notional four streets delineating the Quartier du Temple – the rue du Temple, the rue du Bretagne, the rue de Picardie and the rue Béranger. Nothing of the original edifice was left. End of story.

'Well?' Biljana stared at him across the dinner table. It was two hours later. They were eating meze and flatbread, which she had prepared while he was busy reading.

Hart spooned some chopped salad into his mouth and chewed ruminatively – the older, more experienced man patiently according his time to the callow younger woman. 'You know about the Knights Templar, don't you?'

'Of course. I know everything about them. My mother spoke of little else these past two years. I have been doing all her research for her.'

'Ah.' Hart pushed away his plate and spread Lumnije's notes out on the table in front of him. He was relieved to have something neutral to talk about for a change. 'Your mother has convinced herself that the Templars, forewarned, perhaps, of King Philip's intention to destroy their Order and seize all its assets, somehow found the time to immure their immense treasure, plus the mask of Baphomet—'

'The what?'

Chalk one up for the grown-ups, thought Hart. 'The mask of Baphomet is the embalmed face of Christ. The most holy relic in Christendom. Anyway, according to your mother the Templars found time to secrete all this immense treasure inside the vaults of the great Paris temple just a few hours before the shutters came down. And not only that. For despite torture and questioning and the possibility of a martyr's death under the Inquisition, they all steadfastly declared that the treasure had instead been taken away by ship and concealed somewhere in Scotland. Rosslyn Chapel, probably. Or maybe with the Freemasons.'

'You don't sound convinced?'

'Of course I'm not convinced. It's total nonsense. Fool's gold. Your mother should have known better.'

'And yet she did this for you.'

Hart swallowed. Maybe he had been laying it on a little too thick? 'Yes. Apparently she did.'

'And meant it as a gift?'

Hart could feel himself bridling. 'Maybe. Yes.'

'To which she dedicated the final years of her life.'

'Well. Yes. It does seem so, doesn't it?' He slapped the pile of papers in front of him in an attention-grabbing sort of way. 'But she's only theorizing, don't you see? She doesn't actually come up with any cast-iron location. One might as well go looking for a needle in a haystack. I have a profession, Biljana. And it's not treasure hunter. Or fictioneer. Or mythologizer. It's photojournalist, and it pays the bills. Gives me immense satisfaction. Completes me. I don't need this. I really don't.'

Biljana took a letter out of the breast pocket of her blouse. 'No. But you need this.'

Hart looked at the envelope Biljana was holding in her hand. 'What is that?'

'My mother's final letter.'

'So she did write one. I knew you were fibbing.' Hart watched Biljana from across the table. 'And do you intend to show it to me?'

Biljana slid the letter back inside her blouse pocket. 'No. Not yet.'

Hart threw up his arms. 'Bravo then. We are in something of a quandary, it appears. Might I ask if the envelope is specifically addressed to me?'

'It is.'

'Then shouldn't you give it to me?'

'Why?'

Hart made a face. 'Why?'

'Yes. Why?' Biljana made a face back at him.

Hart was nonplussed. What the hell did this girl want from him? 'Biljana, what are you trying to pull?'

'I'm not trying to pull anything. I want to make a deal with you.'

'A deal?'

'Yes. Father to daughter.'

Hart prodded the tabletop with his forefinger. He felt more like striking it with his head. 'Listen. For the very last time. I am not your father. I met your mother around the date you were conceived. Yes. But that's as far as it ever went. We never went to bed together.'

'I do not believe you. You are lying. You are holding something back from me.'

What could Hart say? The girl was right. He was holding something back from her. And he'd continue to hold it back. Just as he'd promised her mother on pain of hell and damnation when he left her at Visoki Dečani Monastery for the final time.

Biljana will survive this, he told himself, without learning the truth from me. She is young. She speaks fluent English. She'll get her life back on track. Maybe even go to school at last. Then on to college. Macedonia was a young country,

187

both in terms of average age and in terms of expectation. Biljana had her whole life ahead of her. Why blight it for her as her mother's life had been blighted? It didn't make sense.

'I'm holding nothing back.' The lie stuck in Hart's craw, but still he mouthed it. 'What you see is what you get. Please give me your mother's letter.'

'No.'

Hart stood up. 'Right. I'm going. It's been very nice meeting you. And thanks for the food. I'm sorry about your mother. I truly am. She was a remarkable woman. I was very fond of her. Very fond indeed. But I am far too old to play games. If you change your mind about the letter you will find me just across the lake at the Hotel Royal View until tomorrow midday.' Hart started towards the door. 'I won't take these.' He pointed to Lumnije's papers. 'Because they are utterly useless to me without the letter you are holding back from me.'

Hart expected Biljana to run after him. To beg him to reconsider. She thought he was her daddy, didn't she? How could she possibly let him go just like that? He was expecting to hear her voice calling after him all the way out to the car.

But it didn't work out that way. Maybe Hart had an image of an ideal fantasy teenager somewhere in his head? Polite. Respectful of her elders. Non-assertive. But that teenager was not Biljana.

He slid into the car, started the engine, and headed up the track for Ohrid.

He had done the right thing, hadn't he? Surely he had? A man of his age couldn't allow himself to be blackmailed by a fifteen-year-old kid.

Why, then, did he feel so bloody wretched? And so all-fired bloody guilty?

THIRTY-NINE

'What deal?'

It had taken Hart less than twenty minutes car time to reconsider his position. He couldn't up sticks and leave just like that, he decided. This girl's mother had been his friend. She had come back for him, risking her own life, when she had thought him dead. He had saved her life in his turn. Which meant that he had saved Biljana's life too, when all was said and done. In the womb. Before either he or her mother had even dreamt of her existence. That meant something, surely?

The fact that she was the Captain's rape child was neither here nor there. As her mother's daughter she had a clear right to his consideration. He carried information about her that could blight the remainder of her life if he was ever foolish enough – or drunk enough – to blurt it out. Surely he owed this vulnerable young woman – his friend's daughter, for Pete's sake – the courtesy of complying with her requests?

Biljana had been crying. This fact so shocked Hart, who had convinced himself by now that the girl was rock hard and emotionally unreachable, that he didn't know how to react.

'I thought you'd left me for good,' she said.

'So did I,' he said. 'Believe me. So did I.'

Hart looked down at her. He held out a tentative hand but she shook her head, too proud to accept what might still prove to be false sympathy.

Hart could hardly blame her. It was he who had behaved like a boor, not she. She'd just lost her mother to suicide. Imagined she had finally found her father after fifteen years. She was in shock. Had to be. And he had acted like a boor.

'What deal?' he said again.

Biljana looked up. She dabbed at her eyes with the sleeves of her pullover.

Hart proffered her his handkerchief but she shook her head.

'You take me to Paris with you,' she said. 'If we find the treasure, half is mine, half is yours. If we do not find it, I give you the letter anyway and you can read what my mother says about you. Then you decide whether to acknowledge me as your daughter or throw me away.'

Hart closed his eyes. He was having a hard time trying to block the 'throwing away' bit. 'You want me to take you to Paris with me? On a sort of glorified treasure hunt?'

'Yes. I have my own passport, you know. And I have my mother's money. I will not be a burden to you. Emotionally or financially. I promise you that.'

FORTY

'So this girl thinks she is your daughter?'

'Yes.' Hart was standing outside the men's lavatory at Skopje Airport. He was talking to Amira on his mobile phone. Biljana was seated twenty yards away in the waiting area, listening to music through a pair of headphones. Her hair was hanging down either side of her head in sheets. The pair of them had barely exchanged two words since Hart had agreed to her deal. 'And she has no one. I mean no one. No friends. No neighbours. No distant relatives who survived the war. Her mother took her to a country where she wasn't known and they isolated themselves in a Christian village, even though they are Muslims. Which is like dropping off the ends of the earth. No one is going to come looking for her.'

'And is she?'

'Is she what?'

'Your daughter.'

'For fuck's sake, Amira.'

'Well, we all know how much trouble you have keeping your dick tucked away inside your pants. They don't call you "Hart the Tart" for nothing.'

'That isn't funny.'

'All depends on which side of the room you are sitting. From my perspective, it's a scream a minute. You always wanted a child. Well. Now you've got one. Your dreams have been answered.'

Hart was tempted to pitch his mobile phone across the terminal. 'You wouldn't feel like that if you were sitting here watching her. What the hell do I do?'

'Do? Do? Why are you asking me?'

'Because you're a woman.'

Amira snorted down the line. 'I'm not a woman. I'm a journalist. And what do journalists know about real life?'

'Amira. Please.'

There was a long silence. 'All right. Do you know what I would do?'

'What? Tell me. I need to know.'

'Take the girl to Paris with you,' said Amira. 'Just as you are doing now. Go through the motions. Give her a nice time. Bond a bit. Offload all the guilt you feel about what you did or didn't do for her mother onto her and then, when it becomes patently obvious that you are not her father – as it will, John, as it will – send her back to Macedonia to get on with the rest of her life.'

Hart let out a long-suffering groan. 'And what does a grown man do with a fifteen-year-old girl in Paris?'

'Look for the hidden Templar treasure. What else?'

'And failing that?'

'There's always Disneyland.'

FORTY-ONE

Hart booked adjoining rooms at the Hotel Les Deux Miroirs. It was cheap. It was central to the Marais. And the manager remembered Hart from a previous trip he had made when he had needed to consult some photo files at the Bibliothèque Française.

'And who is this beautiful young lady?'

'I am his daughter,' said Biljana.

Hart closed his eyes. The manager stared at him. Then at Biljana. 'Ah. A family trip.'

'Yes,' said Hart. 'A family trip.'

The manager gave Biljana her passport back. He somehow managed to contrive an expression on his face which said, 'Well, if you wish to involve yourself with underage young women, that is entirely your own affair. I am a man of the world. Why should I cast the first stone? But if you damage the reputation of my hotel you are dead in the water.'

'Why did you have to say that?' said Hart, as they travelled up together in the lift.

'Because it's true.'

'Look. We don't even share the same surname. He probably thinks I am trying to groom you.'

'Groom me? What is "groom me", please?'

'Oh God,' said Hart. 'Forget it.'

That evening, before deciding on where to go for dinner, Hart took Biljana on a tour of the wasteland that had once been the temple. 'Do you have any idea yet when you are going to relent and tell me where I have to dig? I'm assuming your mother will have given full details of the treasure's location in that letter you have in your pocket. You know? The one that is addressed to me?'

'Let's not run before we can walk, shall we?'

Hart stopped dead in his tracks. He turned to Biljana, an unbelieving expression on his face. 'Did you just say "let's not run before we can walk"?'

'I did say that, yes. It's a good expression, isn't it? My English teacher taught it to me.'

Hart thrust both hands inside his pockets as if this was the only way he could prevent himself from throttling the girl. 'You're not bullshitting me by any chance? There really is a letter? That is not just an empty envelope you have in your pocket that you happened to snatch off the mantelpiece when you thought I might be leaving?'

'No. It isn't.'

Hart still couldn't read the young woman in front of him. However hard he tried. And the more closely he looked, the more he saw of the Captain in her. Maybe being a sociopath was inheritable too? 'Shall we eat?' he said at last.

'Might as well.'

'French? Or I suppose you want a McDonalds?'

'I don't want a McDonalds.'

'Right. French it is then.'

He took Biljana to a small brasserie near the Place des Vosges.

'Will you order for me?' she said.

'Are you sure you want me to?'

'I don't understand any French. I have never been here before. I don't know where to start.' She looked ready to cry again. 'If you don't help me, nobody will.'

Hart's stomach gave a sudden lurch. Looking at Biljana's forlorn face, he could feel the scales slipping from his eyes. How could he have played it so wrong? Sitting across the table from him was his friend Lumnije's daughter. Not some juvenile delinquent who had latched onto him in the hope of a reward.

Hart tried to reimagine the young woman in front of him as his goddaughter, and that he was taking her out for a treat. In Paris. No strings attached. Just a forty-one-year-old photojournalist, on furlough after a traumatic posting, with his fifteen-year-old goddaughter in tow. What was so hard about that? Why, then, was he finding the whole thing so damnably difficult? Why was he making it so complicated for both of them? Why was he feeling so resentful? So put upon?

'Have you ever eaten snails before?' he managed at last.

'No.'

'I will order them then. And Boeuf en Daube. Which is marinated beef in a thick gravy. You drink wine, I suppose?'

'I drink Coke.'

Hart rolled his eyes. 'One cannot drink Coke with a Boeuf en Daube and snails. You shall have red wine. You are fifteen. Almost a grown woman.'

'I am not a grown woman.'

Hart grimaced. 'No. You're not. I don't know why I just said that. I can't imagine what came over me.'

Biljana stuck out her chin. Her lips were trembling. 'Because you wish I was a grown woman. Then I would not be bothering you, would I? You could get rid of me with a clear conscience and get on with your life.'

Hart stared at her.

Biljana stared back.

Hart gave her the briefest of nods. 'Touché.'

He looked up at the hovering waiter. 'Coke it is then.'

FORTY-TWO

They spent most of the next morning scouring bookshops and libraries and museums for any material relating to the Templars. The weather sailed perilously close to perfection. The parks were full. Le tout Paris was outside celebrating spring.

They visited a food market near the Rue des Rosiers and bought a picnic lunch which they ate on the banks of the Seine, on the far tip of the Île St Louis. Hart took Biljana to his favourite church of St Gervais. They bought honey made by the nuns. Had tea sitting by one of the open air tables. By the end of the afternoon they had walked every street and covered every inch of what remained of Templar Paris. And they had found nothing. No abandoned chapels. No Templar churches. No vaults. No catacombs. It was as if the Templars had been struck off the map and their fields sown with salt, like ancient Carthage.

That evening Hart bought tickets to the Opera Bastille via the concierge, who still hadn't decided whether Hart was actually a paedophile, or merely an over-compensating guilty parent. As Hart and Biljana never touched, it was clear that he was still veering towards the paedophile reading.

They saw *La Bohème*. Biljana's eyes never left the stage. She watched the opera as if mesmerized. Hart found himself almost liking her for the first time. Not viewing her as a desperate load he was unwillingly being forced to carry, but as a person in her own right, with feelings, faults, and frailties just like his own. The daughter of a very close friend.

At midnight they sat outside a café and drank hot chocolate with petit fours he had bought at a chocolatier on the Rue Jacob a few hours before. Hart didn't mention the letter. Neither did Biljana. It was like the dark secret a married couple share but which they refuse to confront, fearing the loss of years of fastidiously built up trust. The loss of investment in the substance of their relationship.

When he said goodnight to her that evening she offered him a brief kiss on one check. Chaste. A child's kiss. The sort of kiss a daughter will give her father. And he reciprocated.

Later, much later in the night, he fancied that he could hear her sobbing through the walls of his room. But it might just have been the wind.

FORTY-THREE

The two days Hart had initially allocated to placating Biljana and following up her mother's Templar investigations soon turned into four. Then five. Quite how this transmogrification occurred escaped Hart. But he gradually found himself relishing showing a young person around Paris for the very first time – viewing it as a privilege rather than a penance. And this change of heart appeared to affect Biljana too.

The initial impetus for the transformation occurred after yet another wasted day searching for non-existent clues to a no doubt non-existent Templar treasure. It occurred when Hart discovered that he and Biljana shared a mutual love of film. They were sitting in a café in the Rue de Flore. She was drinking hot chocolate and Hart was drinking Red Label whisky over ice. They had spent most of the day in the Quartier du Temple, as usual, beating their heads against a brick wall. Their conversation was in imminent danger of grinding to a halt.

Casting around for something to ask her that would not risk bringing her mother back into the dialogue, Hart had a brainwave. He would ask her about herself. People always liked talking about themselves, didn't they? And young girls were doubtless no exception to that rule.

'What did you do with yourself?' he said at last, with every appearance of interest.

'What did I do with myself?' she said.

'Yes. You persist in telling me that your mother had no friends. That she never invited anybody back to the house. That she taught you herself. So what did you do with yourself in your spare time?'

Biljana looked at Hart as if he had taken temporary leave of his senses. 'I watched movies, of course. Lots of them. My mother approved of that because it was good for my English. So we subscribed to a film rental club in Skopje. They sent us movies by post. It got to the point where I was receiving twenty or thirty films a month. We got good value out of that subscription, I can tell you.'

'What sort of movies did you watch?' Hart didn't know what he expected to hear, but it was probably along the lines of *High School Cheerleader 4*, or *My Boyfriend is a Vampire*.

'Oh, everything and anything. I watched Bergman and Kurosawa. Scorsese and Coppola. Ford and Hawks. Gus van Sant and David Lynch. Anything I could lay my hands on. By the end they were running out of films to send me.'

Hart stared at her. 'You watched Howard Hawks?'

'Yes. But not only him. I like 1930s and 1940s films the best. Film Noir and cowboy movies are my favourites. Films like *Arizona* and *Out of the Past*. Followed by glamour pics and white telephone movies. Oh, and I like Lubitsch and Sturges comedies. *The Palm Beach Story*. *Sullivan's Travels*. Stuff like that. After that I like the 1970s. Jeff Bridges. Jack Nicholson. Robert Duvall. I watched them all. *Five Easy Pieces* is a masterpiece. *Cutter's Way*. *Thunderbolt and Lightfoot*. *Tender Mercies*.'

'Jesus Christ.'

'Why are you swearing? What have I said?'

Hart shook his head in wonder. 'Biljana, you do realize that Paris is the greatest city on earth to watch old movies in? That it has more dedicated art house cinemas than New York and London put together?'

'No. I didn't realize that.'

Hart felt in his pocket and brought out the tattered copy of *L'Officiel des Spectacles* that he had been using to find them restaurants and art exhibitions. 'Look at this list they've got here. At the beginning. These are all the movies showing in Paris this week. Choose one. Any one. And I shall take you to see it. And to hell with the bloody Templars. You will see the movie as it was meant to be seen. Not on a box the size of a cornflake packet. But on a big screen. Academy-sized.

With an audience of aficionados who all love film sitting around you. You'll be alone but not alone. It's the very best feeling in the world.'

Biljana stared back at Hart, her eyes shining. 'I want you to choose one for me.'

Hart sat back in his chair. 'Are you sure about that? You might not like it.'

Biljana ducked her head and nodded at him. 'I'm very sure.'

'Okay. Then I will.'

Hart cast his eyes down the list. For some reason he realized that the choice he made now would in some way be significant. To both of them. That it would cement their relationship. Take it to another level. How he knew this was beyond him, but know it he did.

'Have you ever seen Charles Laughton's *The Night Of The Hunter*?' he said at last.

'Charles Laughton the actor?'

'Yes.'

'The one who was Quasimodo and Rembrandt?'

'Yes.'

'I didn't know he directed movies.'

'He didn't. Or rather he directed only one. And it received such disastrous reviews that he never repeated the exercise. But in the years since it came out it has slowly been recognized for the masterpiece it is. There is no other film remotely like it.'

'And you would like me to see it?'

'Yes. I would.'

'Why?'

Hart shook his head. 'If I knew that, Biljana, I would be a very wise man. But wise is something I am definitely not. So let's both go and see it. Afterwards, you can tell me what you saw in it. And why you think I wanted you to see it. Maybe then I will be able to make out my own motives. Because I certainly can't now.'

FORTY-FOUR

Biljana handed Hart the envelope. The performance was over. They were sitting in a brasserie across from the cinema. She was eating a Croque Monsieur and drinking an Orangina. Hart was eating a Bayonne ham sandwich washed down by a glass of his favourite beer in the world – a Pelforth Blonde.

Biljana had been crying. Hard. It had started about halfway through the movie, when the two orphaned children, inadvertently hiding their dead father's stolen loot, had escaped from the clutches of Robert Mitchum's evil Reverend Harry Powell and set off together into the night. When the journey unexpectedly turned magical, thanks to Stanley Cortez's extraordinary cinematography, Biljana went very quiet. But still Hart could see the tears coursing down her face and reflected in the light from the screen.

He felt guilty enough about suggesting the film in the first place. By the end titles he felt suicidal. That is until Biljana turned her tear-stricken face towards his and told him how much she had loved the film. Every moment of it. Then she had handed him the envelope.

'Are you sure you want me to read this?'

'Yes. I'm sure. It was addressed to you. I should never have kept it.'

'But you wanted there to be a reason for me to take you away with me? Was that it?'

A fractional hesitation. 'Yes.'

'Well, I want to tell you something.'

She darted a look at him, part trepidation and part despair. 'What is that?'

Hart toyed with his beer glass. He was never comfortable when forced to verbalize inner emotion. His preference was to keep everything safely locked away. But something warned him that vulnerable young women like Biljana – young women who had managed to convince themselves that he might possibly be their father – might wish for something more explicit in terms of a declaration.

'I am very glad indeed that you did what you did. Very glad, too, that you got me to bring you to Paris. Whatever it says in here...' he prodded the letter with his index finger, 'I don't regret these days we've spent together. I've really enjoyed myself. I only wish your mother could have been here to share this time with us. You are an exceptional young woman. You would have made her proud.'

Biljana lowered her gaze in awkward acknowledgement of

Hart's compliment. She had not yet reached the age where she could take such things in her stride. 'Read the letter. Please.'

'Now?'

'Yes.' Biljana sensed him hesitate. 'I'm still thinking about the film. I'll tell you why you wanted me to see it afterwards. Okay?'

'Is this another of your deals, young lady?'

'Yes. You've got to read the letter first, though.'

Hart bent his head towards the envelope. A sense of fatalism overwhelmed him. There were a number of loose sheets of paper and a smaller envelope, still sealed, with his name printed on it inside. 'This smaller one? You haven't read it yet?'

'No. My mother asks me not to read it in her main letter. You'll see.'

'So she expected you to read that?'

'I think so. Yes. She left it unsealed. I would say, knowing my mother, that she knew I would read it. But she also knew that I would obey her about the other sealed letter.'

Hart took a sip of his beer. He was aware of the girl's eyes upon him. In the past few days she had tailed off a little from telling him he was her father. Almost as if she suspected that something was in the offing. Curiously, it had allowed them to draw a little closer one to the other. It was emotionally tiring denying something that you were in no position to substantiate. It was all very well saying you weren't something

209

– harder, though, if you couldn't explain why you weren't it.

Hart looked at the loose sheets. Reams of Templar stuff. Clearly written for Biljana's benefit, by a mother who knew she would read it.

'Okay if I go straight to the other one?'

'It is addressed to you. Please open it.'

Hart glanced one further time at Biljana to monitor the expression on her face, but she was already flicking through the *Officiel des Spectacles*, busying herself marking off potential movies they might go to with a pencil.

Hart felt a rush of affection for her. He was briefly reminded of himself, a generation before, on his first solo visit to Paris, sitting in a bar and doing exactly the same thing. As though, for that seemingly eternal moment, what he was doing had been the most significant action in the world.

How brief youth is, and how short its span, he decided.

My dear friend. May I call you that? John is such an awkward name. At least to my lips. Johannes would be better because the J is soft. That is what your Templar ancestor was called, was he not? Johannes. The one I read about in the articles written by Amira Eisenberger. Is she your girlfriend? I suspect so. She writes about you as if she loves you. But then we women are sensitive to such things, whereas you men are not.

By the time you receive this letter I shall be dead. Do not be sad. I have been dead ever since the Captain killed my family and destroyed my honour and my innocence. And you are right. The Templar material I researched with Biljana is so much stuff and nonsense. But I wanted something – anything – that would allow her to connect with you. But do not worry. I do not expect you to act as her father. All I want is for you to ease the first few weeks of my loss for her. Then you are free to go. I have left her a little money. The house, too, is in her name, thanks to my father's foresight in keeping his assets outside the country during the Kosovo War. Biljana is an intelligent girl. She will manage very well. But she is entirely unaware of her past. I have spared her that. And I ask now that you do the same.

I know Biljana will assume that you are her father. She will grow out of this. I have neither said it was so, nor have I denied it. The subject of Biljana's paternity has never come up between us. In this I have been rigorous. I know, when you took your vow, that you did not know that I was pregnant. Neither did I. But if I had done, I would have asked for your promise, that day when you left me at the monastery, never to tell any child of mine how it was conceived. I ask this of you again now.

Have a good life, John Hart. I have thought of you many times over the years. Of your madness in saving me from that house of shame. Of your foolhardiness in confronting the Captain. Of your steadfastness in *carrying me to safety. For if you had not chosen to come back from the dead the Captain would surely have killed me. Twisted passions such as his are invariably lethal.*

Please forgive yourself for leaving me at the monastery. You had your life to live. I had mine. There was no connection between us beyond that created by happenstance. I am sorry to have to call on you now. Consider it the price one has to pay for thwarting fate. One intervenes in this world at one's peril. It makes you not a good photojournalist, John, because you are not able to detach. But it makes you a good man.

Now I think about it, maybe you were born to be a priest? Yes. I think that is what you should have been. Like your distant ancestor before you. A soldier priest. A Templar.

Lumnije Dardan

Biljana was staring at Hart with a curious intensity, as someone in the jury at a trial might stare at a prisoner accused, but not yet convicted, of an atrocious crime.

'What is it? Why are you staring at me like that?' he said.

'Your face.'

'What about my face?'

'It has gone white. Bleached of all blood. Like you have seen a ghost.'

Hart managed a hollow laugh. 'Maybe someone just walked over my grave.'

Biljana's eyes flared in shock. 'My mother you mean?'

Hart shook his head. 'You know I didn't mean that. It's just a stupid expression. The sort you toss out without thinking.'

Biljana held out her hand. 'May I read the letter now, please?'

Hart looked at her in consternation. 'Of course not. It is addressed to me. You told me so yourself. Your reading it wasn't ever part of the deal.'

Biljana sat back in her seat. Not once, in the entire course of the movement, did her eyes leave Hart's face. 'Are you still pretending you don't know why you wanted me to see the film?'

Bravo. Biljana had wrong-footed him again. Hart felt himself flush with outraged virtue. Far from wanting to know what the film signified, all Hart wanted to do was to thrust the letter inside his jacket pocket and forget all about its existence. Then he wanted to spring to his feet and run out into the street yelling for a taxi to the nearest airport. 'Tell me,' he said at last. 'Tell me why I wanted you to see the film.'

Biljana collected her thoughts. The effort was clearly visible on her face, for her features were so expressive that each action she took was semaphored ahead as if by advance messenger. 'You wanted me to see the film because you unconsciously wished me to understand how lies can blight a person's life. That's so, isn't it? But you were unable to tell me so yourself.'

Hart groaned.

213

'You see. I am right. The two children in the film were lied to by everybody, weren't they? Only their father, who was a criminal, and was destined to hang, told them the truth. Because he had nothing left to lose. Other people, in positions of power, always abused them. And you are in a position of power, just like them. You may or may not be my father. You tell me you are not. But you will not tell me who is. By what right have you, a stranger, to dictate my life to me? That is what the film has told me. That is the message you wanted me to receive, is it not? That you are a good man. Not like the people in the film. Not like the reverend. But you do not behave like a good man should.'

Hart closed his eyes. He felt as if he had been caught napping by a freak wave and swept under by its weight. Part of him almost wanted to drown. To let himself sink inside the groundswell and have done with it. 'I am not a good man. You've got that bit right.'

But Biljana was not done with him. 'Does my mother, in that letter, direct you to lie to me?'

Hart glanced down at the letter on the table in front of him. Suddenly, for no reason that he could fathom, he pushed it towards Biljana. 'Why not read it for yourself and see? That's what you want to do, isn't it?'

Biljana's hand froze halfway towards the envelope. 'Is this a trick? Is the letter about something else entirely?'

Hart shook his head. 'No. There's no trick. It's about you.'

'Why now then? Why not before?'

Hart gazed at her. 'Because you could have read it any time in the last week and you didn't. And because you're right, though it crucifies me to have to admit it. I owe you the truth. Your mother is dead. You are living. There's a difference. The dead should not be allowed to dictate to the living. That would be both morally and ethically wrong.'

'So you won't be breaking any vows in showing it to me?'

'No. Your mother didn't know she was pregnant when she asked for my promise never to tell anyone what had happened to her. By killing herself, and by calling me over to look after you in the aftermath of her suicide, I figure that she broke any deal that I originally made with her. If I were you, I'd want to know who my father is too. So I've got no right to treat you in a way I would refuse to be treated myself. Read the letter, Biljana. Then ask me whatever you want to ask. No more lies. No more prevarication. You can have the truth. Though you may not thank me for it in the end.'

'Like in the film?'

'Oh yes. Just like in the film.'

FORTY-FIVE

It wasn't an easy few hours. Biljana veered from anger to tears and then back to anger again, often in the space of a few minutes. At first Hart tried to control the situation, but he soon realized he needed to let Biljana expend herself in whatever way she saw fit.

They spent some time in the back of a taxi. Later they sat in one of the countless small parks dotted around the centre of Paris. Still later he tried, but failed, to get her to eat something in a late-night café that advertised twenty-four-hour meals.

At a little after two in the morning they returned to their hotel and Hart helped put Biljana, still fully clothed, into bed. Later, hearing her crying through the walls of his room, he was tempted to go into her room to see if he could help, but finally decided against it. He wasn't her father. And young girls, especially young teenage girls full of hormones and without fathers, were prone to inappropriate crushes. He was sure of himself, but he wasn't sure of her. The last thing he wanted was for his and Biljana's relationship to veer off into dangerous territory. She was far too young and far too vulnerable for him to take those sorts of risks.

Over breakfast the next morning Hart made Biljana the offer of formally adopting her, or, at the very least, securing a special guardianship order until she was eighteen. He told her that this was so she would be guaranteed a modicum of security and some sort of still centre inside the vortex in which she now found herself. The offer surprised him even as he made it. Although he had always wanted children, Hart did not, in his customary perverse manner, see himself as a particularly paternal man.

'But I already have a father. I know that now. I would have liked him to be you. But he is not.'

Hart stared at her across the breakfast table. He didn't know, for a moment, whether to laugh or to cry. 'But the Captain's a war criminal, Biljana. A rapist. He's also a Serb, and, in theory at least, a Christian. You are a Muslim. The situation is impossible. Added to which he's probably dead. And if he isn't, he should be.'

'I want to meet him.'

Hart tried to rein in his sense of frustration. 'Even after what he did to your mother? Even after all the horrors he perpetrated on God knows how many innocent victims? The killings? The torture? The man is a monster. He killed your grandparents, Biljana. He killed your uncle. I know this is true because your mother told me so. She watched him do it.'

'But he is my father. I need to see him.'

Hart felt as Pandora must have felt when she first opened the box. Pandora had managed, so it was said, to seal in hope. Hart didn't give much for his chances of pulling off a similar trick. 'That's an impossible request. He could be anywhere. If he's alive he'll be in hiding, for he'll certainly be on the United Nations watch list. Which means that if he shows his face in any civilized country he'll be immediately imprisoned and sent to trial at the International Criminal Court in The Hague. He'd be lucky to escape with thirty years. In any rational society he'd be put up against a wall and shot.'

'Will you help me?'

Hart threw his hands up in the air. 'Help you? How can I help you? What you are asking me is insane.'

Biljana cocked her head to one side as a person does who is estimating whether or not the individual they are talking to has a somewhat limited mental capacity. 'You said you last saw him at the monastery. The one in Kosovo. The one you call Visoki Dečani. Take me there then. We can talk to the monks. Maybe they will know what happened to him?'

Hart shook his head. 'That was fifteen years ago, Biljana. And even if we found him, what good would it do? What would you be after? Revenge? Is that it? Because I refuse to

218

have anything to do with that. I will not help you blight the remainder of your life. That would be letting the bastard win. He and his kind did what they did to produce exactly this kind of response in their victims. The whole thing was prejudged. Coldly calculated. Like what the Russians did to German women at the end of the Second World War. And even if he is alive somewhere, he won't be interested in you. You'll be tearing yourself to bits for nothing. Trust me in this. Go back home. Think over my offer. It won't involve you in anything. But it will mean that if anything ever happens to me, you will be taken care of. They do insurances for us, you see. War risk. Hostage taking. Death by misadventure. Only our immediate families can benefit.'

'So you think you are going to die too?'

Hart rolled his eyes. 'No. I'm not saying that. Of course I'm not. But look at you. You're fifteen years old. You've just found out that your father is a rapist and a war criminal. I would have spared you that, believe me…'

'And you would have been wrong.'

'Maybe. Maybe not. It's not for me to decide. But what is done is done. Why not let sleeping dogs lie? Come back to England with me. I want you to meet someone. Amira Eisenberger. She's a journalist. And a good friend. She could be of enormous help to you in any career you later choose. You can go to college. The whole world is open to you. You just have to reach out and grab it.'

'Will you take me to Visoki Dečani?'

Hart flipped the lid of the coffee pot down with a bang. He cleaned his hands on a paper napkin, balled the napkin up, and stuffed it into his cup. 'No, Biljana. I've told you. No. Wild horses wouldn't drag me back to that place.'

FORTY-SIX

'So you told her about her father?' Amira's voice was pitched an octave higher than its usual smoky drawl.

'I thought it was her right to know.'

'You never could keep your trap shut about anything.'

Hart let that one slide by. Amira was never happier than when she had a reason to castigate him for things she would have done in exactly the same way were she in his place.

'But what, in heaven's name, caused you to go one further and agree to help her track him down?' she said.

'I couldn't have her going off on her own. She's fifteen, for Pete's sake.'

'So you let a fifteen-year-old girl pin you against the wall and force you to do her will?'

'It wasn't quite like that.'

'It sounds very much like it to me.'

'Listen. I shot myself in the foot. I let slip the name of the monastery where I left her mother. It didn't seem significant to me at the time. But of course the moment she had it, she fixed on it. She had a trail. Wild horses couldn't have stopped her then.'

Hart hunkered back against his pillows. He was sitting up in bed, fully clothed, trying to figure out how to escape from the disastrous mess he had got himself into. Amira was his first – and only – port of call.

'So what do you expect from me?' Her tone was heavily ironical.

'Some advice? A plan, even?' There was a protracted silence. 'Are you still there, Amira?'

'I'm thinking.'

'Thank God for small mercies.'

There was a *harrumph* from the other end of the line. Then the sound of a match being lit. A pause while she took the first drag of her cigarette. 'Yes. I can see that. Someone thinking must make a welcome change from your perspective.'

Hart knew better than to comment when Amira was in full flow. He switched the phone to loudspeaker mode and rested it on his knee. He cocked his head to one side and stared at it as one would stare at a strange-looking beetle that has deplaned from out of nowhere.

'Listen, Marco Polo. Did you personally witness the Captain murder those unarmed people on the track when he was following you and Lumnije?'

'No. But I heard the shots.'

'Not good enough. Did you see him rape anybody?'

'No.'

Amira gave a grunt. 'Did you see him kill anybody at all? The two women who escaped, for instance?'

'There were three women. And no. I told you. I saw him try to murder someone. Me. But I didn't witness him actually killing anybody.'

'That's a shame.'

'What are you getting at?'

'I'm getting at whether we can turn this whole thing to our advantage. Capture ourselves a war criminal. Bring the bastard to justice.'

'He's Biljana's father, for Pete's sake.'

'So what?'

'I can't serve two masters, Amira. I've agreed to try and help her find him. When I've done that, I'll need to take my cue from her as to what I do next. Not from you.'

'Has anyone ever told you that you're a big girl's blouse?'

'Yes. You.'

'I knew the insult sounded familiar.'

Hart caught the sound of a soft knock on his bedroom door. 'She's here. Biljana's here. I have to go. We can talk more later.'

'So you're really intending to take her to the monastery with you?'

'I've got no choice. She's set to go anyway. And I owe this

much to her mother. With any luck the trail will go cold there and that will be an end to it.'

'And what if it doesn't?'

'I'll jump that fence when I come to it,' said Hart. 'Look, I have to go.'

'Wait. One more thing before you open the door.'

'Yes?'

'The Captain is the scum of the earth, isn't he?' Amira had on her journalist's voice again.

'Yes. He's one of the worst. He used to boast to Lumnije about the bestial things he'd done during the war. As if it might give him kudos with her. Turn her on. He tried the same trick on me when I had him handcuffed. Probably hoping I'd go crazy with the horror of it and give him an opening. The guy is a mass murderer. He's filth. He's the crud you find in the dishwasher filter.'

'Elegantly put.' Amira hesitated. 'But Lumnije's dead, isn't she? So there are no witnesses left to what he did?'

'Yes. She is. And no. There aren't. None that I know of, at least. But there'll be living victims scattered right across the Balkans if half of what Lumnije told me is true. They won't be that hard to round up now that the Serbs are gone. The War Crimes Commission will have collected interviews and affidavits. That's what they do, don't they, when a conflict is over?'

'All right, then,' said Amira. 'Go to the monastery. See what you can find out. I'll do some digging here.'

'Why would you do that?'

Amira laughed. 'Because I am first and foremost a journalist, lunk head. And because I've learnt a few things about you in the past few years. One thing in particular.'

'And what's that?'

'Where you go, stories go.'

FORTY-SEVEN

Visoki Dečani Monastery was sealed off when Hart and Biljana arrived at the gates, forty-eight hours later. Half a dozen KFOR vehicles were blocking the main entrance, alongside two blue Carabinieri Land Rovers.

'What's going on?' Hart asked one of the heavily camouflaged Italian troops guarding the entrance. He flashed his press pass to avoid the soldier closing him down. NATO's peacekeeping operations were a bureaucratic nightmare, and Kosovo Force was one of the worst. Veteran journalists called it the 'snake with two heads'.

'The abbot is showing our admiral and some other VIPs round the monastery.'

'May I ask why?'

The soldier hesitated.

'Off the record,' said Hart. 'My niece and I just want to visit the monastery as tourists. I'm not here on any assignment. We'd like to know whether or not we stand a chance of being allowed in today. If we don't, we'll clear off. You could save us a lot of trouble by simply answering my question.'

The soldier nodded. His eyes travelled over Biljana in an automatic masculine assessment. Biljana made a face and turned her back on him. She glared out at the surrounding forest as if she expected it to burst into flames at any moment as the result of a napalm attack.

The soldier gave a half smile, as though he and Hart, both being men, would understand what had just occurred without any need for further explanation. 'Last week the KLA threatened to burn this place down. There is nothing new in this. A year ago the monastery was attacked by a man with rifle grenades. By visiting like this, KFOR are showing these fucking Albanian whoresons that they take guarding the monastery seriously. This place is a UNESCO Endangered World Heritage Site, you know?'

'My niece is Albanian,' said Hart. He stared at the soldier, his gaze unwavering.

The soldier stared back. 'I'm sorry. I really am. But sometimes we can't pick our relatives.'

The admiral's arrival, accompanied by the abbot and a number of his long-haired, black-frocked priests, plus a phalanx of men in brown, beige and off-grey acrylic summer-weight suits, neutralized the imminent showdown between Hart and the Italian soldier.

'You were going to hit him, I could see it,' Biljana said later, when the admiral and his KFOR escort had disappeared in a cloud of dust back towards Peć. 'You didn't like what he said about me and you were going to hit him.'

'One doesn't hit armed soldiers.'

'I don't believe you. I could see it in your eyes. You were angry. You are still angry.'

'Shows how dumb men can be,' said Hart. 'I'd avoid them if I were you.'

Biljana wrinkled her nose. 'He was quite handsome, though, in a Genghis Khan kind of a way.'

Hart gave her a look.

Biljana stared directly back at him. When she was certain she had his full attention, she fluttered her eyelashes melodramatically.

The abbot cleared his throat.

Hart turned to greet him. He managed to wipe the burgeoning grin off his face. Biljana's expression turned abruptly serious too.

'I am so sorry,' said the abbot. 'You wish to see around the monastery perhaps?'

'We were hoping to see the tomb of St Stefan. Yes. But we will come back tomorrow if it is more convenient.'

'No. No.' The abbot waved one hand. He toyed with the cross hanging on a silver chain around his neck. 'I will not hear of it. We have already delayed you quite sufficiently. I shall show you and your daughter round personally.'

'My name is John Hart, Father. And this is Biljana Dardan. But I must tell you that Biljana is not my daughter. She is the daughter of a close friend, recently deceased.'

The abbot made a sad face and inclined his head. 'Biljana? That is an Albanian name, no?'

'Yes,' said Biljana. 'Albanian Muslim.'

'All are welcome here,' said the abbot, pretending that he had not noticed her prickliness. 'Christians. Muslims. Buddhists. Jews. Just so long as they are not wearing explosive vests, of course.'

FORTY-EIGHT

The monastery seemed unchanged since Hart had last seen it. It was a shade neater, perhaps, with the grass tended just a little closer to perfection. But the stones still looked as if they had been scrubbed by invisible hands, and the trees as though they had been pruned by someone with a mania for expressive topiary. The vines on the hillside behind the monastery stood to attention like Napoleon's Imperial Guard, and the river flowed clean and crisp through the valley as if it alone might wash away the discordant memories that infected the place.

Hart caught himself staring, despite his best intentions, towards the room in which he had said his last goodbyes to Lumnije on the final morning of his sojourn at the monastery. The memory remained fresh, as though it had occurred only a few days before.

He glanced guiltily at Biljana, as though she might

somehow succeed in picking up the memory by osmosis and making it her own, but she was staring across the hillside, her expression blank.

'This is not the first time I have been here,' Hart said to the abbot.

'I'm afraid I do not remember you,' said the abbot, frowning. 'No. I definitely do not remember.'

'You were probably not here then,' said Hart. 'It was fifteen years ago.'

'Oh, I was here,' said the abbot. 'Only I looked like Peter over there.' He pointed to one of his young priests. 'I didn't have this impressive hat for a start. Neither did I have grey hair.'

Hart laughed. 'I don't remember you either, I'm afraid.'

'Ah. That is the way of things.' The abbot stopped by the open abbey door. 'This was during the war, no?'

'Yes,' said Hart. 'I left someone here. A war victim. This young lady's mother, in fact.'

The abbot turned his gaze towards Biljana. 'Your mother?'

Biljana nodded silently.

'We were being pursued at the time. By a man called the Captain. A war criminal. A killer.'

'A Serbian?'

Hart nodded. 'I'm afraid so.'

'And he pursued you here?'

'Yes. But your abbot kindly took us in. I owe the monastery my life. Biljana's mother too.'

The abbot smiled. 'Yes. That happened much around this time. Our Venerable Father Visarion was a holy man. A good man. To him all human beings were created equal in the likeness and love of God.'

'No. He got that bit wrong. The Captain wasn't. No one can convince me of that one. God missed a trick with the Captain. The same sort of trick he missed with Adolf Eichmann. And Idi Amin. And Saddam Hussein.'

The abbot inclined his head. He was not going to offer any argument.

'So we have come here to ask—'

'About your mother?' The abbot was staring at Biljana again, as though her face might reveal some secret that only he held the key to.

'No. About my father,' she said.

'Your father? But I don't follow you.'

'The Captain was my father. Now that my mother is dead, I want to find him.'

'Understandable. Quite understandable,' said the abbot. 'A child needs both its parents. Even if one of them leaves much to be desired.'

'The Captain raped my mother, Father Maksim. After killing my grandmother and my grandfather and my uncle before my mother's eyes. That is how he came to be my father. And that is why I wish to find him.'

The abbot looked at her for a long time. 'So you do not wish to see the tomb of St Stefan?'

232

'No.'

'I see.'

Hart watched the abbot carefully. But Father Maksim was giving nothing away.

'You will dine with us tonight?' the abbot said at last. 'We could offer you a good stew. Our own wine and rakia. Accommodation. We have a guest dormitory, you know. Would this be acceptable to you both?'

'Very acceptable,' said Hart, more quickly than he had originally intended, but with more relief in his voice than he either cared, or knew, how to express. 'Very acceptable indeed.'

FORTY-NINE

The rakia was the best grape brandy Hart had ever tasted. Biljana, no doubt still under the influence of her trip to Paris, managed to force down a little red wine with every appearance of relish. The fourteen monks, most of them surprisingly young men, did not stint themselves either. The stew was a mixture of rabbit, venison and local beef. It was heavily spiced, more in the Hungarian than the Kosovan style. The accompanying vegetables were fresh from the farm. For pudding they ate homemade yoghourt sweetened with local honey. The monks, who had not eaten since eight-thirty that morning, ate as only young men who have been working in the fields all day, or painting icons, or making candles, can.

Hart followed each face, each movement the monks made. After an hour, an elderly woman came in to clear away for the guests. Each monk took away his own plate and tumbler, leaving the half dozen outsiders to finish their coffee alone.

The abbot beckoned to Hart.

Hart glanced at Biljana, then stood up.

'None of my monks are able to help you,' the abbot said, leaning close. 'I have asked them. I am the only one of our community still here from that time. Apart from the archimandrite, our spiritual leader. And he is on a retreat and will speak to no one.'

'So why did you ask us to stay over, Father?'

The abbot indicated the serving lady with an inclination of the head. 'Because of Maria. She has been here for forty-seven years. She remembers the Captain well. Which is scarcely surprising, in the circumstances. For she is related to him.'

Hart looked across at Biljana to see if she had heard, but she was immersed in a pamphlet detailing the history of the monastery. 'She's the Captain's relation?'

'She is the Captain's great-aunt, I believe. This is not something…' The abbot hesitated, lowering his voice even more. 'Shall we say that this is not something of which our lovely Maria boasts. My sense is that she will not speak of it to you either. But…' He shrugged his shoulders. 'You and Biljana are our guests. It seems only reasonable to apprise you of such facts that are certain to my knowledge. The rest is up to you.' The abbot backed away a little and inclined his head. 'I must regretfully say goodbye to you now. We have busy

235

nights here at the monastery. And tomorrow I must attend committees. The day after as well. So I shall not be here to say goodbye to you. This, too, I regret.'

Hart shook the abbot's hand. 'Can I ask you one final thing?'

'You wish to know why I am helping you?' The abbot smiled.

'Yes.'

'I am a Serb. I am a priest. I am a man. One day soon I shall be an archimandrite, and shall be called upon to oversee abbots such as myself in terms of their spiritual welfare. When this occurs I must, like the present archimandrite, occasionally go into retreat.'

Hart nodded in understanding. 'Your conscience, you mean? You could not square not helping us with your conscience?'

'Yes. Yes. My conscience. If that is what you call it.' The abbot drew in a long breath. 'I am horrified by what has been done in the name of Greater Serbia these last twenty years. If I were to say as much in certain circles, I would be lucky to make shepherd, far less archimandrite. Is that not how you say it? To make something? Instead, to make archimandrite, I hold my silence. This is necessary to secure the monastery. Otherwise men would be here who might abuse this priceless gift we have been given. But there is only so far one can keep silence. If you choose to write about what I am doing for you, then I accept this. But I would ask that you do not. It would be a catastrophe for us.'

'I will not write about it, Father. Neither will anyone else.'

'I thank you. This place is precious to me. Perhaps, before you leave, you will ask one of my monks to open the cask of St Stefan for you after all? You may touch the saint's hand. He is very well preserved, I promise you, and he does not smell. If you crawl underneath the casket, you will be healed of all that ails you. Will you do this? Biljana too. It is a heavy burden that she is carrying. I would not see this in one so young.'

'But she is a Muslim.'

'Really? She is a Muslim? There is no God but God, is that not what the *tahlila* says? Muslim, Christian, Jew, where is the difference? We all bow before the same God, do we not?' The abbot beamed. His smile that of a good man, in his element. 'We forget this at our peril.'

FIFTY

'I'm sorry. I cannot help you.' Maria was drinking a cup of tisane in the abbey kitchens. Her hands were red and hard, her fingers gnarled with arthritis. Her white hair was drawn back tightly on her head, outlining the shape of her skull. Her cheeks were sunken from a lifetime of smoking, with lines escaping from her eyes in every direction but upwards, as if God had decided at some point in her life that the sadness of her interior demeanour must be adequately reflected on her face.

The young novice who was doing the translating for Hart hunched his shoulders apologetically, as if he was somehow responsible for his charge's intransigence.

Hart took a sip of his tea. He met Biljana's eyes and lowered his own melodramatically, so that she would know not to intervene.

'That's fine. I never quite believed the abbot when he said you were a relation of the Captain's. A woman such as you,

238

serving the monastery for – I believe the abbot said forty-seven years, did he not? – well, it would be unthinkable for a person such as you to be related to a war criminal.'

The young novice havered for a moment, as if he didn't quite approve of what he was being asked to transmit. But then, with a small sigh, he translated what Hart had said.

'A war criminal?' said the old woman.

'Didn't you know?' Hart put his cup down with a shocked expression on his face. 'Yes. The Captain killed and tortured and raped in the name of Greater Serbia over a period of close on six years. His victims are beyond counting. He even raped this young lady's mother. That is why she is here, you see. To confront her father.'

'To confront her father?' Maria seemed entirely out of her depth.

The young monk was looking more uncomfortable by the minute, as if he had stumbled into an orgy peopled by individuals he had previously thought better of. At the very least, Hart comforted himself, the abbot must have spoken to the young man beforehand and given him some indication of what he was entering into. Either that, or the boy would be experiencing a vastly accelerated moral education.

In for a penny, in for a pound, Hart decided at last.

'We quite appreciate,' he continued, 'that if you were related to such a man, you would not be keen to acknowledge the fact. It is for this reason that we will fully understand if you decide not to cooperate with us.'

Maria looked startled. Her eyes, widened in shock, made her face look briefly younger, as if the lines her life had marked her with had temporarily been scrubbed away. 'The Captain raped your mother?'

'Yes,' said Biljana. 'He kept her in a rape house for three weeks. He raped her every day. He wanted her to become pregnant. Wanted her to have a child. I am that child.'

'You are a Christian then?' The old woman's expression was pained, as if the question had had to be forced out of her.

'No. I am a Muslim. My mother was Muslim. My father was a Serb. But one could hardly have called him a Christian, could one? Would you have expected me to take on the religion of my father given the circumstances surrounding my birth?'

Maria began to cry. Biljana ran to her, but the old lady brushed her off – kindly but firmly. 'It is not because you are a Muslim,' she said, awkwardly. 'It is that I do not like to be touched by anyone.'

Biljana froze, her face stricken.

Maria glanced at the young monk, almost as if she were seeking his approbation for what she was about to say. 'You see, I too was...' she hesitated. Then the words came out in a rush, following each other like dice thrown onto a table. 'What happened to your mother happened to me.' Maria drew in a long breath. 'In the war. The Germans. They created the Ustaše. The Croatian Fascist State. You have heard of the Serbian Genocide?'

Hart shook his head. Biljana sat down near the young monk, who was looking more stricken by the minute at what he was being asked to do. She shook her head too.

'Five hundred thousand Serbs, Jews and Romanis killed. In one camp alone – Jasenovac, Heaven spit on its name – fifty-two thousand were murdered. In 1941 I was eighteen years old. Eighteen. How old was your mother, child, when the Captain touched her?'

'Sixteen and a half.'

'And how old are you?'

'Fifteen.'

The old lady nodded slowly. 'The Ustaše used a Srbosjek on their hands to quickly kill their victims. This is an agricultural knife worn over the hand like a glove, with the blade facing downwards, the palm protected by a copper plate. It is the sort of knife a small farmer will use in the fields even now to cut his wheat.' She gave another quick glance at the novice monk.

He was sobbing. But still, through his sobs, he continued with the translation.

'They nicknamed this knife the Serb Cutter. One downward blow on the neck and a person will bleed out to death within twenty seconds, like an animal. Of course, many times they missed. Then it would take many blows. Much longer to die.'

The young monk wiped his eyes on the sleeves of his habit.

The old lady handed him her cup of tea and he took a small sip and returned it to her, smiling gratefully.

Hart was gradually becoming aware of the multifarious tendrils of relationship available within the monastery environment. And of how close the young novice might be to this otherwise forgettable old woman.

'But I was young and pretty,' Maria continued. 'Yes. It is hard to believe now. But so I was. And the Ustaše were young and all-powerful. And I did not want to die. By this time in the war the Ustaše were scared. They took to using the Granik to kill their victims. This is a special hoist traditionally used to unload goods from the Sava boats. The crane quickly transforms into a gallows. The Serb prisoner would be stripped and beaten and chained and carried to the Granik like dead meat. Weights would be tied to his chains so that his arms were bent out of shape. The Serb's stomach would then be slashed so that his intestines fell out. His neck would be slashed. Then he would be struck on the head and plunged into the river. Later, because this method was too slow, Serbs were tied in pairs. Then their bellies were cut and they were thrown into the river alive. One man, Petar Brzica, because of a bet, killed 1360 people in one day. He won prizes for it. A gold watch. A silver service. A bottle of Italian wine. A roast suckling pig. He was very happy. Another man, Mile Friganović, tried to make an old man called Vukasin bless the name of the criminal, Ante Pavelić, who was the father of the Croatian fascist movement. The old man refused. Friganović cut off Vukasin's ears. When Vukasin refused again, he cut off his nose. Then he ripped out his tongue. Finally he cut out the old man's eyes, tore out his heart, and slashed his throat until he died. You see, my dear,' Maria held out her hand to Biljana. 'You see why I let them touch me?'

Biljana, her eyes damp with tears, took the old lady's hand.

'Good.' Maria nodded her head a number of times. Then she raised Biljana's hand in hers and kissed it. 'Some touch is good. Your touch is good. Now, my child, I have something for you. Open your hand.'

Biljana opened her hand.

Maria slipped a piece of paper into it. 'I am still in touch with my niece. The mother of the man you are seeking.' She shrugged. 'There are evil men everywhere. Of every race. Of every religion. No one is exempt. No country is without stain. One does not choose to whom one is related by blood. Remember this.' She glanced at the young monk, as if willing him to pay particular attention to her words. 'Remember this, too, Biljana, when you think of your mother. Remember what happened to me. And do not judge her too harshly.'

FIFTY-ONE

Hart and Biljana were seated in Hart's bedroom, a table between them. The piece of paper, still folded, lay on the table like the reminder to the timing of an execution.

Hart pointed to the paper. His hand, without his knowledge, took on the shape of a pistol. 'Before we open it, I want you to promise me something.'

Biljana was having trouble focusing on Hart's face. Part of her was elsewhere. From her expression, it was not a comfortable place. 'What is that?'

'If this paper holds nothing of any use to us in finding the Captain, I want you to promise me that we finish this thing right here. In this room. That we let it rest. You come to England with me. I introduce you to my friend Amira, as we agreed. We do some nice things together. Then we decide on your future.'

Biljana lowered her head.

'Can we agree this?'

'What if there is something in it that we can use?'

Hart squared his shoulders. It took some effort. 'Then I will do exactly as I promised, and help you to the best of my ability. But I will not kill the Captain for you. And I will not resort to violence of any sort. I will simply try and arrange a meeting between the two of you. After that we will decide where to take things. You know my feelings in this. You know that I would rather not do it. This man is filth. The lowest of the low. He tried to kill me. He raped your mother. He murdered your relatives. He tormented and killed many others. But I'm according you the courtesy of imagining that you know your own mind.'

'Okay then.'

Hart straightened up, surprised. 'Okay to everything I just said?'

Biljana nodded. 'Yes. I promise. Okay.'

Hart flared his eyes for a moment, as if he didn't quite believe her. Then he thought better of it, and inclined his head in grudging accord. 'Then open the paper. Let's see what she's given us.'

Biljana spread the paper out on the table in front of her.

There were two words on it, written in pencil and capitalized.

FFL and *DJIBOUTI*.

Hart suspected that the old lady, accustomed only to the Cyrillic alphabet, had got the young monk to write the words out for her. And that she had elected to hold the paper back as a final resort until she had decided whether or not she wished to help the two foreigners.

For one dreadful moment Hart found himself interpreting the initials *FFL* as Freshly Fucked Look, which had formed part of a communal wish-fulfilment fantasy about girls at his school twenty-five years before. Then he saw the word *DJIBOUTI*, and he knew.

'What does it mean?' said Biljana.

'It means that your father is a member of a branch of the French Foreign Legion which is based in Djibouti. This doesn't surprise me. For a man like him it makes perfect sense. He'll have known that he was a marked man after Kosovo. But you can join the Legion and mask your previous identity. I've visited Djibouti twice on assignment. We all have. It's the arsehole of the world. The 13th Demi-Brigade of the Foreign Legion is stationed there. Alongside the Yanks, the Brits, the Japanese, the South Koreans and pretty much anyone else who can come up with enough moolah to interest the president. It's a country you buy your way into. The place is strategically vital. The Gibraltar of the Red Sea. Which is lucky. Because it's got nothing else to offer.'

'But Maria has not given us the Captain's true name?'

'Foreigners hardly ever register under their own names when they join the Legion. They are allowed to choose pseudonyms. That's part of the attraction. You can abandon your old life and start fresh. I think Interpol do check on each candidate now, though. But the Captain may have got in before that. And I doubt due diligence is retrospective. The French don't faff about. They tend to make their own laws.'

'So how do we find him once we're out there?'

'You really mean you want to go out to Djibouti and confront your father? You mean to take it that far?'

'Yes.'

Hart threw up his hands. 'Then that's what we must do then. We'll not find out about him through the Legion, though. I can promise you that much. They are notoriously difficult to penetrate. Once a man has been taken in he will be protected. They will not release his identity to anyone bar the police. And only then if there is good reason. I've run into the Legion fairly often while I've been on assignment. They are like the Marines. Or the combination locks at Fort Knox. A closed book.'

'Then how do we find him?'

Hart shrugged. 'There you've got me. We'd better pray for a mass parade and a high-powered pair of binoculars. Otherwise we're going to need luck. And lots of it.'

FIFTY-TWO

The roads around Djibouti were like the roads at the ends of the earth. Slate-grey hills, slate-grey fields. A few scrubby trees. Electricity pylons marching into infinity. The occasional off-white town surrounded by a sea of plastic junk and litter. Not a crop. Not even a productive bush. The shadows on the mountains were the only things to remotely break the endless monotony.

The few local people visible outside town seemed to be nomads. A few sheep. A few half-starved camels. The occasional moveable hut sheathed in plastic and corrugated iron. Even the rocks seemed out of place. If she had had to describe the scene to someone who had never been there, Biljana would have said it was the death of landscape. The entrails of the earth. Sixty percent of the country and a hundred per cent of the animals lived below the poverty line. Eighty-five per cent of Djibouti's urban population was out of work. Corruption. Inertia. Bad luck. The average life expectancy was forty-three years.

But the place was a strategic minefield. It was located close to the world's busiest shipping lanes and to the oilfields of Arabia. Every army and every tin-pot security firm on the planet had a piece of Djibouti. During the twenty-minute drive from the airport to their hotel she saw Foreign Legionnaires from the 13th Demi-Brigade cruising the marketplace in their ridiculously abbreviated budgie-smuggler shorts. She saw Yankee officers in dress whites from the US-led Horn of Africa anti-terror force at Camp Lemonier emerging from shiny black limousines. She saw under-funded British soldiers in hand-me-down camos, shabby Number Twos, and emergency desert kit trying to kick start their malfunctioning Land Rover Wolfs. She saw earnest Germans. Happy-go-lucky Dutch. Snap-happy Japanese. Even the South Korean military had got into the act. The bar fights, her guide book insisted, were legendary.

And the Djibouti government raked in the service dollars with an extra-long croupier stick and then sent ninety per cent of the cash abroad to a series of foreign bank accounts that had very little to do with national reconstruction and a heap of a lot to do with personal gratification. This was the country she had come to in search of her father.

'Not a chance,' Amira said to Hart down the phone. 'You know that just as well as I do.'

'Not even with your connections?'

249

'Not even with my connections.'

Hart glanced at Biljana and shrugged his shoulders. She shrugged back. She started to unhook her earpiece, but he shook his head. He still wanted her to listen.

'Any bright suggestions, then?'

'Only the old one. You cut me and Rider in.'

'Rider? The misery guts who was with us out in Tal Afar when we ducked out from under IS? Is he your new best mate?'

'He might be a misery guts but he's a first-rate journalist. And eight eyes are better than four. After Biljana gets to talk to her father, she lets Rider and me step in and grab him. That's the deal.'

'You grab him? You and Rider? And who else's army?'

'Djibouti allows citizen's arrests.'

'By foreigners?'

Amira made a sort of *humph* sound. 'We hold him until the Yanks or the Brit military can take him off our hands. We get Biljana's exclusive story for our Sunday issue. The newspaper gets full credit for running down a war criminal and bringing him to justice. The French get egg on their faces. Apart from him and them, everyone goes home happy.'

Hart glanced at Biljana. She looked as though she'd just been tasered. 'You can trust Amira,' he mouthed. 'She's straight. It's our only chance.'

'But I get to see him first? Alone?' she mouthed back. Her face was sheet white, like that of a cancer patient suffering from platelet collapse.

Hart cleared his throat. 'Biljana gets to see him first. Alone. Agreed?'

'We can do that. As long as she doesn't interfere when we grab him.'

Hart raised an eyebrow at Biljana. She gave a curt nod.

'It's a deal,' he said. 'Couldn't happen to a nicer guy.'

Amira somehow managed to talk and exhale her pent-up breath at the same time. 'I knew you'd see it our way. Rider's already on his way out to you. He's got all the kit. All we need is to find ourselves a safe house close to the French camp. Then we watch the comings and goings. You'll recognize him, won't you? The Captain?'

'Unless he's had a facelift, yes. For certain. His physiognomy is – how shall I put it? – memorable. We spent a fair amount of time together, remember? Time I won't forget in a hurry.'

'So it'll be like a reunion of old friends?'

Hart glanced across at Biljana. 'Amira. I somehow don't think Biljana shares your sense of humour.'

FIFTY-THREE

Rider rented a two-bedroom apartment overlooking the entrance to the French Foreign Legion HQ. The only problem was that the FFL did most of their training way out of town, in a camp situated off the main road. Which made observation of that aspect of the Legion's routine almost impossible.

So they concentrated most of their efforts at night. Rider, Hart and Amira took it in turn to cruise the clubs and bars of the old town on the off chance that they might encounter the Captain on one of his evenings off. It was during one of these forays that Hart found out that the main rump of the 13th Demi-Brigade had recently decamped from their headquarters at the Quartier Général Monclarin to somewhere in the UAE, at Abu Dhabi, leaving only a minor detachment back in Djibouti town to clear up.

'Chances are the Captain will have gone with them, I'm

afraid. We're on a hiding to nothing here. And Abu Dhabi is not like Djibouti. Women can't walk around freely. The military nightclubs are in closed environments, not available to tourists. If he's not here, we don't find him, it's as simple as that.'

But still they persisted.

On the twelfth day Hart made friends with a German major. They swapped drinks and stories. Hart said he was preparing a piece on what Foreign Legion soldiers did in their spare time. The major, already deep in his cups, was mightily amused. Hart asked him about his experience of the Legion. Who were the best soldiers? Who were the worst? The German was paternalistic. Old School. Claimed to stay back with his men at Christmas time because most of them had no homes to go to any more. Still. He had opinions. And wasn't shy of giving them.

'Let's start with the worst then. That will be the Chinese. All they want to do is cook. Next worst are the Americans. And you British, of course. Forever complaining about living conditions. You are soft. Given half a chance you will desert. No wonder you've lost all your recent wars.' He thought for a moment. 'The Koreans are the best soldiers amongst the Asians. The French themselves? They are crazy. Flaky. Like pastry mixed with too little sugar and butter. Best of all are the Brazilians. They even keep themselves and their billets clean.'

'You get many Serbs?'

'Serbs? No. Not any more. But we got a shedload after the Kosovo War. Tough as hell.'

'I was in Kosovo,' said Hart. 'I did my first major piece on that war. You got anyone with you from that time?'

The major laughed. 'Yes. We got two. But they won't talk to you. They won't talk to anyone, if you take my meaning.'

'Officers?'

'One is, one isn't.'

'You're holding something back, major. I can tell by your face.' Hart was into his sixth beer by this time. The German had probably sunk eight, each accompanied by a schnapps chaser.

'Too fucking right I'm holding something back.'

'Can't you tell me?'

'Why do you want to know? Are you a spy?' The German's face had changed from inebriated vacancy to a sort of drunken suspicion.

Hart slapped his press pass down on the table between them. 'I'm no fucking spy. Look. All you have to do is Google me. You'll see the sort of stuff I do. I'm just trying to chisel a story out of nothing. It's how I make my living. It's a sort of bum's rush. With me as the bum, and the newspaper doing the rushing.'

The German seemed, temporarily at least, placated. 'Don't go near the Serbs, then. That is my advice. I've heard them boasting of what they did in Bosnia and Kosovo. The Captain is not a good man.'

'The Captain?'

'Yes. One of them is a Captain. The other is a *brigadier* – what you would call a corporal.'

'Do you know the Captain's name?'

'Aha. That wouldn't do you any good. The Serbs give themselves new French names the moment they sign up. Part of the deal is that they have to learn French. Respect the hierarchy. Toe the line. Their past is used to turn them into good soldiers. We do the rest. The Captain started out as nothing. A trooper. He worked his way back up the hierarchy. There are people in this life whose destiny it is to command. The Captain is one of them. Within two years he had all the shitheads and the crazies – and trust me we've got a few – eating out of his hand. If you believe half of what he says he's done, you wouldn't want to stay in the same room with him for five seconds. He'd skull fuck your grandmother for ten euros. The man's a self-proclaimed war criminal. If he wasn't protected by the Legion, they'd have locked him up years ago. Prison is the best place for filth like that, as far as I am concerned. I disagree with the Legion on that one point. Fighter or no fighter, a man who abuses civilians puts himself beyond the pale.'

Hart couldn't disguise the look on his face.

The German shook his head in wonder. 'You know him, don't you? This man I am talking about? All this *Schweinerei* about building a story out of nothing. You've already got your story, haven't you? You've been feeding me beer and schnapps with one hand, and milking the hell out of me with the other. Is that how to treat your friends?'

Hart let his head drop onto his chest in feigned submission. It wasn't difficult with the amount of beer he, too, had on board. Added to which Hart had never found it easy to lie. It was why he took photographs. Journalists revealed their biases every time they wrote copy, but photographs always told the truth. One particular truth, at least. It was the nature of the beast.

'Yes. I lied. And no. It's not the way to treat your friends.'

The German shrugged. 'You know something? I'm too damned drunk to take offence. What's more I like you.' He cocked his head to one side as though listening for distant drums. 'So. Are you going to tell me? Are you going to be honest? Are you going to – what do they call it in England – play cricket?'

Hart told the German major everything. From the beginning. He could see the officer falling in and out of drunkenness again, like a man trying to clear his eyesight after having a drink dashed in his face.

'*Jesus Christus Gottes Sohn!*' the German said at last. 'You are crazier than a shithouse rat. Isn't that the expression you Brits use? You should not let a fifteen-year-old girl anywhere near that bastard. Even you…' The officer shook his head emphatically and made a poking motion with his forefinger. 'Even you should steer well clear.'

256

'But I've promised. Promised the girl that I would arrange for her to confront her father.'

The German slapped the table angrily with his hand. A few of the other drinkers turned round to look. But it was a military bar. People were used to sudden outbursts of sozzled logic. 'Look. You listen to me. The Captain is posting out to Abu Dhabi in six weeks' time. I know this because I prepared his orders myself. I am going too. The Legion are closing up shop here for good. Why not lie to her? Tell her he's already gone. Even she can't be so crazy as to imagine that she'll be able to go over to Abu Dhabi and run the man to ground out there. Abu's not a piss-hole like this is. It's one of the richest cities on earth. The FFL will be kept well out of town, this I can promise you. To protect the tourists, the carpet-buyers and the gold-purchasing mothers-in-law from being outraged by our riff-raff. He goes there, you've lost him.'

'And here? Will I be able to find him here?'

The German half-closed his eyes. 'You've not listened to a word I've said, have you?'

'I've listened to everything,' Hart assured him, with what passed for honesty in a drunken man. 'Every fucking word. I promise you that.'

'Well, you are truly making a very good try at forcing me to think otherwise.'

FIFTY-FOUR

Hart took Biljana on a visit out to Lake Assal, using as his pretext that they needed an outing. Lake Assal was situated seventy-five miles west of Djibouti City, and purported to be Djibouti's answer to the Dead Sea. At 509 feet below sea level, it was both the lowest point in Africa and the world's largest salt reserve. When seen from outside the protection of the tourist coach, it seemed to Hart both beautiful and horrifying at the same time. The water colour was of an incredibly vibrant blue, but the lake itself was surrounded by an ugly mass of volcanic detritus, sludge, pumice and God alone knows what else, and was subject to seemingly endless storms. Real scalp-lifters.

As the major had told Hart during one of their drunken, rambling conversations, '...thanks to the high salt content it would be the ideal place to get both proscribed and preserved simultaneously. It is why the Legion trains there. We like places that resemble hell on earth. It makes us feel at home.'

'So you've finally run him to ground? My father?' said Biljana, as she hunched forwards against the wind.

'How did you guess?'

'The binoculars.' She pointed to his chest. 'And the fact that Rider finds it utterly impossible to keep a secret.'

Hart shook his head in despair. Rider was known as Radio Free London amongst his journalistic peers. Add to that the fact that Rider and Biljana had become firm friends in the past week or two, with Rider acting as her mentor in all things journalistic, and the chances of Rider keeping his mouth shut must have fallen to about nil.

'We know where he is. Yes.' Hart held his hand up in front of his eyes in a vain attempt to protect them from the eternally shifting sand. 'Thanks to a German major I met who feels the same as I do about war criminals.'

'And can I see him?'

Hart took Biljana by the shoulders. He lowered his head in an attempt to seem less intimidating. 'Listen to me, princess. The major has described your father to me in detail. Both physically and in terms of his behaviour. In the fifteen years you have been present on this earth, the Captain has got worse, not better. I know you don't want to believe this about him, but I am not making it up. The only thing that has controlled him all this time has been the Legion. The fact that he belonged to a bona fide army unit that was happy to use his undoubted skills and not bother themselves overmuch as to where and how he acquired them. The Captain, in his turn, needed the protection of the Legion to escape from his persecutors – all the decent people who would love to bang him up for war crimes committed during the Bosnian and Kosovan wars. And whatever you say about the Legion, they do protect their own. So he is still free. And likely to remain so unless we actively intervene. But – and this is of crucial importance – he has been contained. Do you understand what I am telling you?'

'That he is like a piece of ammunition that has not yet gone off?'

'Something like that.' Hart couldn't help smiling at Biljana's ability to cut a direct path through all his guff. 'No. Come to think of it he is more like a booby-trapped barrel bomb that might still have a few nasty surprises left after a devastating initial detonation.'

'So why have you brought me out here then?'

Hart smothered a sigh. 'I have brought you out here so that you can take a look at him safely and from a distance. Under cover of all these tourists. But not to speak to him. Yet. I want you to see him. Weigh him up. And only then tell me whether you still want to continue with this madness. Or whether you will allow Amira, Rider and me to intervene with the Legion authorities and have him taken into custody. Because even the Legion can't argue when proof of a man's true identity and his past outrages is slapped onto the table in front of them.'

'So he is here at the lake? As we speak?' Biljana couldn't mask the excitement in her voice.

'Yes. The Legion are training out here. The major tells me that today they will be formally parading near the salt flats. It is customary for tourists to watch the parade. The Legion considers it good PR, apparently. So we'll be safe inside the crowd.'

'But you. The Captain, my father, knows you well, doesn't he? He will recognize you, surely?'

'I will wrap a keffiyeh about my head. With this wind it won't seems such a strange thing to do. Even my mother wouldn't recognize me dressed like that.'

'And where will the Captain be?'

'As the most senior officer present, he will be running the parade. So we'll have no problem in identifying him. Personally, I remember the bastard as if it was yesterday. He can't have changed that much.'

Biljana was silent for a while, digesting both this new information and the tone of Hart's comments about her father. 'And we will really be safe?'

'As safe as anywhere. He can't do anything in a public place.'

'All right then.'

Hart shook his head forlornly. The words of the German major kept echoing and re-echoing through his head. 'Daughter or no daughter, you should not let a fifteen-year-old girl anywhere near that monster.'

Hart felt as if he were walking on eggshells. On one side lay his present loyalty to Biljana. On the other side his memories of her mother and his historical duty towards her. But surely Lumnije had abrogated all her rights when she committed suicide on her child's fifteenth birthday? It had been a dreadful act. No wonder Biljana was not showing the sort of sympathy towards her mother that the grotesque details of her conception might presuppose.

Biljana and Hart passed the hours until the midday parade admiring the salt sculptures on sale near the edge of the lake. All the time the wind howled and the salt and the sand beat at their unprotected faces. Hart put on his keffiyeh, and wrapped a hijab, which he bought from a roadside stall, around Biljana's head to protect her eyes, ears and mouth from the saline dust.

'This place is hell on earth,' said Biljana.

'That's what my German major told me. But try down on the Red Sea shore,' said Hart. 'It will be even worse down there. Part of the tourist deal I've bought today is that we have lunch down on the beach near the L'Île du Diable after the parade. You'll be lucky if your plate doesn't take off and skitter along the sand pursued by seagulls. With you windmilling along behind it with your tongue flapping out.'

Hart's levity fell on stony ground.

At dead on twelve o'clock the Legionnaires assembled for the parade. About a hundred stricken tourists, from three separate coaches, gathered to watch them. The Legionnaires were wearing desert-sand camouflage and white kepis on their heads, with the officers wearing black kepis with red tops. Even the fifty battle-hardened types present on parade appeared to wince as the salt and sand granules picked holes through their specially designed clothing.

'Jesus,' said Hart. 'I don't believe it.'

'You've seen him?'

'Yes. I was expecting it, but it still comes as a shock after all these years. He's the one wearing the three gold bars. With the black cap and the red top with all the gold braid in front. It's absurd. He doesn't look a bloody day older than he did back in Kosovo.'

'That's my father? The one standing alone?' There was an edge of yearning in her voice.

'Strictly speaking, yes. But anyone less like a father than the Captain would be hard to find. Just please, please, don't go building any illusions about him. He'll shatter them as soon as look at you.'

'Do you think he has any other children?'

Hart could feel himself colouring beneath his keffiyeh. Biljana's comment had caught him catastrophically off guard. It had never occurred to him to address this other aspect of the Captain's life. 'I believe he is – or at least was – married. And with a child. A son, I understand. Or so your mother told me.'

'So I have a half-brother?' Biljana took hold of Hart's sleeve. 'Why have you never spoken of this before?'

'Hell, Biljana. Because I never thought about it. And what did you expect to do if I had told you? Wander up to his wife – whose whereabouts we don't know and who may not have survived the war – and trill, "Hey, I am your husband's rape child. I just thought I'd pop by and pay you both a visit"?'

Biljana fell silent. She stood beside Hart and stared at her father, fifty metres away. The Captain, who must have been about the same age as Hart, looked hard and fit, with no excess fat. He had the sort of physique you get from hard running – not pumping iron in a gym and popping steroids.

'Can I have the binoculars, please?'

Hart grunted and handed Biljana the binoculars.

She put them to her eyes and stared at her father. She spent a long time perusing him. 'He has a scar on his face, same as you. He looks like Charles Bronson in *Once Upon A Time in the West*.'

Hart nearly choked on the can of Coca-Cola he had been sipping from to cleanse his throat. 'Jesus Christ, Biljana. This isn't one of your movies. This is real life. And this man is no hero like Bronson. He's the Henry Fonda figure in the movie. Remember? The one who kills an innocent young boy seconds after he's massacred the child's entire family. And I don't remember him having any scar. That must have come after my time.'

'He's missing a finger on his left hand too. Did you notice that?'

'It couldn't have happened to a nicer person. I wish it was me that shot it off.'

Biljana put down the binoculars and stared at Hart. 'Are you sure he's done all those things you told me about?'

Hart's could sense the girl's pain. The urgency of her need for good news after a lifetime of disappointments. He wished that he could lie. Tell her that everything was all right. That it had all been some bizarre misunderstanding. That her father was a fine man. A good man. That he had been waiting all this time for her to find him so that he could enfold her in his arms and squeeze her so tight that all her ills would be cured.

'More than what I've told you, sweetheart,' he said. 'He's done more. I've held back on most of what your mother told me that he boasted to her about doing. And what he told me himself while I held him prisoner. What's the point in gilding the lily? The man is a monster and there's an end to it. He's not worth the effort of debating.'

Hart knew that he was playing the whole thing wrong. That he risked alienating Biljana with his prescriptiveness. But he couldn't help himself. The sight of the Captain after all those years – the sight of the man who had tried to kill both him and Lumnije – was proving massively unsettling. Hart could feel the kernel of fear he had harboured back then reigniting in his belly. He suspected – no, he was certain – that the Captain would kill him without hesitation if he became aware of his presence. And the bastard would probably laugh while he was doing it.

'Have you seen enough? Our bus is about to leave.'

'Yes. I've seen enough.'

Hart tried to ignore the condemnation in Biljana's voice. 'Do you still want to meet that man one-to-one?'

'Yes.'

'Oh God, Biljana. Can't you just leave well enough alone?'

'Would you?' Biljana was crying now. 'Would you leave well enough alone? If you suddenly found, after fifteen years, that you had a father? Would you not at least want to meet him? To hear him speak? To give him the chance to defend himself?'

'What can I say? What can I tell you? You've spent the last fifteen years longing for a daddy. And suddenly one pops out of the woodwork. Trouble is, though, that he isn't quite the knight in shining armour you might once have craved. Those sorts of illusions are hard won. And even harder to discard. So whichever answer I pick you won't believe me. You've already made up your mind, and you simply want me to double-stamp it.'

Biljana raised her chin pugnaciously. 'To triple-stamp it. Yes.'

Hart threw the tail of his keffiyeh around his head and strode back to the bus. For a moment there, he had found himself thinking that he didn't much give a damn whether Biljana saw her father or not. What was it to him? The girl wasn't his daughter.

Then he remembered their time together in Paris, and he despaired.

FIFTY-FIVE

In his dream the Captain is back at Srebrenica/Potočari again. During the Bosnian War, 12–13 July 1995. With the Scorpions. The date is categorical. Deeply imprinted in his unconscious mind. The heat is overwhelming. Just as it was back then. The sort of heat that drives you to do something. Anything. Just to keep moving.

This kind of recurring dream is plaguing him more and more recently. Disturbing his sleep. The dream always takes the same linear form, mimicking what really happened. Retelling the historical truth.

First the gang rape of the young Bosniak girl alongside the three other Scorpions, none of whom he knows or will ever meet again. The holding up and spreading of her legs. The gagging of the girl with a rag. One man helping the other. Comrades.

While he is waiting his turn for the rape, the Captain keeps a wary eye on the Dutch UNPROFOR troops to see how they will react. But the Dutchbat forces don't react at all. They leave the White House, and everyone in it, strictly alone. It's as if they are mole-blind. Small, sniffling creatures with blunted teeth. Irrelevant.

Then comes the killing of the Bosniak kid and the cutting off of his nose, ears and lips by the bearded Scorpion. Why does the guy do it? The Captain cannot say. But it makes a crazy sort of sense.

The Captain is only a second lieutenant at this stage of his military career. Twenty years old. But the sudden realization that a man can do anything he wants if only he does it forcefully enough is a liberation. Like the loss of one's virginity. You realize that no one really cares what you do any more. That no one minds so long as you don't parade it beneath their noses. There is a craziness in the air. No one will protect these people. No one will fight back on their behalf. It is the gifting of total power. Something the wet-behind-the-ears kid that is the Captain has never experienced before.

The dream then follows its usual trajectory. An honest trajectory, which reflects what really happened during those two empowering days.

All through the night and into the next day the Captain rapes and kills with impunity. Each detail is clearly etched into his unconscious. Each movement is pre-programmed – endlessly repeated. As always the Dutch soldiers stand by and watch, like the captive audience at a cinema. The Captain and his people kill the Bosniaks on an industrial scale. They illuminate the killing fields with their arc lights. Cart the bodies away in their trucks and their bulldozers. Bury them in mass graves like cattle suffering from mad cow disease. Rape any available women when they fancy a break from the killing and have got their sexual energy back. Sometimes in front of their fathers and mothers. In front of their children. A rape break, thinks the Captain, crippled with laughter. Not a coffee break. A rape break.

Some of the victims they bury alive just to see what will happen. Nothing counts but what is occurring in that precise moment. The Dutch soldiers have their Walkmans on. These guys are listening to music while the raping and the killing and the mutilation go on. How does one account for that?

The Captain is half crazy by this time. Out of control. He and his unit have gone too far to ever stop now. It is here, at this point in his dream, that the Captain remembers the suicide stories. Of the people in the refugee camp killing themselves rather than waiting for the Scorpions to come and claim them. Hanging themselves from the chainlink fence surrounding the White House. Like pheasants displayed outside a butcher's shop.

Yes, thinks the Captain to himself. This is total power. This is total war. Action. Pure and simple. No holding back. You act as you see fit. When and how you see fit. You are God. Because there is no God. How can there be? How can any God let this happen? Or is it that He doesn't care? The Captain remembers the Serbian Orthodox priest blessing his unit before they started in on the killing. How can anyone take God seriously after that? When even the priests reckon God must be on your side while you murder people?

The Captain wakes, just as he always does, with his face slick with sweat and his T-shirt dripping. Some of the officers in the dormitory are complaining about him crying out and disturbing their sleep. Trying to get him moved to a single room. This happens regularly now. But the Captain doesn't care. Most of his contemporaries in the Legion have never seen combat – nor are they likely to. They have never killed in the heat of battle. They don't know what real rage is like. Or the damage done in its aftermath. And they are scared of him.

Look at the Kraut major sitting over there on his bed. The man is a wet flannel. Thinks his men actually care that he stays back with them over Christmas rather than going home to visit his family in Germany. It makes the Captain sick to his stomach. Sick to his soul. That's not leadership. That's moral cowardice.

He calls out to the corporal to fetch his shaving water. The corporal fought alongside him all the way through Kosovo. They signed up together with the Legion when things finally became too hot to handle back home. The stupid bastard even made it as far as lieutenant once, but the Legion cashiered him when he tried to go AWOL and sneak back to Serbia to see his family. Broke him back to *brigadier*.

Bloody fool. The man was a cipher during the war, and he is a cipher now. Cipherdom suits the bastard. But it is good to talk Serb nonetheless. To reminisce about the old country from time to time. The corporal is useful for that much, at least, if he is good for nothing else.

The German major sidles over in that way he has and tells him about this new chess prodigy they've discovered in town. A young girl. Sixteen maybe. At the chess club. A mind like a computer they say. The Captain, in the major's opinion, won't stand a chance against her.

'What do you mean "won't stand a chance"? I am top marker. I am the best player in the whole of Djibouti.'

'Not any more you aren't.'

'This girl. She is Arab?' The Captain puts a sneer in his voice, as if an Arab would find it impossible to compete on a similar level to himself.

'I don't know. I only hear what I hear.'

The Captain brushes away the corporal with his shaving water. 'I play her. Will she play me?'

'I'm sure she will,' says the German major. 'I can arrange it if you like. At the club. Do you want an audience?'

The Captain shakes his head. 'No. No one else there.'

'In case you lose?' crows the major.

'I will not lose. No girl will ever beat me. It's an impossibility.'

The major smiles. 'So? I'll arrange it then? For this Sunday? Shall we say ten o'clock in the morning?'

271

FIFTY-SIX

'The dossier has come through on the Captain,' said Amira. 'Why don't we give it to your tame major now and have done with it?'

She was facing Hart across the table at their rented apartment. She had caught the sun during the past few days because she refused to wear any head covering when she didn't need to. Djibouti, though a Muslim country, valued its female foreigners and their currency far too much to be prescriptive on that subject.

'Because we said we wouldn't,' said Hart. 'Do you generally go around telling people one thing and doing another, Amira?'

'I'm a journalist. So yes. I do.' Amira manufactured a grin. 'I suppose you don't, Mister Whiter Than White?'

Hart made a *pah* sound. He got up and walked over to the window.

'Are you sure this German major of yours is kosher?' she continued. 'I mean, can we trust him not to purposely lose the Captain's dossier and then wave the bastard off to Abu Dhabi where we'll have hell's own chance of ever running him to ground again?'

'We can trust him. Yes. I'd stake my life on it.'

'Why?'

'Because he's got a personal interest in the thing. He hates the Captain. The pair have what amounts to a vendetta going on between them. The Captain undermines the major at every opportunity. Chisels away at his authority. I suspect it's why the major drinks. He knows the Captain wants into his shoes. He'll be only too pleased to see the man go down. Believe me.'

'So what do we do? Let Biljana talk to her father, and then turn him straight in?'

'No,' said Hart. 'We let her call it, as we promised. She'll need some time to think. To decide how she feels.'

'What if she says no? What if she falls in love with Daddykins and wants to continue the relationship? I may be a dyed-in-the-wool feminist, but I don't have any illusions about women. I see us realistically. And one of our major flaws is that we really believe that we can change people. Look at me, John. I thought that being loved by me would transform you from the gormless idiot that you were into Prince Charming. How wrong can a girl be.'

Rider guffawed.

Hart rolled his eyes. He studied the street with even more attention than before.

'Where is she at the moment?' said Amira.

'In the Souk. She's promised to be at the chess club by ten.'

'What do you want us to do in the interim?'

Hart shrugged his shoulders. He was still smarting from Amira's barbed comments. 'How do I know? Hang around outside maybe. Identify the Captain's car. Be available. One thing I know. Something like this is going to play itself out in a completely different way than we anticipate. The Captain is arriving at the club assuming he is going to play chess. When Biljana tells him who she really is, he is going to imagine he's walked into a trap. God knows how he'll react. Our only advantage is that Biljana is fifteen years old, and hardly threatening. When he gets over his initial bout of the wobblies, he'll probably calm down and listen to what she has to say. That's if he hasn't already frightened her the hell away.'

'Where will you be while all this happens?'

'In the men's lavatory, listening. The major has described the place in detail to me. The layout is straightforward. The toilet is situated directly off the main clubroom. I can leave the door cracked.'

'Will Biljana know that you are there?'

'No.'

Silence.

Hart hesitated for a moment, then broke it. 'Do you see a problem with that, either of you?'

'No. I think you're doing the right thing in the circumstances,' said Amira. 'However dangerous it is. Will you be armed?'

'With what? A howitzer?'

'How about a baseball bat?' said Rider. 'You could sally out to the rescue waving it around your head like Joe DiMaggio.'

'Thanks, Rider,' said Hart. 'Thanks for your input.'

'You're welcome.'

Hart gave a final glance at his two companions. 'Right. I'm about to get moving. I need to be in place well before Biljana gets there.'

'Remember to take a book,' said Rider. 'You might get caught short. And waiting can be painful when there's no place else to sit but on the bog.'

'So can left hooks to the kisser,' said Hart. 'And believe me, right now I'm sorely tempted to give you one.'

FIFTY-SEVEN

The Captain arrived at the chess club an hour early. To practise his openings, he told himself. In fact he was suspicious of the German major's unlikely interest in his chess game. He and the major were mortal enemies. They despised each other. The major had understood long ago that the Captain envied him his position in the hierarchy, and would do anything he could to undermine him in the eyes of the men. So what was going on?

By the time he'd unlocked the front door and finished his rounds of the premises, the Captain had managed to convince himself that all was above board. All the major wanted was to see him publicly humiliated by a girl. And if it didn't happen in public, the major was sure to noise the Captain's defeat around at the first available opportunity.

The place itself was empty as the grave. And public opening wasn't until three o'clock that afternoon. The

Captain definitely had the place to himself. So he sat down and went through the motions. If this girl was as good as they said she was, he would need to protect his king from her from the word go. He began with the Ruy Lopez opening, therefore, and played against himself for five minutes just to see what would come of it. Then he tried the Giuoco Piano with the Evans Gambit variant. The kid was sixteen. How could she possibly know about this?

Later he tried the Sicilian Defence. Followed by the Caro-Kann. The Captain enjoyed the challenge of chess. It was one of the few things that allowed his mind to relax and not dwell on the past. That and the brain-dead physical training he was required to do for the FFL. Both methods worked in their separate ways.

He finished off with the King's Indian and the English opening, which would have the virtue of surprising the hell out of her if it did nothing else. He sincerely hoped that she would not feel the need to come with a chaperone of some sort. He disliked distractions when he played. The thought of five hours clear, and playing against a worthy opponent, stimulated him beyond measure. The general standard of game he encountered at the club was abysmal. Even the German major – when he deigned to play – was prone to desperate flaws thirty or so minutes in. It was like the Germans during the Second World War. Fantastic opening. Useless end game.

The Captain made himself a cup of coffee at the machine behind the bar. Perhaps the girl would be pretty, he told himself. That would make a change. Sixteen was a tricky age. Some girls still retained the gawkiness of childhood. He was not interested in these. But others already held the promise of what would come later. This was a different matter entirely. He was tired of the Djibouti brothels and the jaded women he found there. When he thought back to the delights he had experienced during the Bosnian and Kosovo wars, it made him want to weep. How had he come to this? Through cowardice? The fear of being banged up for war crimes he and every other red-blooded Serb had committed simply because they could? Just because he had been a Captain at the time, and nominally in command? The whole damned thing was bitterly unfair.

By the time the clock hand moved round to ten o'clock, the Captain had managed to make himself very angry indeed. The catalyst for this state of affairs was a mixture of outraged virtue and nostalgia for an impossible-to-replicate past. Things didn't happen in threes. He knew that he had benefited from a crazy concatenation of events in two religious and ethnically centred wars. Such a thing would not happen again in his lifetime. And he was getting older. His past now felt like an elusive utopia that was rapidly coming to seem as if it had happened to somebody else.

And what was he doing now? Playing chess against teenagers.

It made the Captain want to vomit.

FIFTY-EIGHT

Hart saw the Captain's car pull up. The man was ridiculously early. Hart had secured a duplicate key to the chess club from the German major, but this was immediately rendered useless by the Captain's arrival. The Captain, as club secretary, also had a key, and there was only the one main entrance. His plan for hiding out inside the club was effectively scuppered.

Hart called Amira on his mobile phone.

'The bastard's arrived early. And I mean really early. I should have known he would. Lumnije used to call him "the superman". He would think everything through twice as fast as everybody else and outflank them. It was sheer luck that we got the drop on him back then. He couldn't have foreseen that my telephoto lens would deflect his bullet.'

'John, this is irrelevant. Where are you now?'

'In a coffee shop on the opposite side of the road to the chess club, fuming with anger. I can see the front door clearly. The Captain's car is parked directly outside.'

'What sort of a car is it?'

'A four-wheel-drive Jeep Renegade. The number plate is half in Arabic, half Western numbers. It looked like 394D36. But I only saw it for a second so I may have got it wrong. The man drives like a psychopath. He even parks aggressively. As if he expects someone to sally out and dispute the space with him. Do you think we ought to abort? I can catch Biljana before she goes inside. I don't feel comfortable leaving her in there with that maniac without being able to see and hear exactly what is going on.'

'No. We don't abort. The girl would never forgive you. You've watched her building up to this ever since her mother's death. What are you going to do? Ask the Captain for a bloody rain check?'

Hart gurned at his reflection in the café window. 'You've got a point.'

'Of course I have. Listen. I'm going to send Rider out to put a tracker on the Captain's car. Just in case. Is the car locked?'

'How the hell do I know if the car is locked?'

'Well, the emergency lights would have flashed when the Captain left it, John. That's what usually happens in these cases.'

Hart smothered a groan. 'I'm sorry. I didn't mean to be grumpy.' He didn't often apologize to Amira. He could sense her unbending over the telephone. 'I don't know, is the answer. I was too busy monitoring war criminals.'

'That's okay. I know you wanted to be inside the building, watching things from close by. But I'm sure Biljana can take care of herself. It's probably safer this way. What if the Captain needed to piss and caught you hiding in there? At least this way you'll be outside in case anything untoward happens. And with the tracker we'll have the advantage of being able to follow him wherever he goes. If Biljana gives us the nod, we can take him out easily. Listen to me, though. I'm still tempted to bring the Americans in on this. You know what the French are like when it comes to foreigners interfering in their internal affairs. I call it "ex-colonial power syndrome". Djibouti was theirs once upon a time. They probably still think they own it.'

'Believe me, Amira. The German major will be quite enough without the Americans. I've primed the man. He knows what the Captain has done. And he wants the man's blood. The Legion, too, doesn't want any bad publicity. If they are the ones to take him out, they can publicly boast that they protect their own. If the Yanks come in on it, you'll just be throwing oil onto the fire. The French and the Yanks have a curious relationship. It's not what you would call close.'

'Okay. So where are we now in terms of the girl?'

'She knows to be here at ten. Alone. She also knows that I'll be around somewhere. But I have promised her that I am going to keep my snout out of it. The thought of sitting over here without being able to see what is happening makes me sick to my stomach. But I don't see what else I can do. The bastard is her father. Not mine.'

There was silence on the line.

Hart bulldozed on, on the verge of panic. 'Are you thinking what I'm thinking? That maybe we're playing this whole thing completely wrong? That we ought to intercede before Biljana arrives and have done with it. Scoop the Captain up. She can go and visit her father in the prison stockade. Under vastly more controllable conditions. Okay. Maybe she'll hate us. But the Captain will be neutralized.'

'John, your needle's stuck. Weren't you the one who told me we needed to listen to her and do exactly what she wants? That we owed her that much consideration on account of her mother. Are you seriously intending to change horses midstream?'

'No. No. Of course not. I'm simply getting the collywobbles. The man does something to me. You should have heard some of the stories he told me. It's hard to believe that any human being could do such things to another human being. It puts what IS are doing in Iraq into grim perspective. The Captain was there first. IS learned their trade, and what they can get away with, from people like him.'

'Men have always done such things to each other.'

'I know. I know. So why are we so different then, you and me? Why don't we go around raping and killing and mutilating? Why do we have a moral conscience? Answer me that.'

'Because we've had the opportunity to be different, John. We've had it easy. We've inherited the fucking peace dividend. Think what the Russians and the Germans did to each other during the Second World War on the Eastern Front. Think what happened in the concentration camps. We were spared all that because of the actions of our parents and grandparents.'

'Okay. You can lay off with the lecture. I get the point. I'm just trying to make myself feel better.' He raised his head. 'Look. I can see Biljana now. She is walking down the street towards the chess club, carrying her shopping from the bazaar. The kid looks like she's on a Sunday outing to the big city. You wouldn't think she's just about to meet the man who raped and abused her mother.'

'She's her own person, John. You can't live other people's lives for them. However tempted you may be to do so. You're not a magician. You're an ordinary man.'

'Thank you, Amira. Thank you for reminding me.' Hart's tone was heavily ironical. 'I was, of course – but only for a second there – in sore danger of forgetting that fact. I'm glad I can count on you to always keep me in line.'

FIFTY-NINE

This is no Arab, thought the Captain to himself. The girl isn't even partway brown. She is as white as a lily. Maybe she is some administrator's daughter? Or a half-breed with more than a little French blood in her veins? The Captain watched her walking towards him through the clubhouse. She was carrying two bags. Maybe she had been to the Souk? It was Sunday after all. The Souk was always packed out on a Sunday.

He got up and moved towards her. Strange. The girl looked young for sixteen. And she had Slavic cheekbones. Almond-shaped eyes. A strong nose. If he had to guess, now that he could inspect her more closely, he would have marked her down as Bulgarian. Ukrainian maybe. Even Serb. He'd forgotten now what the major had said she was. Maybe he hadn't asked. Maybe he hadn't been interested enough. But he was sure as hell interested now.

'Hi,' he said, in French. 'Are you the chess genius?'

'I'm your daughter,' Biljana said, in Serbian. 'The rape child of Lumnije Dardan.'

The Captain froze, his eyes wide, his mouth a little open, as if someone had slapped him unexpectedly on the back to cure him of the hiccups.

Then he ran past Biljana and threw open the street door.

Hart, who had been half expecting this reaction, watched from his sheltered position in the coffee bar opposite.

The Captain looked both ways down the street. Then at the building opposite.

Hart buried himself behind his newspaper.

The Captain slammed the door and went back inside the clubhouse.

He strode past Biljana and on into the lavatory area. She could hear him kicking open the cubicle doors one by one. Then he hurried upstairs. She heard his feet drumming on the floor above her head. Part of her wanted to run. She could still do it. Easily. She would be out of the front door before he knew it. But she stood her ground. What was Hart always saying? *In for a penny, in for a pound.*

The Captain came downstairs again. He stopped a few yards away from where she was standing and looked her up and down. 'What age?' he said.

'What?'

'What age are you?'

'Fifteen.'

'Ah.' He walked back to the front door and locked it, replacing the key in his pocket.

Biljana clutched her bags to her chest as though they might protect her from his anger. She had never encountered anyone who exuded anger the way the Captain did. It petrified her. Made her incapable of thinking.

'Sit,' he said, pointing to a chair.

Biljana sat, still clutching her bags.

'Fifteen-year-old girls don't travel alone to Djibouti. Who is with you? Where are they now?'

'My mother is with me,' said Biljana, although she did not know where the idea to say this had sprung from. What quiet despair had produced it. 'She is at the hotel.'

'What hotel?'

Biljana thought quickly. 'The Sheraton.'

'Is the whore rich all of a sudden? Where does she get the money from to come out here? To stay at the Sheraton? How did she find me? What are you both doing here?' The Captain's eyes were wild. Like those of a feral animal caught in a trap. 'How did you get the major to talk for you? That miserable worm? To arrange this? Does he know who you are? Where does he figure in this? Is it a trap?'

The Captain was standing a few yards from her, his upper body hunched towards her, his arms hanging down like a gorilla's arms in front of him, the fingers flexing and unflexing. Spittle flecked the Captain's lips as though he were suffering from rabies.

Biljana fell silent. She was incapable of speech. She stared at the Captain as if he was an alien being which had suddenly transmogrified from its human form directly in front of her.

'You're my daughter, you say?'

She nodded. Her head felt stiff on her neck. Her right eye had begun to twitch as it sometimes did after she had been crying. She wondered where Hart was. What he was doing. Why he was not intervening. She had never before in her life felt so frightened as she was of the Captain. He was a primal force unleashed.

The Captain walked up to her and took her face in his hands. Biljana wanted to cry out, but the sound froze in her throat.

The Captain tilted her face first to the left and then to the right as you would do that of a puppy you were thinking of purchasing. 'Yes. Could be.'

Biljana feared for a moment that he was about to force open her mouth and inspect her teeth.

'Why is your mother not here with you?'

Biljana swallowed. She wished the Captain would let her alone. His hands were hard and calloused. The hands of a man who ignored the niceties of life. 'She did not want to come to Djibouti, but I persuaded her. She doesn't want to see you again. Ever. She didn't want me to see you. She thinks no good will come of it.'

The Captain gave a single bark of laughter. He was master of the situation now. He understood what he was dealing

287

with. 'But you wanted to see your daddy? See what he looked like? Is that it?'

Biljana nodded. She began to cry.

The Captain freed her face and stepped backwards. 'Now tell me how you found me. Everything. Hold nothing back, or I shall know.'

Biljana swallowed her tears. She could feel the imprint of the Captain's fingers on her cheeks as though he was still gripping hold of her. 'Maria told us. The woman who serves the monks at Visoki Dečani. We discovered she was your relative. Your great-aunt. That she keeps you informed about your family. She told us you were out here. That you were in the Legion. I persuaded Majka to bring me out. We looked for you.'

'And the major? Where does he come into all this?'

'Nowhere. Not really. My mother spoke to him. Persuaded him of who I was. She thought an officer in the Legion would know of any Serbs in its ranks. And he did.'

'Did she tell him everything? About how you were conceived, for instance?'

Biljana had the sudden, inescapable conviction that she was arguing for her life. That if she told him anything resembling the real truth, the Captain would kill her. Instantly. With no discernible emotion. And to hell with the fact that she was his daughter. 'No. No, of course not. She just said we wanted to find you. That you might want to see me. It has been many years. My mother feels differently about things now. I feel differently. We mean you no harm. I just wanted to meet you.

This was the only way.' Biljana prayed that the Captain would not see through her lame fabrications.

The Captain stared at her. Biljana felt as if his eyes were eating her up. She realized, with a sudden, shocking insight, that she and this man were of one blood. She had always expected to recognize him in some way. Feel some familiarity with him. Some conjunction. But this? This blood curse? With a man who tortured, raped and murdered at will?

'Are you Christian?'

'Am I what?'

'You are my daughter. So are you Christian?'

'No. Of course not. I am Muslim. Like my mother.'

'That will be changed.'

Biljana felt the hand of fate descend upon her. The Captain's gaze was unwavering. Unholy. His eyes were ice cold.

'What does it matter what I am?' she yelled. 'Why should it matter to you? You raped my mother. How can you expect me to take the religion of a man capable of doing something like that?'

The Captain slapped her. The movement was so sudden, and the pain so intense, that Biljana had no time to respond. She fell sideways off the chair onto the floor.

The Captain kicked her in the side.

Biljana rolled herself into a ball and covered her head with her hands. She was no longer thinking. Only reacting. She felt something break inside her heart.

'Please,' she said.

The Captain grabbed her by the throat and began to squeeze.

Biljana's eyes filled with tears. She felt a long way away from herself. She could hear her mother calling, in exactly the tone of voice she would use when ordering Biljana inside the house as a child. From where had she summoned her mother like this? And why had her mother chosen just this moment to come to her, after depriving her daughter of her presence so categorically via the cowardice of suicide? And why had she said what she had said to the Captain? There was no sense to any of it.

A profound sadness suffused her. The sort of sadness a child might feel when parted from someone to whom she was deeply attached.

She closed her eyes and drifted into unconsciousness.

The Captain stepped away from Biljana's body. He walked across to the bar and ran some water into the basin. He washed his hands roughly, and then his face. He caught sight of himself in the bar mirror and looked away.

If Lumnije Dardan was here in Djibouti, he was doomed. The woman he remembered would not hesitate to hand him over to the authorities. And there was no way that same woman would have allowed her daughter to come and see him alone. No. Biljana must have been lying when she said that. She must have run off on her own accord. Slipped the tether.

But by gifting herself to him in that way, Biljana had inadvertently gifted him a priceless handle over her mother. Maybe the whore would not be so keen to turn him in when she knew he had her daughter in his hands?

He walked over to where Biljana was lying and prodded her with his foot. She was still out cold. Well. All the better.

He dragged her as far as the front door. Then he went back into the clubhouse, collected her shopping bags and dumped them into one of the trash bins in the utility room. He walked back to the front door of the chess club and unlocked it. He stepped out into the street. The heat hit him like a solid force. He looked to his left and to his right and stepped across the pavement to his car. He opened the front door and left it hanging.

He lit a cigarette. The chess club was situated in a quiet cul-de-sac. Apart from the café opposite, there was nothing here to attract passing trade. He waited five minutes until there was no one within fifty yards of him, then he flicked away the cigarette and hurried back inside the clubhouse. He swept Biljana into his arms and lumbered out to the car with her. He dropped her into the passenger well at the rear of the car and slammed the door. Then he got into the front.

He engaged Drive and forced his way out into the traffic without caring about other cars. A horn honked behind him. Someone doing a U-turn. He opened his window and raised his fist. The horn fell silent.

This was it, he thought to himself. The Great Change. He had been expecting it for years and it had finally arrived. Well. He would visit Lumnije Dardan at the Sheraton Hotel and tell her exactly what he would do to her daughter if she grassed him up to the War Crimes Commission. Then he would call the corporal at Camp Lemonnier and tell him the moment had come to gather together certain items they would be needing over the next few days. Civilian clothes. False passports. Guns. Emergency cash. Stuff like that. Stuff he had been hoarding against just such an eventuality.

The Ethiopian border was two hours away by road. About a hundred kilometres, if you travelled via Ali Sabieh and the RN5 to Dewele. It was Sunday morning. The corporal could follow him out in his own car. They could meet at the border post. He and the corporal would be long gone before the Legion, or the police, were any the wiser.

They would buy their Ethiopian visas at the border. Border guards, in his experience, were always bribeable. And the Ethiopians notoriously so.

Once he and the girl were safely out of the country, he would be home free.

SIXTY

Watching the Captain smoke his cigarette in such a relaxed way had lulled Hart into a false sense of security. He had assumed, wrongly as it turned out, that the Captain had been suffering from nerves on meeting his daughter, and had needed to go outside and smoke a cigarette to calm them. And then the impossible had happened, and he had seen the Captain running towards his car with Biljana in his arms.

Something closed down in Hart when he saw the Captain carrying Biljana. It was as if a portcullis had rolled down over his heart. He began to hyperventilate like a man caught out by a freak wave.

He threw down his newspaper and ran outside, but the Captain's car was already fifty yards down the street and accelerating all the time.

Hart pulled out his mobile phone and rang Amira.

Before she could answer, he said, 'The Captain's taken her. She's gone.'

'What do you mean?'

'I mean she's gone. The Captain carried her out to his car and dumped her in the back. He was off before I could get to him.'

'Was she alive?'

'I don't know. But even the Captain wouldn't stoop to murdering his own flesh and blood. No man could do that? Surely?' It was clear that Hart didn't believe his own protestations. 'She must have been unconscious. Maybe he got angry and hit her? That must have been it.' He stood for a moment, staring up the road. 'What have I done? What the fuck have I done?'

Amira was shouting down the phone. 'Wait for us. Don't move from there. Don't, above all, do anything stupid. We can rectify this. We can get her back.'

Hart tried to damp down his rising panic. 'Listen. Did Rider manage to plant the tracker in the Captain's car?'

'Yes. He'd left the thing open. Rider crawled along the pavement as if he was looking for a dropped mobile phone. He cracked the rear door and sneaked in from the side. No wonder you didn't see him.' Amira bit back the rest of what she had been about to say. It had become almost automatic with her to needle Hart. To remind him of his shortcomings. There were times when she wondered if it wasn't some form of unconscious revenge for the fact that he had been the one to break off their relationship after she had aborted their child, not her. Either way, this wasn't the moment to plunge the dagger in any further.

'So wait there. Do you understand? We're coming. We'll be with you in five minutes.'

Hart stepped inside the clubhouse. He expected to see upset chairs – some evidence of a scuffle – but there was nothing. It was as if Biljana had never existed.

He sat down at a table and put his head in his hands. What had got into him? How had he ever allowed a vulnerable fifteen-year-old free rein to put herself into danger? What insane stupidity had caused him to call everything so wrong?

He looked around vacantly, as if the walls themselves might choose that moment to open up and explain what had occurred within their purview.

But they were silent.

SIXTY-ONE

The Captain pulled up outside the Sheraton Hotel. He checked in the back of the car but the girl was still out cold. There were moments when he didn't know his own strength. She'd angered him so much about the Muslim thing that, for a second there, he'd come perilously close to killing her. Which would have been seriously counterproductive. A wise man doesn't shit his pot full and then insist on turning the thing over to see the full extent of the mess he has created.

The Captain felt inside Biljana's jacket and came up with a purse and her passport. Well. That would make things easier. He looked inside the passport. Biljana Dardan. And her date of birth. Yes. It all made perfect sense. She was his all right. No doubt about it. He had sealed her mother in her room at the rape house for three solid weeks. Only he had had access to her. No one else. Those had been the good times.

He locked the car and stepped inside the hotel. The

hall porter pointed to his car and hunched his shoulders interrogatively. The Captain passed him a five-dollar bill. 'I'll be five minutes. A buck a minute suit you?'

The man saluted and stepped backwards.

The Captain walked to the hall desk and confronted the clerk. 'I found this passport in the street outside the hotel. Is this young lady registered here? If she isn't, I will take the passport along to the police.'

The desk clerk looked at the passport. Then he checked his computer. 'No. She is not registered here.'

'Maybe her mother or father registered under another name? Looks like the owner of this is only fifteen.'

The desk clerk shook his head. 'We would have checked this passport and registered the young woman under her own name. That's the law. Every passport must be checked. Each individual consolidated against their own identity papers. She would be on our records. No one of this name is staying at our hotel.'

'Consolidated?' The Captain rolled his eyes. 'Consolidated against their own identity papers?'

'Consolidated. Yes, sir.'

'Okay. Right. I'll take this along to the police station then. Thank you.'

'You're very welcome, sir. She's a lucky girl that you found her passport. There are people passing by outside who would have stolen it as soon as look at you, and then sold it onto the black market.'

The Captain manufactured a dramatic double-take. 'A Macedonian passport? Who in his right mind would want one of those? They're not even in Europe yet.'

'You'd be surprised, sir. Believe me. There is more evil on this earth than we can reasonably give credit for.'

'Asshole,' muttered the Captain under his breath as he exited the hotel. 'Reasonably give credit for? Bumptious little asshole.' He manufactured a fond picture in his inner eye of him carving off the desk clerk's head, just like the Daesh did with their prisoners in Iraq. There were times when he bitterly regretted the good old days. Then, you just acted as you saw fit. You possessed total power. Now, in the so-called civilized world, the Captain felt like a furious misfit. A square peg in a round hole. Still. He couldn't very well join IS. They'd take one look at him and lop off his head.

The Captain went back to his car. He looked inside. The girl was still curled up in the rear footwell. He leant in and checked her eyelids. No flaring. She'd be okay when she came out of it. A headache. Maybe a sore throat. But she'd be okay.

The Captain eased himself into the front seat. So she had been lying about her mother. That put a very different perspective on things. Maybe, though, she'd just lied about the name of the hotel? To put him off the trail? He got out again and searched Biljana's pockets for a hidden mobile phone. A crumpled piece of paper. A bill.

Nothing. That would have been too much like good luck.

He called the corporal again. Checked on how he was making out. 'We'll meet at the border. Take both cars across. Then we can sell yours for cash. This one has four-wheel drive. We may require it before we're through.'

'Are you sure we need to do this? To slink away with our tail between our legs. We're not being premature?'

'Dead sure. I've got an unconscious girl in the back of my car. The major knows I was meeting her this morning. Chances are he suspects a lot else. You know what the man's like. He's got a ramrod stuffed up his arse. It would give him immense pleasure to send me to the stockade. My true name will be high up on the War Crimes list. Yours too. And the Legion has them somewhere in their records. All they need to do is look. We can't risk it.'

'What do we do when we get to Ethiopia?'

'How the fuck do I know? All I know for certain is that we'll be beyond the clutches of the Legion. That's the first item on the agenda. We can take it on from there at our leisure.'

'What'll you do with the girl?'

'Same answer. I'll decide when we get there. Her mother is lurking around some place. We need to silence her. While I have the girl she'll keep quiet. So the kid's worth her weight in gold to me.'

'How do we get her through the border?'

The Captain laughed. 'I have her passport. Plus I'll scare the living shit out of her. She'll fall into line.'

'They're not going to be happy seeing two grown men travelling with a fifteen-year-old girl.'

'Bullshit. The Ethiopians couldn't care less. They get married at twelve there. Even before. They'll probably offer to buy her off me. Always assuming the bitch is still a virgin.'

'You wouldn't sell your own daughter?' The corporal sounded almost shocked.

'That all depends. Maybe if someone made me the right offer?'

The corporal fell silent.

'Jesus, Danko. I was joking. When will you get your fucking sense of humour back?'

SIXTY-TWO

'What's the range of your tracker, Rider?' Hart was sitting in the back seat of Rider's hire car. He was concentrating all his attention on the road ahead. His face looked drawn and pinched.

'The makers claim eight miles. Considerably less in an urban environment. But that's all malarkey. We have to keep within a mile of the target in case we need fuel. Otherwise we risk losing them.'

'How accurate is it? Really, I mean. Forgetting the publicity.'

Rider sat forward in his seat. He always got excited when talking about technical matters. 'Very accurate. It'll pinpoint the target car's position to within ten feet. And before you ask, the battery lasts for two months. And it's satellite, not cellular. Cellular would have been a waste of frigging time out here.' Rider jerked his head at the windscreen. 'God, this is a forlorn bloody country. Look at all that litter. How do they manage to pin plastic bags to every frigging thorn tree? Takes real skill to do that.' Rider cracked the car window, hawked and spat.

'Does it do anything else?' said Hart.

'Like what? Tie its own bootlaces?'

'Can it, Rider. You know what I mean.'

'It can monitor conversations if you get close enough,' said Rider. He looked like a man demonstrating how to conjure a rabbit out of a top hat.

'You're kidding.'

'No. Truly. Only trouble is, Biljana and the Captain will be talking to each other in Serbian, won't they? Do you happen to speak Serbian, Hart? Is that one of your many accomplishments?'

Hart looked at Amira for support. She stared straight ahead at the oncoming traffic.

'Well, at least we'll be able to confirm that Biljana's still alive.' Hart sounded bereft.

'Yeah. We'll be able to do that. Sure thing, Hart. Sure thing.' Rider's tone, exceptionally, was almost kind.

'How far are they ahead now?'

Rider glanced at his laptop computer. He'd set it up in the centre of the dashboard to the detriment of forward visibility. 'Seven miles. At the outer edge of reception, I'd say.'

'Shouldn't we be speeding up then?'

Rider made a face. 'Look at the map, Hart. We couldn't

lose him if we tried. This road only goes one way.'

'And where's that?' said Hart.

'Ethiopia,' said Rider. 'My guess is he's making for Ali Sabieh. Then he'll cross the border and head for Dewele. There aren't many more directions he can go. Only a frigging nutcase would go to Somalia.'

'The Captain is a nutcase. Haven't you realized that yet?'

'Not that much of a nutcase,' Rider said. 'Believe me. He wouldn't make it past the first border post. They'd have his money, his car and the girl off him in two shakes of a lamb's tail. And not necessarily in that order.'

'And in Ethiopia?'

'Ethiopia is a civilized country, in case you hadn't heard. They have a booming tourism industry. The Captain will have no problem getting in. Once he's in, he can head for Addis Ababa and get a plane to wherever he wants. The world is his oyster after that.'

'How long will it take him to drive to Addis?' It seemed to Hart as if he was going through the motions. That nothing he said could have any influence on the outcome of what was occurring.

Rider shrugged. 'If he drives straight there, maybe ten hours. But Ethiopian roads are piss awful. The Chinese are busy building new ones, but they haven't quite finished yet. So it could take a lot more than ten hours. Especially if it rains. Ethiopian roads transform into mud slicks in the rain. You're lucky if you don't drift over a ravine.'

'Sounds like you've been there?'

'I have.'

Hart pondered that for a moment. Then he discarded it. 'We need to hit him this side of the border then.'

'Easier said than done,' said Rider. 'The bastard is averaging around eighty. Which is a stretch for this sardine can with three of us on board. We'll not catch him in time. We'll need to go into Ethiopia after him.'

'Got your passports?'

Amira and Rider nodded. 'We're journalists. What do you think? Of course we bloody have.'

Hart cleared his throat. 'Are you both still up for this? I don't want to drag you into anything that could turn dangerous. And this could.'

'I could do with a change of clothing,' said Amira. 'But apart from that I'm as ready as I'll ever be. I'll do pretty much anything for a story, short of actual murder, as you know. Rider's the same. He's a newshound like me. You're the one we're always wondering about. Whether you've really got the flannel to be a photojournalist. Or whether you're as half-arsed about it as you always seem.'

Hart ignored the jibe. He was used to Amira riding him. Despite all the bombast and the hard talk, he sensed that she was worried about Biljana too. The two women had bonded during the days they'd spent together in Djibouti. Amira was even in danger of becoming something of a mentor figure to the girl.

'Have we got anything resembling a weapon?' he said.

'No.'

'Great.'

Amira twisted in her seat and looked at Hart. 'We weren't expecting to have to do this, John. Seems to me we've done pretty well so far. And Rider set up the tracker. Without that, we'd be nowhere. You need to give us a little credit.'

'I know. I know.' Hart hung on to the seatback in front of him. 'I'm just worried about Biljana, that's all.'

'We all are. But worrying won't get us anywhere. We need to outthink the man. He's going to imagine his cover is blown. That goes without saying. And we have to assume that he will prise the fact of our existence out of Biljana sooner rather than later. She's fifteen. She won't be able to hold out against him for long. But he won't know about the tracker because Biljana doesn't. Once he's in Ethiopia he'll relax his guard.'

'Are you sure the tracker's safe, Rider? If he finds it we're blown.'

'He'd need a GPS detector to find it. And someone to use the detector while he's driving. Chance would be a fine thing. He won't find it. I guarantee it.'

'So now.' Hart looked sick. 'The big question. Why has he taken Biljana with him?'

'That's simple,' said Amira. 'He did it by default. He'll reckon her simple presence at the chess club means that people already know about him. So he'll have taken her to give himself an edge. And to guarantee himself a regular source of information. My guess is that once she regains consciousness – assuming for the moment that that's the significance of what you saw when he carried her out to his car – he'll want to debrief. Find out everything she knows. So maybe he'll stop on the way to Addis. Spend the night. That's when we can intervene.'

'Without weapons?'

'The Captain won't be gunned up either. He left too abruptly for that. So let's buy ourselves some knives. Or a machete. Or a fucking sickle. Strikes me that Ethiopia is just the sort of country where people use those sorts of things in the normal course of their day. And we're three against one.'

Hart shook his head. 'God, we sound like a bunch of bloody amateurs.'

Amira smiled. 'That's what happens when you let the enemy take the battle to you. We missed a trick in Djibouti. We underestimated the bastard. We felt he had too much to lose to risk monkeying with Biljana. When, as far as he was concerned, he stood only to gain.'

SIXTY-THREE

'So you're awake?' The Captain glanced round his headrest at Biljana, who was struggling to get out of the footwell.

Biljana didn't answer. She eased herself onto the back seat and rubbed her throat, which was still sore from the Captain's pawing.

'Cat got your tongue?' The Captain's Serbian seemed rusty. Almost old fashioned. As if he had not been speaking it on a regular basis.

'You tried to kill me.'

The Captain laughed. 'You'd be dead if I'd tried to kill you. You angered me, so I punished you. If you anger me again, I will punish you again. Is that clear?' The Captain glared into his rear-view mirror. 'Is that clear?'

Biljana nodded.

'Good. I'm glad we've got that straight.'

'Where are you taking me?' Biljana coughed to try and clear her airway.

'Ah. A sensible question at last.' The Captain pulled the car over onto the side of the road. 'Get out. I've decided I want you sitting next to me, not behind.'

Biljana stared at him. 'I need to… you know.'

'You can go the other side of that tree. I'll watch you.'

Biljana's breath caught in her throat. 'I can't go if I'm being watched.'

'Yes you can,' said the Captain. 'In fact you'll have to. Because I'm not letting you out of my sight from here on in.'

Biljana eased herself out of the car. She felt in her pockets.

'They're empty,' said Captain. 'I have your purse. And I have your passport. Here.' He threw her the purse. 'You can have this back. I don't take money from widows and orphans. The passport I'm keeping.'

Biljana stared at the Captain for a moment, looking for more significance in his words. But there was none. She stepped behind the tree. 'You could at least turn your back.'

The Captain hesitated. Then he made a curious spitting noise with his mouth and turned his back.

Biljana started running.

She had made barely ten yards before the Captain reached her and grabbed her by the hair.

He yanked her head back and slapped her hard across the face.

Biljana fell forward onto her knees and started crying. A bus drove past in a clatter of gravel. Biljana could see the faces of the passengers staring blankly at her through the windows. But the bus didn't stop. It disappeared over the crest of the hill in a cloud of diesel fumes.

The Captain straight-armed Biljana's hands behind her back and forced her towards the car.

'I still need to pee.'

'So piss yourself. Do you think I care any more? People who get up to dirty tricks always end up paying for them. That's life.'

Biljana snatched one of her hands back from his grasp and turned to face him. 'What do you want from me? Why are you doing this? Why are you behaving like such a beast?'

'Your mother,' said the Captain, a half-smile on his face. 'I want your mother's silence. It's as simple as that.'

Biljana stared at him as if he had taken leave of his senses. Then she remembered what she had said back at the chess club. About her mother being still alive and in Djibouti. What had she done? How could she have been so stupid? 'I lied to you back there. I was frightened. My mother's dead.'

'Don't give me that.'

Biljana scrubbed the tears from her eyes. 'It's true, though. She committed suicide a month ago. I came out here on my own.'

'Rubbish.' The Captain rolled the word around his mouth

like a boiled sweet. 'You're a fifteen-year-old girl. Do you think I was born yesterday?'

Biljana managed to put the vestige of a sneer into her voice. It was surprisingly easy given the way she was starting to feel about her father. 'Fifteen-year-olds are considered young adults by the airlines. We can travel wherever we like unaccompanied. I can't believe you don't know that.'

The Captain shook his head as if an insect had unexpectedly settled on it. 'How did your mother kill herself then? Tell me that. Fast. Don't stop to think.'

He listened to Biljana's explanation, his head cocked to one side like a bird-dog. 'So. What were you doing living in Macedonia? In a Christian village? You told me you were a Muslim back at the chess club. This makes no sense.'

Biljana took a step towards him. 'Majka was only trying to protect me. She knew nobody would ask questions she couldn't answer in a Christian village. It was the one way she could think of to give me a decent upbringing.'

The Captain grunted. 'So she told you all about me? A wet-behind-the-ears teenager like you? I don't believe you. She'd have tried to protect you from the truth. I know your mother, remember. Better than you think. She was tougher than she looked.'

'Then how did I know where to find you?' shouted Biljana. 'How did I know about the monastery? How did I know to search out Maria and ask her where you were? Tell me that.'

The Captain shrugged. 'There's more to this than you're telling me. You're smart. But not that smart. You must have had help. It goes without saying.' The Captain thought for a moment, his brow creased in concentration. 'So, whatever happens, I'm keeping you. I'm going to give you six hours – until we get beyond the border and find somewhere to spend the night. Then you're going to tell me everything.' He squinted into the sun. 'I'm halfway willing to buy this notion of yours of your mother's suicide. For the time being, at least. She was that sort of a woman. Selfish enough to off herself on your fifteenth birthday and leave you to fend for yourself.' He straightened up. 'But I'm not willing to buy the rest of it. All this crap about you travelling alone. You can forget it. There's something or someone else behind all this, but I haven't got the time to find out now.' He waved his hand. 'You can climb back into the rear of the car. I've got child locks. I don't fancy you sitting in the front with me any more. You'd probably throw open the passenger door and bounce out and break your neck just to spite me.' He shook his head. 'That was a damned stupid thing to do, running away like that. I'm in the Foreign fucking Legion. I jog five days a week. I can outrun you with my eyes shut. Don't ever try it again, or I'll break your leg for you. Then you won't be running anywhere in a hurry.'

Biljana made a face at him. 'Why are you so disgusting? What did I do to deserve a father like you?'

The Captain threw back his head and roared with laughter. Then he bundled Biljana into the back of the car and set the

311

child locks. He got back into the driver's seat, started the car and continued onwards towards the Ethiopian border.

Biljana shuffled in her seat and stared at the nape of his neck. After a while he looked away from the rear-view mirror and began to avoid her stare, just as she had planned.

She found the tracker just over an hour into their journey.

Back in their flat in Djibouti she had questioned Rider endlessly about his technical gizmos. He had finally explained to her about the tracker, and what he intended to do with it. Where best to hide it in a car. Just how effective it was.

While the Captain was concentrating on his driving, Biljana had been feeling furtively beneath the front seats. She knew what the tracker looked like because Rider had shown it to her. When she felt the small square box tucked tight up against the back corner of the passenger seat, a warm rush of comfort suffused her.

Rider had done just as he had said he would. Hart, Rider and Amira would be following her.

She was no longer alone.

SIXTY-FOUR

'Where have you hidden the guns?' said the Captain.

'Beneath the spare tyre,' said the corporal, pointing to the rear of his car. 'I've wrapped them in burlap.'

'A brilliant plan. No one will ever think to look for them there.'

'Where else do you suggest?' The corporal sounded peeved, as if the Captain had turfed him out of bed too early in the morning. 'And why should they bother to check on us anyway? They've got no reason to give us more than a cursory glance. We're Europeans. Not bloody Eritreans.' The corporal glanced at Biljana. She was watching him quizzically through the back window of the Captain's car. 'You didn't hurt her any more, did you?'

'I cut off one of her fingers,' said the Captain. 'She's tamed now. She'll do anything we ask of her.'

The corporal stared at him. 'I wish you wouldn't do that. Say those sorts of things. Even in a joke. She's your daughter.'

'She's the intended product of a rape. The fact that she happens to be my daughter is entirely coincidental. You've probably got half a dozen brats of your own out there somewhere. You weren't so squeamish in Kosovo, as I remember. We were trying to repopulate the world with Serbs. Or have you forgotten?'

'That was in Kosovo. We were young. It was shameful what we did. I regret it every day of my life.'

'Why not give yourself up to the authorities then? Stand trial? You'd feel better, I'm sure, if they put you on show and then imprisoned you for life with a bunch of African shirt lifters. But you'll forgive me if I don't partake in your bleeding-heart penance.'

The corporal turned and stared back down the road. It was always dangerous to question anything the Captain did, unless you were prepared to play tough yourself in return. Toughness was the only thing he seemed to understand. To the Captain, life was a constant struggle, with the Victor Ludorum going to he who remained angriest and held out the longest. 'No. You did the right thing breaking away. I just think the girl is a mistake. We're at the border now. Why not chuck her out and leave her? Once we're across we're home free. The Legion holds no sway in Ethiopia. Nobody much does. We can take a plane to Kenya. Or South Africa. Hire ourselves out as instructors to the army. Wipe the Legion's dust from our boots.'

'I'm not leaving the girl.'

'What?' The corporal hitched his shoulders back as if he'd been slapped. 'Don't tell me you're getting paternal feelings all of a sudden? You haven't seen your wife and son for ten years. I've never noticed you mourning them.'

'This is different,' said the Captain. 'There's something wrong here. And I want to get to the bottom of it. I don't believe she did all this alone. If she won't tell me voluntarily, I'll force it out of her.'

The corporal shrugged. In all the years he had known the Captain, he had never been able to change the man's mind by so much as an iota once he had made it up. 'So we take both cars across?'

'Yes.'

'How do we guarantee the girl won't sing out at the border crossing?'

The Captain grinned. 'Because we're going to tie her up and gag her and put her in the trunk of your car.'

'My car?'

'Yes.' The grin turned into something colder. 'Didn't you just tell me that there was no reason for them to bother to check us? That we're Europeans, not Eritreans? I'm only taking you at your word.'

The corporal closed his eyes. He knew a fait accompli when he saw one. The Captain had decided to use him as a stalking horse. So what else was new? He'd spent half his existence being used by the Captain. Why change the habit of a lifetime?

SIXTY-FIVE

'They're static,' said Rider.

'What do you mean "they're static"?' said Hart. 'Can't you speak in plain English?'

'I mean they've made it through the border crossing and have stopped near Dire Dawa. Biljana and the Captain. For fuel or for the night. It's eight o'clock in the evening. What's your guess which of the two he's chosen?'

'How far are they ahead of us?' said Amira.

'Seven. Maybe eight miles,' said Rider. 'We lost precious time at the border getting our visas issued. We've made most of it up since, though. Do we close in?'

'Yes,' said Amira.

'How will we get the Captain back across the border if we do manage to take him?' said Hart.

'We don't,' said Amira. 'Too dangerous.'

'What do you mean?' said Hart. 'We made a deal with the

German major that we would hand him back to the Legion. That's the only reason the major agreed to our plan.'

'Out of sight, out of mind,' said Amira.

'Impressive,' said Hart. 'I so love watching ethical journalism at work.'

Amira flashed a look at Rider, who glanced guiltily away. 'I have more control over the story if we give him over to our own people here, you see. My newspaper has connections with the press office at the British Embassy in Addis. The embassy will eat him up. It'll be a major coup for British diplomacy. The Captain can spend a well-deserved couple of years in an Ethiopian jail while we rustle up the right papers to have him transferred to the International Criminal Tribunal for the Former Yugoslavia in The Hague. Those guys have a lot of pull. But they don't move quickly. It took them seven years to indict and sentence Zdravko Tolimir.'

'Who the hell was he?' said Hart. He had long ago decided it was a waste of effort arguing with Amira about what constituted principled behaviour and what didn't.

'Assistant Commander and Intelligence Chief of the Bosnian Serb Army.'

'So what? Where's the connection?'

'He took part in the Srebrenica Massacre. Just like your friend.'

'What did they hand down to him?' said Hart.

'Life imprisonment.'

317

'It couldn't have happened to a nicer guy,' said Rider. 'I bet he liked puppies and small children too.'

'Stop the car,' said Hart.

Rider looked seriously perturbed by Hart's sudden volte-face. 'You aren't going to be sick, are you?' he said. 'I know I piss people off sometimes. But this is ridiculous.'

'Look over there,' said Hart. 'Looks like a farm store, doesn't it?'

'So?'

'I don't know about you, Rider, but I don't want to go up against the Captain without some sort of weapon in my hand. Even if it's a sickle. We're a few miles or so off a major city. I'd rather buy whatever it is I'm going to buy here. Where no one gives a damn.'

Rider gave a relieved laugh. He eased the car onto the hard shoulder in front of the shop. When they emerged from the car, everybody in the street stared at them. Hart decided that it probably wasn't every day that three conspicuously white-skinned people visited what amounted to a one-horse dirt-road town ninety-five miles from the Ethiopia/Djibouti border. And in which the average colour of the inhabitants' skin was an elegant dark ebony.

Two gaudily painted buses took up most of the available parking spaces in front of the shop, and a number of dust-stained sheep patrolled the main street in search of something elusive to eat. A man carrying fifty empty plastic water canisters on his head stumbled past them on his way to... *Where?* thought Hart. *Purgatory?*

Hart had to duck to enter the shop, which was protected by a fragmentary fly curtain. The shopkeeper was a young girl of little more than ten years of age. She was wearing a bright-pink school uniform and a white headscarf. Hart looked around before speaking. Ethiopia was one of the few countries on earth that had never been colonized apart from a brief period of forcible occupation by the Italians in 1936, so he didn't quite know what language to begin with. He knew no Amharic, and his Italian was rusty. He decided to try English by default.

'Do you have machetes?' he said.

The girl let out a long, extended wail.

Hart froze. He could feel the back hairs on his head rising. 'I mean...' He paused. 'An implement to cut things with.' He searched desperately around for something concrete to point at, but the wall was hung with buckets, double spades and hand clippers for shearing sheep. The only visible thing that could cut worth a damn was a scythe.

Rider chose that moment to enter the shop, accompanied by Amira.

The girl backed towards a corner.

'What have you done to her?' said Amira. 'She looks terrified.'

The girl's father entered from the rear of the shop. He smiled and patted his daughter on the head. She grabbed him round the middle and held on tight.

Hart, Amira and Rider left the shop ten minutes later armed with three Ethiopian Lizard machetes. The knives were about two and a half feet long, with wooden handles and a curved tip ending in an upwards point, like a question mark. They were made in Tianjin, China. And they were blunt.

'Great,' said Rider. 'How are we meant to sharpen these? With this sharpener he's given us…' Rider held up a rectangular whetstone for everyone's inspection, 'I reckon it will take us a good three hours per knife.'

'But they look good, don't they?' said Hart. 'Wouldn't you think twice if someone came at you wielding one of these?'

'I'd think twice if someone came at me waving a stick of rock,' said Rider. 'But that's just me. I'm made that way. I have a strong suspicion the Captain isn't.'

It took them another hour to reach the outskirts of Dire Dawa, thanks to a combination of bad traffic and unchecked animal incursions onto the highway. During all that time the tracker in the Captain's car remained on standby.

'I don't like the fact that Biljana has been alone with the Captain all this time. It's not like when she's travelling with him in the car. He has other things on his mind then. Do you think he'll feed her, at least?'

'Oh, for God's sake, John,' said Amira. 'There's only so much we can do. You have to give the guy some credit for a little humanity.'

'No I haven't.' Hart rapped the windscreen with his knuckle. 'Wait. Look over there. That's his car. The Jeep Renegade. Parked tight up against the white Peugeot. Do you see? At the Saypress Hotel?'

'Saypress?'

'I suspect they mean Cypress,' said Hart.

Rider pulled over to the kerb opposite the hotel. 'We're in luck. They may call it a hotel, but this looks remarkably like a motel to me. Chances are he'll have the room directly back from where his car is parked. We won't need to go inside to check it out. We won't even need to register. So who's volunteering?'

'I'll go across,' said Hart. 'I got Biljana into this by acting like a damned fool and agreeing to bring her with me to Djibouti. I should have put my foot down right from the start.'

'She wouldn't have listened to you,' said Amira. 'She would have done it on her own.'

'Yes. But it would have been a whole hell of a lot harder, wouldn't it? Chances are that she would never have found her father on her own.'

'If it makes you feel any better. Yes. You're right. A lot of this is on you.' Amira was fast losing patience. 'But that's rather missing the point, isn't it? We're here now. Not somewhere back in Cloud Cuckoo Land two weeks ago. Are you going to recce that motel room or not? We need to get this thing on the road. Our best time to break in would be at about three o'clock in the morning. When everyone's asleep. We can bind and gag the Captain. We could be outside the gates of the British Embassy in Addis by early afternoon. But we need you to reconnoitre first, John. Like, now.'

Hart threw open the car door. After a final, weary glance at Amira, he started across the road. He reckoned the chances of the Captain choosing just the moment he was approaching the motel room to come out searching for ice were pretty remote. Still, just to be on the safe side he cut round the rear of the motel and approached what he assumed was the Captain's room from the side opposite the road.

When he was twenty feet shy of the room, he ducked into the shadows at the edge of the building and inched towards the first of the room's two windows. He could see Rider and Amira monitoring his progress from their car, fifty yards away across the main road.

Hart hunched down near the windowsill and duck-walked the last few feet. It was then that he heard the sound of raised male voices from inside the room. Speaking what he was pretty sure was Serbian.

Two men? Two men in the room? Where the hell had the second man sprung from?

Hart thought swiftly back to what the German major had told him. Yes, the major had confirmed that the Captain was one of two Serbs currently serving with the FFL. One an officer and one not. The major had been oddly coy about talking about them. He had mentioned the second man just a few moments before he had accused Hart of being a spy. And then he had never mentioned him again. Maybe this was him? Maybe the Captain had warned his mate that both their covers were blown? It would make perfect sense. But it set the cat amongst the pigeons in terms of their plans. Busting into a room in the middle of the night and taking two men prisoner – and two highly trained soldiers at that – more than doubled their chances of failure. It meant the odds rose exponentially.

Hart eased his way to the edge of the window. The curtains were tightly shut. He listened for Biljana's voice, but he could only make out the sound of the two men going at one another. Maybe they were arguing over her? Maybe – and here his heart turned over in his chest – maybe one wanted to kill her and the other didn't? If not, why were they arguing?

Hart crept towards the second window. There was a crack between the curtains in this one. But the crack was high up. Nearly eye height.

Hart tried to work out in his head whether easing his way up close to the crack, or distancing himself from it to gain some perspective, was the better thing to do. Distancing himself, he decided. But then he would see next to nothing. No. He would have to get up close and personal. Maybe he could adjust his angle of vision so that he wasn't instantly visible? He wished he'd had time to practise somewhere. It would have been such an easy thing to do. Pull shut a pair of curtains, leaving a peephole. Then look through it, with someone positioned on the other side to yell out the instant you became visible to those in the main room. He should be so lucky, he told himself. Life, he decided, had a way of serving you blinders when you least expected them.

He edged up to the gap in the curtain and looked through it at an angle. He could see a man. Not the Captain. The man was gesticulating. All his attention was on his interlocutor.

Hart craned his neck so that his head was a little closer to the gap. He froze. Laid out on the nearest bed were three pistols, an assault rifle and a sawn-off shotgun. He could also make out Biljana's feet on a second bed. He knew the feet belonged to her because he recognized her pink-and-white striped ankle socks. She had bought them in Paris. At the Monoprix Saint Paul in the Marais. As he watched, the feet moved. So she was alive. Thank God.

Hart could no longer help himself. He needed to know her exact condition.

He stepped across to the gap, hoping that the sudden, fluid movement, would not capture anybody's attention.

Biljana was sitting on the bed staring at the two men. Her arms were tied. But apart from that she seemed okay. No bruises. Hair all over the place, but then that was to be expected. Hart knew Biljana well enough by now to be able to read her body language. It was clear from her expression and the position in which she held herself – skewed to one side and tense with apprehension – that the men were arguing about her, and that she was scared.

From his position at the window, Hart could take in Biljana, the unknown man, and the guns. But he couldn't see the Captain. As he watched, Biljana's eyes met his.

She opened her mouth, then closed it again, damping the words she had been about to utter. But it had been enough. The curtains were torn apart.

Hart sprinted away from the window and towards the car. He heard the door of the motel room being thrown open behind him.

Right. The two of them are now going to shoot me, he told himself. And it will be my fault entirely. They are going to shoot me in the back and in the head and God knows where else and I shall plunge into the dirt and that will be the end of the matter.

Hart reached the car without a shot being fired. Rider had the door already open waiting for him.

Hart turned round.

The Captain was standing in the full glare of the light emanating from the open door of the room. The second man was standing next to him. Neither of them was carrying a gun.

As Hart watched, the Captain grinned and curled his right hand into the shape of a pistol. He raised it and pretend-fired it three times, almost as you would ring a handbell. Then he smiled again and shrugged his shoulders as if, what the hell, it wasn't a personal thing, this future killing of Hart and his companions. Simply routine.

Hart eased himself backwards into the car. His eyes never left the Captain's.

When he was inside, Rider engaged first gear and they pulled away.

The Captain and his friend watched them all the way up the street.

SIXTY-SIX

'Leave your car behind,' said the Captain. 'We travel together from now on in.'

'Why not take mine then?' said Danko.

'Because it's built like a lean-to,' said the Captain. 'The usual French tat. And we're going to need a four-wheel drive where we're going.'

'Where are we going?' said Danko, as he hustled Biljana into the back seat.

'Not in front of the girl, you idiot. Some of these trackers can pick up conversations. And then she could relay what I just told you in English.'

'Trackers?' said Danko.

'Yes. There must be a tracker in the car. How else could they have followed us without our being aware of it? The minute we get a spare moment we truss the girl up and we go over the vehicle with a toothcomb. Before that we keep stumm. Or only talk in Serbian. If the girl tries to speak English, knock her out.'

'Surely that's another reason to take my car?' said Danko.

'Don't be absurd. Didn't you ever stop to think that the tracker might be in your car, not mine? No. Leave your car open. Keys inside. My guess is that in this place, it won't even last the night. The local Mafiosi will have the Djibouti plates off and Ethiopian plates on it in no time. It's an even better way of getting rid of it than burning the damned thing. We wouldn't have got much for it anyway. The crate's been clapped out for years.'

Biljana huddled onto the back seat. She composed her features into a neutral, submissive mask so that neither of the two men would notice that she was taking in every word that they said. But beneath the beaten exterior, and the clearly visible apprehension she was manifesting as to what might happen to her, she remained alert.

So the Captain was wise to the tracker, was he? She would have to deal with that before he had a chance to inspect the car. Her one big advantage was that he had already searched her. Unless he was hyper-vigilant, he would probably not feel the need to search her again, especially now that she appeared to be so frightened and broken down. Biljana decided that she would make good use of this fact.

She let her mind begin to range a little. The relationship between the man called Danko and the Captain was a fascinating one. For some reason, even though Danko was cut from precisely the same cloth as the Captain, she didn't fear him in the visceral way that she feared her father. There were moments when they mimicked each other's tone in the way men with a long history of partnership seemed prone to do. At other times Danko defied the Captain, and tried to rein in the tyrant's worst excesses. The difference in behaviour fascinated her.

Just before the disturbance at the motel, for instance, the Captain had been threatening to resort to torture to find out the names of whoever had travelled with her and put her up to the Djibouti trip. Danko had noticed the horror and revulsion reflected on her face, and had made a point of arguing openly against the use of more violence. Almost as if he wished to pass her a subliminal message. At one point it had even looked as though the two men were set to come to blows over her. Then Hart had appeared at the window and she had given him away with her surprised face.

Nothing escaped the Captain. He was always alert. Like a feral cat. A puma maybe. Or a lynx.

Danko struck her as more like a former Macedonian neighbour's neutered Maine Coon.

'So who were those people?' said Danko.

The Captain snorted. It was half a laugh, half an expression of mild astonishment at his own stupidity. 'The man at the window was the Englishman you and I followed from the rape house in Kosovo all those years ago. The one who freed Lumnije Dardan and the three other bovines. I shot him in the back an hour or two after you left us. But the bastard has the luck of the devil. My bullet deflected off the telephoto lens on one of his cameras. He survived to shoot me back. I then spent a day and a half as his prisoner. I'm hardly likely to forget the cunt's face, now, am I?'

'Why did you never tell me about this? We all wondered where you'd gone. And when you came back all those days later you were silent as the grave. We reckoned you'd found a woman some place and gone to ground. We never thought you'd been bushwhacked by a Britannia and taken prisoner.'

Danko was on the verge of laughing out loud until he caught sight of the Captain's expression. This was clearly no laughing matter as far as he was concerned. Danko switched tone as smoothly as the automatic gear change on a Rolls-Royce. 'Are you seriously telling me that this is the same man who freed this girl's mother?'

The Captain darted a glance at the back seat. 'Yes. This little cocksucker's mother.'

Danko couldn't help himself. 'For pity's sake, man, can't you control your language? We're not in barracks now. The girl is only fifteen.'

'Then she probably knows better than you what a cocksucker is. What do you think she is? A virgin?'

'I am a virgin,' Biljana declared in a shaking voice from the back seat. 'And I'd appreciate it if you did what Danko says. Your language is disgusting.'

The Captain lunged at her, but Biljana was too quick for him. The fact that he was trying to drive at the same time as hitting her didn't help matters.

The car fishtailed across the road. The Captain righted it with a single wrench of his shoulders. 'You'll regret that. You've got a belt coming. The minute we stop I'm going to give it to you. You won't walk straight for a week.'

'No, you're not,' said Danko, with surprising intensity. 'We're a team. And this girl's our trump card. Yours *and* mine. You've got to leave her alone from now on. She's only useful to us if she's undamaged goods.' He glanced pleadingly at Biljana, making sure the Captain didn't see him. 'I'm sure she'll open up now. She has no reason to hide anything any more, has she?' He narrowed his eyes encouragingly. 'We know we are being followed. And by whom. So the cat's already out of the bag. No point shoving it back inside again, is there?'

The Captain jerked his chin in Biljana's direction. 'Well? Come on then, Joan of Arc. Cough up. Who were the other people in the car your mama's friend was running towards? And what's the bastard's name anyway? I don't think he ever got round to telling me back in Kosovo.'

Danko grinned reassuringly. He dipped his head as if he would have liked to have given Biljana an emboldening nudge with it.

Just like horses do when they get impatient, Biljana thought to herself. Or when they're after carrots. The man is a complete mystery. Why is he always so explicitly trying to protect me? Have they worked out some sort of nice man, nasty man routine between them? That would be just like the Captain. Strangely enough, though, in her heart of hearts, Biljana was tentatively inclined to trust her initial instincts about Danko. Maybe he really did mean her well? She could do with an ally. Each time she talked back to the Captain it cost her more than she cared to think of in terms of Dutch courage.

'Hart,' she said at last. 'His name is John Hart.'

'Now we're getting somewhere,' said the Captain. He seemed ridiculously pleased with himself. As if he really believed that his threats of physical violence were hitting home. 'On to the nitty-gritty. It looked to me like there were two more of them in the car, sitting there waiting for him. A man and a woman. Come on. Spit their names out.'

Biljana havered for a moment longer. Then she decided that, just as Danko was always implying, there was no real harm in telling the Captain at least a part of the truth. It might even force him to control himself a little. To ratchet down the tension. She was privately frightened that he would lose his temper one time and really kill her.

'They're journalists. British journalists. One's called Rider. That's the only name I know him by. The woman is called Amira Eisenberger.'

'I should have known,' said the Captain, hammering the steering wheel. 'I should have bloody known. That Hart bastard who kidnapped your mother was a journalist, too, wasn't he? Festooned with cameras like a paparazzi.' He flicked his front tooth with a fingernail. 'Is that what he is? A fucking paparazzi?'

'You should be so lucky,' said Biljana. 'No. These are real journalists. And they've got a file on you a foot thick. They are going to make sure you are imprisoned for war crimes. You'll probably be banged up for the rest of your life. It's a shame they no longer have the death penalty where you are going. That would even things up a bit. For my grandmother and my grandfather. For my uncle. For my mother.'

The Captain made a disgusted sound with his lips, like someone tasting sour milk.

'Do they have a file on me too?' said Danko, in a vain attempt to ease the atmosphere. To distract the Captain from responding in his usual way whenever the girl defied him.

'Of course they fucking do,' said the Captain. 'What do you think? That you somehow managed to waltz through two wars, raping and torturing and killing like Genghis Khan, without anybody fucking noticing?'

Biljana stared at Danko. This was new. Danko came over as such a reasonable, tolerant man. So unlike the Captain. It was hard to see him as a murderer and a rapist.

'Did you really do those things the Captain says?' she said to Danko, before she was able to stop herself. 'Did you rape and torture too? Did you rape my mother?'

Danko shrank back against the dashboard like a frightened dog. He opened his mouth to speak but nothing came out.

'I'll answer that,' said the Captain. 'Your mother was mine. Exclusively. So you're my little brat whether you like it or not. And Danko? Yes. He did all those things and more. Didn't you, Danko?'

Danko stared at Biljana. She stared back.

Finally, infinitely slowly, Danko nodded his head. 'Yes. I did do them. I was young. And I thought the war gave us the right. I'm ashamed of who I was then. Of what I did. I would like to take it all back. But I can't.'

'Your victims must be gambolling about in their graves,' said the Captain. 'Desperate to climb out and get on with their miserable lives again. If it wasn't for the unfortunate fact that you killed them all stone dead.' The Captain lipped a cigarette from his pack and lit it. 'Listen, my little pudding. Danko is the sort of man who will always bleed with pity after the event. But remember. I've seen him in action. You haven't. Don't think for a moment that all this mild talk of his – the sticking up for you – the worrying about my swearing – is the real Danko. Far from it. The real Danko raped six women in one day. I saw him do it. He headed round the room doing one, then the other, desperate to break Fat Anda's record. Didn't matter how many times they'd been raped already. Danko still chalked them up on the blackboard.' He blew cigarette smoke at the rear-view mirror. 'I've seen him kill unarmed civilians too. I saw him kill an innocent old man once, six hundred yards away, just to prove the value of a looted sniper rifle he wanted to sell on to one of his war buddies. Is that the man you recognize sitting here? Is it?' The Captain spat what remained of his cigarette out of the car window. 'If I left you alone with him, he'd probably rape you too. Old habits die hard, you know?' The Captain brushed a strand of tobacco from his lip with the back of his hand. 'Well, at least you're safe from all that stuff with me. I'm your father. And daddies don't rape their little virgin daughterkins, though, do they? Not unless they are made very angry indeed.'

Biljana stared in horror from one man to the other. Danko would no longer meet her gaze. The Captain turned round and leered at her as though he'd just won a chess game in record time.

Biljana bent forwards at the waist as if she was crippled with grief. But there was a cold edge to her crocodile tears. The Captain's diatribe had freed her from feeling even the slightest vestige of sympathy for either of the two men in front of her. Disguising the movement with her body, she felt under the passenger seat with her right hand. When she encountered the tracker she levered it first to the left and then to the right. She knew exactly how it would be attached to the seat, because Rider had shown her.

When she had the box safely in her hand she threw herself backwards and curled up on the seat, still sobbing. When she was sure that the Captain was bored witless with her outpourings, and that she was no longer being monitored by either of the men, she slipped the tracker down the front of her jeans.

At last she had been able to do something to make up for her stupidity back at the motel. At last she had been able to do something to make Hart proud of her.

SIXTY-SEVEN

'Now what do we do?' said Rider. 'Head back to bloody England? Looks like we've blown it big time.'

There was a period of silence while everyone digested what had just happened.

'No. Too late for that. We continue following them,' said Hart. 'Just like before. But this time we get as close as we can. It won't take the Captain long to figure out we've planted a tracker in his car. He'll find and destroy it and then we'll have to rely on keeping him in range visually.'

'What a result,' said Rider. 'Good guys zero, bad guys one. How many guns did you say you saw on the bed? Before you had to hightail it back home?'

Hart gave an embarrassed shrug. 'Three pistols, an assault rifle and a sawn-off.'

'So why don't we simply bring in the Ethiopian police then? It can't be legal to drive around with an arsenal like that in your boot.'

Amira, who had been holding her fire while the men snapped at each other, chose that moment to cut in. 'Because they'd be massacred, that's why. This isn't Addis Ababa, Rider. This is the bloody countryside. The police out here aren't even armed. They carry batons. And maybe a can of pepper spray if they're lucky, and the budget runs to it. We can't afford to put Biljana's life at risk because some local cop over faces himself running up against a man like the Captain. No. Whatever we are going to do to save Biljana, we'll have to do it ourselves.'

Rider flicked a finger at his computer. 'Well, lookie here. The tracker's still working.' He shook his head. 'I don't get it. If the Captain suspects we planted one. Well, like Hart says, surely he'd have winkled it out by now?'

'Where did you hide it exactly?' said Hart.

Rider grimaced. He knew what was coming. 'Underneath the passenger seat.'

'Great,' said Hart. 'What a masterstroke. That's the last place anyone would look.'

'There wasn't much time for niceties,' said Rider. 'Or have you forgotten?'

They were silent for the next hour.

'No change,' said Rider at last. 'The tracker's still online. Incredibly. It tells me he's turned right at Āwash. Towards the Aledeghi Wildlife Reserve. You don't think he's being cute and has hooked the tracker onto the underside of a tourist bus, do you? And we're shadowing a Women's Institute outing?'

338

'No,' said Hart. 'I don't. He's not that smart. He must think we were following the second car and got to him that way.'

Rider tapped a few coordinates onto his laptop. 'So if it's true, and it really is him, it means he's no longer heading for Addis. He's heading from south to north up the country.' He lowered his head until it was nearly touching the glass. 'Maybe he knows about the tracker and he's using it to lure us somewhere isolated? Maybe he intends to bushwhack us? That's what I'd do in his place.'

Hart hitched his chin in Rider's direction. 'What's ahead if he keeps on going as he is?'

Rider shrugged. 'If he keeps on going far enough he'll hit Eritrea. But he'd be shooting himself in the foot if he did that. The Eritreans and the Ethiopians don't see eye to eye. They waged a vicious war from 1998 to 2000, which cost more than seventy thousand lives. If he tries to cross the border from Ethiopia into Eritrea, the Eritreans will boil him alive in a hot kettle. Biljana too.'

'So where does that leave us in the general scheme of things?' said Hart, rolling his eyes. 'Anyone care to sum up our position for the record?'

'I'd say that was pretty clear,' said Amira. 'Bad news first. Three rank amateurs, armed only with blunt machetes, are facing two heavily armed and highly trained professional soldiers who are holding as hostage a young woman that the amateurs feel personally responsible for. The amateurs have inadvertently revealed themselves to the enemy, forfeiting any small advantage they might previously have possessed. All clear so far?' Amira put on a fake smile. 'Now do you want to hear the good news?'

Hart grimaced. 'Okay. Tell me the good news?'

'The amateurs outnumber the enemy by fifty per cent.'

SIXTY-EIGHT

The Captain wriggled out from underneath the Renegade and stood up. He brushed absent-mindedly at his clothes, but it was clear that all his attention was focused on the road behind them. 'There's no tracker here. Inside the car or out. It must have been concealed in your car, Danko. This vehicle is clean as a nurse's snatch.'

'I don't get it,' said Danko. 'Why would they place a tracker in my car and not yours?'

'Because they were being cute,' said the Captain. 'They knew it's the last place we'd ever look. Plus they'd never have suspected that we'd sacrifice your car as our contribution to the Ethiopian black economy.'

Danko gave an emphatic shake of the head. 'I don't go for it. Couldn't they have been following us conventionally?'

The Captain eased the knots from his body. He glanced across at Biljana, who was propped up against a tree with her

341

hands tied in front of her. 'No. I was on the lookout all the time. They'd have needed an armada of different vehicles at their disposal to hoodwink me. Which I suspect they didn't or they'd have pulled me over back in Djibouti. Same reason we weren't stopped at the border crossing. They couldn't get their act together in time.' He chucked his chin at Danko. 'How about you, though? Were you wise to every car that followed you? Were you on the lookout for a tail?'

Danko made a face. Finally, after giving it serious thought, he shook his head. 'No. I wasn't. So I could have been followed, I suppose. I could have led them to you. But I don't reckon I did.'

'Nobody ever does,' said Captain. 'That's the beauty of it. None of us ever think we're that significant. But we've got the girl. And as far as Hart is concerned, I'm the guy who raped his girlfriend and then tried to shoot him. So he's got a pretty strong motive for revenge.'

'His girlfriend?' said Danko.

'I'm not saying she was his girlfriend when I raped her. But afterwards? Who knows. Women are renewable fixtures. And stranger things have happened on this earth.' The Captain glanced again towards Biljana. 'Then she ups and goes and kills herself. So who's he going to come looking for, heh?'

Danko shrugged. 'You believe what the girl says then? You think the mother really did kill herself?'

'I know she did,' said the Captain. 'I've still got connections back home. People who served with me and didn't get picked

342

up after the war. Before I phoned you and set this whole thing on the road, I got a friend to check the Macedonian death registrations for June/July. It's easily done. It only takes a phone call. Lumnije Dardan killed herself end June. Drowned herself in Lake Ohrid. They called it "death by misadventure" on the certificate. But I don't believe that for an instant. The Dardan woman was a Muslim. They don't go much for suicide within that culture. So whoever filled in the records cut her some slack so she could be legally buried. That's my theory at least.'

'Muslims not going for suicide? You've got to be kidding me. What about the Daesh suicide bombers? What do they call it over there? *Istishhad?*'

The Captain hawked and spat. 'That's bullshit, and you know it. As in every culture, the priests and the imams say exactly what suits them at a precise moment in time and then justify it later. When suicide bombing suits them, the imams find examples from the Hadith that support that. If it doesn't, they don't. When in doubt, they know they can always use donkeys to carry the bombs. That won't offend anybody but the British.'

'God, you're a cynic,' said Danko. But he couldn't help laughing.

'I wouldn't have it any other way.' The Captain cleaned his hands on a rag. 'Now untie the girl and shove her back inside the car. We've got some serious driving to do.'

Danko did as he was told. All through the process, though,

he was aware that the girl was no longer looking him directly in the eyes. She had obviously changed her mind about him since hearing the details of his wartime exploits from the Captain. This wounded Danko.

For in the years directly following the end of the Kosovo War, Danko had changed his manner of thinking entirely. He now sincerely regretted many of the things he had done as a young man. At heart he believed himself to be a fundamentally good person. A man who missed his family and his country and the closeness of relational ties. Hell, hadn't the Legion cashiered him when he had tried to sneak back into Serbia illegally to see his wife and children? Would a mass murderer have done a thing like that? Risked everything like that? Danko desperately wanted Biljana to understand that he had changed. That he was no longer the man he had once been. And he wanted to see this understanding reflected in her gaze.

Okay, he had done some of those things the Captain had boasted to Biljana about. He had behaved dishonourably on occasion. But he had been eighteen years old when he had shot the old man with the sniper rifle. And raped all the women. Couldn't a leopard change its spots? Wasn't it possible to regret what you had done in your early youth and make some sort of amends?

But he hadn't made amends yet, had he? He'd simply closed the door on his past like a coward, and buried his head in the sand.

Danko found himself thinking how he might make amends now. How he might turn things around.

Could he help the girl in some way maybe? Nobody's daughter deserved to be treated the way the Captain treated Biljana. It was almost as though the Captain blamed her for being his flesh and blood. Blamed her for reminding him of the sins of his past.

Danko glanced across at the Captain. He sighed inwardly. God forbid, but the man was relentless. He wouldn't be easy to trick. And if Danko somehow contrived to let the girl escape, he knew, without a shadow of doubt, that the Captain would kill him.

Was the risk worth it? Would it serve to give him closure on all the evil memories that proximity to the Captain had summoned up?

Only time would tell.

SIXTY-NINE

'I don't get this,' said Rider. 'I don't get it at bloody all.'

Amira was taking her turn driving. Rider was in the front seat fiddling with his laptop. Hart was in the rear opening and shutting his window depending on the quantity of passing cars and the amount of dust they raised.

'What don't you get?' he said.

Rider sniffed. 'We're three miles behind them. And they are twenty miles or so short of Gewanē.'

'So what?'

Rider tapped some more instructions into his laptop. 'Gewanē is the town at the entrance to the Yangudi Rassa National Park.'

'And?'

Rider shrugged. 'I've knocked about Ethiopia a bit in my time. I covered the police massacres in 1995, for instance, and the subsequent riots. The tail end of the Eritrean war in

2000. I may never have been to the Yangudi Rassa National Park, in other words, but I got to visit Simien, which is smaller but otherwise much of a muchness. And one thing I know for sure. They don't just let you drive into these places. You have to register before you go in at park headquarters. And you have to de-register when you leave. If you don't, they won't let you in past the turnstile.'

'So what?' said Hart. 'Are you saying we descend on the three of them while they're busy filling in their entry forms?'

'No,' said Rider. 'But a strange thing happened when we went to Simien.'

'Which I'm sure you're going to tell us,' said Hart.

Rider looked up from what he was doing. He gave Hart his most engaging grin. 'Yes. Because they insisted each separate car take an armed guard with us all the time we were in the park.' He nodded a few times like a man revisiting past accomplishments in his mind. 'Didn't cost us much. And the guy more than earned his tip collecting wood and making himself useful about the place. But he sat with us all the way through our visit, clutching his rifle to his chest. Never let the thing out of his sight. I suspect he was only there to frighten off the baboons if they got too curious.' Rider allowed his grin to slip. 'The point I'm trying to make is that Yangudi Rassa is twenty times the size of Simien. And it marks the split in the territory of two tribes, the Afars and the Issas, who hate each other's guts with a vengeance. My guess is that they'll have much the same system here. You register to go into the park, and you get your guard. And you don't lose him again till you leave.' He shrugged. 'Do you reckon the Captain will know this? Because I don't. It came as a total surprise to me when we entered Simien. Nobody warned me. Nobody said anything about it before it became a fait accompli. Truth to tell, it didn't bother us any. But it'll bother the hell out of the Captain and his chum. Even if the guard is a congenital idiot, he must realize that something is very wrong indeed with their set-up. That the girl is there under duress. They won't want that.'

'Are you suggesting we can use the armed guard for our own purposes?' said Hart. 'Pounce down on them and get him to do our dirty work?'

'Of course not.' Rider seemed almost irritated. 'Our guard in Simien was about seventy years of age and half blind with it. I reckon the park authorities only use the position to pension off their grandfathers. No. I think when the Captain finds out about it, he'll just refuse, turn round and head back the way he came in.'

'Right into our laps, you mean?'

'Something like that.' Rider didn't sound enthusiastic.

'So what the hell do we do?' said Hart. 'Ram him? Like in the Battle of Actium?'

Rider made a face. 'Sounds like a plan. Anyone have any more bright ideas?'

Amira shook her head. 'I think you're wrong, Rider. I don't

think he'll turn round. I think he knows exactly where he's going.'

'How bloody come?'

'Because when we smoked him out from the motel at Dire Dawa, he didn't hesitate for a moment. He drove straight to Āwash and hung a right. And even a cursory glance at the map shows that Ethiopia isn't chock-full of alternatives. Once you're on a road, you're on it. Highway 1, which we're following now, is the only main road in the whole area. Highway 2 is fifty miles to the west of us, with not a single road leading to it from Highway 1 until you get to Mile, eighty miles ahead of us inside the park. And down to the east of us there's sweet fuck all for three hundred straight miles until you reach the Somali border. Unless you go back on your tracks, as you suggested, and follow the road we came in on.'

'So?' said Rider.

'So my reading of the Captain tells me he's heading north because he means to,' said Amira. 'Straight through the National Park. And guess what? Plum in the middle of the park you get to Mile, as I just said. And a few miles before you get to Mile you are presented with a choice. You either take Highway 1 back to Kombolcha, which is the only sensible way to get back to Addis should that happen to be your inclination, or you head on a few miles and hang a left west to Chifra, which will eventually take you back to Highway 2 and the road north. Straight towards the Eritrean border.'

'But we've already discussed Eritrea,' said Hart. 'Only a maniac would head there. Didn't Rider say something about being boiled alive in a hot kettle?'

'Rider,' said Amira, looking directly at Rider, 'will say anything at all to get a reaction. He's hard-wired that way. Like a kid perpetually asking his parents *Why this? Why that? Why the other?*'

Rider gave a grunt. But he didn't put up a fight.

'So you think they're headed for Eritrea after all?' said Hart.

'Yes, I do,' said Amira. 'The Eritreans are just as corrupt as the Ethiopians. Maybe more so. And the Captain must surely have twigged that we're journalists by now. We know for certain that he recognized you back at the motel because he made the pistol sign at you – that was recognition if ever I saw it. Pure hate. It wouldn't take a genius to put two and two together after that. And my guess is that Biljana will have had the good sense to feed him whatever information he wants about us as she must know it no longer matters worth a damn anyway. He's already on his guard and he will remain so.' Amira lit her second cigarette in as many minutes and blew a controlled stream of smoke out of the car window. 'Added to which he has to think that we might benefit from a certain amount of pull in Addis thanks to the newspaper we work for. That if he goes anywhere near the capital he will risk being picked up. Out here, in the boondocks, he's safe as houses. We're hardly likely to fly in Delta Force to apprehend him, are we? And the local police clearly aren't worth a damn. If he gets to Eritrea and manages to bribe his way across the border he's home free. He and his chum can make for the coast and blag their way aboard a boat to the Yemen. The world's his oyster after that.'

'And Biljana?' said Hart.

'That's obvious,' said Amira. 'She'll be surplus to requirements.'

'What the hell do you mean?'

'I mean that unless he's bonded with her in some obscure way – surprised himself, and us, by a sudden unexpected surge of paternal feelings – he'll act just like he's always acted and get rid of her.'

'Kill her, you mean?' said Hart.

'Why would he do that?' said Amira. 'As you say, she's his daughter. Even if she's one of possibly many. No. He's made his contribution to the Serbian gene pool, and that's as far as it probably goes with him. My guess is that he'll simply dump her somewhere convenient when he has no more use for her. Most likely in Eritrea. And Christ alone knows where she'll end up after that. She's fifteen. And scared. And she's female. Do I need to draw you a diagram?' Amira twisted round in her seat. 'You're all that girl's got in the world, John. No one else gives a damn. If you don't reach her before he offloads her, no one will.'

SEVENTY

The Captain stared at the old man with the rifle. 'You've got to be kidding me.'

Danko glanced swiftly back at the car. Biljana was sitting in the rear seat, looking out at the unlikely trio, the ghost of a smile hovering about her face. The Captain had spent a great deal of time impressing on her that if she so much as squeaked while they were at the National Park entry post, he would take out the pistol he had tucked into the back of his trousers, under the flap of his Guayabera-style shirt, and kill everybody in the vicinity.

Biljana had believed him. But there was still a mischievous edge to her that was enjoying his discomfort at this new and unexpected spanner in the works.

Now she watched the old man who had been allocated as their park guard walking towards the car, with the Captain and Danko following him. One glance at the Captain's face and she knew that she held the guard's life in her hands.

'Move over,' said the Captain in broad Serbian. 'Granddad is coming to sit beside you. I hope to blazes he doesn't stink, because if he does, I'm going to kill him just for the hell of it and pitch his body over the nearest cliff. I'll also kill him if you do anything – anything at all – to make him suspicious of us. Between you and me, I want the bastard to continue breathing. I'd like to be able to drop him off before we get to Chifra, body and rifle intact, so he can go back and dandle his grandchildren on his knee. But I won't hesitate to fry his liver if you give me any reason, any reason at all, to do so. Do you understand me?'

All the time he was saying this, the Captain was grinning at Biljana as if he was sharing something nice with her. Recounting the delights of the National Park. Outlining their future plans together.

Biljana shunted up on the seat and let the old man climb in beside her. He didn't smell at all. He was dressed in baggy grey trousers over open-toed plastic sandals. He wore a blue shirt under an off-white, four-layered linen *gabi*, which covered his shoulders and most of his upper body like a cloak. The outfit was topped off with a matching linen turban and a neat pepper-and-salt beard, which was missing only the moustache part. Everything the guard wore was scrupulously clean.

'Hello,' said Biljana.

'Hello,' said the old man, touching his forehead in greeting. 'My name is Gersem.'

'And my name is Biljana. You speak such good English. Where did you learn it?'

Gersem smiled. 'In my youth I am guide. Now I am guard. Speak many English. What language you speak with men?'

'Serbian.'

'Ah,' said Gersem. He shook his head in wonder. 'I never hear this before.' He glanced through the car window at the Captain, who had just ordered Danko over to a nearby booth to buy them all a picnic lunch. 'He your father? He look much like you.'

Biljana smothered a groan. She was scared for Gersem and scared for herself. She knew all about the Captain's short fuse. Knew how easily the situation could move from awkward harmony to outright murder. 'Yes. He is my father,' she said grudgingly.

'Other man your uncle perhaps?'

'No,' she said. 'He's a friend of my father.'

'Ethiopia beautiful place,' said Gersem, settling back in his seat. 'We see many animals. Oryx. Gazelle. Zebra. Flamingo. Bastard.'

'Bastard?' said Biljana.

'Big bird. Run very fast.'

'You mean a Bustard?'

'Arabian Bastard. Yes.'

Biljana just about managed to maintain a straight face.

Suppressed anxiety was taking her dangerously close to a fit of the giggles. 'Why do you have a rifle?'

Gersem made a shooting motion with his hands. 'Bad baboon. Big males can attack. Need frighten off. Also tribe. Sometime take hostage. European. American. Hold for ransom. This very bad also. I make see off. No come while I am here.'

'That's wonderful. Thank you,' said Biljana.

'Is okay. What I am for,' said Gersem.

Danko eased himself into the front of the car and handed Biljana the plastic bag containing their lunch. He glanced at Gersem, then back across to her. He appeared to be trying to communicate something to her with his eyes, but Biljana turned her head away and refused to look at him.

Gersem started to get out of the car to put the plastic bag in the rear luggage well.

'No. No. Don't do that,' said Danko sharply, in English, fearful that Gersem would stumble onto the guns. 'The boot's full. You can keep the bag on the seat between you. We'll stop in a couple of hours and eat it anyway.'

Biljana smiled at Gersem in an effort to defuse the tension. But it was clear that Gersem had already picked up on the atmosphere between her and Danko. Biljana knew that she must swiftly put on a believable act or she would give herself away. That she must make an attempt to pass off the charged edge in the atmosphere as nothing in particular.

'Thanks, Danko. We'll do that. I'm looking forward to it. I shall be famished by lunchtime. Mmm.'

Danko did a slow double-take. Then he looked at the guard. It belatedly dawned on him that Biljana was doing her level best to protect the old man from the Captain.

'Sure,' he said with a lop-sided grin, pleased that she was connecting with him again, even if only on a nugatory level. 'Sure. We'll have a great picnic. This is going to be one hell of a trip.'

SEVENTY-ONE

It was Rider who called for the unexpected halt. Sharply, and with an edge to his voice. The Captain had pulled off the main highway. Rider had almost missed the signs. He had lost concentration.

'The bastard can't be more than half a mile ahead of us,' Rider hissed, furiously tapping at his computer. 'If we carry on as we are going, there will be a disaster. Either that or we will have to accelerate past the Renegade, leaving the Captain to bring up our tail.'

Hart was inured by now to Rider's fervid taste for melodrama, so he paid scant attention. Once they were stopped, he separated himself from the others and started off up a nearby hill, armed only with a camera and a pair of binoculars. Their guard seemed ready to object, until Amira explained that Hart was a fanatical ornithologist, obsessed by vultures and rock finches, and that if he went everywhere accompanied by an armed man the birds would simply fly away. Such a catastrophe would, Amira assured the man, impact on the scale of tip the guard could expect when they reached the far side of the National Park. The choice was entirely his.

The guard proved instantly amenable. His English wasn't good, and his commitment to actually guarding them seemed lukewarm at best. Amira busied herself feeding him sandwiches and sodas from the picnic lunch they had bought back at Gewanē, while Rider sat hunched over his laptop under the shade of a baobab 'dead rat upside-down' tree, communicating with the ether.

With a final backward glance at the guard, Hart eased himself along the crest of the hill, making sure that his silhouette didn't fracture the skyline. When he saw a giant lobelia, surrounded by half a dozen clumps of ground-hugging shoots, he crawled across to it and sheltered beneath its shade. Once he was certain that no one looking up the hillside below could possibly see him, he brought the binoculars to his eyes and scanned the road.

Yes, it was just as Rider had suspected. About five hundred yards away from him, and maybe three hundred feet below where he was lying, the Captain's Renegade was drawn up facing the road. It was parked in a sort of natural lay-by. All four doors were open.

Hart allowed his binoculars to range to the left and right of the SUV. The first thing Hart saw was the Captain's

Ethiopian guard, sitting cross-legged on a waist-high stone about forty yards from the vehicle. The man was eating a sandwich. His rifle was cradled in the crook of his free arm. He seemed a very different sort of man indeed from the lacklustre guard his own party had inherited. A dozen yards beyond him, the second Serb was sitting on the ground, a few feet from Biljana. They were eating too.

Hart spent a long time with his binoculars focused exclusively on Biljana, monitoring her body language and the expression on her face. To his astonishment she seemed entirely at ease with her situation. At one point she called something across to the guard, and they both laughed. Hart felt good about the presence of the guard. While he was around, Biljana would be respected and treated in a halfway civilized manner. His presence offered her a certain degree of security.

Next, Hart focused his attention on the Serb. The man seemed a few years younger than the Captain. Hart estimated him at not much beyond thirty-five years of age. He had a more open expression than his older companion too – boyish even. An almost man. One glance at the Captain's face, and you had no doubt whatsoever about his chosen profession. The man was born to be a soldier. Hard-faced. Grim-featured. Implacable. This other man seemed almost tame by comparison. A waiter maybe. Or a garage attendant.

Despite the apparent dichotomy, Hart noticed that Biljana never looked directly at the second Serb – and neither did they speak. Once or twice, when the man was turned away from her, or had allowed his attention to wander, Hart could see Biljana furtively studying him, as if he were a rare species of moth pinned to a lepidopterist's table. But the moment he looked towards her again she mimicked losing interest, and turned away.

Curious.

When Hart was satisfied that Biljana was unharmed and in good spirits, he searched around for the Captain. But the man was nowhere to be seen. Then, about twenty yards below where he was lying, Hart heard the rattle of a handful of small stones as they pitched and tumbled down the hillside.

Hart shrank back inside the cover of the giant lobelia shoots. The Captain had clearly had the same idea he had. He was making his way to the top of the hill to get a look back along the road behind him. To gain a perspective. To spy.

Hart eased himself as deep inside the bower of shoots as he could get. The edges were sharp and unpleasant to the touch, but Hart didn't care. He just wanted to be invisible. To disappear into the undergrowth.

When he was buried to the full extent of his body, he twisted round so that his head was pointing back over his right shoulder, its outline disguised by the largest of the shoots. He could see the Captain clearly now. The man was standing in full view, about five yards to the right of where

Hart was stretched out. If the Captain turned round for any reason, Hart would be instantly visible.

As Hart watched, the Captain felt beneath his shirt and brought out a pistol. He stared at it lovingly for a moment. Then he ejected the ammunition clip, popped the clip into his top pocket, and checked the mechanism. Hart could hear the click-click-snick as the Captain tested the slide, followed by the hiss of expelled air as he blew down the barrel to clear it. When he had finished preening, he snapped the ammunition clip back into its original position and tucked the pistol inside his trousers, tight up against his spine. He settled his shirt over the pistol so that it was invisible again, and gave an appreciative grunt.

Hart looked frantically round for something to defend himself with. Two feet to his right he saw a stone. Maybe three pounds in weight. And small enough to fit into the palm of his hand. Anyone struck with that would know they had been struck. But to reach out and get it would be to reveal most of one arm. If the Captain turned and saw him, he would be for it.

Hart didn't have a great many other options. He was lying prone, and in an awkward position. It would take him all of three seconds to get to his feet and into action. By that time the Captain would have drawn his pistol and shot him. And there was a fair chance from up here that no one would hear the shot. The Captain could conceal Hart's body beneath the giant lobelia, where it would moulder quietly away and eventually be eaten by termites, or a passing lynx. Either that, or he would take advantage of Hart's fortuitous absence from the race to sneak up on Amira and Rider and clear the decks of them too. If he hid their bodies as well, he and his sidekick could probably make it as far as the Eritrean border before anyone thought to raise the alarm. Cross-border cooperation between Eritrea and Ethiopia was non-existent. The Eritreans would probably applaud.

Pre-crisis adrenalin surged through Hart's body. He didn't doubt for a moment that the Captain was capable of murdering them all. And the sheer size of the park played directly into his hands. The roads until now had been remarkably clear of vehicles. Tourism to the park was minimal. And as far as the indigenous population was concerned, all they'd come across so far had been one Ethiopian road gang led by the usual, near ubiquitous, Chinese gang boss. The place was a murderer's paradise.

As Hart watched, the Captain raised his arms, elbows extended.

So he was using binoculars too? Hart couldn't quite see to make sure. Either way, the Captain's full attention seemed focused on the group below him. Hart would never have a better chance.

He rolled out from under the lobelia in one fluid movement, picking up the three-pound stone as he did so.

The Captain turned towards him, his mouth part open, his binoculars at half mast.

Hart launched the stone full force at the Captain's head.

The Captain twisted away from the incoming missile. He threw up one arm to defend himself. The stone missed his hand and caught him on the rear side of the skull, near to the occipital bone, just a fraction to the right of the spinal canal.

The Captain pitched forwards onto his knees.

Hart kicked him between the shoulders, and then once again, as the Captain instinctively curled into a ball, catching him a glancing blow on the right flank. As the Captain crumpled in front of him, Hart dropped to one knee and snatched the pistol that was now clearly visible inside the Captain's belt.

Hart stood up. He aimed the pistol at the Captain's head.

'Get up, you bastard. You must be losing your touch. This is the second weapon I've taken off you in fifteen years.'

Hart was only half conscious of a noise below him and somewhere to his left. It was the sound a branch makes when it snaps in the wind.

Something warm brushed past his head.

Hart turned towards the direction of the noise, his attention no longer on the Captain.

The Captain's Ethiopian guard was shooting at him.

As Hart watched, the snapping noise came again. Hart threw himself to one side. The bullet sliced a frond off the giant lobelia directly in front of him. The vegetation parted as if it had been split by a machete.

Hart sprinted down the hill towards his car. There didn't seem to be a lot else he could do. Stay on the summit, and the Captain's guard would shoot him. Or, worse than that, the Captain would recover from the blow to his head and force Hart to kill him. And given what the guard must think he had seen, Hart could see himself facing half a lifetime in an Ethiopian jail. That would be the crowning irony, wouldn't it? A murderer and rapist like the Captain transformed into a victim and posthumously sanctified.

Hart waded like a spaceman through the scree that littered the downward slope of the hill. When he was somewhere near the bottom he forced himself to slow to a walk. He covered the final few yards to where Rider and Amira were standing in the full knowledge that the Captain's Ethiopian guard might at any moment appear at the top of the hill and take another pot shot at him with his rifle.

'What was that noise?' said Amira. 'It sounded like shots to me.'

Hart glanced towards their own park guard. The man was finishing his second sandwich and sipping from a bottle of Mirinda Orange. He seemed achingly unconcerned by anything he might have heard from the other side of the valley.

Hart raised his voice so that the guard would pick up everything that he was saying. 'It was nothing. Nothing at all. Only another party ahead of us frightening away some baboons. The guard was firing into the air. I saw him through my binoculars.' Hart glanced nervously up the hillside behind him. 'Look, you two. I fancy I've done something rather stupid. I think I've left one of my camera lenses back at the entry post at Gewanē.' Hart made a face. He wasn't good at play-acting, but it was either that or giving the game away by hustling everyone into the car without providing a reason. 'It's a particularly tricky piece of kit to find. And damned expensive. So I'd rather not lose it. Do you mind if we go back the way we came and see if we can locate it?'

Hart kept his back to the guard so the man wouldn't see the expression on his face. To Amira and Rider, it was abundantly clear that something was very wrong. Hart rolled his eyes dramatically to get them to hurry up.

Amira strode back to the car, calling on the guard to accompany them. Rider packed up the remainder of his kit.

In a little more than five minutes they were heading smartly in the opposite direction and back down the road they had arrived on.

'Look,' said Hart. 'Do you see the road that curls away there? Down to the left? Pull over for a moment so that I can have a quick check inside my bag. It would be stupid to drive all the way to Gewanē and find I had the thing with me all the time.'

Rider didn't take much convincing. He pulled off the road and parked five hundred yards along the incline.

Hart told their guard he could remain in the car. He got out and walked a few yards from the vehicle. He squatted down over his lens bag, and pretended to search inside. He waited for Amira and Rider to join him.

'What the hell's going on?' said Amira, when she reached his side. 'Those were shots, weren't they? And don't give me any of that baboon bullshit you foisted on the guard.'

Hart glanced up at her. 'Yes. They were shots. By sheer good luck I managed to brain the Captain with a piece of rock and get his pistol off him. It's tucked beneath my shirt. Here.' He pointed behind himself. 'I had the bastard covered when his park guard started shooting at me. He must have thought I was about to kidnap his precious client. There's no way he could have taken a good look at me, though. I must have been close on five hundred yards from where he was standing. And uphill too. And these guys don't seem to run to telescopic sights, thank God.' Hart jerked his chin back towards the guard in their car, with his open-sighted rifle. 'Do you think Calamity Jane back there will give us any trouble?'

'No. He's clearly used to hearing gunshots. He scarcely flinched. Just carried on eating his sarnie.'

'Incredible,' said Hart. 'Do you think he's deaf?'

'No. Just unmotivated.' Amira straightened up. 'So what's all this baloney about your losing a lens?'

'I wanted to get us away from the road in case the Captain decided to come after us.'

'Hardly likely, now he knows that we're armed,' said Amira. 'You brained him with a stone, you say?'

'Yes,' said Hart. 'I got him a good belt on the back of the head. Then I kicked him. He was all over the place. It was the last thing he expected. I had the pistol off him before he knew what was happening. It's good to know he's mortal like the rest of us. That he can make mistakes.'

'He'll be seriously pissed off,' said Rider.

'My heart bleeds for him.' Hart shouldered his lens bag. The worried expression on his face didn't quite match his defiant words. 'What do you think he'll do now?'

Amira turned to Rider. 'Might he get the guard to report us? Try to nobble us that way?'

Rider shook his head. 'It would be a hard thing to prove. If what Hart says is true, and the guard was five hundred yards away from the action, it will be his word against ours. And nobody was killed.'

'We'd better get rid of the pistol, though,' said Amira. 'That's the only evidence against us.'

'Over my dead body,' said Hart. 'It nearly cost me my neck getting it. And if the Captain talks about the pistol to anyone, he'll be as good as admitting he smuggled it into the country. The police will go through his car with a toothcomb. No. I think we can assume we are still in the clear as far as that goes. The pistol can stand as evidence later when we hand him in. It might be traceable. You never know.'

'And Biljana? Did you see her?' said Amira.

'She's fine,' said Hart. 'Frightened, but fine. I saw the other Serb too. He doesn't seem cut from quite the same boilerplate

367

as the Captain, but who can tell? Take Eichmann. He looked like a postal clerk. But he was personally responsible for managing the logistics of the Holocaust. Either way, we can't afford to leave it too long before making our move.'

'We'll have to leave it until we get out of the park again,' said Rider. 'We can't risk involving these guards in anything else.'

'Fair point,' said Hart. 'Should we go out by a different route from the Captain then? Just in case he can't persuade his guard to keep his trap shut? I mean, what if the guard flags down a police car inside the park and tells them about us?' Hart ran his finger across his throat.

'Then they'd be waiting for us at all the exits.' Rider started back towards the car. 'It wouldn't matter which way we went out. But I don't think the Captain will let him get anywhere near a police car. Reason dictates that he'll be more chary than we are of involving the local authorities because he's got more to lose. Either way, we need to keep following him. He's got two ways of making for Eritrea. The Bure route to the east. And the Adigrat route to the north. No telling which way he'll choose. But in many ways the Bure route would be his better bet. It's shorter. And it leads straight to Assab on the Red Sea coast. A few hours on a ferry from there and he'd be in Mocha.'

'Maybe I gave him a slow-burning brain haemorrhage when I hit him with the rock?' said Hart.

'Yeah,' said Rider. 'Maybe you did.' He grinned. 'And maybe pigs can fly.'

SEVENTY-TWO

Danko stared at Gersem in astonishment. The man was standing on a rock. He had his rifle up to his shoulder and had just fired two single-spaced shots towards where the Captain was located a third of a mile away at the top of the hill.

'Your friend,' Gersem shouted. 'He is being attacked.' Gersem leapt off the rock and began running up the hillside at a speed more suitable for a forty-year-old than for a man well into his sixties.

Danko glanced at Biljana. Then back up the hill. As he did so, he found himself overwhelmed by a sudden revelation. This was it. This was surely it. The moment he had been waiting for for the past fifteen years. Danko understood this more certainly than he had ever understood anything in his life.

'You come with me,' he said to Biljana.

Biljana straightened up. She looked like a fawn that has been spooked by a lion. 'No,' she said. 'Why should I?'

Danko drew the pistol from his belt. 'I am not arguing with you. We have very little time. I am taking you back to your friends. If you do not believe me, I do not care. But you are going with me. Now.'

Biljana stared at him. It was the stare you might give to a vagrant who was trying to convince you that you had just won the national lottery. And, what's more, that he was the man who had been detailed to hold the cheque for you. 'You are going to deliver me back to my friends? What do you take me for? A fool?'

'Hardly that. Get into the car.'

Biljana did as she was told. There was something about Danko's expression that gave an added weight to his words. The man was as scared of the Captain as she was. That much had been clear to her for some time. Maybe he really was looking for a way out of their dilemma? But what did she care? Anything that took her away from the Captain had to be good. If she had ever held any illusions about his position as her father, these had been shattered into a thousand pieces a long time ago.

Once Biljana was safely inside the Renegade, Danko threw himself into the driving seat and engaged gear. He slewed the car round and headed back the way they had come.

Biljana watched him steadily from the passenger seat. 'You're really serious about this, aren't you?'

Danko nodded. 'Absolutely serious. This is our last chance. The last chance for both of us. I am going to trade you for my freedom. So your friends will not pursue me for war crimes. So they will not follow me any more.' Danko's eyes filled with a wild hope, like those of a man reaching for the only remaining tuft of grass at the top of a sheer cliff. 'I want to go back to Serbia. I want to see my family again. I am tired of running. Tired of being a soldier. This is the only way that is left for me.'

'But what about the Captain?'

'What about him? He is insane. If we stay with him we will die. He will bring disaster down on everyone's heads. Just like he has always done. I cannot understand why I ever followed him.' Danko's eyes flashed sideways, as if testing the effect of his words on Biljana. 'I have been a fool. I shall be a fool no longer.'

'Look,' said Biljana. 'Down there to the left. A car.'

'Is that their car?' said Danko. 'Do you recognize it?'

'I think so.'

'Why are they stopping here? Are they mad? Don't they understand who they are dealing with? I thought they would head straight back to Gewanē, and that we would catch up with them there.'

Biljana didn't answer. She felt a sudden sense of doom. As if an unexpected shadow had passed over her on a sunlit day. She turned her head away so that Danko would not see the expression on her face.

Danko steered the SUV along the slip road. He had begun to sweat. His shirt was dripping with it. The back of his neck was slick with perspiration. He wiped both his palms on his trouser legs so that the steering wheel would not slip out of his hands.

He pulled the Renegade up a few yards short of Hart's car. He could see the three of them – Hart, Rider and the woman – what had Biljana called her? – Amira, Amira Eisenberger – clustered in a group together and staring at him. Like alpacas. Yes. Like a herd of alpacas. Their necks all stretched out and quizzical. The man called Hart had a pistol which he was pointing at the Renegade. Danko recognized the pistol. It was the Captain's. Maybe Hart had killed the bastard? Because the Captain wouldn't be an easy man to deprive of his weapon if he was still alive.

Danko drew his own pistol and covered Biljana with it beneath the level of the dashboard. 'Step out of the car. Slowly. Do not try to run or I will shoot you.'

Biljana's eyes went dead. 'But I thought you said you were going to hand me over to them? Why are you pointing your pistol at me again? You've changed your mind, haven't you?'

Danko shook his head. He lowered his voice to an anxious whisper. 'I shall hand you over. Just as I promised. But I need to protect myself first. We need to reach an agreement. All of us. Out in the open.' He motioned to her with his pistol. Then he called out in a loud voice for the others to hear. 'Go on. Over there. I shall slide out afterwards and stand behind you.'

Biljana got out of the Renegade. Danko came after her. He edged round the car, using it to protect himself from Hart.

'The girl is not in any immediate danger.' Danko's voice broke unexpectedly. He was forced to clear his throat like a man with laryngitis. 'I promise you this much. But I want you to lay down your pistol. I am a trained marksman. Which I suspect that you are not. I can easily shoot you from here. Tell your guard to get out of the car too. And to leave his rifle inside. I don't want to see it.'

Hart glanced at Amira. Then he took a further step towards Biljana. 'Are you okay?'

'Yes.' Biljana flapped her hands. 'Please do as he says. He wants to bargain with you. I trust him. I don't want anyone else to be hurt.'

'You trust him?' said Amira. 'He's standing behind you with a pistol to your head and you trust him?'

'Yes. Yes, I do. I know it seems crazy, but I do. He has behaved kindly towards me. He wants a deal.'

Hart could feel the hand of fate descending upon him. It was true. He was certainly no marksman. He'd fired a pistol, as opposed to a rifle, maybe three times in his life. This man could probably shoot him dead before he even took aim with his own weapon. Shoot them all dead. The fact that he hadn't done so yet told Hart something.

He laid his pistol carefully on the ground. Then he beckoned their park guard across from the car. The man eased himself out along the back seat and joined them, leaving his rifle. He didn't seem sorry to be abandoning his weapon. He seemed more bewildered than anything else. As if he was attending the dress rehearsal of a play in which he had a minor part and for which he had long since forgotten the lines.

'Did you kill him?' said Danko.

'Kill who?' said Hart.

'The Captain, of course.'

Hart laughed. The laugh came out as a nervous bark. 'Unfortunately not.'

'How did you get his pistol then?' said Danko. 'I cannot imagine he gave it to you willingly.'

Hart manufactured a grin. He still didn't know whether he was dealing with a maniac of the same ilk as the Captain, or a man who genuinely wanted to parley his way out of a cul-de-sac. 'I belted him on the head with a stone when he wasn't looking.'

'Impossible,' said Danko. 'The Captain would not let himself be bushwhacked by an amateur.'

'I was lucky.' Hart took a few more steps towards him. 'Believe it or not. As you will. It's all the same to me.'

'Stop right there,' said Danko. 'I have Biljana covered. I will not hesitate to shoot her if you give me just cause. Or you, for that matter. I will shoot you in the leg. It will hurt a great deal.'

'You'd better tell us what you want,' said Hart. 'We're none of us comfortable standing out here in the open. How about putting your gun away as a sign of trust? You can easily draw it again before I have time to reach down and pick mine up.'

Danko stepped round Biljana. He slid his pistol inside the waistband of his trousers. 'This okay?'

'It's a start. Now tell us what you want for delivering the girl.'

'He wants his freedom,' said Biljana. 'He wants to know you won't pursue him and cause him to be put on trial for the war crimes he has committed.'

Hart had difficulty suppressing a laugh. 'They've probably got a file on him a foot and a half thick back in The Hague. We can't do anything about that. What's done is done.'

'You could tell them that I am dead,' said Danko. 'You are journalists. They would believe you.'

'What did you die of?' said Hart. 'Remorse?' He scratched his head theatrically. He was feeling more confident by the minute. 'Old age?'

Danko grimaced. The sweat had begun to leach through his T-shirt. More of the garment was wet than was dry. 'I'm sure you can think of something. In fact you must think of something if you want the girl back. Otherwise I will take her with me.'

'And do what?' said Hart. 'Adopt her? It strikes me your heart's not in this any more. If it ever was. Why not get back in your car and take your chances? We'll give you an even break if we can. But we won't lie for you. That would be an insult to your victims.'

Danko took a further step forwards. He appeared to have forgotten about Biljana. 'But you won't actively pursue me?'

Hart shrugged. 'We won't actively pursue you. No.' He glanced at his companions. Rider and Amira nodded their assent. 'Let's face it. It was never you we were after. As far as we're concerned, you're in the clear. Your freedom for the girl's. It's a fair price to pay. But much good it will do you.'

Danko's head exploded like a watermelon that has been cleaved in two by a hatchet. The accompanying rifle crack came a millisecond later.

Hart sprinted towards Biljana and swept her to the ground in a flying rugby tackle. All the colour had drained from her. In the fraction of a second before Hart took her down, she had been staring at what remained of Danko's head with an expression of unmitigated horror.

The front window of Hart's car starred and shattered.

Hart and Biljana took cover behind the Renegade. Rider, Amira and the Ethiopian guard were lying flat on the ground, in full view of whoever was up on the hillside doing the shooting.

Hart didn't doubt for one moment that it was the Captain. He must have overwhelmed his own guard, taken his rifle and made his way across the intervening valley towards them. Hart cursed himself for not having driven further away before stopping to check on his stupid lens. It never did to underestimate a man like the Captain. Look at Danko. Lying there in the dirt with his head blown off. It wasn't a pretty way to die.

Hart eased open the Renegade door. 'Climb inside. Quick. We have to get across to Amira and Rider before the Captain picks them off. He won't expect us to take his car. That's why he smashed the windscreen on mine.'

Hart wriggled across to the driver's seat. Every moment he expected to hear another shot. But nothing came.

Four rounds. Two used on him, one on Danko, and one on the car windscreen. Maybe four rounds was all the park guard had in his magazine? If that was so, they still had a chance.

Hart started the Renegade and engaged gear. He accelerated over to where Amira and Rider and the park guard were lying and threw open the passenger door to cover them. 'Get in. I think he's out of ammo.'

'You're sure of that?'

'We're still alive, aren't we? He would have picked you off otherwise. You were sitting ducks out there.'

'We have to get to our car,' said Rider. 'We need my laptop.'

'Not any more we don't,' said Hart. 'The bastard is probably sprinting down the hillside as we speak. We need to get out of here fast. Let's face it. I may be wrong about the ammo.'

When they were all safely inside the Renegade, Hart sheered away down the valley, leaving Danko and their damaged car behind them.

'Did anyone pocket the car keys?'

'No. They're still inside the car.'

'Damn. We can't risk going back now. We need to make as much time as we can getting out of here. We're ahead of

377

the game for the time being. We've got Biljana. The four of us are intact. It's close to a miracle, given what might have happened.'

'Meanwhile he inherits our guard's rifle, Danko's pistol, which you dropped, and our car.' Amira looked across at their guard. 'How many bullets are there in the magazine you left in the car?'

'Four,' said the guard. 'We are all given four bullets. I do not know why. Maybe to stop us selling them?'

Amira shook her head in mock amazement. 'You were right. There had to be a reason he didn't take us out while we were lying out there in the open. Should we go back? Now we know he's unarmed?'

'He's not unarmed any more.' said Hart. 'He must have reached our car by now and found the rifle our guard left in it. Plus my pistol is lying out there in plain sight. Want to risk it?'

'Hell, no,' said Rider. 'But he's going to regret like hell taking that windscreen out. This country is fifty per cent dust and the rest mud.'

'He probably thought he had half a magazine left when he did it.'

'Yeah.' Rider grinned. 'He would have thought that, wouldn't he? Couldn't have happened to a nicer guy. Shall we head for Gewanē?'

'We cannot go back towards Gewanē,' said Biljana. 'We must check on the other guard. He is called Gersem. He is a good man.'

Hart stared at her. 'What? The guy who just tried to kill me up there on the ridge?'

She nodded. 'He was only doing his duty. He thought you were attacking his client. We cannot leave him. He may be injured.'

Hart glanced at Amira. Then at Rider. Then at their park guard.

When he was through with his inspection, he raised an eyebrow and sighed. 'I'm relieved someone here apart from me still has a moral conscience.'

SEVENTY-THREE

Hart switched to four-wheel drive and aimed the Renegade at the top of the hill on which he'd cold-cocked the Captain. They didn't have a lot of time. But Biljana was right. They couldn't leave the guard alone out there. The man might be badly injured. There were lions living in the National Park, and Ethiopian wolves. Even baboons were known to relish a diet of flesh when they could get hold of it.

'Look. There he is.'

Gersem was stumbling towards them. His face was bloody. He was holding his right arm tightly against his body.

Rider groaned. 'This is going to be a tight fit.'

'Get a grip, Rider. You climb in front with Biljana. Amira knows first aid. She can see to Gersem while we put a bit of distance between ourselves and the Captain.'

'You don't think he'll follow us?' said Rider.

'Yes I do. He's an angry man. He's killed once already.

He'll kill again. He's used to this, remember. Human life means nothing to him. Back in Kosovo, Lumnije and the other women he kept in the rape house used to call him "the superman". Because the bastard never gives up. Because he never loses.'

'I don't buy it,' said Rider. 'If he has any sense he'll get out of the park by the way he came in. Before we have a chance to report him.'

'He knows we're not going to report him.' Hart glanced back at Gersem and the other park guard. 'We've already had far too much collateral damage since Djibouti. He's got a second rifle now, with four slugs in it. And a pistol. If we bring in the authorities there will be a bloodbath. He'll make sure of that. No. I've made my decision and I'm sticking to it. The rest of you can do whatever you want.' He hitched his chin at Amira. 'Is Gersem okay?'

'He'll live,' she said. 'The Captain sucker-punched him when he was expecting a pat on the back. Then our hero kicked him in the side for good measure. Gersem's arm might be fractured. But that's the full extent of the damage.'

Hart fought back a sudden attack of the guilts. The Captain had only done to Gersem what Hart had done to him. The physical parallels were too close for comfort. 'Gersem, listen to me. We can't risk bringing in the local police about this. Do you understand? If the police try to stop the man who struck you, there will be much killing.

And the authorities will more than likely take us in too. On principle. Before we are able to explain how we came to be involved. The Captain is a very bad man indeed.'

'He is an evil man, yes,' said Gersem. He looked at Biljana. 'He and the other man were keeping you prisoner, weren't they? You kept quiet to protect me?'

'They would have killed you,' said Biljana. 'I knew this for certain. That is why I stayed silent.'

Gersem nodded slowly. 'Then I made a very bad mistake. My soul told me something, but I did not listen to it. I should not have shot at your friend.'

'No,' said Biljana. 'You did the right thing. You did what you had to do. We owe you a great deal.'

Hart checked his wing mirrors for any sign of pursuit. After having been the pursuer for so long, he didn't like the switchback feeling of being pursued. Especially not as the man behind him possessed a rifle capable of killing someone at more than a mile, together with the will to do it. 'Gersem. I need to ask you and your companion something. A favour. A big favour.'

Gersem looked up. Amira had bandaged his head. She had also fashioned a sling for him out of the Mexican *rebozo* she had been wearing. It gave him a devil-may-care air. Like a latter-day pirate. 'I am listening to you.'

'If we drop you off before we reach the park exit. In a nearby village, say. Will you give us a little time before you call in what has happened? Time to entice the Captain away from the park? To ensure that no more innocent people are drawn into this?'

'What do you intend to do?'

Hart glanced at the others. 'I intend to lure him as far away from civilization as I possibly can. Well outside the National Park area, anyway. Up into the mountains somewhere. Along the way I'm going to drop these three off. Somewhere safe. Where they can rest up.'

'But he has Fikre's rifle. He will kill you from a distance.'

'There's an automatic weapon hidden in the back of this vehicle,' said Hart. 'What they call an assault rifle. I've seen it. And a sawn-off shotgun. I also pocketed back his pistol. That's more than enough artillery for what I need to do.'

'And what will you do?' said Gersem.

'I'm going to set up an ambush.'

'And you are going to kill him,' said Biljana. 'You are going to kill my father.'

Hart reached across to her, but Biljana turned away from him.

'Biljana, I have no choice,' he said. 'You must understand this. You've seen what he's capable of. Look what he just did to Danko. What if I promise to try and take him alive if I can? If he'll let me?' Hart glanced up from his driving, but Biljana wouldn't meet his eyes.

Hart switched his attention from Biljana to Gersem. He could see Gersem's face in his rear-view mirror. The man exuded an acute intelligence. As different from the

383

other guard beside him as it was possible to be.

'Have you heard of a place called Debre Damo?' said Gersem.

Hart shook his head. He glanced at the others. They shook their heads too.

'No. Why do you ask?'

'This is the sort of place you must lead him to. If you are sure he will follow. I can guide you there.'

'You? Guide us? Why would you do that?' said Hart.

Gersem lowered his gaze. But not before Hart saw him looking at Biljana. There was gratitude in his eyes. Gersem knew that the girl had been trying to protect him. To save his life at the risk of her own.

'What is Debre Damo, Gersem?'

'It is a monastery. An ancient monastery.' Gersem crossed himself. 'High on a hillside near the Eritrean border. The only way up is by a rawhide rope. A monk holds one end of the rope in a hut fifty metres high, jutting from the wall of the hill. The climbing man holds the other part. You scramble up a sheer cliff. There is no other way up or down.'

'What's up there when you've done the climb?' said Hart.

'An ancient church. Many cells in which the monks live.' Gersem's gaze turned inwards, as if he were picturing the monastery in his mind's eye. 'There is good cover. Few people. No woman has ever been allowed on top of the mountain since the monastery was built by Abuna Aregawi fifteen hundred years ago. So the Captain cannot take hostages.

The monks, for themselves, will not mind to die. They are close to God anyway.'

'Why there, Gersem?' said Hart. 'Why there in particular?'

Gersem half inclined his head. 'My brother is a monk at Debre Damo. If we climb to the top, we can talk to him. I may be injured but it might be possible to pull me up, with the rope beneath my arms. When I tell my brother about the Captain, he will arrange it so the Captain can climb up too. Then we will have him. It will be impossible for him to escape. How can he climb up with a rifle on his back? And with both hands occupied, how will he be able to defend himself?'

Hart shrugged. But he could feel hope burgeoning inside him. 'The monks will hardly let me climb up with an assault rifle on my back either.'

'But a pistol?' said Gersem. 'This they will not see. And if I am drawn up behind you? With the shotgun concealed in my *gabi*?'

Hart laughed. 'Your brother will never forgive you.'

Gersem grinned. 'My brother is a pragmatic man. As are all monks. When he sees what the Captain has done to me, he will soon forgive and forget.'

SEVENTY-FOUR

They dropped Fikre off at a village on the edge of the National Park. Gersem had spoken to him at length in Amharic. By the end of the conversation, Gersem assured them that Fikre would hold his tongue just so long as they promised him his rifle back, together with the four cartridges the park authorities had allocated him to protect his tourists. He feared for his job otherwise. He had a large family to support. And he had no other source of income. As far as the dead man was concerned, he had seen and heard nothing.

When Amira gave him fifty dollars with which to tide himself over, Fikre put both hands up to his eyes and saluted her.

'Three days,' he said. 'I will be silent for three days. Is this sufficient?'

'If it isn't, we're in serious trouble,' said Rider.

'Aren't we forgetting something?' said Amira. 'What about Danko's body?'

'If I know the Captain,' said Hart, 'he will have settled that little matter for us. He's hardly likely to leave a man's carcase around if it might remotely lead the authorities back to him. I know there wasn't much left of Danko's face. But do you remember? They photocopied all our passports at the border crossing before they gave us our visas. I'm sorry to seem morbid, but I'm pretty sure there was enough left of Danko for a positive description.' He flashed a glance at Biljana in the rear-view mirror to see how she was taking his words. 'No. By now Danko is pushing up the daisies somewhere. Or his corpse is feeding a pack of baboons. I can't pretend I'm mourning him. God alone knows how many people he raped and killed during the Kosovo War. Backdated remorse is all very well, but it doesn't mend bullet holes and broken hearts.'

Rider cleared his throat. 'So what do we do about my tracker?' He pointed under the seat. 'The Captain has inherited my laptop. If he's halfway computer literate he'll be able to follow us just as we followed him.'

'That's a question I've been meaning to ask you,' said Hart, turning to Biljana. He was still treating her with kid gloves. Her relationship with her father was a psychological minefield. 'Just how did the Captain manage to overlook our tracker?'

'I stuck it down my pants,' she said.

Amira burst out laughing.

Biljana surprised them all by grinning in return. 'He'd already searched me. So I pretended I was bawling my eyes out and hid the tracker. Then when he ransacked the car he couldn't find it. He thought you'd all been incredibly clever and hidden one in Danko's car instead.'

'Credit where credit's due,' said Amira. 'That was a moment of pure genius, Biljana.'

'Agreed,' said Hart.

Rider shook his head. 'Genius or no genius, all I know is that when the Captain finds out the tracker's still switched on, he's not going to take long to twig that we want him to follow us. We've underestimated him before. Once bitten twice shy, I say.'

Hart grunted in affirmation. 'What else can we do? We can't bear down on him head on. He's got a rifle. All we can do is lead him away and hope that he's so pissed off he will decide to follow us.'

'And what if he doesn't?' said Rider.

'Then we've lost him. It's a risk we'll have to take.' Hart grinned. 'But we have Biljana back. Which means that we're already ahead of the game. Why not look on the bright side for a change, Eeyore?' Hart fixed Rider with a gimlet eye. 'If the man gives up and goes off in a huff, we might even manage to make it out of this country with our necks intact.'

SEVENTY-FIVE

The Captain dragged Danko's body into the defile. He spent a moment looking at what was left of Danko's face. Then he reached across for a stone and pounded the remainder of the face into pulp. When he was finished, he blocked up the entrance to the defile with rocks, leaving just enough room for an animal the size of a fox, or maybe of a small baboon, to squeeze through and luck into a free meal.

The Captain found a bottle of water in Hart's car and rinsed his hands. Then he wrapped a towel around his fist and smashed out what remained of the windscreen. He drank some of the water and checked the state of his armaments. Four rifle bullets. Four. Whose sorry idea was that? What sort of an asshole gives you four bullets in a magazine that should take a dozen? He could have been killed. Still. Four were better than nothing when push came to shove.

The Captain checked Danko's Beretta. Thirteen Parabellum rounds in that one. Unlucky for some. The Beretta 92SB semi-automatic pistol used to be issued to US marines before they switched to the 92FS. You couldn't buy it in gun shops any more but it was easily available on the black market if you knew where to look. The Captain was more than capable of a ten-shot, three-inch grouping at fifty metres. Not as good as Danko's numbers, but good nonetheless. And Danko sure as hell wouldn't be taking his marksmanship skills with him to wherever he was going next.

The Captain stared down at his right arm. It was damaged, that much was for sure. How bad was hard to say. Hart had kicked him hard in the scapula as he was going down. Now the whole of the arm was numb. Painful and numb. Although you would have thought that the two things were contraindicatory.

The Captain's head, too, was damaged. The back of his neck felt tender. Swollen and tender. And he had a splitting headache. Heads do that if you pelt them with heavy stones.

He searched out the woman's suitcase. Yes. Here were some Advil. You could always count on women to have strong painkillers somewhere around.

The Captain took four and chugged the rest of the water alongside them.

He would enjoy taking his revenge on Hart. The man had the luck of the devil. He had an uncanny knack of getting himself into the right spot at the right time. But he'd never once faced up to the Captain man to man. That would have a very different outcome. Take away the luck and Hart was just a sorry journalist with no skills beyond camera-clicking. The Captain had spent the past twenty years hard-training his body and working on his frame of mind. No contest.

The Captain powered up the laptop. It didn't take him long to find out that it belonged to someone called Leo Percival Rider. And that Rider must have been online when Hart had told him to leave his laptop alone and get into the huddle the Captain had found the trio in a few minutes before he'd shot Danko through the ear. With a few taps of his finger, the Captain ordered Rider's computer to remember its new password, just in case the laptop powered down unexpectedly.

Another five minutes online and the Captain was following Rider's tracker programme.

'Fuck,' said the Captain. 'How the hell did she do that?'

The tracker in the Renegade was still *in situ* and communicating. And yet he had gone over the vehicle with a fine toothcomb. He was near to one hundred per cent certain that he hadn't missed anything. The only possible way for him to have missed the tracker was if Biljana had been concealing it about her person. Hmmm. What had Sherlock Holmes said? 'When you have eliminated the impossible, whatever remains, however improbable, must be the truth.'

So that's what must have happened.

The Captain smiled. Maybe Biljana was a chip off the old block after all?

Now that he was on the road again, the Captain found the wind buffeting through the smashed windscreen bracing, to say the least. And when he passed the occasional car travelling in the opposite direction, the dust swirled and jigged around the cabin as if he had stumbled into the eye of a sandstorm. The prospect of a sudden rain squall didn't bear thinking about.

Two hours of such self-imposed hell was enough. The Captain had just passed through Mile when he saw the nearly new Mazda CX-9 by the side of the road. He pulled over onto the hard shoulder. He sat in the car for a moment staring at the Mazda. Why shouldn't he steal it and make straight for the Eritrean border? And to hell with Hart, Biljana and the rest of them. He had close on sixteen thousand dollars rainy-day cash with him, tucked away inside a money belt. And when that was gone he could steal some more.

But would Hart and the others leave him be? Hardly likely at this late stage in the game.

The Captain watched the Mazda as if it might tell him something.

Biljana. His daughter. What of her?

Well. When it came down to it, he could take her or leave her. Blood didn't mean a damned thing to him. If it had been more convenient to kill her at any stage over the past few days, he would undoubtedly have done so. Was he angry in retrospect about her tricking him over the tracker? Hardly.

In her eyes she'd been doing the right thing. But he was detached. Yes. That was the way he felt. Detached.

So it came back to Hart. As it always did. The man had dogged him all those years ago, and he was dogging him again now. It was Hart who had forced him to leave the Legion. Hart who had made him shoot Danko. Okay. Danko may not have been much to write home about, but he had been the Captain's creature. And Hart had forced him to turn on the one man he owed loyalty to. A fellow Serb. A man he had history with. The Captain found he minded. Considerably.

The Captain watched the Mazda some more. Pretty soon the owners would come back. Then he would need to decide. He'd let it come down to a mathematical equation. Simple as that.

He heard their voices first, through his smashed windscreen. American voices. First a man's, then a woman's. Next, a foreign voice, speaking broken English. Probably the Ethiopian park guard. Then the first man's voice again. A man, a woman, and the park guard. The maths didn't add up.

Then he saw the second man. Walking a few yards behind the first three. Taking photos. Stopping every now and then to frame something using his thumbs and forefingers. Pretentious bastard. Just like that idiot Hart.

Well. That did it. The maths added up.

The Captain got out of his car and strolled towards the approaching party. Thinking, as he did so. Weighing up the odds of what he was about to do.

He glanced around. No cars approaching. Nobody visible. He could feel the excitement building deep inside his gut. Just as he had felt in the run-up to the Srebrenica Massacre.

'Hi,' he said, raising one arm. 'Can I ask you guys a favour? I've had an accident.' He pointed towards his shattered windscreen. 'A stone fell off a cliff and bounced through my screen. It hurt me on the arm too.' He pointed to his right hand, which he had tucked inside the middle two buttons of his shirt. 'It hurts me to drive. Can I possibly hitch a lift with you to the next outpost of civilization?'

The woman was the first to reply. Needing to please, thought the Captain. Needing the approbation of the men.

'Sure. That's okay. Isn't it, Hank?'

Hank was the alpha male of the party. That much was clear.

'For a ten-buck tip, I'm sure our guard will drive your car on ahead of us, windshield or no windshield,' said Hank. 'In fact, he'll probably throw in his sister for free.'

'*Hank!*'

The Captain privately reckoned that the woman probably called this man *Hank!* in that fake-outraged tone of voice maybe a hundred times a day. Multiply that by, say, a period of ten years, and you had three hundred and sixty-five thousand outraged *Hanks!* under your belt before you knew it. Well, she was truly off the hook now.

The Captain shot Hank in the face. Next he shot the photographer. It was a longer shot, but he got him high on the temple, well within the Legion's three-inch grouping, given that he'd been using the man's right-hand eye as his target. The woman turned round and began running, her arms and legs windmilling in panic. She looked like a moving swastika.

The Captain shot the park guard lower down in the body. No need to disguise this one's identity. In fact better to keep him clean. The first shot took him through the lungs. The second through the heart.

The woman was thirty yards away by now and accelerating with each passing second. Maybe she was a jogger? Maybe she and Hank – *Hank!* – went out jogging together in the early mornings, when the air was fresh, and there weren't too many people out yet, pre-breakfast? One thing the Captain knew for certain. Hank would never, ever, have let this woman overtake him. Hank would always have needed to be the number one. Just like he'd been number one to die. Being the alpha male was a hell of a responsibility. You had to live up to it right to the end.

The Captain took the woman right at the edge of the invisible fifty-yard ring he had constructed in his mind. Straight through the back of the head. Straight through the occipital lobe and on through the temporal lobe and far into the cerebral cortex. It was a fair shot, given that she was a moving target. God alone knew what the front of her face now looked like. These Parabellum cartridges were neat going in, but they made one heck of a mess coming out. Mushrooming, the pinheads called it. Sick bunch of bastards.

Now that the four were safely dead, the Captain raised his game a little. He got into Hart's car and backed towards the first three bodies. He piled them onto the rear seat. What with each corpse's dead weight, though, and his own damaged arm, it wasn't an easy trick to pull off. He was sweating by the time he had finished. His injured arm felt as if it had been picked apart, sinew by sinew.

Next he hefted the woman's body and placed her in the front seat, after inching forwards so that he wouldn't have to manhandle her on her back through the dirt. When she was safely in place he continued on a couple of hundred yards towards the cliff edge and parked.

Now that he was out of sight of the road he switched the four of them round, like you would seat people at a dinner party, eventually putting Hank in the driving seat. Appropriate, that.

'Hank!' he shouted, in a high-pitched, mock-outraged voice. '*Hank!*' Yes. He had her voice down to a T.

The Captain collected up the passports and placed them in his jacket pocket. The woman, just as he'd figured, had been married to Hank. The third man was the gooseberry. The audience. Because a guy like Hank would always need an audience. Someone he could show off in front of. A gallery he could play to. And – the Captain checked the woman's passport – Loren would have been more than happy to join in with his power games. That had been her kick, surely. Endlessly stomaching Hank. Complaining about him to her girlfriends. *He's so dominant. You wouldn't believe what he makes me do.* Whisper. Whisper.

When he was finished with his arranging the Captain made sure all four bodies were securely fastened into place. And that their faces were messed up enough to puzzle the authorities. Especially when they were handed John Gilbert Hart's, Leo Percival Rider's and Amira Elizabeth Eisenberger's passports on a plate. He also pocketed the deceased park guard's four extra cartridges. That gave him eight now. Eight long case shells. A whole lot better than nothing.

He took Hank's car keys and Hank's cash. The guy must have been an old-fashioned type, because he still used American Express traveller's cheques. The Captain confirmed Hank's signature in his passport and matched it against the signature on the cheques. Yes. Not too hard to fake. He'd cash the cheques in another country first chance he had. Because traveller's cheques are eternal. And they never ever bounce. At least according to American Express.

When he was through, the Captain tore up one of the woman's blouses and fed it down the fuel tank. When he was sure the far end was drenched, he switched ends and left the drenched end hanging out about two feet down the side of the car.

He turned on the engine and let off the handbrake. The car edged towards the lip of the cliff. But the Captain had judged it well. He could control the car with little more than a shove from his still good left arm.

He lit his lighter and touched it to the end of the fuel-soaked blouse. Then he hurried to the rear of the car and shunted it, full force, with his good shoulder.

The car teetered on the lip of the cliff and tipped over the edge.

The Captain backed off fast in case the fumes from the fuel ignited too early.

The car careened down the cliff, bouncing higher and higher as it gained pace. Halfway down there was a whoosh, followed by an explosive crump. The car was alight.

It gathered speed, jumping and careering over boulders and outcrops, twisting and jinking like a cat with a burning newspaper tied to its tail.

About two hundred yards down, the gradual incline turned into a full, perpendicular ascent. The car fishtailed end on end, thick gouts of smoke billowing in its wake.

The Captain lost sight of it.

There was a long period of silence, and then the car exploded somewhere beyond his sightline. Around him, the birds fell silent. The Captain could feel the heat of the plateau like a lover's arms pressed tightly against the back of his neck.

He felt for the four cartridges in his pocket.

As he walked back towards the Mazda he played with them, like Humphrey Bogart with his stress relievers in *The Caine Mutiny*.

'Eeny meeny miny moe,' he sang, fingering the cartridges one after the other. 'Catch a tiger by his toe. If he hollers, don't let go. Eeny meeny miny moe.'

SEVENTY-SIX

Hart's party spent the night at a town called Qwiha, about four hours by road from their final destination of Debre Damo. By that time they'd been driving for sixteen hours straight, and no one was in the mood to hurry on fate.

They had decided between them that they would give it another twenty-four hours. If the Captain didn't follow them to Debre Damo, then they would call the embassy and put the gears into motion. But each of them knew that if the Captain had decided to make a break for Eritrea, any such action would be way too late. He'd be across and free by nightfall of the next day. The important thing, though, was that they had Biljana. The Captain could wait. Without the protection of the Legion he would be that much easier to trace. The Legion would have photographs of him, which could be published in the newspapers. It would be only a matter of time after that.

After a brief discussion, Hart, Rider and Gersem agreed to split the guard duty between them. Amira didn't argue. Her brand of feminism had always been invested with a certain degree of enlightened pragmatism. What suited her, suited her. What didn't, didn't. And Biljana had never fired a gun in her life. And couldn't, furthermore, be expected to take up arms against her biological father. So that ruled her out from the start.

Hart took first watch. He sat outside in the Renegade, the assault rifle cradled across his lap, his eyes like a lion's, half open. The hotel's car park had been designed to take upwards of three hundred cars. There were four cars in it. So maybe the rest of the empty places were for weddings? Festivals? Stuff like that? Either way it was convenient, as Hart had a 360-degree clear view in every direction. No one could sneak up on him. The nearest anyone could lie up to take a shot was 150 yards away. And with no lighting in the parking area, they'd have trouble finding a target unless Hart was crazy enough to switch on the interior light and strike a pose.

For whatever reason, though, Hart chose to sit in the back seat, with his head well off to one side and partially protected by the metal struts holding the rear screen in place. If the Captain took a pot shot at the driver's seat, he'd at least have some warning. And Gersem had the sawn-off shotgun, while Rider had the Captain's Beretta. No single man was going to rush that hotel room and get away with his hide intact.

Despite all these precautions, Hart still felt furiously exposed. What if a coach party suddenly pulled in? Or a group of partygoers returning from a local knees-up? Such things always happened when you least expected them. He'd be a sitting duck.

Hart thought back to what he knew about the Captain. The time he'd spent with the man when they were dragging Lumnije's unconscious body through the undergrowth back in Kosovo all those years ago. How had he got from there to here? And how were people like the Captain created in the first place? Could a man be solely motivated by greed and lust? Wouldn't self-consciousness cut in somewhere and leaven the mess? Maybe the Captain was what they called a pure psychopath? Or was that simply a copout? Maybe he just enjoyed it? Most men, if they were honest with themselves, fantasized at some time or other about being given carte blanche in the sexual arena. Maybe, if he'd been brought up surrounded by violence – or if violence had been the key to advancement in his profession – he'd have been tempted by a get-out-of-jail-free card too?

Hart almost missed the flicker of movement at the very edge of his vision. He opened his eyes as wide as they could go and focused on the same spot again. Nothing happened.

Hart reached up and deactivated the interior light. Then he cracked the back door on the side away from where he'd seen the movement and slipped out of the car.

Maybe it had been a cat? Or some night animal, perhaps? Whatever it had been, he suddenly didn't feel safe locked inside a metal pod, at night, in the middle of a vast sea of emptiness. He needed some elbow room.

He crawled round the car until he had the place where he'd seen the movement back in sight again. He crouched beside the rear tyre, with the assault rifle cradled against his cheek.

How had he allowed himself to be spooked like that? The Captain wouldn't just ignore the Renegade and go reconnoitre the hotel room, would he? With anyone concealed in the Renegade calmly monitoring his back? He wasn't that stupid.

The feral dog broke cover and trotted out into the open. Another dog followed it. The two of them did a sort of dance round each other. Then the bigger of the two dogs climbed onto the back of the smaller one and began thrusting away.

Hart muffled a groan. Great. Now here he was, outside the safety of the car, an assault rifle clamped to his ear, watching two dogs having sex.

Hart heard the crunch of gravel about eighty yards to his left. *Not again*, he found himself thinking. *Why does this always happen to me while crouched down behind inadequate cover?*

He eased himself to his feet and laid the assault rifle silently across the Renegade's roof, with his cheek to the stock.

Yes. It was the Captain. Moving towards the Renegade, the rifle steady in his hands. At what the military would call the porte-arms position. Meaning you were ready to fire at the drop of a hat.

Hart squinted along the rifle. Even though there was little light, it was more than enough to make out the Captain's silhouette.

One of the dogs howled and the Captain stopped dead in his tracks.

You crafty son-of-a-bitch, thought Hart. *You saw the dogs. You knew they would take the attention of whoever was in the Renegade. And you reckoned you would take advantage and creep up behind them and take them out.*

Hart was never going to get a better sitting target than this, the Captain frozen to the spot in the middle of a third of an acre of empty concrete. Like a tin duck at a fairground.

He squeezed the trigger.

Nothing happened.

Hart tried again.

The trigger was immoveable.

Hart felt frantically for the safety catch. He switched it backwards and forwards. Tried both ways. Nothing. The rifle might as well have been a block of ice.

The dogs had drifted apart by this time. As if they had never met. The male dog went one way, the female dog another.

The Captain was moving towards him again.

'Freeze!' shouted Hart.

Which is pretty much what had happened to his rifle.

404

The Captain reacted instantly. He dodged to the left and then zigzagged back towards the heavy cover at the outer edges of the car park.

Hart tried again with the rifle. No go.

The two dogs were pelting off in opposite directions. It was almost comical. The Captain headed one way, the two dogs another. Hart hunching over the Renegade with a useless rifle in his hand.

'Get back inside,' he yelled, when he saw Gersem and Rider, alerted by his shout, standing by the opened door of the hotel room. 'And cut the fucking lights. You're sitting ducks.'

He slid into the Renegade and gunned the car across the car park. He stopped outside the door of the room. Every moment he expected the sudden shattering of glass beside him. The numbing blow of a deformed slug tearing through his face.

'Get in, everybody. We've got to leave. Now.'

Nobody asked any questions. Nobody froze. They knew each other – and the situation in which they found themselves – too well for that. They'd prepared for it by leaving all their possessions in the car. The women's faces were serious and drawn. Still half asleep.

'I'll drive,' said Amira. 'You men can get some sleep when we're clear of the area.'

They took off out of town without a backward glance.

Hart sat in the passenger seat, the rifle cradled between his knees, shaking his head.

'What happened?' Amira said at last.

'I saw him,' said Hart. 'Creeping up on the Renegade. He'd chosen his moment well. By pure luck I was outside the vehicle—'

'Taking a piss…' said Rider.

'Whatever,' said Hart. 'It little matters. What does matter is that I had the Captain in my sights and I didn't hesitate. I took the shot.'

'Why's he not dead then?' said Rider.

'Because the rifle froze. That's the only way I can describe it. The damned thing froze on me.'

'You probably had the safety on,' said Rider. 'Happens all the time.'

'No,' said Hart. 'Not this time. I tried the safety both ways. Nothing doing.'

'Bullshit,' said Rider. 'You're just covering your arse. Here. Hand the thing to me.'

Hart handed the assault rifle to Rider. Rider stared at it. Finally he cracked the window and aimed the rifle outside. 'Cover your ears.'

He pulled the trigger. Nothing happened.

Then he flipped the safety and tried again.

Still nothing happened.

He slid out the magazine, tapped it a few times, checked that there were bullets in it and went through the firing process again.

'You're right,' he said. 'This gun is frozen. Shame we never had a chance to give it a test run. The bloody thing is useless. Maybe it's one of those replica thingies? Maybe it's not a real gun at all? Maybe the Captain just used it to frighten people?'

'No it is not,' said Gersem. 'It is a real gun. Give it to me, please.'

Rider handed the rifle to Gersem. Gersem ran his fingers around the position of the safety catch. 'Yes. Here.' He showed the rifle to Rider. 'You see this small hole?'

'Yes. What is it?'

'During the 1990s,' said Gersem, 'certain arms manufacturers began fitting their guns with a locking mechanism. It was designed to protect children who found the rifle and thought it was a toy. The lock must be deactivated by a special key before the gun may be fired.'

'A trigger lock,' said Rider. 'Yes. I've heard of them.'

'Well, I haven't,' said Hart. 'When the thing didn't fire I nearly shat myself. I can't take too many more shocks like that to my system.'

'You were going to kill my father,' said Biljana. 'Just like you would kill a deer.'

'I had no choice,' said Hart. 'He was armed and approaching my position.' He turned round and stared at her. 'Listen to me, Biljana.' He cleared his throat a couple of times. He was not on comfortable ground. But he knew that he needed to get his point across now to avoid a tragedy further down the line. 'There's one major difference between your father and a deer.'

'And what is that?' said Biljana, with a disbelieving shrug, as if she thought Hart might be about to attempt an inappropriate joke.

'Deer don't shoot back,' he said.

SEVENTY-SEVEN

They drove most of that day on a mixture of dirt roads and ungraded tarmacadam. Road gangs were everywhere. Thirty or so Ethiopian workmen would be overseen by one or two Chinese. It was clear that in ten years' time the Ethiopians would have a halfway decent road system. Meaning that these same Chinese could then rape their country of whatever remained of its natural resources, Hart decided. Ethiopia, like Thailand, had largely avoided the colonial axe. But these newly fledged neocolonial executioners, chopper in hand, camo paint firmly in place, were sure as hell creeping up on her by the back door.

In the meantime, the existing roads were poor to catastrophic. Around midday the rain began to fall. Even the Renegade, with its four-wheel drive, slewed across the rain-slick road like a tap dancer negotiating an olive oil spillage. There was much jubilation in Hart's party at the thought of what the Captain must be having to endure with his shattered windscreen. Only Biljana kept herself apart from the forced levity. A part of her was still in shock, unwilling to fully believe the extent of the Captain's perfidy. She never went as far as making excuses for him, but neither did she appear to relish the prospect of his downfall.

By mid-afternoon they were still thirty kilometres short of Debre Damo. The rain was sheeting down like blood from a ruptured artery. Gersem indicated a track off to their left.

'We go country road now,' he said.

'Country road?' said Rider. 'What do you call the roads we've been surfing down so far? Highways?'

Gersem held his hand up to his mouth and laughed uproariously. 'These are big roads. Major roads. Now we find bad one.'

Watching the interplay between Gersem and Rider, it suddenly occurred to Hart that there would be no more stops from now on in. No more breaks. This was it. Once they committed to this road there would be no turning back for any of them.

'Does this track lead anywhere beyond Debre Damo?' he said.

'No,' said Gersem. 'Road end there. Eritrea a few kilometres further on. Many military. Impossible go further.'

'Military, you say?'

Gersem made a face. 'Maybe you call these militia, not military. Mostly are local people with rifles. In case the

Eritreans come across the Tigrayan Mountains and attack fresh time.' Gersem made a cutting motion across his throat and down along his chest. 'These Eritreans very bad. They take our country. We not like them. People fight.'

Hart stopped the car. He looked round at the faces of his friends. The engine ticked away in the background like fate's timepiece.

'We're a democracy,' he said. 'Right? Here in this car?'

'Right,' said Rider. He answered so fast that there was no chance that he'd had time to think about Hart's words, let alone what they might mean.

'Right,' said Amira. 'So what do you expect us to do? Take a vote on something? At this stage in the proceedings? You must be joking.'

Hart looked momentarily taken aback. 'I thought you just agreed we were a democracy?'

Amira shook her head in mock despair. 'Despite all that's happened to you over the past few years – all the scrapes you've got yourself into and, more importantly, that you've slithered out of – you still persist in misunderstanding yourself. And, even worse than that, you persist in misunderstanding everyone else around you.'

Hart made a face. 'How do you mean?'

Amira hunched forwards. 'You're good at what you do, John. Surprisingly good.' She registered Hart's shocked face – he wasn't used to receiving compliments from her. She hurried on, not wishing to lose her temporary advantage.

'I mean you think on your feet. Instinctively. No need for a bloody vote.' She sat back triumphantly. 'Twice you've nearly put one over on the Captain. Twice. Something I'd have thought impossible before we set out on this charivari. We need you to continue doing it.'

'Charivari?' said Hart.

'A mock serenade,' said Rider. 'An elaborate way of taking the piss out of something.'

'Amira?' said Hart, rolling his eyes in disbelief.

'Shut the fuck up, Rider,' said Amira. 'You could complicate Armageddon.'

There was a sustained silence. Everybody was uncomfortable with it. But no one wanted to be the first to break it.

'What I'm really saying,' continued Amira, after the prolonged pause had gone beyond uncomfortable, 'is that we want you to decide for us. Since Danko's death this whole thing has taken on the quality of a nightmare. We are all exhausted. Physically and mentally. You started this thing, all those years ago in Kosovo. We need you to finish it.' She held up one hand to stop Hart interrupting. 'We have been leading a homicidal maniac by the nose around a country none of us except Gersem either knows or understands. Now we appear to have backed ourselves into a corner. The Captain may or may not be after us. Personally, after last night's fiasco, I very much hope that he's broken away and made for Eritrea. But I suspect that he hasn't. You've humiliated him on two separate occasions now. He got back at you once by executing Danko in front of Biljana and your friends. He'll want to get his own back on you again. Which means that Biljana is still vulnerable. And will remain so until he's out of the game. Because how best can he harm you?'

'Through her,' said Hart. His voice sounded tired. As if it was struggling out from under an extreme weight.

'You bet.' Amira glanced at Biljana to see if she was listening.

Biljana's eyes were steady and straight. Her entire attention focused on Hart.

Hart stared down the road behind them.

'Yes. He's coming,' said Amira, catching the direction of his gaze. 'You can count on it. He's probably only a mile or two behind us as we speak. Look at this road. Our car is loaded to the gills. His car, even though it doesn't have four-wheel drive, is carrying just one person. He'll have made time on us coming up here. And he has a rifle. If he gets up on one of these...' She hesitated.

'*Ambas*. These hills are called *ambas*,' said Gersem.

'If he gets up on one of these *ambas*, he can cover the road a kilometre ahead of him. He can pin us down.'

'Even with four bullets?'

'If even one hits home, he'll have us.'

Hart put the car into gear and began driving again. 'You say they don't let women climb up to the monastery?'

413

'No,' said Gersem. 'No woman, not even a female animal, has been on the plateau for sixteen hundred years.'

Hart shook his head in disbelief. 'Is there anywhere else we can leave them then?'

'You mean like a hotel? Or a guest house?' said Gersem.

'Yes.'

'There is nowhere like that,' said Gersem. 'There is just a village with a few huts. This is not a tourist place.'

Amira's words had spooked Hart, as they were meant to. They had also galvanized him into action. He kept looking in the rear-view mirror as if he expected the Captain to appear behind them at any moment. 'Anywhere near the monastery then? Someone's house maybe?'

'No,' said Gersem. He cocked his head to one side as though it might facilitate his thinking. 'But there is a tomb.'

'A tomb?'

'They bring bodies there,' said Gersem. 'People who want to be buried near the monastery because it is a well-known holy place. Both men and women can be buried there. It is near to the spot where we climb up. It is not a pleasant place. But people could hide in there. It is very big.'

'Rider?' said Hart.

'Yes?'

'Have you found the key yet?'

'The key?' said Rider.

'To the assault rifle.'

'Yes, boss,' said Rider, snapping out a mock salute. 'It was in a zipped compartment in the sleeve. Shame we didn't think to look in there before you got the drop on the bastard.'

'Can you use a rifle?' Hart said.

'Can I shoot, you mean?' Rider made a face. 'If I have to. I believe they trusted me with a .303 Lee Enfield once while I was still at school. The one time they let us into Bisley for some sort of inter-schools competition. This one here on my lap can't be much different. Trigger. Magazine. Firing pin. What's not to like?'

Hart rolled his eyes.

Amira caught the look. 'I can use a rifle too.'

'Right.' Hart nodded his head emphatically. 'Then you three hide in the tomb. I will climb up onto the plateau with the pistol and then I will get a couple of the monks to help me drag Gersem up with the sawn-off shotgun hidden about his person. There's only the one way up to the top, right?'

'Yes,' said Gersem. 'Only one way.'

'And your brother is up there?' said Hart.

'Yes.'

'Well,' said Hart. 'You wanted a plan. That's it.' He negotiated his way round a particularly pernicious hole in the road. 'Will we make Debre Damo before nightfall?'

'Yes,' said Gersem. 'We should be up there before it gets dark. This will be to our advantage. If the Captain follows us, he will be highlighted against the setting sun. We will have the protection of the hut on the cliff face. He will need both his arms to climb.' Gersem's voice tailed off. He wasn't convincing anybody, not least himself.

'The moment he starts up,' said Rider, 'I can emerge from the tomb and cover him from the bottom. I'll let him climb up about ten yards, so he'll be really vulnerable. He'll have no choice but to chuck down his pistol and give himself up.'

'Will the three of them be well enough concealed inside the tomb?' said Hart. 'Are you sure of this?'

'Yes. There are many catafalques,' said Gersem. 'Many hidden corners. It would take a man much time to investigate them all. Especially in the dark. There is no electricity anywhere in the valley.'

'What if he brings a torch with him?'

'Still.'

'And I'll have taken him prisoner by then anyway,' said Rider. 'My assault rifle to his blunderbuss. Hey, Amira. If the newspapers call Hart "the Templar", what will they decide to call me after you've written me up in your piece?'

'My encomium, you mean?' said Amira. 'The piece of hagiography I will design especially around you?'

'Yes,' said Rider.

'The "Tosser",' said Amira. 'Nothing else would be remotely appropriate.'

SEVENTY-EIGHT

The Captain glanced down at Rider's laptop on the seat beside him. It looked to him as if Hart and his party must have stopped once again for the night.

The Captain typed in a request for an accurate position. The computer came back with the words *Debre Damo*. The Captain Googled the place. After a moment he laughed out loud.

'Clever bastard,' he said. 'Talk about a cul-de-sac. You must have known about this somehow, John Hart. No one comes across a place like this accidentally. Not even you have that much luck.'

He read some more about Debre Damo. Whichever way you looked at it, there didn't seem much alternative but to climb to the top of the *amba* using a rawhide rope. The priest who originally discovered the place had apparently enlisted the help of a flying snake during his first ascent. But one could hardly count on that at this stage in the proceedings. And if the Captain climbed up via the rope, he would be a sitting duck. Which was presumably the plan. Added to which, given that the place was a monastery, no one would be happy to see him slinging a rifle onto his back before he began scrambling.

What the Captain couldn't work out was whether Hart had simply chosen Debre Damo as a safe place his party could lie up in and regain their energy. Or whether this was the place where he intended to confront the Captain once and for all.

Which was when the Captain read about the 'strictly no women' rule.

So this *is* it, the Captain said to himself. The showdown at the OK Corral. Hart was sending him a subliminal message via the very laws of the place he had chosen. He was telling the Captain that this time the women must be kept out of it. That they would be placed in safety somewhere, upon which Hart would confront him on a ground of his own choosing.

Well. The Captain would see about that. He wasn't a gentleman and he wasn't a player. And as far as he was concerned this was no game. May the worst man win.

It didn't take the Captain long to find the abandoned Renegade. They had left it at the bottom of the hill in what he supposed was the tourist parking area. Though the Captain had difficulty imagining much tourism going on in a godforsaken place such as this.

He drew the Mazda up beside the Renegade and cut the engine.

The late-lamented Hank had obviously had a weakness for expensive toys alongside his number-one hobby of pissing off his wife, because there was a two-thousand-dollar pair of Swarovski binoculars tucked inside the glove compartment.

The Captain scanned the surrounding hillside with his new acquisition. The sun was only just beginning to set, so that there was more than enough light left to see. And the binoculars were magnificent. Crystal clear. Yet another posthumous gift from Hank to go alongside the Mazda.

An Ethiopian man was in the process of being hurried up the cliff. A rawhide rope was looped underneath his armpits, and two men were manhandling him from above. He was about halfway up the fifty-metre cliff. By the look of him, the Captain reckoned the guy must be on the far side of sixty.

Then the Captain steadied the binoculars and looked closer. Yes. He was sure he'd recognized him. It was his park guard. Gersem. The one he had bushwhacked and whose rifle he had stolen. So Gersem had switched sides? That explained how Hart had found this place so quickly. There was nothing lucky about it.

The Captain focused the binoculars above the climber's head on the entrance to the hut that the monk in charge of the rawhide rope used for shelter during inclement weather.

Yup. There was Hart, tugging away at Gersem's rope. True to form, Hart was poking his head out from cover like an eager schoolboy on a school corps exercise. An elderly monk was hunched up beside him, helping him manage Gersem's weight. Had Hart noticed the Mazda far below him? Would he work out it was the Captain's new car? Or would he still be expecting the Captain to be driving the wreck with the shattered windscreen he had inherited from the journalists?

The Captain was tempted to take a pot shot at Hart just for the hell of it, but the range was too far over open sights and in such poor light. It would just be a wasted bullet. The Ethiopian would make a better target, drifting on the cliff face like a hangnail, but why kill him? He didn't figure in anything much. And he was clearly injured worse than the Captain had figured at the time, or he wouldn't have needed hauling up. Perhaps there was a medic up there? That would tie in with Hart's tender-minded and flatulent thinking. The man seemed obsessed with making himself vulnerable when he didn't need to.

The Captain checked around some more. No sign of the women. Which was not surprising, given the sexual apartheid prevailing upon the mountain top. Human beings were asses, thought the Captain. When they were handed their freedom on a plate, they insisted on sabotaging their good luck with crazy rules.

So where did you leave them? the Captain mouthed silently to Hart. *Where did you dump my daughter and the Eisenberger woman?* The Captain scanned the village below him. Fifty huts. Maybe more. But no hotels. No guest houses, no electricity, not even a fucking windmill. It would be impossible for him to check out every one of the habitations, which had presumably been the point of the exercise. So maybe they were hiding out in the open? That would have been the sensible thing to do. He would never find them then.

But these were Western women, the Captain told himself. Their natural instinct would always be to search for cover because that is what they were used to. And if the rain started up again at anything like the level of that afternoon, cover was what they would assuredly need.

The Captain slung the rifle over his shoulder and slid the pistol inside his belt. Then he locked and secured the Mazda. When he was finished making his preparations he crouched down beside the Renegade and let all the air out of the tyres. Why not? It never did to leave possible escape routes open behind you if you didn't need to.

When he was satisfied that no one would be driving away fast in the Renegade, he cradled the rifle and moved off to the right. Anyone imagining that he would calmly climb up the rawhide rope and straight into a trap must need their heads examining.

It took the Captain twenty minutes to find the entrance to the tomb. No one was around to guard the place. There was just a barred gate, with a chain and padlock securing it. The Captain checked the padlock. It was unlocked. Anyone could go in or out at will.

He stepped inside the tomb and looked around. The place had originally been a cave. It was maybe one hundred metres wide by about two hundred metres long, spread out beneath the *amba* like a Bavarian beer cellar. The perfect place.

'Anybody home?' shouted the Captain.

Did he hear a furtive reaction from somewhere deep inside the natural crypt? Or was it only a rat, jinked by the unexpected sound of a human voice?

The Captain ventured further inside.

'The big bad wolf is coming!' he intoned. 'Fee-fi-fo-fum. I smell the blood of an Englishwoman. Be she alive or be she dead. I'll grind her bones to make my bread.'

The Captain was enjoying himself all of a sudden. What did he have to lose? Hart, the Ethiopian guard and, in all probability, the man called Rider were no doubt planted up there on the plateau, busily counting sheep. He'd already left a pile of charred bodies in his wake. A few more would make no difference now. He might as well relish the process. It was almost like the good old days again, back when Serbia swept everything before her by sheer force of will.

The Captain decided to change tack. He forced a little candour into his voice, as if he was engaged in selling encyclopedias door to door. 'If you are here, Biljana, step forward alone. The others can stay behind. They will be safe. You can come with me. Your father. I guarantee that no harm will befall you.'

The Captain's major disadvantage was that he possessed no

torch. Hank had let him down on that one. But the walls of the tomb gave off a sort of mild luminosity, as if they were coated with some form of radioactive substance. Radium, perhaps.

Using the eerie half-light given off by the radio-luminescence, the Captain strolled past the stone coffins and the catafalques, kicking up the dust. Making noise. Some of the bodies, mostly decomposed now, had been left out in the open for the elements to toy with. The place reminded him of a trip to Mexico he had made with the Legion a few years before. On a day off from their official duties, he and a few other legionnaires, including Danko, had visited the famous Mummies of Guanajuato – a bunch of naturally mummified bodies that had been preserved in the mud, beyond all natural logic, after a cholera outbreak in 1833. Some of the victims appeared to have been buried alive, given their extreme facial and corporeal contortions.

This being Mexico, therefore, the cemetery workers had soon seen the wisdom of charging people for the privilege of seeing the bodies. The Captain reckoned that the Ethiopians were missing out on a similar trick here. One mummified woman he remembered from Guanajuato had even chewed off part of her own hand after finding herself, one presumed, prematurely entombed. Hell of a way to go. Well. You couldn't have everything. True, the Ethiopians were missing out on some of the more gruesome aspects of the Mexican museum, but this place still ticked most of the boxes. It was a goldmine in waiting.

The Captain spent twenty futile minutes checking out the areas that were easiest of access, but he soon realized that he was on a hiding to nothing. The women could be anywhere. And if they didn't give themselves away by mewling, bleating, or otherwise trying to escape, he could easily waste another hour traipsing round and not getting anywhere.

If it was Hart who had suggested they conceal themselves somewhere inside this open-plan sepulchre, he'd done a heck of an efficient job for a change.

SEVENTY-NINE

Rider listened to the Captain clomping round the tomb area with a rising sense of panic. At one point the cocky bastard had even begun singing, quoting from the same Jack and the Beanstalk nursery rhyme Rider had learnt as a child in kindergarten. Where had a Serbian got that from? Did they teach it universally now?

Rider could feel Biljana shaking with nerves beside him. He couldn't blame her. He was pissing with fear himself too. The design of the underground cave ensured that it acted as a sort of gigantic acoustic resonator. The Captain's voice, in consequence, sounded as if it was a few feet away from them. It was enough to rattle the nerves of a water buffalo.

'Shall I fire at him?' whispered Rider. 'Force the bastard's head down?'

'No. For Christ's sake, no,' said Amira. 'He doesn't know

for sure we're in here. He's just toying with us. And you can't see him anyway.'

'But if I fired a burst it would spook the hell out of him.'

'No, Rider. No. Do you hear me?' Amira was struggling to keep her voice down to little more than an angry whisper. But her message was getting across. 'We need him to give up and go outside. Then we need him to imagine the coast is clear and climb up the cliff behind Hart and Gersem.'

Rider tapped his temple. 'He'd be crazy to do that. This is a fucking useless plan. I knew it from the start. There's no way he's going to make himself into a sitting duck just to suit us. He'd be far better off just returning to his car and waiting there for daylight. We haven't got him trapped. He's got us.'

'Don't say that,' said Biljana.

'What? Because it's true?' Rider eased himself into a more comfortable position. 'He's still walking around out there. Fifty yards away from us. I can hear him. Maybe he'll decide to spend the night here? How would you like that?'

'Last chance!' shouted the Captain, from somewhere over to their right. There was an enormous crash, followed by the sound of a bullet ricocheting off the wall ten metres or so behind them.

'Jesus Christ. Do you think he heard us?'

'No,' said Amira. 'But keep your voice down anyway. He's just trying to frighten us. Now he's wasted one of his precious four rifle bullets.' She waited for the echoes to die away.

426

'Maybe that was just a pistol shot?' said Rider. 'He'll have plenty of bullets left if he was using his pistol. Hart told me the Beretta magazine holds thirteen.'

'Shut up, Rider,' said Amira. 'You'd turn the Dalai Lama into a depressive.'

Biljana hunched forwards. 'Do you think the sound of that shot will bring someone?'

'What?' said Rider. 'From fifty metres up on the hillside? Or from a village half a mile away?'

'I suppose not,' said Biljana.

There was total silence for around five minutes.

'Do you think he's gone?' whispered Rider.

'I think he wants us to think that,' said Amira.

'Well he's succeeding,' said Rider. 'I can't take much more of this.'

Amira punched him on the shoulder. 'Well you're bloody well going to have to.'

EIGHTY

Hart heard the distant crack of the bullet from where he was crouching up on the amba. Gersem was just climbing over the lip. With his arm still injured from the Captain's attack, being pulled up by rope had clearly taken it out of him. Hart and the old monk levered him onto level ground.

'Did you hear that?' said Hart. 'It sounded like a rifle shot.'

'Yes,' said Gersem. 'I believe it came from the tomb.'

'But he can't have found them?' said Hart. 'That place is immense. It's like the Père Lachaise Cemetery in Paris.'

Gersem shook his head, not quite picking up what Hart was talking about. 'Perhaps he hope to frighten them? It is what I would do.' He was clutching his right arm and leaning back against the stone wall of the hut, his mouth set into a rictus of pain.

'You mean go in there and fire a random shot? Hoping that someone will make a break for it and run?'

'Yes.'

'I'm beginning to think this whole thing was a very bad idea indeed,' said Hart. 'And I'm responsible for it. We should never have split up. The chances of the Captain deciding to come up here after us are infinitesimal. Would you climb up in his shoes? When you know you will be a sitting duck?'

'If I am angry enough. And have enough...' Gersem hesitated. 'What do you call it when a man is very pleased with himself?'

'Vanity?' said Hart.

'Yes,' said Gersem. 'If I have enough vanity I will do it.'

'Well, the Captain sure as hell has enough of that,' said Hart.

Gersem leant forward and whispered into the ear of the monk who had been helping Hart haul him up.

The monk acknowledged Gersem's words and hurried away.

'What did you just say to him?' said Hart.

'I asked him to go and fetch my brother,' said Gersem.

'Why did he make that weird salutation with his hand?' said Hart.

'Because my brother is the abbot,' said Gersem. 'It is a sign of respect.'

'The abbot?' said Hart. 'Your brother is the abbot? The boss of this whole place?'

'Yes,' said Gersem.

'Why didn't you tell me this before?' said Hart.

Gersem sighed. 'Because I was not sure of you, that is why. Because I did not want to put the monastery in danger. Later, when I saw what the Captain was capable of, it was too late to tell you. What would have been the point? We had committed ourselves to this action by then.'

'He's going to be angry, isn't he, your brother?' said Hart. 'Angry that we are trying to draw an armed man up here? To this place of peace?'

'No,' said Gersem. 'He will not be angry. He will understand. He is a better man than me.'

Hart stared hard at Gersem. The Ethiopian was curiously unfathomable. One minute you thought you understood him, and the next you were as much in the dark as you ever were. 'You're quite something, you know that? Taking us all under your wing like this. Backing our play. When you could have jumped ship any time you wanted to and been in the clear. Like your friend whatever-his-name.'

'Fikre.'

'Yes. Fikre.' Hart reached forward. 'Here, let me check on that dressing.'

Gersem proffered his arm. He glanced one more time down the cliff face, and then allowed Hart to open his dressing and reset the bandage.

'Do they have a doctor up here?' said Hart. 'You need some proper care with this. That climb you just made has broken the wound open again. If we're not careful it will become infected. You don't want to lose your arm.'

'There will be one up here who understands such things,' said Gersem.

'Just how many people are there up here in the final analysis?'

'The entire community is three hundred and fifty strong,' said Gersem. 'One hundred and fifty monks and two hundred deacons. There will be those among them who specialize in nursing the others too. I will be in good hands.'

'What?' said Hart. 'Three hundred and fifty people? All living up here on this plateau? You're kidding me?'

'No I am not. I am not kidding,' said Gersem.

'And we're enticing the Captain up here?' said Hart. 'Like a fox amongst the chickens? I can't do it, Gersem. I just can't do it. You should have told me.'

'So what are you going to do?' said Gersem. 'Are you going to climb down again? Now that you know for certain the Captain is below you? With a rifle that he is aching to use? He would enjoy the target practice, I believe. When he has dealt with you, he will have ample time then to find the others. And what do you think he will do with them? Will he allow them to go free and write about him, do you think?'

Hart shook his head. He felt closer to despair than ever.

'My guess is that he will try to come up here in darkness,' said Gersem. 'Late in the night. Hoping we will have lowered our guard by then. Or maybe have fallen asleep in one of the many huts scattered about the plateau.'

'And what if there's another way up?' said Hart. 'A way no one knows about? The Captain is capable of just about anything. Physically, despite his injury, he will still be very strong.'

'How do you know this?'

'Just a hunch,' said Hart.

'There is that too, of course,' said Gersem. 'Another possible way no one knows about. But do not let him under your skin. The monks will be watching now. They will all know what is happening. My feeling is that when the Captain finally appears at the top of the *amba*, from whichever direction he chooses to come in, he will be somewhat surprised at the warm welcome my brothers shall have prepared for him.'

EIGHTY-ONE

For a long moment, Rider didn't notice that Biljana had slid the rifle off his lap. He was listening hard for any sounds from beyond the entrance to the tomb. The creaking of the gate. More singing. Another random shot. Anything along those lines. His concentration was elsewhere.

'Biljana,' Rider said, when he discovered the empty space in front of him where the rifle had been. 'Please stop pissing about and give me the rifle back.'

Biljana held the assault rifle tightly in her arms. Her face, in the dull ambient light, looked oddly determined. 'No.'

'Sweetheart,' said Amira, in a low, intense whisper. 'Hand the bloody rifle back to Rider. This is no time for teenage stuff and nonsense.'

'This is not teenage stuff and nonsense,' said Biljana, clutching the rifle tightly to her chest. 'You are not a judge and jury. Any of you. I will not let you kill my father.'

'Is this what this is all about?' said Amira. 'Killing your father? Come on, girl. No one is going to kill him. We are aiming to capture him, that's all. That's why Hart and Gersem have taken themselves up onto the plateau. So we can conduct a sort of pincer movement and catch him where he can't injure anybody. And when we have him, we are going to hand him over to the criminal court in The Hague. They'll make sure justice is done.' Amira put on her most empathetic smile. 'That way you will have a chance to get to know him, you see? To help him if you want. I'm sure they will let visitors in to see him at the prison. We're a civilized society.'

'I do not believe that this will happen,' said Biljana. Her eyes were locked onto Amira's with unsettling intensity. 'You are just saying that to sway me. To keep me in line. I can tell by your face.'

'Do you deny that your father killed Danko?' said Amira, no longer able to hide her irritation. 'That he raped your mother? And connived at the rape of all those other women during the Kosovo War? Alongside God knows what else? The murder of your uncle and your grandparents, for instance?'

'I know that he is a bad man,' said Biljana. 'Yes. But he is still my father. The only remaining blood of my blood. I cannot feed him to the pigs. You heard what he said, didn't you? He promised no harm would come to me. And that you would be safe.' Biljana sprang to her feet. She turned on her heel and sprinted towards the entrance to the tomb.

Cursing under her breath, Amira followed her, with Rider hard at her heels.

When Biljana reached the gate, she saw that it was half open. The Captain had already left.

Something closed down in her heart when she realized that the Captain had not been sure that they were hiding in the sepulchre after all. He had sounded so positive when calling out to them. So sure of himself. As he always did.

Biljana was the first to admit that she found her father's powers of persuasion unsettling. She was more than half aware of her own susceptibilities in the matter. But something, nonetheless, was forcing her to play the dangerous game she and the Captain were involved in to its bitter end.

She eased herself through the crack in the gate and pulled it to behind her.

Dusk had fallen. Around her she could see the silhouettes of swooping bats feeding on the last of that day's harvest of insects.

She stood with the rifle cradled in her arms, searching for signs. When she heard Rider and Amira approaching behind her, she turned back towards the gate, unhooked the padlock, reset the chain, and clicked the padlock shut.

'What have you done, child?' said Amira. She tugged at the padlock, but it was locked tight. 'Don't do this. Don't go looking for your father out there. You'll be making a serious mistake. Please go and hide. Please. Leave him for Gersem and Hart. They know what to do.'

Biljana ignored her. She walked slowly towards the cliff face. She could just make out the rawhide rope and the accompanying safety rope swaying gently on an evening zephyr. Stationed near the rope was a man's figure. The man had a rifle slung on his back. He was looking up at the cliff edge through a pair of binoculars.

Biljana raised the assault rifle to her shoulder and started towards her father.

At first he did not hear her. She was wearing espadrilles. Their rope soles were completely silent against the rocks. Thirty yards out, though, Biljana trod on a dry stick. The crack of the stick sounded like a rifle shot in the night's vacuum.

The Captain turned abruptly. He let the binoculars fall onto his chest.

'Don't touch your rifle,' said Biljana, moving towards him. 'I have you covered.'

The Captain reached for his rifle with one fluid movement. 'That sort of assault rifle needs a key, you know. It's useless without it. This one doesn't, though.'

Biljana fired a single shot. She aimed it maybe ten feet over her father's head. The bullet struck the cliff face above him and ricocheted away with an angry whine. The sound of the shot reverberated over and over again down the valley, until it gradually faded away into the distance like a forgotten curse.

The Captain instinctively ducked his head, even though the bullet had struck high above him. He looked amazed that his daughter had managed to summon up the courage to fire a warning shot over his head. He let go of his rifle.

'We found the key,' said Biljana. 'The one you were talking about. The rifle, as you see, is unlocked. I will shoot you with it if I need to.'

The Captain let his hands fall to his sides in seeming capitulation. 'So what do you want me to do? Climb up this rope? Hand myself over to those two arseholes cowering up there on the ridge? You know what the do-gooders in The Hague will do to me, don't you? They'll lock me up and throw away the key. I'd be better off hanging myself with this.' He pointed to the rawhide rope dangling behind him. 'Would you really do that to your own father?'

'My own father?' said Biljana. 'Is that what you are?'

'Like it or not,' said the Captain, with a grin. 'That's what I am. You're blood of my blood. You've only got one of me. You'll only ever have one of me.'

'One is quite sufficient,' said Biljana.

The Captain laughed. It was a sudden, ragged bark. More like the hack of a jackal or of a prowling fox than anything resembling a human sound. He raised one hand and took hold of the rawhide rope, as if he wished to demonstrate how a man could hang himself on it.

'Let go of that,' said Biljana.

The Captain let go of the rope. It swung to and fro behind him like a pendulum. 'So what are you proposing? To keep me prisoner? Or are you intending to let me go, perhaps?'

437

'Yes,' said Biljana. 'I am intending to let you go.'

The Captain straightened up as if someone offstage had barked out an order to stand to attention. 'You're joking, surely?'

'No,' said Biljana. 'I'm going to give you one final chance. You can take your car with you. Make for the Eritrean border. I will give you the gift of this one night only. Rider and Amira are locked inside the tomb. They cannot get out. Hart and Gersem are up on the plateau. The only way down is by this rope. But I will not let them descend it. If they try I will fire so that they must keep their heads inside the hut. No one else will come. It is night-time. People are frightened of gunfire at night. Look. There have been two shots in the past twenty minutes. But no one is here.'

'You are really going to let me go?' said the Captain. 'Just because you are my daughter?' He shook his head in disbelief. 'So blood really is thicker than water? Is this what you are telling me?'

'Yes,' said Biljana. 'Our shared blood dictates that I refuse to be responsible for your downfall. You will doubtless manage that yourself in your own sweet time.'

The Captain laughed again. This time it was more of a guffaw. The sort of a guffaw a man will give when he thinks he has the edge on a certifiable lunatic. 'So you are searching for someone to love? Is that it? Is that what this is all about?'

Biljana shook her head. 'I don't love you. I hate you. For everything you have done.' The end of her rifle twitched.

The Captain lurched spasmodically on the spot, in a mirror movement to the rifle's, as if he expected to be shot at any moment. 'I hate you for driving my mother to suicide,' Biljana continued. 'I hate you for killing my grandfather and my grandmother. For killing my uncle. I hate you for killing Danko. And for all those other innocents whose lives you have ruined along the way.'

'Then,' said the Captain, 'I don't understand. Why the fuck are you letting me go?'

'Because I am not Allah,' said Biljana. 'Because I will not set myself up in judgement over you. Because I will not have your death on my conscience. Alongside all those other deaths that, by virtue of my tainted blood, I share responsibility for.'

The Captain took a step forwards. He shook his head like a dog attempting to rid itself of fleas. His face was streaked with sweat. Perspiration was leaching through his shirt. 'There's one problem with all this,' he said. 'And it's a dilly. I can't possibly leave all these people alive behind me. You must see that?' He took another small pace towards her. 'It wouldn't sit right with me, you understand? I know their sort. They will never give up pursuing me. While they are still alive, I will need to spend the rest of my life glancing back over my shoulder. And I am not prepared to do that. So I am going to take this rifle...' The Captain began unhitching his rifle 'And I am going to walk past you back towards the tomb. Once there I am going to kill the man called Rider and the

Eisenberger woman. They are sitting ducks. You have made sure of that. I will make their deaths quick and without pain, I promise you. Then I will stand beneath this cliff, with my rifle pressed to your head, and I will call Hart down. And do you know what? He will come. Because I will offer him a hand-to-hand fight. On the square. Man to man. And when I have killed him, and only then, will I get in my car and drive to Eritrea. At this point you can come with me or not. The choice will be yours.'

'Don't free your rifle any more.' Biljana's voice was trembling. 'I will kill you.'

'No you won't,' said the Captain. 'You won't kill me because a killer is not what you are. You are better than that. Far better. You'll maybe find this hard to believe, Biljana, but I am proud of you. Proud of what you have become. Proud of your decency. I'm sorry to have to let you down. But, you see, I am not even a halfway decent man.' The Captain finished unslinging his rifle and raised it to cover Biljana.

Gersem, fifty metres above the Captain, chose that moment to pick up the rock that had fallen at some previous time down from the ledge above. He had marked the rock for possible use earlier. As something to be shunted towards the edge of the cliff face. Just in case.

The Captain was standing exactly one metre away from the rawhide rope. The rope, Gersem decided, would act as his guideline. Either way, the dropping of the rock was a long shot. But Gersem had picked up the tone of every word that had passed between Biljana and the Captain, even though they were talking in a language that was entirely unfamiliar to him. When the Captain raised his rifle to cover his very own daughter there was no longer any option. Gersem knew that he must act. In Ethiopia it was inconceivable that a man would use a weapon to threaten a member of his own family.

Hart reached out to stop him. The Ethiopian was still in considerable pain from his shoulder. He was unable to both heft the rock and hold it steady at the same time. The unexpected weight was forcing Gersem perilously close to the edge of the cliff face.

Hart grabbed Gersem by his linen *gabi* and dragged him backwards. 'The girl, you fool. You could hit the girl. Put the rock down.'

The sudden movement was enough to unsettle Gersem's left hand and cause him to lose control of the rock.

The rock pitched over the side of the *amba* and started downwards. Fifteen feet below the lip, it struck an outcropping spur and changed direction.

The Captain heard the angry snap of rock against rock and looked upwards.

Later, Biljana would come to doubt the evidence of her own eyes. The sudden movement her father had made as if he had been intending to protect her.

What she did know for certain was that he had put out his hand and pushed her away. Had he been trying to disarm

441

her? Had he still intended taking her hostage, as he had been threatening? Or was it the unlikely manifestation of a genuine change of heart?

The rock struck the Captain on his left shoulder, a fraction more than six seconds after it had left Gersem's hands. The Captain pitched to the ground.

Hart threw himself over the lip of the cliff. He scissored his way down the rope, letting the rawhide slide between his hands until his palms were bloody. All the time he was glissading, he could hear Biljana wailing. Each cry was like a knife thrust through his heart.

When he reached the rope's bottom he ran to her, but she turned from him, her weeping done, her wails transformed into silence.

Hart turned round.

The Captain was lying prone upon the ground. His left arm was partially sheared off. In his right hand he held Danko's Beretta pistol. It was loosely aimed at Hart. The Captain's face was pale and wild. The face of a man unexpectedly confronted by his own mortality.

'Move,' said the Captain. 'Move away from the girl.'

'What?' said Hart, his damaged hands held flat against his sides. 'Don't tell me that you are afraid of a bullet passing through me and hitting her?' As he talked he watched the blood steadily pulsing from the Captain's arm onto the rocks surrounding him. It would not be long now. Surely it would not be long.

442

'Yes,' said the Captain. 'My aim, you know. I sense it will be off. But still. It's worth a try, isn't it?'

The Captain raised the pistol and tightened his finger upon the trigger.

The crack of the assault rifle from behind him caused Hart to spin round as if the bullet had been meant for him, and not for his assailant. He was not certain, immediately, quite what had happened. Had the Captain fired? Had Biljana fired back at the Captain?

Biljana stared at where the Captain was lying, her face bereft.

Hart turned round. The bullet from the assault rifle had taken the Captain full in the chest. It had knocked him at least three feet backwards, so that his right arm, still clutching the pistol, was swept upward as if in a salute. The remnants of the Captain's left arm lay a foot or so beyond him, thrown there by the force of the bullet's centrifugal throw-out.

Endeavouring to mask the Captain's body with his own, Hart gently, ever so gently, prised the rifle from Biljana's hands.

EPILOGUE

It took seven months for Hart to complete the initial part of the formal process of adopting Biljana. First there was the problem of her religion, Muslim. And Hart's, Church of England. Next there was the fact that he was an unmarried middle-aged man and she was a female teenager. From Macedonia. Via Kosovo. And stations in between.

Hart nearly gave up on countless occasions. For a start, only two per cent of adoptees were between ten and fifteen years old. And only one per cent were over sixteen. He needed to get on with it. But everything seemed to mitigate against him. Heterosexual couples, despite everything he had heard to the contrary, were Social Services' first choice. Single females were second. Single males were off the damned scale. They figured below lesbians, gay men and transsexuals.

Then the adoption panel wasn't impressed with his profession. Photojournalist. Frequently in danger spots.

Irregular income with vast fluctuations. Hart came close to losing his rag on countless occasions, but Amira, who had agreed to shadow him while he was undergoing the Home Study, somehow kept him in check. He made it through to Matching Panel. It was a miracle he didn't blow that when one of his interrogators, leafing through his press cuttings, suggested that he suffered from a death wish.

Finally, largely thanks to the kindness of the Macedonian authorities, who were as chalk to cheese compared to the English, the adoption was formalized and Biljana could stay with Hart by legal right, as opposed to by choice. The Macedonians, unlike the British, believed in something called a direct adoption, which entitled the child to reside with the potential adoptee before the actual adoption was finalized. This meant that Biljana was able to live with Hart in both England and in Macedonia, under the proviso of regular visits from both countries' social services. The fact that Biljana was nearly sixteen by the end of the process undoubtedly helped curtail the red tape. As a fifteen-year-old, Biljana was also consulted as to whether she was willing to let her Macedonian nationality lapse, and she stated that she was. Macedonia meant nothing to her, she told the panel. It was simply the country in which her mother had died.

Last on the agenda was the possible name change. Hart skated around the issue like a man aware that he is hovering on perilously thin ice but, once again, Biljana proved that she knew her own mind better than he did. She would be called, from henceforth, Biljana Andronika Hart.

Later, when all had been said and done, the pair of them returned to Kosovo, and to the Visoki Dečani Monastery. After seeing the abbot and thanking him, and explaining to Maria what had happened to her great-nephew, they retraced the journey Hart and Biljana's mother had made sixteen years before.

They never found the rape house where Biljana had been conceived, however, for Hart pretended he had forgotten where to look for it, and Biljana allowed him to imagine that she had been taken in by all his many protestations of ignorance.

ACKNOWLEDGEMENTS

I'm very grateful, as always, to my agent, Oli Munson, of A. M. Heath, and to my long-time publisher, Sara O'Keeffe, Editorial Director of Corvus Books. Also to Louise Cullen, who edited me so effectively, and to Michelle O'Connell, who reads my books as I write them and keeps me in line. Finally, to my wife, Claudia, and my granddaughter, Éloise, for riding shotgun so efficiently, and reminding me why I write in the first place.